Kathy

Frias

The

Seed

Hunters

Published by White Feather Press. (www.whitefeatherpress.com)

ISBN 978-1-61808-137-7

Printed in the United States of America

Cover design created by Ron Bell of AdVision Design Group (www.advisiondesigngroup.com)

White Feather Press

Reaffirming Faith in God, Family, and Country!

Settings and Characters

Calneh: One of the cities built by Nimrod, west of Shinar

Martu: Warrior and citizen of Calneh

Simirra: Citizen of Calneh and wife of Martu

Madai: Descendent of Japheth whose forefathers traveled west after the confusion of tongues. Once married to a young kinswoman named Ido, he found himself widowed and came to question the truths of God which his tribe carried with them from the scattering. Bereft, he sailed east across the Brine Sea in search of original truth. As well, deception and idolatry had infiltrated his family and clan. He met Job, Nimrod and Noah and found the truth of a Creator God that he had come searching for.

Kittim: Madai's companion who met him on the shore as Madai completed his voyage eastward across the Brine Sea. He traveled with Madai to meet Job and Noah.

Iscah: The slave-wife of Hamonheb, a young girl rescued by Madai and **Kittim**. She had been a goat herder's daughter who was stolen by Sabeans and sold in Shinar, later sold to Hamonheb.

Hamonheb: The brewer of Gerar, the city from which Iscah was rescued. It is the first city Madai comes upon while on his quest.

Nammim: Priest of Shinar

Nimrod: Wicked King of Shinar, killed by the armies of Shem.

Semirramis: Wife of Nimrod who claimed his throne upon his death.

Tutan: Man of the Orient who met Madai, Kittim and Iscah as they journeyed eastward. He was also searching for God.

Reenah: Exotic tradeswomen, adopted niece of Job.

Arphaxas: A lone man with an unknown past.

The Seed Hunters

Book Two

PROLOGUE

SIMIRRA

"**Y**OU WILL RUN!" A WOMAN COMMANDED HERself even as she fell, betrayed by the constrictions of her own belly. Like a blistering wind she was ravaged. But she swallowed a scream both of panic and pain, waiting for it to pass.

Then came the calm, enough to take another breath.

That breath was full of the sweet scent of desert rose that she so loved, tainted most unkindly by the pungent smell of her own fear. She snatched a glance behind, then like a thief in a melon patch, hugged her belly as she ran again. Thorny branches tore at her, sweat burned and blinded her. She was in heavy labor and desperate.

High servants of The Light of Heaven had arrived from Shinar demanding a sacrifice. She clamped her lips shut to bite back a cry, which kept just behind her teeth for she was in mortal danger, she and the babe. She was glad of a whole moon as she fought through the brush that ringed the city of Calneh. She stopped suddenly and grabbed at a stalk, mindless of its barbs. She closed her eyes and braced against the next mounting pain, which climbed a mighty effort across her body.

The announcement brought by the Servants of Heaven – that a son was born to Nimrod – was the root of her trouble. It was surely the work of the gods, this babe, Tammuz; for Nimrod was dead now and more months than nine. Had the city not been delivered the great King's arm? Severed and delivered by those sons of Shem – enemy to the gods, not to be admired. And yet...

There had been a story told by a dear, dead father. He had believed in a One True God and not the fables of Shinar. But choosing the old religion against the new had always stood her family apart. It was the reason her father was dead. It was, perhaps, the reason Martu would do this thing now.

Suddenly and before she was even aware, Simirra was on her knees again, nothing of herself but a demanding belly. There was something going to happen, no holding it off now. She chewed the soft insides of her cheeks tasting blood. She also heard a branch snap behind her. It made a sound more terrible, louder than a thunder clap. She shrank against the earth. He was coming.

She knew he was driven by a grand ambition. To be the father of a fire-spirit was a high calling. It would suit him. She had seen it in his eyes. He would rip his seed, freshly bloomed, from her womb, with not a moment's regret nor pause.

She held her breath, listening to hear if the twig-snapper had indeed been a man. She arched her back against the pain even as a footfall came near. He smelled like Martu.

A TOMB; SHE WAS A TOMB, STRETCHED OUT ON HER COT. Simirra's cheeks were tight across her skull with a crispy skim of salt. Her throat hurt; her eyes hurt. All that she was, was certainly dead now. Her body had not moved, not even a tic since the babe was born and Martu had...

The violent weeping was past. There was just an unexpected stray tear sliding from the outer edge of her eye, an alien tear, coming from... somewhere. Still she did not move. She lay without sight or sound or presence. Being apart from the body was a wonderful sensation – necessary. Until there came a scratching. It came from some foreign place and settled on her forearm as a quiet prickle – persistently, wickedly growing, exploring her arm.

A rebellious hand rose to scratch the spot. It moved unbidden to her shoulder where the prickle had also moved and she was betrayed. Prickles pinged to life in all sorts of places till she was thoroughly Simirra again, fully and dreadfully. It was unavoidable, like a twilight waking from a terrible dream to find it all true. There was a dull ache in her back, a rhythmic pulsing where the child – O the child! – had emerged, and the quiet constant warm flow of liquid.

She jolted upright. She scrubbed her mind clear to take in the mess – the bright red and sticky pool. That was when she started shaking, a violent first and feral instinct. Martu! He would find her this way; wounded, weak, newly robbed! Quickly, she stuffed a rag between her legs and tied it in place with another.

She swung her legs over the edge of the cot as though she had not been dead a moment before. Her head whirled with a violence to send her spinning but that she braced a hand against the wall – strangely cool to the touch. She stood. She groped for her clothes, spattered with mud and torn where he had dragged her home. Suddenly she froze, remembering something else, the Akkadian girl Martu had brought from a raid. She would hear!

Simirra hugged her belly, instinctive but pointless now, and listened to the silent house. But of course – the girl was gone – she was at the temple. All of Calneh was at the temple. Her child was at the temple!

Simirra was suddenly seized by a wild notion and shaking so violently she had to grab at the edge of the bed.

Why... she could save her baby!

NAMIM

Another man, a priest, was fresh from a journey. His name was Namim and he settled into a silken cushion. How good it felt against his saddle sores! It had been a brutal trip from Shinar, at least for an untraveled man of temples. Even so, he had to restrain a smile. Such a reverence shone on those faces watching him! He savored it as he might have a honey-sweetened plum. Not so ill a fortune to be emissary of a dead king – entirely more agreeable than to be his poppet! Namim, in fact, had hardly born the rabid appetites of his once King. He sniffed. He dabbed at his nose with a square of blue silk, pining even still for a young man, Tazek. For on that night, glorious as it was for the sake of Nimrod's demise, the high priest had lost Tazek as well; disappeared into the chaos of a lost battle. If there had been others, they had not been so loved.

He shook himself, remembering his duty which was an honor after all. He was to introduce the tale; a sort of post-mortem jeer, after so many come from the other way. Semiramis had born a child, and certainly not by Nimrod. He knew that first hand for Namim himself had provided the seed that produced the boy, which made it all the more delicious. Certainly no other man kept Semiramis's bed and no one would suspect him! It was inconsequential that she claimed herself visited by the spirit of her lost husband. It was no matter. Namim knew the truth; Tammuz would be a king. He was father to a king and Nimrod was still dead….

And so the high priest told the story; announcing, proclaiming, attesting by the weight of priesthood that the ancient of prophecies was at long last fulfilled. If Nimrod had rearranged the star stories – making them direct the fates of men with their orbits – a piece of the authentic had been retained. It was the legend that a Son of God should be born to a virgin of man. It was a stuff of nonsense to such men of learning as Namim, but widely spread amongst the rabble. At this point Namim could not restrain himself a smile. Nimrod, being such a son of god, had made it a king's obsession to fulfill the prophecy , and used the kingdom's little virgins to do it. That it took the great king's own death to fulfill the prophecy, he had not foreseen.

Namim's smile broadened to show his teeth, turning his thoughts, even as he spoke of worthy virgin mothers, to Semiramis. The Queen's rather scandalous reputation was known to the farthest regions. But belief in the potent spirit of Nimrod could apparently be squeezed out of the superstitious, for Semiramis's infamy was proving but an insignificant technicality. None seemed willing to protest, nor suggest a more probable paternity.

Namim's eyes actually twinkled. He was not bothered to defend himself as a father and kept no affections for the son, the little pinch-faced god. An extravagant sum of self-esteem leaves room for little else. It was, in fact, the deception itself that kept Namim safe, as he was now High Priest to the young god-king, practically immortal himself.

He watched the crowd a moment, looking for any hint of disbelief, before he began the second purpose for his journey. This purpose hit him at a deeper, more personal level, and stole the smile from his lips. It regarded the spies, they who had robbed him of Tazek; Madai especially, Madai and Kittim.

"There are servants of Shem on the plain now," he spat, his voice rising with a great passion, "those who conspired against The Light of Heaven, as you know. Catch them. Bring them to Shinar and you will be rewarded. The new Light of Heaven – your own god, Tammuz – must be protected against them and avenged his father."

Namim waited again, to see if the crowd would question him. It was a tricky balance – men of that flood God, The Huwah, overrunning the Light of Heaven and threatening his spirit child. The quartering of Nimrod, which had given Namim a secret thrill, had also put terror into these Calneh citizens. Terror, Namim could argue against. Competing gods could go either way.

"Lord Nimrod's great spirit lives," he pressed, "and walks among us. There is Tammuz to prove it! You shall be guarded for his sake. Only bring your offerings, one for the virgin's babe and one for divine protection. There are many of you after all, with only two spies. Rid this plain of the man, Madai, and his servant, Kittim, and Shinar will make you rich!"

He watched them again, knowing how well ambitions can clad a man with armor. Whether allegiance or want of gold was no matter if the desired end be achieved and the end of Madai was what Namim desired.

He watched their faces absorb the information. He watched their budding courage.

He watched as their own priest acquiesced to him with hooded eyes. The Calnehan holy man signaled to his underlings with the delicate twitch of a finger. They stoked the fires afresh, which burned red in the belly of Baal. Namim folded his arms across his chest agreeably. Now he would simply enjoy the rituals. It did bring him a warm thrill to take the soft flesh of a babe to Baal – and there were so many ways to do it.

He missed Tazek so….

A man with a hawkish nose and weathered face stood up. Namim could see the fire reflected in his eyes. He could also see the life force of this fellow, visible in an arc of light, telling him that this one's homage was false. But the hawk-man offered the first sacrifice, fresh from the womb. Namim smiled, forgetting him and sniffed up the smoke from the altar even as he felt the presence enter him, rushing through his veins to all his prized parts. Had he seen himself, he would have seen his own eyes dilate, his face flush red and glisten like dew in the morning. He hardly heard the man's name, as it didn't really matter. Martu.

MARTU.

A GREAT CROWD SURROUNDED THE TEMPLE FILLING the wide steps. Only the privileged few smelt the whole of the aroma inside. It was a beautiful smell, fresh herbs and oils devoted to the mighty god, Baal. With Tammuz newly born, the city was awash with optimism – a new god, or an old one re-born! That made Semiramis divine herself, the god-wife and virgin mother. The more gods, the more power, the more protection - an auspicious occasion in every respect!

There were however, others assembled, men who did not share like passions as the mob. Martu was one and among the privileged. His new wife was with him and wearing an under-dress of silver that had been sacked off some chieftain's woman in Akkad, or another campaign perhaps. With Nimrod gone, there had been many campaigns, for Martu was a restless man, an ambitious man. The confines of Nimrod's reign had not been born willingly with so much wealth to gain.

It was a calculation that brought Martu so promptly with the first sacrifice, for there had been many raids after Nimrod's death. Martu had elevated himself somewhat quickly and with no little bloodshed. That had been, perhaps … impolitic, especially if new governance was in the air.

The raid of Akkad was one of questionable merit, for example, as she was sister-city to Calneh, both built by Nimrod at the apex of his power. But they had each strained at the bit, being ruled by the far off capital and more than ripe for a king from their own.

Nimrod with his vast army had been entirely ravaged by the Shemites for which men like Martu were not altogether ill pleased. Not so, such proclamations of a divine royal birth, though he had made the best of it.

Martu's child, his fire-spirit, was in the belly of the beast. Its wailing was past. Its smoke perfumed the air. Martu had held up his new wife with a commanding arm when she had threatened to sag at his feet. It was a weakness he would need to deal with if he were to keep her. And he would like to. She had brought a fire to his bed that was lost with Simirra long since. The irony made him chuckle, as he watched flames lick out of the altar's open belly.

Simirra gripped the knife so tightly in her hand that her nails dug into her palm. But that was nothing to her as her belly tightened again, trying to pinch off the last flow of blood. She looked a wild woman, hair tossed by a whirlwind and oiled with sweat, gown torn and muddy and streaked down the back with blood. She was enough to frighten a child; a mad woman.

She and Martu had lived in a wealthy house within the shadow of the temple. She was surprised, none the less to find herself so quickly at the sacred site with scarce another thought save to rescue her babe. But the Temple steps were blocked. It appeared that all of Calneh had come to watch her child die. She pushed, only to be swatted back like a fly. She tried to squeeze between, and was harangued at by a woman smelling rank as he-goat.

"Wait like the rest of us," the woman spat, finishing the tirade. She leered back at Simirra, only to dismiss her with a look of disgust. "Go clean yourself up," she hissed. "The Priest of Shinar is in there."

"What is happening?" Simirra heard her own voice, sounding strange and grim.

"Feeding Baal," the woman answered, showing Simirra a toothy grin.

Simirra swallowed. She pulled the knife closer to her side, feeling it cold against a leg hot with fever. "Who?" Simirra's lips could scarcely form the word.

But the woman turned back to the friend beside her and leaned toward her ear. They laughed, as the friend glanced across her shoulder to have a look at Simirra. She turned back and shook her head.

"Your eyes are happy with wine, Picca," the friend scoffed. "The Lord Martu has his wife with him – in there."

"She isn't one of us," the first woman insisted. "I knew her mother."

"I tell you, she is inside."

The woman looked at Simirra again, a cagey look, resentful. "You want to go up?" She asked.

Simirra nodded.

"They say Martu-An has burned a son."

Simirra felt herself sway.

The woman grinned, shrewdly, and leaned back to whisper at her friend again.

"Simirra."

Simirra whirled around.

"Leave now, Simirra."

Even though the Voice seemed as close as her ear, Simirra could see no one. She was the last at the back of the crowd.

"Leave now."

Simirra felt herself back away – even as her hand gripped the knife tighter, even as she strained her eyes for a way through the throng, even as the woman's friend turned to look at her again.

"Who are you?" she whispered, her lips like wood. And, though the Voice did not speak again, Simirra wanted to obey, against reason, for the weight of knife in hand was persistent. She watched the second woman turn away with another shake of her head, to engage the friend and make her laugh.

Simirra blinked and shook her head ever so slightly. Then she backed away, crossing the width of the Temple courtyard, shielding the knife in the folds of her skirt.

As when she had made her way to the Temple, she found herself at home again and entirely a-tremble. She glanced around herself, at the entry and all its tidiness. It awakened something in her, something past shock. It was a duality of emotion, both of rage and fear. She was ashamed to be afraid of Martu again with all his strength and calculation. But there was an urgency in her now, to be away. She hurried through the breezeway into the bedroom, where the crime was done.

She removed the rags from between her legs and piled them on the bed. She was methodical, gathering up what she could carry. She wrapped the knife in a piece of silk, like a gift, which she promised herself to unwrap at a later time. She tied the whole bundle as she had seen Martu do it, and tested it on her back. It was heavy. It cut through the thin substance of her dress.

Hurriedly, she dropped the pack and pulled off the garment. It was appallingly stiff and streaked with blackish, dry blood. She scrubbed at her legs… had it just been this morning? Then she grabbed a pair of her husband's leggings. He was not as tall as some. The thought made her smile.

Simirra was a tall woman. It had always given her a certain grace. "Leave now," she heard the Voice again.

Simirra skirted the nearest buildings cautiously, though it seemed that all of Calneh had been at the Temple. She gained the woods and retraced the path she had taken only the night before, running away from her husband. It was only after she had walked for an hour that a profound weariness set against her. It brought a sense of herself again, of being fully a part of the world with everything aching and amiss. She felt hot, and somehow cold. Had she truly just been to the temple? Where was she now? She sagged against the trunk of a near tree. She leaned her face against its rough skin and closed her eyes. And she wondered for the first time about the Voice.

ARPHAXAS

ICY FINGERS OF CLOUDS CREPT ACROSS THE SKY AND settled above Calneh's temple. A quenching rain drove the smoke of infant sacrifice back to earth, dappling mortals with its first frigid drops and turning the crowd off the courtyard with wet, unrestrained fury. A wind chased after the rain, howling out against atrocities… and men.

If the storm's bluntest fury was hurled against the temple, its rain stretched into the glades to wet its farthest corners. A very tall, rosy-hewed man pushed the coals of his fire under an overhang and cursed at the sky. He was wearing a once-brilliant skin of dragon, now scuffed and worn. The man pulled it over his head and hugged it closed at his chin to sit out the onslaught. How unpredictable were the harvest storms. Some rich lord's crops would rot. The man took a measure of glee in the thought, though not enough to outweigh his own misery.

He took a charred carcass off a spit, only half eaten, and began to gnaw it. He would never be hungry again! He grinned at the thought, proud of himself and his skills. He exposed an arm just to look at it: thick, running with sinew, hard as stone. His face gleamed with pride as he finished the last morsel. But it was not enough to quash what seemed a boundless appetite and the man cursed again, never patient and needing the rain to stop.

But the sky was not finished. It pelted the earth with hail, turning the ground white like a winter's coat. Branches cracked and groaned as the man stoked his fire and forgot about his stomach and wondered if The Huwah would ever leave the world alone. He was tired, a sudden cold penetrating to his bones.

Crack! The man snatched his head up, looking into the night. Crack! A branch snapped by a footfall, the sound a human makes in the dark in unfamiliar surroundings. He pulled a polished scimitar from the scabbard on his hip, as he threw the dragon-cape off his shoulders to pull himself up and out of the overhang. He was a terrible sight of a man, skin quickly drenched and gleaming in the firelight, head ablaze with hair the color of sun and clenching a curved blade with eager affection.

A hump-backed man of unremarkable stature stumbled out of the bushes, wet as a river seal. The man took a step toward Arphaxas's fire, looked him in the face and promptly crumpled to the ground. The red haired Arphaxas lowered his scimitar in a wave of disappointment. Hail peck, pecked at the stranger's soggy back. Arphaxas picked a bit of flesh out of his teeth, sheathed his weapon and sat back at the fire. He pulled the dragon's cape over his head again and closed his eyes.

SIMIRRA TUCKED HER HEAD INTO MARTU'S COAT. SHE hugged her knees up to her chest and tried to lie still, still enough for the red giant to forget about her. She had been drawn by his fire, but instantly terrified by the wildness of his appearance. He was sitting in front of that fire, a long time now. He was feeding it, little bit by little bit. He had not looked at her again. Thank the gods the hail had stopped! Still, the ground was cold as ice. And she might have dared to crawl back into the brush but for the pack. It weighed her down, pinned her like a grouse in a snare.

In time, there came a rumble from inside the man's cave. She listened, just to be sure, peeking at him from the crook of her arm. He was still huddled above his fire, his chin dropped down to his breast. Simirra inched her hand out of the coat and slowly pushed herself up. The ground was frozen except for where she had lain; there it was mud. The pack was stiff. It did not want to yield its shape enough to let her stand, so she began to crawl. How she would like to have made for that fire! But she was afraid, and started for the underbrush.

A hand suddenly latched onto her pack and snatched her off the ground. A tie snapped and she fell free of it, snagging herself on a thorn. She yelped and tried to scramble away. But the giant grabbed her coat in his fist and picked her up again.

"Be still," he snarled.

Simirra would surely not have obeyed the command, but her vision began to close in from the sides and black spots slid across her eyes till everything was dark.

HE DROPPED HER AT THE FIRE AND KICKED HER FOOT away from the flame. Then he sat down and studied her. She was tall for a woman, so much so that he had thought she was a hump-backed man. The hump had been the pack. He dug through that. A legging. He measured the pants against his own legs with disappointment. A jar of – stuff. A dagger wrapped in silk. He smelled the silk, felt it across his face and grimaced. He crumpled the silk in his fist and threw it in the fire. He searched for anything of interest. Not even a scrap of food! How does a woman run away without food?

Arphaxas emptied the rest of the pack with a disapproving grunt. He pushed the contents toward the woman with his foot. She moved at the sound, lifted her face and gaped at him.

"Your stuff, woman," he muttered. "Why are you out here without food?" It appeared to him that she was a mute.

"Have they run you off?"

She snatched at the pile from her pack. She dug through the discard, looking frantic. Arphaxas watched, then held up the dagger with a thin smile.,

"Looking for this?"

At the very sound of his voice, she pinned herself back against the rock that overhung his fire. It was the sight of her, like a cornered rabbit, that tipped a scale inside Arphaxas and he slowly held the knife out to her.

"Take it," he said, "and go."

Simirra was not at all sure she had heard him correctly. He was certainly the sort of brute that was more beast than man. But he was holding Martu's knife out to her. She reached for it gingerly, trying to move without disturbing his mood. She plucked it up from his hand.

"Go." He repeated.

She kept her eye on him, picking up stuff with her free hand. The pack was on the ground beside him, and she needed that if she was to carry all that she had brought. A whimper escaped her throat, for which she was profoundly ashamed. But the fire was so warm; she was so cold and suddenly shaking… uncontrollably. But she re-claimed the pack. She inched her way out of the overhang, into the rain. She felt as though she was weighted down with immeasurable weakness. The length of the night, and perhaps a fever, had managed to turn The Voice with its curious confidence into a whisper.

She took another step into the rainy dark. "I don't know where to go," she whispered.

She could not help but see him from the corner of her eye and through the strands of her filthy hair. He was sitting dispassionate, completely still and perfectly indifferent.

"What is that to me?" He growled.

The icy rain pelted through to her scalp. She was starved and starting to shake with such violence that she could hardly stand. If it made her a traitor to her poor dead babe to think of such things as food, she could not stop herself.

"I'm hungry."

He turned slowly and looked at her.

"Only for the night," Simirra heard herself beg. There was just the sound of the rain in answer.

When he finally spoke it startled her, as though she had drifted away somehow. It was more a grunt, though she perceived a sort of permission in what she could understand. If she had not been quite so miserable, she would have feared the company of this inhospitable stranger more than she did. She was, instead, quite shocked at what he said next, a concession of unexplained pity:

"You will leave in the morning."

Simirra closed her eyes, unable to restrain a quiet sigh. She felt her knees give. She felt herself being pulled through the mud toward the fire and under his rocky overhang again. Only her feet lay outside and she couldn't seem to move them as they turned to senseless weights of useless flesh in the cold.

CHAPTER ONE

<u>60 A.D.</u>

A VERY LARGE MAN SAT IN FRONT OF HIS FIRE FID-
dling with a bag of ancient stones, which hung around his neck. He
was watching a ship hoist its foresail to come ashore after a long
and stormy night. His own vessel was safe in harbor, moored like a minnow
beside a great Alexandrian and waiting out the storm on this tiny island. His
ship was a broad-bellied boat, fit for shallow coasts or deep. Cynwrig pulled
on his beard, conscious of its red blaze. It did set him apart in these regions.

The broad-chested man was a wanderer, an adventurer, a lover of marvelous things. He had a bit of the artist in him, hidden though it was by his
appearance. He was, in actuality, a merchant –   a disguise in itself, meant to
lend some practicality to his wanderlust. He would trade for spices, pick up
something frivolous for his sister and do it all the while for the freedom he
enjoyed at sea. Some might begrudge this stop off on the miniscule isle; it was
in fact, a miserable coast. But it was another land, be it small, that he would
explore after the rain to see what sort the people these were and to hear their
tales. He knew his ship was safe with his brother still aboard. His brother was
called Arthfael and only wanted to get rich in Egypt and bring himself home
to his bride.

Cynwrig heard an ominous rumble and suddenly jumped to his feet. The
ship he had been watching seemed to shudder, with waves piling up against
her. It appeared she was, in an instant, at the first calamitous moments of running aground! The rumble was followed by a terrible grinding, heard even
above the sound of the surf. Terrified men were yelling. He deserted his fire to
run at the sea, knowing as a seaman does, that the ship was doomed.

As he ran, he could see its sailors jumping off into the waves, a great number of them and – Cynwrig strained his eyes – there flew her standard. It was a
Roman ship! His sympathies died in the instant. He stopped. Men do die every

day. He folded his arms and waited, dispassionate now.

It took a good while, but he watched in near fascination as it seemed the shipwrecked men were none succumbing to the waves. Cynwrig saw it all from the spot where he had stopped running. They looked like drowned dogs with their clothes slicked down or ripped off, showing rib -cages and scrawny limbs – these men dragging in from the sea. They were coming ashore on whatever would float. Town folk had arrived to help the weakest ashore. Others were piling up brush for a fire to dry out survivors and warm them up. That struck him uncomfortably, as he was not an unkind fellow. But it was a Roman ship. Now he could surmise that it was also a prison ship, which meant the people of this dismal port were not after pillage and it did make him feel miserly.

Cynwrig slowly returned to his fire. He pulled out a limb for its flame and retraced his steps to the growing pile of brush. He poked the limb under a bit of tinder and backed away. The brush lit like a pyre, despite the rain. He began collecting brush beside the others, building the pile higher. It satisfied his conscience.

"Get back, man!" he suddenly heard, and turned to see what had put terror in the speaker's voice. There was one of the prisoners helping with the fire. Men were fast backing away from him. When Cynwrig focused on the man he saw a brush viper fastened to his hand. It was a particularly deadly serpent indeed, making the ordeal of dying a gruesome business.

The doomed man simply looked at it. He shook it off into the fire – altogether calm. There was courage to be admired in that!

"The gods wanted this one dead," he heard being whispered. "He must be a murderer."

"It's the fates," another replied.

"Pity to lose a whole ship over it, though."

Cynwrig watched the unfortunate prisoner, fascinated, seeing that there was no appearance of fear or concern. It was, in fact, a Roman centurion who seemed the most distressed. The soldier hurried to the stricken man and spoke to him. Then it seemed to be the captive who reassured the keeper – most peculiar.

"Let's wait to see what happens," the whispers continued.

Cynwrig kept his eyes on the pair. He scratched his beard then slowly returned to his own fire. Squatting there, he watched and waited. It was the peaceable manner about the prisoner that fascinated him, made him curious. He waited all morning.

After some hours passed, the prisoner showed no ill effects from the viper. So hearty he was, in fact, that the town folk were amending their first and hasty verdict. This prisoner was now, most assuredly, one of the gods.

Cynwrig chuckled at the efficiency of polytheism. He reached for his flask of dark ale and drained it.

"Have you another, brother?" a stranger, indeed, one of the shipwrecked, asked him. The man's clothes wore a thin skim of powdery white from a salt-water drenching.

Cynwrig looked up at him, the last of the beer still damp on his whiskers. "On my ship," he replied in the local Greek despite a brogue, which hinted that his roots were distant. "But I think there is ale aplenty over there," he nodded toward the crowd surrounding the snake-charmer-god.

The stranger smiled. He was clean-shaven, one that usually summed Cynwrig up in a scornful glance.

"Ah yes, my companion."

"O!" Cynwrig exclaimed, slightly embarrassed by his own enthusiasm, "Do you know him?"

"I do."

"Who is he? That serpent was one of Malta's worst!"

"He is a great teacher, and he was saved by the power of God."

Cynwrig frowned, always dubious, not willing to take the stranger at his word. Even so, he knew, in his experience of venoms, no other explanation. That the man was a prisoner of Rome, however, was a valuable recommendation.

"What do the Romans want with a teacher?" he asked suspiciously.

"His God is not Caesar."

"Nor mine."

"He teaches The Christ."

Cynwrig's frown deepened. "What do you mean, Christ?"

"The Son of God." The man answered, smiling easily.

Cynwrig laughed outright, taking full advantage of his position as barbarian on these shores. "Which one of the gods?"

"There is only One God, my friend."

It caught the laugh in Cynwrig's throat. He leaned forward to inspect the man more closely. He did appear to be Greek…

"Who are you?" he asked.

"I should rather tell about my God."

Which might have been true, but Cynwrig was no raw youth. He shrugged, "You Greeks have many gods."

"A regrettable error."

Cynwrig slowly stroked his red beard, stretching time, maintaining a neutral pose. It gave him the time to refocus on the immunity this stranger's friend seemed to enjoy of viper's poison, which was a curiosity he was more willing to explore. He was so absorbed, in fact, that he did not hear the girl as she came up to their fire. It was approaching nightfall.

"Pardon, my lord," she said softly. "Will you come to my master's house? He has sent me for you and… him." She nodded at the teacher.

"Who is your master?" the stranger kindly asked.

"Lord Publius, my lord," she answered, keeping her eyes fixed on the sand.

"And my friend here?"

It surprised Cynwrig. He watched the girl looking startled as well, and doubtful. "I can't say, my lord."

"Come then," the stranger said with smiling confidence. Cynwrig felt himself stand, all but stupefied.

"And what is your name, my friend?" the stranger asked.

"I am Cynwrig of the Northland," he answered, finding himself following the pair. It was a surprise to him that he would so obey the stranger, but he did and crossed the sand toward a gated estate.

ONCE INSIDE, CYNWRIG KEPT HIMSELF WELL BACK IN the room. He knew this was the house of the island's chief official.

His own status as barbarian did not mix well here and yet he was brought a cup of wine and some bread. He would like to have left the estate for his ship, and felt certainly free to do it, but there was stirring in him too great a curiosity to know about the men from the shipwreck. He had a brief concern for his younger brother left behind in their ship and if Arthfael should wonder what had come of him. Though only briefly, because the servant girl had found him again.

"My Lord's father is healed!" she exclaimed, taking hold of his sleeve. "The man called Paul put his hands on him! Surely we are visited by the gods!"

Cynwrig would not believe her tongue, but he must believe her eyes for they were ecstatic. "Did he say that?" Cynwrig whispered suspiciously.

"Say what?"

"That he is a god."

She shook her head. "No," she answered. "He said it was another god… Jesus, the Christ."

Cynwrig felt oddly glad to hear that, for he had seen in his travels, too many ports with too many gods and too much self-importance. Something inside Cynwrig had wanted to trust the stranger, though he did not know why, and it would have rubbed against the hair to find him but another ambitious rouge.

"I am going for my mother," the girl whispered as though she had been distracted from her errand. Then she left him and dashed out the door, leaving it to stand open. Once again, he might have left as easily, but he turned back toward the door at the end of the hall instead. He had the quiet prickle feeling that an important thing was afoot. It was an intuition, a sort of seeking and was in keeping with the heritage of his family.

It was a short wait. The stranger opened the door and found Cynwrig's with his eyes. He came swiftly down the corridor and to him directly, all smiles, hiding nothing from his face. It occurred to Cynwrig that the cover of a beard might serve the stranger well as he displayed himself openly.

"What did I tell you?" the man announced, overjoyed. Cynwrig shook his head in puzzlement.

"I am a physician, my friend Cynwrig. That poor man was going to die but for the Spirit of Jesus the Christ!"

Again it was the man's face that was convincing. Cynwrig felt his blood shoot cold down his legs and up to his scalp. Despite himself and a penchant toward the skeptical, he took hold of the man's arm with an embarrassing degree of urgency – and glad his brother couldn't see it. He bent down, because he was a tall man, and leaned forward to whisper, "Who is this Jesus the Christ?"

"The only Son of God!" the stranger answered as he had on the beach but with no quiet voice and no impatience. He spoke, in fact, with genuine concern, as if Cynwrig was as important to him as a brother.

But the girl was suddenly back and fairly dragging a stooped beggar woman behind her. The girl looked at the stranger, right in the eyes. "My mother…" she pleaded.

The physician instantly turned away from Cynwrig and toward the pair. He put his hands on the old woman's back. Cynwrig was caught by the tenderness of that gesture. He watched the man bend down to look in her face. He smiled and said something most quietly. The woman yelped. It was a great surprise to Cynwrig that she should have such strength for such a yelp. Then she stood straight up and her arms shot up toward the ceiling. She started to whirl. Cynwrig might have thought she was a young girl!

The two women hugged each other, laughing, crying, then abruptly stopped. They fell at the stranger's feet. He bent and touched the mother's shoulder again. "Stand up," he said kindly. "You are healed by The Christ. Thank Him."

"Who is this Christ?" Cynwrig heard the question, louder this time, and realized it had come from his own lips. He also realized how urgent was his desire to hear the answer.

BUT IT SEEMED THAT WOULD HAVE TO WAIT. COMING with the boldness of a sort of desperation were great crowds which filled the house of Publius for three days. All who came were sick of some disease, or crippled as the servant girl's mother, and all healed as she had been. The teacher, whose name was Paul, and his companion, whose name was Luke, were kept busy mending them all. Cynwrig was like a forest owl, all eyes and silent, watching the care they took with each one, be they beggar or rich. It was nothing he had ever seen before.

On the second day, his brother Arthfael found him, because the island was a-stir with word of the healers. And Arthfael had lost his urgency for Egypt and home. Even the lovely Aingeal would wait for such enormity as had set the island astir. Cynwrig had finally left the hall; was pushed out, in fact, by the crowd. But he was patient, sitting with his brother at the fire in Publius's courtyard; knowing somehow that the one who had found him three days before would find him again. It was the atmosphere of a spring's fair. The sick were healed, the great storm passed and all was well with the world. Even the centurion, who was a Roman no less, seemed in wonder of the man who was his prisoner.

The servant girl's mother had taken to bringing them food, because it was a-plenty, being brought by the villagers or Publius himself. Cynwrig began to think perhaps the whole of heaven had opened up and all Hades had been set at bay. He believed it was so when Paul came through the doors of the estate for the first time and began to teach. He told of an only Son of God. It could nearly be believed for what was done on Malta!

But what was told next was, for Cynwrig, a step too far: this Christ who, if it could be believed, was murdered, this man of miracles. And miracles, Cynwrig had seen! Why would such a one be killed?

"And three days later rose from the dead."

Cynwrig snatched his head up. "What did he say?" he asked his brother.

But Arthfael was leaning forward, hearing the impossible as though it were true. The servant girl and her mother had taken to sitting with himself and Arthfael. So they had heard it too and seemed as rapt as his brother, who had always been a romantic. Cynwrig looked back at the one named Paul, the prisoner, the one to survive a bush viper. He looked about the crowd to find faces that believed, backs and legs and missing limbs that were healed. He also found the eyes of the physician, Luke, who was looking back at him.

Cynwrig did not hear the last that Paul had to say. He only watched as the teacher seemed to finish speaking and Publius came up beside him and kissed him on both sides of his face. Then Paul disappeared into the crowd as any ordinary man. And that was when Luke found Cynwrig again.

"So now you know, friend Cynwrig, who The Christ is," he said, sitting down amongst them as if to resume their last conversation.

Cynwrig could not reply. Magic resurrections were the stuff of fools. He fingered the pouch around his neck, rolling the stones inside it between his fingers. That last was more than a step too far.

"I see you do not believe, my friend," Luke said quietly.

"You do?" Cynwrig found his voice.

Luke nodded, a soft and comfortable smile on his lips. "He is God."

"Did you see him then, this Jesus?"

"No. But Paul saw Him, and he knows the many others who knew Him."

Cynwrig thought as much, though he did not take Luke for a fool. There were, after all, the miracles. That could not be ignored, this undeniable power to heal. He scratched his beard, "So," he muttered, "You did not know him... yourself."

"I know him," Luke replied.

"But you said..." Cynwrig did not finish the sentence. It was a riddle for which he had no patience. "Who saw Him alive then," Cynwrig pressed, "after the murder?"

"Many did. His disciples."

"Did Paul?"

"Yes. Paul saw Him."

Cynwrig stopped. It was an answer he had not expected. But why should that really make the difference, that Paul had seen Him? It was only three days ago, perhaps four that Paul had come ashore with the others, a half drowned rat. Even as he thought it, Cynwrig knew Paul was not to be compared with the others, nor Luke. Who did he know, after all, that could shake a viper into the fire and heal and entire village? And it was not that Cynwrig was a godless man, or wanted to be. It was that their people had waited so long, had waited till they had all but stopped waiting.

He was suddenly struck with the possibility that perhaps the man, Jesus, had not really died. Cynwrig had seen men before who only seemed to die. But he would not ask that question, because he would not insult the healers

"Tell me," Cynwrig asked instead, "this Hebrew, Mary, she was a virtuous woman?"

"A virgin you mean?"

The servant girl was young enough to blush.

"Everything is just as Paul taught you Cynwrig. Mary was a virgin and she bore the child Jesus – the only Son of God."

Cynwrig could not restrain the skeptical smile. Here it was – the old story – resurrected like an alleged Son of God. He glanced at Arthfael who appeared to be thinking the same.

"Begotten of God, eh?" he whispered, leaning toward his brother, glad to see Arthfael was not twice deceived.

Luke looked slightly injured, "What are you saying?" he asked.

"Sounds like an old fable," Cynwrig replied ironically, glancing back at the physician. "It is told from our first forebears that there is written with the stars a virgin who will bear the seed that will stomp his heel on the head of the serpent. We once waited a month long, after a betrothal, to be sure the bride was not the virgin of the stars. It's an ancient tradition not kept anymore," He shot a look at his brother and the servant girl was blushing again.

"How do you know this?" Luke asked sounding incredulous.

Cynwrig nodded his head at the shore and at his ship that was docked there. "Our ancient Father. My ship is named for him, The Madai."

Luke looked at the docks. "The one without a figurehead…"

"We also do not believe in gods you can see," Cynwrig answered, nodding proudly at his ship. It was moored beside a great Alexandrian, whose figure-head was the twin gods Castor and Pollux. "Our Family has always held to the One Creator God," he told them.

"But you are a Norse!" the servant girl exclaimed, disbelieving and meaning of course that he was a barbarian and eater of children. She was scarlet now with her hand over her mouth as though she had stunned even herself.

"I am no…" Cynwrig stopped himself, unwilling to voice the dreaded name.

"Pagan," he finished instead.

"We are not!" Arthfael insisted indignantly.

"They came from the North to invade the land in the days of our forebear, Madai. A few survived it, we sons of Madai, and we keep the first ways." Cynwrig let his voice trail. "Now you tell me that this Crushing Seed is born…"

"Born to a young Jewess maid by the Spirit of God," Luke agreed, "died for the sins of the world, risen from the dead and returned to heaven."

"Hmm," Cynwrig mused, stroking his beard, "A Hebrew…not of Japhet…but of Shem."

"To make all men holy, be they Jew or Gentile."

Cynwrig's mouth literally gaped. He swung round to stare at Luke with his green eyes blazing. "What did you say?"

"The Christ has come for the Jew and the Gentile."

"What of holy?"

"Jesus came to make all men holy, those who will have Him."

Cynwrig didn't answer but only looked at Arthfael with a great intensity. "What puzzles you, friend? Luke asked, "Is it too much for Him?"

"It is only that…"

But they were joined at that moment by Paul himself. He sat down without formalities beside his companion, Luke, and as though he was any ordinary man.

"You must hear this, brother Paul," Luke exclaimed. "This man is from a people with ancient tradition.

They have been waiting for The Christ."

"Are you Jews?" Paul asked doubtfully, leaning forward to look at Cynwrig and his brother more closely. They shook their heads. Cynwrig might have been insulted if not that these Jews were children of Shem, who was greatly admired.

"But you were looking for Messiah? How did you know?"

"Our ancient Father, Madai, brought the truth of the stars back from Ab Noach himself!" Cynwrig answered using even the Hebrew endearment and watching as his words both amazed and impressed the two healers – which had been his intention.

"I think we should like to hear this story," Luke began just as a middle-aged woman fell against Paul with a storm of tears and kisses. They were her thanks because she could not speak the words for her joy.

Paul responded as if she were a precious mother or a sister and that impressed Cynwrig again because the man had to be exhausted, being pressed on every side for days long.

"Let us go inside," Luke suggested when the woman was gone.

"We have something for you to see…" Arthfael interjected, speaking for the first time and passionate. "Will you come to our ship?"

Cynwrig watched Paul glance across the courtyard at the centurion and he was reminded again that Paul was a prisoner of Rome. As though the soldier was tuned to Paul's very look, he crossed the cobblestones toward them.

"This brother wishes to take me aboard his ship," Paul began.

The centurion looked doubtful but a moment. "Of course, citizen," he responded. "I need your word."

"You have it."

And that is how the little group left the courtyard of Publius and came to be escorted onto Cynwrig's trading ship by guardians of the Great Roman Empire.

A<small>RTHFAEL CROSSED THE CRAMPED CAPTAIN'S QUARTERS</small> of The Madai to a small cabinet, which was built of ordinary timber but fastened with an iron lock. The lock and hinges were a craftsman's work of art, scrolls and swirls of great beauty beyond their purpose. It gave the cabinet a look of importance, which out-shined its quite ordinary surroundings.

Arthfael unlocked the cabinet and reached inside. He drew out a roll of hide. Carefully pulling back the hide, he exposed another cloth of fine weaving, blue in color, which swaddled something long and flat. He reverently passed the object, still in its wrappings, to his older brother. Cynwrig laid it on a table and folded back the cloth. He looked up then with the fine lines of pride framing his eyes.

"A plank of the very Ark!" he announced. His audience had a look of puzzlement.

"The Ark of Noah," Cynwrig pressed. "Brought by our ancient father, Madai himself."

Paul sat down at Cynwrig's table and put his hand on the old plank. "The Ark can still be seen today," he rebutted quietly. *

"Perhaps," Cynwrig conceded. "But can it be taken and received from the hand of Shem himself?" The two healers looked at each other. "I think we had better have your story," suggested Luke.

CHAPTER TWO

"START WITH THE ARK OF NOAH," SUGGESTED the servant girl, who had followed and been almost forgotten. She put her arms on the table and leaned forward to see Cynwrig in the eyes.

"No, brother," Arthfael replied quietly, "start with the question."

"What question?" Paul asked.

Cynwrig shrugged. It was a question that was said to have followed the wise Madai all his days. It seemed quite an indulgence, after so much time and blood. It was not a thing to ponder overlong, at least for men, most especially in these modern days. And yet Luke had said it: "to make men holy, be they Jew or Gentile". It did seem too absurd, for Luke had said this too, that it took the murder of this Christ – who, if he was what Luke claimed, the long a-waited Crushing Seed and only Son of God – that it should take his death to make men holy. If God were God, surely He could simply have spoken it so. Never the less, it made the rather numerous hairs on his neck stand straight up.

"Answer!" came the sharp bark of the Roman, which wrenched Cynwrig back to the moment.

"A philosopher's question, sir," he replied sardonically.

"Tell us, brother," Luke urged.

But Cynwrig began the story at the beginning. He told the quest of their long ago hero, Madai, who had sailed the Great Brine Sea to the coast of Mizraim, crossed the plains of Shinar to do battle with spirit and with flesh. That flesh, he told them, had been the Mighty Hunter, Nimrod himself. He told how Shem with his army had defeated Nimrod in an epic battle, had then taken Madai to the foot of Mount Ararat and to Noah, the Ancient of Ancients. It was a long story and he told it uninterrupted. But he told it quickly in deference to the Centurion, though he was loath to admit it, until he came to the setting of Madai's last and enduring question, "What can make men holy?"

Cynwrig stared at the Roman as he recited the words, near to daring the man to laugh. The Centurion appeared unmoved but for a slight pull at the corner of his eye.

"It was in the house of Job," Cynwrig continued. "After Madai and Kittim had returned from Ararat, that Madai could not sleep and he asked that question of their young companion, Iscah."

Possibly this was the part Arthfael liked the most and it made Cynwrig nearly smile, deciding to tell it, because as the story went, it was when Madai came to know that he loved Iscah first and Arthfael was a true romantic. You had only to ask his new young wife, Aingeal, for confirmation of that. All the details of it were kept in song over all the ages past. It was as dear a tale to The Family as any tales of Pollux or Castor were to the Greeks.

"Madai was sitting with Iscah," he said, "those many years ago, before the hearth in Job's grand estate. They were each waiting for Kittim…"

"Who is Kittim?" the servant girl interjected. But Cynwrig continued on as though she hadn't asked.

MADAI

THEY WERE WAITING, JUST THAT WAY… WITH THE PROMise of Iscah's fingers on his hand when Madai heard a footfall at the door. The weight of her hand was child-like, but with the prospect of a woman. And when Iscah stood, crimson silk rustling happily, the depth of his sentiment was realized, embellished by the girl's brilliant eyes. In that initial moment, Madai forgot her face was not for him, but for his excellent friend.

"Kittim!"

Madai heard Iscah's voice enunciate the name hopefully. He stood up beside her, turning to face the door. She was very close. He could almost feel her heart racing.

"Kittim," she cried again, and hurried forward.

Kittim entered. In that moment, Madai could feel the atmosphere change, when he had sat with her and pondered imponderable matters and felt her head against him, her fingers on his hand with affection. Now it was broken entirely. Only the stars remained the same, blinking out their story. But how does a man of flesh walk with Mighty God again as prophesied by Enoch and promised by Job? How does a man occupy an Eden at the side of a Holy God?

Madai turned slowly away from the window, reluctantly toward the drama of Iscah greeting Kittim. It wrenched him through the heart.

KITTIM

KITTIM THOUGHTFULLY MASSAGED HIS CHIN. HIS ATTENtion was for Madai. Though Iscah had pounced at him with irrepressible glee, it was Madai's questions that occupied his thoughts. "I don't know the answer, Madai," he replied. "I would surely like to know."

Kittim moved to the open window. He looked at the same night sky that had arrested Madai and birthed the question as well. There was bedazzled there, a fine tapestry – a foretelling of mysteries and planned before the creation of the earth, already done – yet to come. He remembered a first and glorious Shout! A great, epic explosion of devastating, magnificent light, and after that – other inconceivable dimensions of wonders! Ah, but the power of The Voice was equaled by an ordination, a mystery, a tragedy, a love story for which he was… jealous.

What would make men holy? Kittim could not imagine.

"I do not know," he quietly replied.

MADAI GOT UP; ENOCH'S CRYPTIC PROPHESY AS MUCH A mystery as when Job first recounted it. Madai paced to his friend, suddenly taken aback at the look of his face and more in doubt than before of his question. It took a moment for Kittim to look back at Madai with real comprehension in his eyes. Madai gripped him by the shoulders and gave him a shake.

"It's not so terrible as that, Kittim, if you don't know."   He tried to laugh. "What I don't know will fill the sea. Ask Iscah."

ISCAH

BUT ISCAH WAS NOT INTERESTED IN MADAI'S IGNO-rance, vast as it was. How Kittim had turned her aside to drink in Madai's question was at her forefront. Unknowable questions were Madai's specialty. And she was vexed sorely, yet again, at the power he seemed to wield, at the question that had shaken her unshakable Kittim.

She rustled her gown to draw their attention. "I think Madai wants to go home." She announced abruptly.

Kittim's rich brown eyes widened with pleasure, but no surprise, and to her great dismay. "Yes," he answered. "Madai is going home a teacher."

"Not before the lambs are weaned," Madai interjected. "Job still needs us."

Kittim nodded. "Of course, my friend. And we cannot forget, there is coming a wedding." That statement pleased Iscah. There was true pleasure in Kittim's face, thinking of Tutan's wedding, which proved he was not adverse to such things. And besides, dear Tutan, their Eastern companion who had come seeking God just as Madai had come – how he had pined for Reenah! Iscah knew the woman was excellent of face and now, of character. Why… there was the answer to Madai's question! He had only to open his eyes. Love of God made men holy. Madai made such complications of it all!

CYNWRIG QUIT THE TALE TO LOOK AT PAUL. "THE QUES-tion, you see."

Paul nodded.

"Are you stopping now?" the servant girl asked with disappointment. "What about Iscah and Madai? And who are those others?"

The sun shone a last and orange glow through the open door of the captain's quarter. Cynwrig carefully wrapped the ark plank back in its weaving and then the leather. He gave it to Arthfael, who placed it reverently inside the cabinet.

Cynwrig watched Luke watching them with interest even as the Roman soldier scuffed his boot against the newer planks of their merchant ship.

"My Roman friend cannot leave me here," Paul explained quietly. "It would cost his neck to have a man escape."

"I have your word," the centurion replied as quietly.

Paul nodded and a look passed between the two. "It encourages me," Paul began, looking away and at Cynwrig, "to know there is such knowledge on your shores. All men be they far or near are loved of God and He would have them hear the good news of His Son. I fear my days of preaching are nearing an end."

Cynwrig believed he caught a pallor cross the centurion's face at such a declaration.

"If it would please the rabbi to hear about the gods of your lands, then it is of small cost to me that we should hear it," the centurion announced, in what was as modest a tone as Cynwrig supposed possible for such a one.

The Roman brought a stool up. He sat in front of the door, which led onto the deck of The Madai. He nodded once at Cynwrig.

Cynwrig kept a stony face, looking back at the soldier, though he felt somewhat tempered by what appeared an unexpected benevolence in the Roman toward the healer. As if to acknowledge the sentiment, Cynwrig brought out the best of wine from Iberia, intended for Arthfael's first night home with Aingeal. And when his brother did not complain, but replaced the old candle with a new one, Cynwrig produced two mugs, which would have to be shared, he supposed.

He poured the wine, savored the expensive flavor and slid the cup across the table toward the physician. The servant girl, her name was Corinna, smiled rather shyly at him. There was anticipation in her eyes, waiting for him to tell all about Iscah and Madai. Arthfael too was waiting and keenly because he knew his oldest brother was no willing romantic.

"I shall tell the wedding, old brother," Arthfael said with a laugh. "I have the experience."

"Then tell it quickly," Cynwrig replied. "There's stouter stuff to follow."

Arthfael acknowledged Cynwrig with a wink. He started his story with Madai, who was, in Arthfael's opinion, much like himself.

MADAI WAS HAPPY FOR HIS EASTERN FRIEND AND SLIGHT-ly envious. O, not that he begrudged Tutan his happiness, but that he missed his own. He was reminded of his wedding day on this, Tutan's wedding day. He was also watching Iscah, trying to picture her in the Dance of Maidens, a clan rite that lined the Family's daughters opposite the sons, and waving boughs of seed grass. She clapped her hands together then in such a way that reminded him of how she had taken delight in the sight of shaggy flightless birds whose eggs she had shown them how to steal. There was such richness in her; the way she viewed the world, which was mystery enough in itself – that she could endure what she had with an unspoiled soul. He realized in that moment that she was made of a substance that was part of his own song now and she would fit his world, be it even across the Sea.

"Is it not marvelous, Madai? And see Tutan!" she exclaimed.

"That old hawk!" Madai replied, "He has his prize. Not so consecrated after all."

Kittim joined them. "A wedding is…divine inspiration," he opined with a curious expression, "for a worthy bride."

ISCAH WATCHED KITTIM AS HE SPOKE TO MADAI. HE could be so serious, and at so happy occasions as this!

But they were in their own mysterious world again, Kittim and Madai, where she felt excluded. There were moments when Kittim could see only Madai with an intensity that irritated her. She turned away, slightly wounded, to ponder the wedding herself. But Kittim had spoken of 'a worthy bride' and she hoped he did not hold Reenah's past idolatries against her as the woman had ground them all to dust and sacrifice was made for her. One precious lamb, at a time when Job's little herd was tenuous at best.

Well, he was blessed of God once again, for which Iscah was deeply glad of heart.

She thought the bird enclosure was never more splendid, repaired of the neglect it endured during Job's trouble. It rang a chorus brighter, perhaps than ever before. It sang of sweetest spring, a glorious feathered chorus. And well it was that their voices filled the air, and their plumage painted the trees, for their one time mistress, Reenah, would be married here today.

There stood Tutan, and there, Reenah who was dressed in a silk of more beauty than any Iscah had ever seen. Her veil seemed to waft in and out at her every breath.

REENAH WAS A-TREMBLE AS IF SHE WERE A MAIDEN. SHE felt Tutan beside her, though they did not touch.

She heard the voice of Job but as a backdrop to the bright melody of his birds. He was speaking now of Eve… and ribs… and replenishing the earth. She felt herself blush behind the veil, and was truly surprised by it.

Tutan lifted her veil. He was her beloved. She was, even now, amazed, looking into his eyes, slightly crimped and full of admiration. He took a silver cup from which he drank and offered to her. She smelled the sweet new wine and felt it trickle cool down her throat. It was their covenant making, and her hand was shaking. When they turned toward their friends, they brushed against each other and she was shot through with icy fire and glad for the coming days of seclusion, seven in all.

The music began. It was Lehabim, playing the reeds. Reenah began to dance. She did not think she had ever danced so well. She turned, raising her arms skyward and feeling silken veils billow around her ankles. She read Tutan's intention in his eyes. She was no young girl now, but greatly desired. The paint of love, it is perfect.

ISCAH WATCHED THEM. NEVER HAD SHE BEEN SO WED, though she had been second wife to an aging idolater, Hamonheb. She had not known the wonder of a marriage of love before and was suddenly threatened with deepest remorse. But she straightened her back and watched the couple, and thought about Kittim. She let herself imagine it would all turn out well, that she would wear a silk so beautiful and drink from a silver cup one day, that Kittim would look at her as Tutan was looking at Reenah.

So she joined the dance as she once had danced beneath the desert stars, though with only a dog, Aten to see. At her every revolution, there were faces of friends now: Lehabim, of course, being unabashed, Madai watching her with a curious expression, The Lady, blissful, an artful swaying beside her husband. She glimpsed Marisheba and lastly Kittim. He seemed uncharacteristically intrigued – a hopeful sign.

When the dancing was done, the feasting began. Tutan's glad face encouraged her. Had she ever seen him so happy? She remembered him at the top of that mountain, the head of the Pishon with no Eden. And yet, he had been at peace, confident of God. If she were assured of any man's allegiance, it would be Tutan's - Kittim's being presupposed. She knew that his love for Reenah did not worsen his love of Mighty God. She had been jealous of that once, but she was older now. Yes, truly, her love of Kittim beat stronger every day, and did not chase aside her God. Iscah lowered her lashes to still a rising flood of crimson and took a sip of wine.

So soon the feast was ended, though Iscah imagined it was endless for Tutan, who was now lifting his bride to the back of her horse. He touched her so tenderly. He climbed with a great exuberance onto Cusah and only then turned to wave at Iscah. He wore a sheepish smile. She knew it was for his once proclamation that he had altogether withstood a carnal life, consecrated to God in the entire.

Iscah waved back and watched them go, galloping toward Reenah's cottage. After a time, she lowered her arm, slowly flooding with a wilted sort of feeling. The festivity was ended, Kittim was walking back inside with Madai and she…was well acquainted with the carnal. How she was reminded of that at the most inopportune of moments! Taken by Sabeans and sold at the Shinar market, her carnal experience was thrust upon her when she might still have claimed the description, 'child', of which she was no more, but robbed. Perhaps it was her hopes for Kittim, which made her own lost virtue rise up to insurmountable heights.

'And yet,' she suddenly thought, 'Reenah's stain was surely darker – an idolatress by choice.

Still she is reclaimed by a lamb's offering and the love of Mighty God, praise His Name!' Iscah watched the dust begin to obscure the distant riders. 'Claimed now by the love of a virtuous man.' She thought, certainly nearly as virtuous as Kittim… Iscah encouraged herself. She waved again at the dust kicked up by the horse's hooves, more vigorously now, to assure Tutan of her joy at his joy, and to chase away old regrets.

CYNWRIG HAD TO ADMIT THAT ARTHFAEL FINISHED THE wedding in a reasonably short telling. Corinna was pleased. Even the learned physician seemed not to mind.

"Madai and Iscah?" the girl prodded. "Or is it Kittim?"

Cynwrig started to protest, because it was just too irrelevant and there were weighty matters to get to. But Luke patted the girl's hand. He had a kindly attitude towards Corinna whose mother he had healed, though he would insist it was The Christ who did it. And indeed, Cynwrig was anxious to know more about this Christ. But Luke seemed to think his Family's story was important, and he seemed to think that the servant girl was important as well.

"This Madai is your ancient father?" Luke asked.

"Well…" Cynwrig began.

Paul leaned toward the two brothers. "It would do my soul well to know the story of Madai; truly well. I will not carry the Name of Christ to your lands. You and Arthfael must do that. But I would like to hear about your people and know how it was you came to look for the Master."

Cynwrig saw how much Paul meant it. There was true longing in his eyes, even love for an unknown people, which Cynwrig could not entirely understand. He was angered again at the Centurion, even if Paul was not, for the Roman was jailer to so remarkable a man. He shot the soldier a look, only to see a deep regret on his face as well. Incomprehensible once again.

"Yes, Captain," Corinna was saying. "Tell us the story."

CHAPTER 3

1900 BC

*M*ADAI AND KITTIM STAYED WITH JOB TILL AU-
tumn, when the lambs were weaned and Job was entirely well
and The Lady was near her time. Marisheba would serve as
midwife. She had delivered all their first sons and daughters. She would deliver Tutan and Reenah's as well, in spring. It was a bittersweet departure.
Also, there was the disagreement.

"You don't know what you are asking, Iscah," Kittim had argued. "Will
you leave your fathers?"

"My father is dead," she had answered flatly.

"Yes," he said, "but Madai's lands are not like these."

By which she knew Kittim was determined to travel with Madai. She had
frowned at him. "But, you are the only family I have."

"There is Job."

"Job has his Lady and will soon have a son. Tutan has Reenah. I shall be
second of heart to everyone."

"Let her come." It had been Madai's voice.

That had startled her. She was enormously grateful and vaguely perplexed...
that Madai was the one to want her. But those three words had brought her
here, sitting on the pony, a parting gift from Job. She had named him Aten as
a token to a brave dog, and she pondered these things.

"It will turn out well," she whispered to Aten and the words, now spoken
aloud if only to a horse, comforted her.

She sighed, readjusted herself in the saddle and looked ahead at the endless
terrain. Madai was in the lead.

Behind him was a camel and affixed to its pack were Ark planks. Madai
had taken enormous care with those planks and with the bone of a baby behemoth turned to stone. They were unwieldy and heavy, but of prime importance

to Madai. They were for his people in the West who were, she could only imagine, so far a distance from the scattering - the deluge so far a history that likely it would do them good to have such relics. She slowly smiled, consoling herself at the thought of a journey so long – long enough indeed to change Kittim's mind.

By noon, she was outrageously hungry. Too many timely meals at Job's table, she supposed. The sun had rained down on them hot, and Aten gleamed with sweat, turning his grey coat black. Their route would bring them soon to the Euphrates. It was parent-river to the tributary that coiled its way behind Reenah's cottage, eventually coming to such depths as to hide Leviathan – which would be a thought to avoid given the tale of Lemmeri and her eaten camel. It was across that river that was slung the hemp bridge. The bridge brought them to the cliff of bones, turned to stone, which in itself had a tale to tell. She glanced up again at such a bone riding low on Madai's camel. Creatures caught in a mighty deluge, washed up and dumped together to wait these long years and whisper a warning to earth's remnant.

She remembered that day well when Madai had chosen so enormous an object to unearth, as hot as today! These plains they rode were sun drenched, ready for harvest and golden. She idly patted Aten's wet hide when, in the distance and to her eye's welcome, there appeared a tiny undulating path of green.

"We shall come upon a river soon," she whispered, an assurance the horse did not need as he could smell it.

But the time in reaching Euphrates seemed longer, in the end, than she had hoped. And even then, they followed it south so far a distance that Iscah felt herself tilting off the horse. Aten stopped every time, which jolted her awake and saved her being found not hearty enough for the journey. Even still, it did not save her being wakened a last time, lifted down by Madai's hands. She was so grateful to rest her head that she did not bother to speak or think of her stomach. She was only glad that Kittim did not point out her weakness, or fuss again about her coming. She insisted to herself that she would bear up better tomorrow as she felt Madai cover her up with a blanket that smelled sweetly of home.

AND IN THE MORNING, IT SEEMED THERE WAS STILL CON-vincing to do.

"So, you are awake!" it was Madai's voice.

She pulled the blanket to her chin, a little shivery and fuzzy-headed.

"It is not too late," Kittim told her.

She thought first that he was consoling her about the hour of the morning…

"You can find your way back," he continued, "Job is but a day's ride."

Those words were a rude slap. She pulled the blanket tight and squared her shoulders. Already, her hair was dry of the oil she used, the braid pulling free and she looked a little like the waif she once had been. But she couldn't answer him. He continued to watch her, his face looking worried. And that, at least, was something.

But it was Madai who offered her something to eat and a look of encouragement.

"What was so bad about Lehabim?" was what Kittim asked next.

Both Iscah and Madai gaped at him in astonishment.

"Well," it was Madai that answered, "He has an intent for her."

Iscah felt, for the first time in all her knowing of Kittim, an ill feeling. It spared her another threat of weepiness. She dropped the carcass of the fish in the fire; a few remains of flesh still clinging to its backbone.

"Iscah will need a husband," Kittim replied quietly, "for protection. She is of age."

Madai fell quiet. It seemed to Iscah that it scratched him wrong, implying Lehabim as her husband. She felt the blood drain from her face in agreement, and hearing the dread words come through Kittim's lips was all the worse.

"I shall protect myself," she answered stiffly. She watched them both look as if to measure her. Madai seemed pleased, even proud, but Kittim seemed... not so sure at all.

"A decision was made," Madai insisted.

"Yes it was. I am only thinking of the journey. It will be... difficult."

"Why so? We've made it before," Madai argued.

There was a moment of quiet before Kittim spoke again. "Yes," he said. "But now there will be resistance."

"What do you mean?"

Kittim gave Madai one of his looks.

"There are ones that will not want you safe, Madai."

"We have bested trouble before," he answered.

"Yes," Kittim replied. "But now you carry a truth with you, and there are ones that scorn the truth, ones that will unleash the worst to keep you on these shores."

Iscah watched the shudder that ran Madai's length. Men always seemed to imagine the worst and she could not forget the affront of Kittim's suggestion – that she should be for Lehabim. It was what was mostly on her mind. Her inclination had been to transfer the first indignation she had ever harbored against Kittim to Madai, for whom she had had many such feelings. But Madai had defended her here. Still... Kittim did seem truly worried...

So she rode through the second day of their journey with a modicum of dignity and a resolution to patience. She did not complain or ask to rest or be the first to mention food. She kept her seat atop Aten without the embarrassing nodding off of yesterday, till it was finally Madai who pulled them up to stop for the night. It seemed early, and she suspected it was for her benefit. It was, to her, no matter what had inspired it. They had stopped; she could eat, bathe, sleep and above all else, wake to a third day with Kittim beside her.

AS FOR MADAI, HE WAS STILL FEELING THE CHILL. THAT human shudder at Kittim's warning was just a small thing, so much smaller than the danger of which Kittim had more than implied, though he had no way of knowing that then. He was presently and pleasantly watching Iscah sleep.

"She's held up well today," he was quick to remind Kittim. They had settled in for the night and Madai was encouraged with their progress. Given a day, perhaps two more and the great mountain of the river, Pishon, would rise on the horizon. Indeed, good progress and no menacing terrors.

He looked at her again, sleeping with the blanket pulled up to her eyes. She was looking like her child self once more, the trappings of civilization being already worn away, the last of which in fact, had been scrubbed clean in the river. Her hair had dried to its springy former condition, giving her face a frame of wild, dark curls. He suddenly thought of Ido with a start, almost feeling the silk of her sun colored hair between his fingers. It impaled his stomach like the tip of a lance.

"Are you sick, Madai?" he heard Kittim ask.

And Madai pulled himself back – just enough to look up. "You've gone pure white, my friend."

Madai looked up at the sky instead of answering. How fast it came dark and filled with stars! "I was thinking of home," he finally replied.

Kittim studied him thoughtfully before he asked, "With so much despair?"

But Ido's ghost was fading and Madai was becoming himself again. He was also thinking about their morning's conversation. "I am wondering why it is that you do not want Iscah with us. What could be worse than the Anak?"

Kittim stirred the fire with a twig before he dropped it into the flames. "She was safe with Job."

"She was safe with us," Madai insisted.

He could see Kittim was remembering their first journey together as the dark man gave him an ironic look and a smile to match. "Well, she was rescued, not once, but twice."

"Lehabim," Madai muttered.

Kittim's smile widened. "Hamonheb," he corrected, and Madai blinked, self-conscious. "Yes," he quickly agreed, "Hamonheb."

But Kittim was uncharacteristically curious tonight. "And now I am wondering why it is that you so much wanted to bring her."

Madai felt the temperature of his face change. Having traveled what seemed another lifetime of adventure, he and Kittim had yet to broach so private a thing. It was a subject, in truth, that still erupted with unexpected contradiction. What was waking his heart awoke his pain.

"I…" he tried to answer. He looked at the stars again. "Had a wife once."

"Yes, you did."

Madai felt a half smile turn up the right edge of his beard. "I might want one again."

30

It was a still night, so quiet Madai could hear Kittim breathe. "O," he answered. And then it was quiet again.

Having said it, Madai felt settled. "Yes," he affirmed. "Forgive me, Madai. I have been thinking of other… things."

"What do you mean?" Madai quipped, "Iscah is… more than only beautiful. You cannot say that you don't know it."

Kittim nodded slowly. "She has ripened well."

Even the night was surprised by Madai's laugh as the river splashed with startled frogs.

"I sometimes forget the sort of things that engage the heart," Kittim continued and Madai shook his head, disbelieving.

"Do not try to convince me that your heart cannot be engaged," he laughed.

Kittim shrugged. "Well." Was all he answered in reference to himself. "She is a highly valued daughter of God," he continued. "She would bring you joy and solace."

Madai clamped his friend on the shoulder with a snort. "You sound like an old man, Kittim." He glanced at Iscah, wondering when it was he had first started seeing her 'that' way and heartily convinced that she would likely be aghast by it.

"But can you protect her?"

"I will protect her," Madai insisted. "What has gotten your confidence?"

"There are wolves in the night." Kittim muttered.

"And dragons and giants. We've bettered them all, Kittim."

Kittim looked Madai full in the face. "But you have something now. Something he does not want you to bring back."

Madai was starting to itch. He wished he had washed off the sweat of the day as Iscah had done. And, Kittim was waxing mysterious again. Madai scratched his scalp. "Who is he?"

Kittim trained his eyes at Madai before he uttered with darkest of tones, "The Prince of these regions."

"Nimrod is dead," Madai declared evenly.

Kittim looked away, appearing as though he was scanning the bushes even now, which gave Madai an eerie chill.

"He is a prince in regions unseen, Madai, and more dangerous by boundless degrees than Nimrod."

Madai froze, still as stone. He remembered an encounter, feeling hunted down and gnawed at by a thing in the dark when he had followed Yamma to find, hiding in his forest, The Banned - plying a new god with naked devotion. It was a time in his life that he had thought to leave behind, having found the Ancient of Ancients, having felt seen again by God.

"Do you mean a spectre?" Madai asked.

Kittim smiled, which seemed to betray an ill-suited emotion, given the question. "That is superstition, my friend," he answered. "This prince is real, slave demon to the serpent, itself." Kittim pointed in the direction of the pole star.

"The Dragon?" Kittim nodded.

Madai felt his heart thump an extra beat especially at hearing demons spoken of, as they are worse than spectres, and he felt stalked by something akin to morbid fear. It was a fear outside himself, but trying to get in.

"Holy God is stronger, Madai," Kittim reminded him. "But the Dragon rules the earthly realms – for now. He will wage a war against us; stop at nothing to keep all you have learned here, on these shores." Kittim looked pointedly at Iscah asleep beside the fire. "Nothing."

And Madai understood. His back ran with a shudder, seeing Iscah there, asleep and defenseless, a woman-child, and already too acquainted with evil. Perhaps the understanding married itself, at that moment, to all the old wound of losing Ido, and his own particular guilt so long ago. He was a selfish man it seemed. He had brought Iscah - into what? And what was worse, it was all for his own hopes, for himself alone.

CHAPTER 4

*T*HEY WERE TWELVE DAYS ON THE JOURNEY AND nothing terrible had attacked them. This night, however, was showing them a savage turn of the weather. Madai's horse was dancing sideways against great pellets of ice. The camel bearing his precious cargo of ark relic and behemoth bone was terrified, with white ringing its great brown camel eyes. Their uneventful journey seemed to have gone wild. It was the roaring storm, whipping at them with a ferocious wind and unexpected hail.

The tether Madai gripped so tightly suddenly ripped through his hands as the camel planted its feet, refusing one step more. He yelled above the tumult at the beast, only to see it hunch up like an old man, prepared to drop to its knees on the path directly in front of Iscah's equally terrified grey horse.

She looked a little like a scrap of flotsam at the mercy of the waves in a stormy sea, there atop her dancing pony. Madai was just struggling to dismount when he saw Kittim suddenly emerge from the dark of the storm. And it was Kittim that leaned over, rescuing her himself.

"We can't stay out here!" Madai yelled at them even as the wind snatched his words away. He turned toward the hillside, looking for any sort of shelter. Lightning splintered across the sky at that moment, to reveal what appeared a kind of outcropping in the rocks above them. He fumbled with the leather reins in his hands, quickly growing stiff with cold, and lashed his horse to a stout limb.

"There is something there," he yelled, pointing at the rocks. "Come," he asked of Iscah, skirting the willful camel now firmly planted to the ground. "We need shelter!" he cried, reaching for her, encouraging her off a horse suddenly quiet beside Kittim.

She slid quickly off her horse and into his arms. He wrapped her round with his cloak. "There's a place up there," he called into her ear. She nodded, her head against him. "What will we do with the animals?" Kittim yelled above the storm. "We need them."

"They'll keep," he insisted. But he tied the camel to the base of a nearby spruce, though it hardly seemed inclined to move again.

He and Iscah started the climb toward the rocks as an icy rain abruptly replaced the hail. Still the wind howled so that Madai believed its ferocity held challenge to the bitterest of his homeland's mammoth plains. He glanced over his shoulder to see Kittim still busy with the animals. The thought that he should be doing the same was fleeting as he felt Iscah shudder with cold. He tightened his hold of her and fairly lifted her across the rocks toward the hollow above them. If it had an ominous appearance, it was surely for the cause of the terrible night's storm. It would be a shelter from the wind and perhaps even dry.

"Nearly there," he assured her. "We'll build a fire."

Together they finished the climb. The rocks were slippery and sharp, coughed up from a fire-mountain, a flinty haphazard heap. It was not the haven he would have chosen were it not for… Lightning shot across the sky again. With that, he ducked his head and entered the mountain's rocky mouth.

"Where is Kittim?" Iscah asked through chattering teeth. "Behind us," he assured.

She pulled out of his arms. "Kittim!" She called. "Here," he answered, sounding close.

Madai heard Kittim's foot dislodge a rock as he reached the cave. A second crackle of lightning lit the dark behind him, stretching a web of brilliance across the night. Thunder snapped just seconds behind, assuring Madai of his decision.

"Come in here, Kittim," Iscah demanded, pulling at his arm. Kittim leaned forward to enter the tiny cave.

Still the night was lit by lightening. Madai found dead branches by its light for a fire. It was a job getting them to start; beginning with a sputter and wafts of accompanying smoke he finally produced a small circle of light and inadequate degrees of heat. Kittim stood at the entrance all the while, reluctant with shoulders hunched for the height of his body against the stature of the cave. He looked out at the night. It had stopped its hailing but continued to weep its rain.

"Was there ever such a storm?" Iscah queried faintly. Madai put another soggy branch beside the fire to dry.

"When this rain stops," Kittim insisted, looking into the darkness, "we need to get out of this cave."

"It's dry," Madai argued.

"Don't you smell it?" Kittim asked, turning to look at them. Madai sniffed. "I smell rain in a storm."

"I smell death," Kittim replied flatly.

Madai frowned, for Kittim's face was deadly serious. "Have you lost your nerve, friend?" he asked, trying for a lighthearted tone. "It is only a night's camp out of a wretched storm. No bears."

"Smell again."

Madai did. Perhaps there was a slight hint of rot… He lit the rusty needles of a dry pine and extended his arm behind them. It lit a dark, shrinking space, revealing nothing to cause alarm. He turned back around. "Nothing, as you see," he said, "and Iscah is wet through."

Iscah looked up at Kittim, having the appearance of a drowned rat in Madai's estimation, with a swipe of dry blood across her forehead.

"We can go," she insisted. The sound of her voice was miserable. Her teeth clicked out a cold rhythm even as she spoke the words.

ONE TINY PAW, INCISED WITH FOUR LANCE-LIKE CLAWS, touched the rocky floor to advance its body forward. A creature shifted its weight to move other appendages and lifted its snout to test a fine thread of aroma on the air. Its nostrils quivered. Its belly rippled. A trail of saliva trickled down its throat even as it opened its mouth to drink in the smell. Saliva dripped through its teeth, hanging by its own ooze a moment, then catching on a jagged rock as the creature moved forward another inch. The host of the smell did not whimper, as did most of what it ate. And there were no wails of pain either. That caused the creature to cock its head, and distend its nostrils again. It might have retreated back to the lair to wait, hoping for the next arrival, had it not been for a sort of prompting, an unnatural fixation driving it forward.

It was not a monstrous sized creature. Not like dragon, which also dwelt these lands, though having been hunted, kept to the highest regions. It was a cousin, a stealthy creature, nubile and efficient. It kept its weapons disguised inside its diminutive frame. Its means of conquest were in its claws, which sunk to a great depth when fully extended, and in the saliva, which crawled with poison and in its dogged ability to hold on.

There were noises coming from the source of the smell. Its brain distinguished differing qualities of sounds. One was a high frequency, the kind that gave the creature a different sort of satisfaction, a cruelty not innate but certainly at work when it was inhabited by the presence. The fact that there were two others with her aroused a primal caution, though the prompting lifted its other paw.

It squeezed through a passage, its face wafted with the billowing fragrance of humankind. All its caution dissolved as it considered the satisfied bulge of its body when they should be consumed. An ingrained inclination to hunt heightened its desire, till the castoffs it was regularly fed lost their appeal altogether.

MADAI SHIFTED. THE FIRE WAS SHRINKING AS IT BURNED. He wanted to keep it all through the night, as the rain showed no signs of slowing. Surely Kittim was over-alarmed. What would be worse, a faint smell of rot or a miserable soggy night under the trees? Perhaps even Iscah would be taken of fever. Madai had an inordinate dread of fevers. He pulled at a composting pile of fallen limbs that lay just outside the cave, under brush and partly dry. He put an end in the fire, hoping to coax out an hour more.

Iscah had fallen asleep. She had changed out of her wet clothes and into something he had gallantly retrieved from their animals tethered below in the trees. She changed behind the protective curtain of Kittim's coat and was wrapped in that now, peacefully quiet of her shivers. Madai did not perceive himself still a boy, with old infatuations part of a long-ago self. He had saved her, with Kittim, from a kidnapping and a lusty old man. She was all a part of a wondrous time in his life, having come through the depths of despair that Ido had left for him. And Iscah was there when he found his God again. Momentous times. Only it wasn't just that. It was her grim hold on a Mighty God when life had seen her abused; it was her gentle hand to nurse an injured stranger; it was her laughing eyes beholding every new adventure; it was her love of marvelous things. Second, truly second – for Madai had tested himself – it was the maiden beauty that had emerged from the frightened child. If she was no maiden in body, though no choice of her own, it was nothing to Madai. Her heart was pure and he had come to love it. Only he must persuade her. For he was to her, merely the friend of a man more loved, Kittim. And he, Madai, might be even still, the unruly miscreant in her eyes, a foolish man seeking truth when it all seemed obvious to her. He hoped not. He hoped at least, that she perceived him a true man of God, for that he was again.

He watched her sleep, the cloak rising, falling in a steady rhythm. How greatly he had missed the lovely life of Ido. How greatly he had missed the pleasant breath of love. He looked away, to protect himself from too great a longing. And he reminded himself of that assurance he was granted in the gathering room of Job's great house when he had asked Iscah a question of principle importance. 'What could be done to truly make men holy?' For Madai had seen the worst of men, even of himself. And in that night's conversation, he had recognized in Iscah, a woman, and seen his own heart toward her, and felt to his core that she would, someday, love him too.

AT A DISTANCE IT READ THEM LIKE A GLOW, AN AURA TO warm the chill of reptilian flesh. There were three spheres of soft radiance. One stood at the edge of its domain, very tall and imposing. It would let that one escape. Its world was housed within the boundaries of this beautiful rock. It had been enough to keep to the depths, taking flesh as it fell from above, always broken at some point but still alive. No excess trouble or running required. And so it had gradually quit the world out there. And quit the goat flesh for something sweeter. It sucked down another stream of saliva, thinking about it.

The one on the ground interested it most. It was the one of the high voice, the one that pleased its indweller the most. She would be tender, it knew by prior experience. It cocked its head again, tasting the air of the one sitting beside her. He smelled of strength but, as he was not standing, did not appear impressive. It flattened against the jagged floor of its cave and flicked its tongue, engorged with the indweller and the unnatural warmth that came with him. It needed that warmth, being a dragon-cousin, after all, and confined to a cave.

JUST ABOVE THAT CAVE, ON THE GRASSY CREST OF THE hill, Namim huddled inside his canopy. Rain was all that was left of the terrible storm, though the hail had dealt the temple a terrific blow. And despite his proclivity toward the cynical, he felt a shudder run through himself, recalling the tales spun by Nimrod that The Huwah was fought in a hail storm. It was all a bad end to what had begun a pleasurable day in Calneh. Had it only been this morning that Baal was fed the flesh of that city?

Then there came this wilting, which always arrived at the heels of every precious offering. It seemed there was never offering enough. Namim shivered, despite his wrappings and decided to think about Tammuz. O, he kept no fatherly affection for the babe, but there was that rarified satisfaction. For, if even a part of Nimrod peeked up through hell, then Namim had given him a show. No seed born of the Annanas, but of Semiramis herself. Namim chuckled. She was surely a sow, no surprise Nimrod preferred younger flesh. Only he, Namim, had got what Nimrod could not; the seed, and Semiramis the virgin. It made him laugh out loud.

A sudden sound drew his attention. It was a scuffle between a large man and his uncooperative slave. The spectacle, though somewhat entertaining, underscored the provincial aspects of Calneh, their amateurism. They should have drugged her. He watched her a moment, clawing for her unremarkable life, then pulled a scarf up over his nose. They must be getting close. O, he was weary, and longing for Shinar's court. Perhaps he would leave at first light.

KITTIM LOOKED VERY DISTRACTIBLE TO MADAI. SURELY he did not still begrudge them their dry place. Kittim had been inspecting the night, stepping back into the rain perhaps to tell if it was slowing. Madai expected it would rain through till dawn. He re-supplied the fire and pulled his coat tighter, hoping for a little sleep.

"I'm going to check the horses," Kittim whispered, which was surprising to Madai, as though his watchful friend was afraid to be heard.

Madai unfolded himself with a sigh and a last check of Iscah. He supposed he must help. Something had set Kittim on edge, be it imagined or no. He inched across the cave's rocky floor to follow his friend into the dark.

THE CREATURE WOULD HAVE SMILED IF IT COULD HAVE. It slid across the rock as though it were a snake, making a faint click, clicking sound with its spike of claws and advanced toward its unsuspecting meal. It was more like a hunt to the creature, awaking its primal brain. The meal made a gentle whooshing sound as she breathed. She lay with one outreached hand, glowing warm in the dark. The creature would find a ledge from which to pounce, but it would smell her first. So pleasant was anticipation.

It inched its snout toward her, head flattened against the rock. Its nostrils flared and it sucked in her scent. It let its tongue flicker out, snatching a taste of her skin, leaving behind a trail of slobber. The taste was more than the little dragon could endure and there was to be no ledge-finding. It drew up its hind-quarters, hunched its back, and ejected its claws to their full glory – and then it heard a familiar thump. A customary shriek and a scrabbling across stones followed the thump. The creature swung its head around, flinging drool.

An offering had arrived.

"STAY DOWN, KITTIM," THE CREATURE HEARD THE sound of a strong man's voice. It snatched its snout up in time to see him duck back into the cave and maneuver his spear sideways. "There are men up there," the voice continued. "They were dragging something."

The creature stiffened. It compressed its body against the stone again and lay perfectly still. Only its nostrils flickered, identifying the intruder's changing positions. It had recognized the pointed end of Madai's lance, schooled regarding such weapons as it carried a ragged scar on its belly. Suddenly the familiar sounds at the back of its lair held a more pleasant prospect than this sleeping she-creature. It retracted its claws to provide for a silent retreat and bent its body at right angles to slink back the way it had come.

The indweller tapped at its hunting nerve again, causing the dragon to twist its head across its back for a last look. But the enticement of a real kill could not outweigh the creature's own wariness, and the indweller's hold was lost.

KITTIM SNUFFED THE FIRE. "WE CAN'T BE DISCOVERED," he whispered.

Madai nodded once. He was as leary of the men on the hill above their cave as Kittim seemed to be and suddenly glad for the steady drumming of the rain. That would cover the noise of their horses below. Perhaps it would hurry them home as well. Whatever they were doing in such a storm he could not imagine. Indeed, to assuage a god of hail with a sacrifice dropped down a chasm would never have entered his mind.

They might both have recognized what was done had the little dragon not snapped the slave girl's neck before she could cry out again. Instead, they listened through the night and guarded against some one of the crowd finding their hiding place. It rained the night through as Madai had predicted. But the sun brought the day with not a cloud and neither of them knew of the danger that had been just turned aside.

CHAPTER 5

NAMIM ROLLED OVER. IT WAS WELL PAST FIRST light and his body was fully recovered from all its exertions of yesterday. Despite the storm, it had been a day of pure pleasure! Baal was fed, as was the town's dragon. Sacrifice upon sacrifice. Yes, he felt more able to endure this Calneh and perhaps he would even oversee the hunt for Kittim and Madai. It was Madai that had cost him Tazek, after all. It would give him a greater pleasure even than the sacrifices to see the Japhethite destroyed.

A girl came into his quarters, having heard him stir. She brought him a bowl of water and a towel. He did love his new position! Semiramis had improved his prospects, and she had also reintroduced him to the pleasures of womankind. Perhaps he would indulge it again with this girl before he rose for the day...

SOMEWHERE IN THE NIGHT SIMIRRA HAD FOUGHT WITH her shivering enough to fall asleep. When she awoke, her hands found her belly unconsciously and she could not stop a soft groan. How could her body feel whole when it was so empty? A prickling at her breast quickly wet her shirt with milk enough to break her heart. 'You will stop!' she commanded herself. She found Martu's knife beside her and closed her fist around it, and then she remembered the red-haired giant.

Turning her head slowly to the side, she spied his boot. She rose up on elbows to see him sitting in just the spot he had been the night before. He was eating. Her stomach was the hollow that only days without food can leave.

"What are you eating?" she heard herself ask. He didn't look up even to answer, "Goat."

"Do you have more?"

He slowly shook his head and took another bite.

Simirra sat up, clutching the knife. She looked at his fire with disappointment, as he had told the truth. "I ate it yesterday," he told her.

She massaged her foot, cold from the night, feeling hungrier now than afraid. "Who are you?" she asked. He chewed a last bite, turning the bone over to inspect it. Then he tossed it in her direction.

"Who are you?" he asked in return. "This is my fire."

She looked at the bone. "I am from Calneh," she answered.

"Of course you are, woman."

She eyed him, not enough care left in her to bother at the irritation in his voice. She laid the knife in her lap, suddenly freed from her cage of fright.

"Do with me what you will," she announced. "Be done with this waiting. Only do not kill me, I have something that needs doing first."

That brought a response to his eyes, and the muscles of his jaw. He stared at her a slow moment as only silence passed between them.

"What needs doing?" He asked at last.

She took a long, calming breath. "A man needs killing," she said.

ARPHAXAS TOOK THE TIME TO PICK HIS TEETH. SHE HAD surprised him. That her mission mirrored his own was the irony. And what had first appeared an uninvited complication might indeed prove... helpful.

"Tell me what went on last night," he demanded.

"What do you mean?"

"In Calneh."

Her hands squeezed into fists. "Dignitaries from Shinar," she responded curtly.

"I know that, woman. Tell me why."

"They came with news," she answered dryly. "And there are spies."

"Who came with news?"

"I am very hungry."

Arphaxas took a piece of black jerky from a sack beside him. "Tell me first," he insisted, holding it just beyond her reach.

He saw her unable to restrain a glance downward.

"The High Priest of Shinar is here," she said, swallowing, "with news of a royal birth, Nimrod's son."

Arphaxas' face stretched into an ugly smile. "But Nimrod is dead."

"The son of the stars," she retorted sounding defiant again and looking up, "or do you not believe?"

"Who is this priest?"

"The Queen's man; he was the King's man before her."

Arphaxas absorbed the information carefully. He gave her the jerky. He watched her eat it like a man would and let her swallow before he asked the priest's name.

"Namim, I believe," she spat, grinding the jerky between her teeth. He blinked, and nodded once. "Now tell me about the spies."

She finished the last morsel before she looked up at him. "Could be you, for all I know. Is your name Kittim?"

"And the other one?" He insisted.

"Madai and a girl," she answered, cocking her head. "There is a reward."

Arphaxas nodded once. He turned away from her, searching his pack for a piece of jerky for himself. "So," he finally replied, "you are after the reward."

He watched her face as possibilities changed it. She was not adept at hiding her thoughts. It was a weakness that might have been admirable once.

"Are you?" she finally retorted.

He allowed a slow smile and looked out from the overhang at the sky. It was grey, but dry. "Who needs killing?" He responded, still looking at the clouds.

"A man of no consequence." She chewed her meat. "My husband."

Arphaxas looked back into her face. Husbands and wives were tricky business, and surely as false an alliance as any other. He glanced at the knife in her lap. "I wish you success," he said.

She nodded, watching as he began to tie up his sack. He dragged it out from under the shelter and she grabbed at his dragon cape with enough strength to stop him.

"You said I could come."

Arphaxas tied the strap of his scabbard to his thigh. "What I do, I do alone."

"What is that, then? Perhaps I can help you."

"For what in exchange?"

"Whatever you ask."

He laughed. It was an ugly sound. "You women think we all have need of you. But it is you that have a need. What is it?"

Simirra waited to answer. He could see that he had stung her, which proved her pride. But her answer was as true as it was quiet.

"I may starve before I can kill him... without you."

It was a simple truth, which he could appreciate. She had news he could use, and if she could keep up... "Tell me what you can remember then," he insisted.

She nodded quickly. He watched as she pulled her pack together and lifted it to her back. "I remember everything."

"Who are these spies?"

"They are enemies of Shinar," she quickly divulged, "part of the rebellion."

"And your husband?"

"Personal," she replied.

THE JOB OF FOLLOWING THE GREAT RED MAN WAS MORE difficult than Simirra expected. His gait was slightly stiff, favoring a right side but not enough to slow him down. She was not quite as able as she hoped, but strong for a woman and tall. Her leg's length would certainly serve her well. But they deserted the night's camp with the meager fare of jerky and an un-shared goat, toward the sacred grove and the high place where the dragon waited to be fed. It seemed that fate would underscore her loss, taking her past another site of human sacrifice. It seemed also, that despite his foreign appearance, they shared a thing – abhorrence for such a practice. He turned to her with it painted across his face.

"Your Calnehan god was hungry last night?" he asked, picking up a woman's broken sandal and peering down into the pit.

"Not my god," she snapped, stepping back.

"You are not religious?" He asked, turning away, starting down the hill. "I am not religious."

It was a stray remark, but Simirra absorbed the information. She had yet to meet a man who did not serve one god or another. She slid down the hill behind him, toward the bottom and a tiny cave.

"See, here," he continued, now on one knee and looking into the rocky opening. "Someone was here." He was pointing at a dead fire and a print in the mud. "Here, and here." He hurried forward, toward a stand of trees. He stopped at a thicket to kneel again and trace the track of a horse's hoof.

"Who was it?" Simirra called, "the spies, do you think?"

Arphaxas stood up, straining eyes at the western horizon and at the muddy signature of too many animals. "They leave an easy trail for spies," he muttered.

"Calneh is behind us," she dared to mention. "Perhaps the ones you want are there."

"I don't think so," he replied, and started west at a fast trot.

Simirra watched him start off in the wrong direction. He was after the men on horse-back, probably the spies, probably not Martu. Her stomach grumbled again, watching him begin to gain a distance from her. She turned back toward the city; there was nothing for her there... no shelter, no food, likely to be shunned as a cast-off, child-less wife. She considered her purpose even as the knife seemed to burn through the folds of her coat. But she was not half-crazed as she had been that first night when she thought she could kill Martu at the temple. The poor babe would not be avenged if she were to fail, after all. In the end, it was Martu's face that decided her – how he would smile that smile after he had escaped her. She quickly adjusted the pack on her back and started a fast clip after the stranger, not having a better plan.

ARPHAXAS WAS AWARE WHEN SHE BEGAN CHASING HIM. He could hear her, even feel her and was beginning to doubt her use. She was certainly too noisy and was, in any case, a complication. He knew he should not have relented in the beginning when she stumbled upon him, but the hail had been ferocious and there were still bits of his soul left.

CHAPTER 6

ISCAH BEAT ATEN'S HEAVING RIBS. IT HAD BEGUN A better day, last night's storm well past, when the air had come alive, whistling with tiny projectiles. They were being rained at, though this time it was not by hail. Iscah all but flogged her horse, demanding its greatest speed. She was untouched as far as she could tell, but Kittim was yelling at them to run.

At first she had thought there was some sort of ferocious insect attacking them. One had struck Madai's camel right under her nose. It was then that her senses had stopped the regular flow of time and she could see that it was just a sliver of bone, sharp and thin.

The camels were fleeter of foot than appearance would tell, but they were no contest for the horses. She sped past Madai with his camel in tow, leaving it to catch more of the spiny missiles. A low hanging branch nearly unseated her as they raced through the trees and she knew in the instant that the attack was launched from the perch of those branches. In the passion of the moment, she could see the little missiles precisely, spinning through the air past her.

Ahead she could see where the sun was just breaking through the trees. She headed there, eyes fixed on the spot. As quickly as she cleared the grove, the hail of little bones began to fall away, proving her assumptions correct.

"THEY WERE IN THE TREES," KITTIM CRIED, DISMOUNTing and looking behind them. Quickly, and with a degree of alarm, he examined the rump of his horse and its legs. Satisfied, he ran his hands over his camel, carefully dislodging one tiny sliver from the animal's pack.

Iscah did the same. "Carefully," Kittim warned. "Don't stick yourself."

"Yes," she understood and cautiously ran her hands along the plains of her beloved Aten.

Madai found three little spears in his camel's rump. Kittim plucked one from the leather coat on Madai's back.

"Who are they? There was a horde!" Madai exclaimed.

"Yes, and they'll be after us," Kittim agreed.

"And these darts are poisoned," Madai finished, recalling the knife blade that had delivered the poison to him on their journey to Job.

"Your camel has taken them. Quickly, undo what we need!"

Madai hastily unfastened the animal's pack. It slid to the ground, drug down by the bone of behemoth fastened to the side. Iscah dug through the pack, pulling out the rice. There were other niceties, Eastern silk, spices, but Madai was after the extra arrows and his great long bow.

"Get those water skins, Iscah," Madai insisted.

They moved quickly, stuffing the packs of the other camels. Madai struggled with the bone, looking for a spot on another animal's back.

"We have the ark planks," Kittim reminded him. "This tells the flood too," he argued.

"We will be chased."

That was when Madai's camel lost its legs. They began to wobble like a newborn lamb till the animal slowly collapsed. It stretched out its neck and looked up at them with its great liquid camel eyes. One leg at a time, starting at the back, it began to twitch. Twitching turned to quaking. Madai ended it all with his knife, impaling the stricken creature between its ribs.

Iscah clamped her hand on her own mouth and checked Aten again. "Come on, Iscah," Madai insisted. He lifted her up to the horse's back.

"Who were they?" she exclaimed.

Madai answered her with the slap of a quirt against animal hide, starting them all galloping again onto the grassy plain. Iscah was hemmed in with Madai at the lead and Kittim at the back. Slowly, there came to the girl a welcome realization: It was dire dangers such as this that Kittim had wished to save her from, which must prove his affections. She started to smile.

ARPHAXAS REMOVED HIS DRAGON CAPE. HE DREW OUT his scimitar from the scabbard and was waiting in the clearing below the assassins. The first man dropped out of a tree; it was an easy matter, and Arphaxas's blade opened flesh like a reflex. The second dropped in time to see a shock of red hair and raise his arm. But his was no better a challenge than the first had been. The third and fourth men came at the same time. They were not caught unaware but they were unarmed, having left their spears on the ground. The fifth man came at him bare fisted, catching Arphaxas in the back. He staggered, robbed of breath, but he whirled round with all the strength of weighty arms and an arc of scimitar. He was surprised himself, slicing the Calnehan's head from his body in a single swing.

Even as the head flipped off the shoulders and the legs gave way, Arphaxas darted his eyes at the trees. He had counted six. But not a branch rustled; not a face exposed itself. There was not a cawing crow, not a tree squirrel, not a sign of life at all. Even still he backed away from the trees, zealously wary of little darts.

He retrieved his cape, wrapping it round himself and pulled up the hood.

It was a protective coating with its close knit scales. Then he listened to the silence as a stalking lion does, waiting for the last of the hunted to betray itself.

"They escaped toward Calneh," Simirra whispered behind him. And he whirled around at the voice. "There were two more."

Two? That disturbed him. He had not reckoned their number correctly. Simirra was waiting just a stone's throw in the shadows and he had not been aware of that either. She was like a prowling animal too, with a face coolly serene.

"May I have a look?" She asked daintily. And she glided past him, lifting each face – coming away disappointed.

"He is not here," she muttered.

Arphaxas watched her, slightly unnerved. "You were hoping for your husband…"

She looked at him as if to say 'Of course'. He noted no squeamishness about her, but a raw intensity as she nodded affirmation in a particularly sane way. Arphaxas wiped the scimitar blade against the grass. He stood up, facing Calneh.

"I cannot catch them without a horse," he muttered. At which she gripped his arm with a grim smile. It was a brave move, but she seemed a creature here in the bloody grove.

"Martu has horses."

"Your husband?"

"My once husband, I redeem myself," she spat.

It was a curious comment to which he did not reply, instead, Arphaxas dragged his eyes from the direction of a distant Calneh to study her. The hate in her eyes was too clear. "Do you lie to me, woman?" he snarled.

And she planted her gaze at him with as much intensity. "They were my father's. And when I help you get them… you will help me."

"I can steal them myself," he insisted.

She smiled at him with ice on her lips. "They know my voice." She replied. "And you do not know Martu."

SIMIRRA WONDERED AT HERSELF HERE IN THE STREETS of Calneh again – as if she had become invisible, invincible without physical needs as sleep or food. A goddess had surely smiled upon her, keeping the god of the moon under covers tonight. The way was dark. And though her house was near the temple, it was still as death itself. The stables were set in the trees, an easy access. She chuckled to herself at Martu's confidence. It was going to see him robbed tonight.

Indeed, her family's best horse-stock greeted her as friends. They had become Martu's by acclamation after her father was executed, which was a rather tidy term, given what was done to him. But he had become a heretic living too near a city built by Nimrod, and refusing to renounce the Maker God. That had left Simirra and her mother unprotected, and soon after that, beggars. Only the Lord Martu had taken pity upon them; taken them with the horses. He planted the best mares of the region in his stable, and Simirra in his bed. That she was beautiful, virginal, of a proud and once wealthy family, left him pleased to make her his wife. The Lord Martu, of the warrior class, was rich by valor and benevolent too, having saved a woman from poverty and an obsolete god.

Simirra shook her head to clear it, then took only the horses that were her father's, with one exception: Martu's great black stallion. That she would bring for the giant. She covered its eyes, tucking a shirt, which smelled of Martu under the straps of the bridle. She thanked the goddess consort of the moon once again, and left to bring the giant what he wanted.

Leaving the city was not as easy as stealing the horses. Here, he was so near. Hate was making her blind again, supposing that Martu slept, and with that soft center of his throat. She allowed herself to touch her empty belly. It had shrunk nearly to its proper size and her milk was dry. If she were to live too many more days, the babe would disappear entirely.

"Go, Simirra."

It was the same command. But the hairs on her arm stood up anyway. It did not occur to her to refuse, or to question the source. She was tugged at, mildly tugged toward the house. Only Martu's throat had taken a duller sheen at the sound of the Voice. Finishing the mission of the horses felt paramount. There was the giant to kill Martu, for he would be riding the stallion and her once husband would not abide that.

THE WAY BACK WAS QUICKER, ASTRIDE A HORSE. EVEN the stallion didn't fight, as if he was glad for freedom. She was first worried to find the red giant again, here in the dark and on this wild plain. But before she hardly knew she had come so far, there was Arphaxas, stepping out from the trees. With only the fewest of stars for light, he was a dark hulk, wrapped in his cloak. He took the stallion from her, as though he knew it was what she had intended. Simirra was surprised then at the way he handled the great horse, like a master. It was then that she first began to consider that his wild appearance might hide another past, not so common a past, improbable as it seemed.

Without a concern or a moment's hesitation he swung up on the beast, this animal that allowed no man but Martu. And he pointed the stallion's nose toward the west, dug heels into its sides and galloped into the dark with no word of thanks. Quickly she started after him, letting the other mares go free.

And she was liberated! How the wind whipped through her hair; how Basar, who she had not ridden since coming with child, chased after the stallion and its rider! Here in the dark there were rocks and holes, impediments she would not dare gallop across without light. But tonight was full of daring and nothing to lose. There rode a giant before her; there rode a knife strapped to her waist – there was Calneh behind…

She suddenly jerked back on the reins. There was Calneh behind – Martu behind!

"Stop!" she cried at Arphaxas.

But she was helpless to stop him, helpless against her own horse that would not relent. They each pulled her away from Calneh and the man she so intended to kill.

THEY GALLOPED THAT WAY FAR INTO THE NIGHT, TILL Arphaxas suddenly smelt a fire. He pulled up in sharp reflex. But the horse that should have been all run out, wanted to run more. Arphaxas pulled at the reins with mastery. He had rejoiced in the ride, recalling another life before this one. Only the campfire smelt close. The woman's horse came to a sudden stop behind him and he was instantly irritated. She would be noisy when he needed stealth.

He quickly dismounted and put his hand over his horse's muzzle. He darted a warning look at Simirra to do the same and pushed the reins of his stallion roughly into her other hand.

"Wait here," he demanded.

Then he crept into the night without a sound.

He followed the scent till he could see the first flicker of light. He dropped to his haunches, eyes fixed on the distant fire. Their very self-assurance annoyed him, sending out such a beacon. It proved both arrogance and conceit, qualities in men that he despised. They could not know what had come of those poisoners from Calneh; still they revealed themselves with a fire. He crept forward into the dark, hand on the hilt of his sword.

ISCAH'S HANDS WERE ICY. THEY HAD ALREADY MADE and abandoned two fires, such an effort when she was cold, tired, and hungry. She was not, however, entirely unafraid, having seen the camel fall. And if all this had been a directive of Kittim's, she might have been less critical. It was, however, Madai who demanded they build such decoy fires. She stumbled, dropping the few sticks she had managed to glean in the dim of starlight. Still, the stars had guided them across the open plain to come upon this dense grove, which gave them cover.

She turned, listening for Kittim so as not to be lost, when to her great relief, she heard his quiet whisper, "Iscah, where are you?"

AS FOR MADAI, HE WAS ADVANCING THE RUSE, SEARCHing out another place entirely to shelter through the night. But it was all a flat plain with the forest behind them. Perhaps he had made a mistake, leaving the trees. He began to doubt himself, remembering Kittim's warning. It had been proven true with poison darts, after all. Who could possibly want them killed so as to lay in ambush? No man that he could imagine…the dragon himself? It ran his blood cold.

Madai decided to pray. Certainly he had found nothing on his own. But he was unpracticed at it. He remembered the way Noah had prayed, head turned skyward, lips moving, soundless, without doubt nor self-conscious.

'A God who answers? Who sees? Was He watching when Ido died? Did He hear you, Madai?"

Madai almost looked behind him, all but hearing the words with ears of flesh. They were words he had not pondered in a long while. A sweat sprang up, even in this chilly night. Which was worse – to be never heard, or heard and yet refused?

He suddenly gave his whole body a shake, as if to unseat the uninvited squatter. "I have made the choice," he hissed at the night.

The voice in his ears fled away.

He turned his face to the night sky, "Show me the way," he whispered. "Where will it be safe tonight?"

He waited. He shivered. It was cold again. It was a hard night to spend without a fire. He stared at the stars and waited for God to answer. He had watched it happen with Noah. That was real.

He found himself holding his breath, just on the chance that God's Voice was quieter than one would expect.

And yet, there came not a word, nothing at all. He waited till the cold brought his toes numb.

"Perhaps it's safe beside the fire after all," he thought, deciphering an answer in the silence. He started his way back to Iscah and Kittim where he could see the lights of three already burning. But he could not deny his disappointment, having not heard nor felt the Great God. Beside the sound of crisp drying grass beneath his feet, there seemed the faint noise of other-worldly snickers.

That was when an improbable urge turned him to the side. And in the dim light of the moon, there loomed a mound of shadows. He started toward them, catching his foot on a rock, and another till he came upon a surround of boulders.

He could have laughed aloud for the relief and utter joy of being answered! He investigated the site. Why, there was even a hollow where a rock had been burrowed under and a fire might be risked! Happily, with what was in his estimation his first direct guidance from God, he began to map out the providential lay of boulders, boulders that would hide them through the night.

Such had ended a day of good fortune. Not one but the camel had been lost to the enemy of which Kittim spoke with such severity. A good plan was both devised and achieved. He had been answered of God. Even as he explored the camp-site, he imagined their return trip in his mind: the Pishon and its lush valley, the crystal river from which behemoth had so calmly observed them. He retraced their journey to the great cavern painted with the adventures of other travelers. All the way to the first city of his quest, the very one that had given them Iscah – and after that, the Brine Sea, and after that… home.

He was consumed with all such pleasant optimism when his head was suddenly pounced upon, driven to his chest. He gasped for breath even as his cheek hit the hard surface of a rocky earth. His arms were pinned as he heard Iscah's startled yelp of fear in the distance.

CHAPTER 7

L IFE'S VERY BREATH SQUEEZED UP THROUGH
Madai's throat in a last gasp as a sharp knee found the small of his
back. His arms were near to wrenched off and his wrists bound so
tight behind him as to end the flow of blood to his hands, which was of small
matter as he should die first of suffocation! He fought to roll over with the last
of his breath when someone laughed, and – excruciating relief – a knee removed from his back. He was yanked up then, by the ties, stretching his arms
in a painful, backward arc.

"Kittim!" He tried to shout a warning, more a croak, even as he remembered with helpless sinking, Iscah's cry.

He was boxed in the head from behind. "Hiding like a mole, atoyak?" the
attacker laughed and pushed him roughly forward.

Madai stumbled as he heard the indecipherable, unappealing garble of
Shinar behind him. He was in a panic to invent a course away from Kittim and
Iscah. But there was their fire, an unmistakable guide. He shoved against his
foe, only to hear him laugh again and push something sharp against his back.
So Madai settled into a shuffle, stretching the time it took, searching his mind
for a plan… finding it empty.

They came into the circle of light, Madai and his captor, to find the situation
worse even than he'd imagined! There lay Kittim sprawled out and unconscious. And there sat Iscah, trussed up like a quail in a snare with a look of
dashed hope in her eyes.

"Madai!" she cried.

"Are you hurt? Is Kittim…"

The Calnehan boxed his head again and spat at him with his Shinar tongue.
He shoved Madai at the ground. "Sit!" he barked.

Madai squirmed up and twisted round to get a better look at Kittim. He
couldn't see in the dark, if his friend was even alive. He darted his eyes from
Iscah to the man squatted behind her. This second captor wore a venomous

expression and seemed to be whittling a piece of twig with an enormous knife.

"Stumbled right into me, Ahbed," the man laughed to his lounging cohort.

Ahbed glanced up, his face sinister in the shadows. He nodded, shaping the branch into a slender point. "Kittim?" Madai whispered at Iscah.

"He came from nowhere," she whispered back, glancing at the man behind her. "Kittim hasn't moved since…"

Kittim moaned softly as if he knew their worries. He tried to lift his head. "Good, atoyak! You're worth more to me alive," spoke the first man.

He was square built, with a day's growth of beard on his face. He had a hawkish nose, a scar on his chin and a piece out of his left ear. He tipped Kittim's face up with the toe of his boot. "Which one are you?   Madai?" He leered at Iscah, then looked at his accomplice. "Put that down, Ahbed you lazy goat and bring us the wine!"

Ahbed gave the man a cagey, sidelong look. He dropped the stick and dropped the coat off his shoulders as well. Madai watched the eyes of his captor go wide and jaw go slack.

"Simirra?" he gasped, even as he was wrapped round from behind by the burly arms of a taller man dressed in a dragon's skin.

THE SCUFFLE WAS SO SHORT AS TO BE HARDLY CALLED A fight. And the one who was first Ahbed and second, Simirra carefully edged her way around Iscah, past the fire to stand face to face with the one whose fortunes had turned in a moment. "Martu," she breathed pleasantly, lifting the knife to his nose. "You are not happy to see me?"

Arphaxas hugged his captive tighter.

"Where's Ahbed?" Martu wheezed, stunned at the sudden appearance of his wife in his partner's clothes. "In hell," she answered quietly, a smile in her voice.

Martu's face drained its last color, facing his exultant wife. He opened his mouth only to sputter, a little like a trout drowning in the air.

All but dazed, Madai watched Martu's face reflect a thousand emotions. His position had changed, but so had Madai's – in an instant. He got to his knees, fighting with the rope that bound him.

"How shall you die, Martu?" Simirra was asking. "Tell me."

Madai heard the Shinar tongue again, watching the woman confront the man. If the precise meaning of her words were unclear, the knife at his stupefied face told its own story. And then there was her look of exquisite hatred…

"Stand away, Woman!" The dragon-clad man demanded.

SIMIRRA ROLLED HER EYES UPWARD. SHE COULDN'T SEE Arphaxas's face, as he was wearing the hood of his cape again. It had frightened her when he wore it before, creating the appearance of some mystical villain. But it didn't seem to matter anymore. She had the decided feeling that she was at the pinnacle of her life, nothing left to see but a once-husband dead. How pleasant it was to watch his face begin to shrivel. Perhaps he knew, after all, that the thirsty god, Baal, kept the regions of hell.

"Stand away, Woman," Arphaxas growled again. Her eyes blinked at him, and she stepped back. Then she watched Arphaxas tie a doomed man to a tree.

She hardly noticed the man on his knees, crawling toward the girl. But Arphaxas turned at him, giving Martu's bindings a last savage yank. He brandished his sword, and the yellow-haired spy stopped. Dispassionately, she watched him trying to speak to the girl with his eyes.

"Tie that one up," Arphaxas growled, pointing with his scimitar at the unconscious man on the ground. It hardly seemed necessary, but she would obey him. He had got her Martu.

Arphaxas shoved the other captive off his knees with the toe of his muddy boot. They were all inconsequential, these three others. All that mattered was the once husband.

Simirra quickly finished her chore. She was obliged to Arphaxas now. He probably wanted the reward. She stretched her back, having tied very good knots. She slowly looked up to find Martu with her eyes. She smiled at him, tied to his tree and already formulating an escape. It pleased her because it would all be futile. She glanced at Arphaxas. He was just discovering a rodent of some kind, charring over the spy's fire. He was a greedy swine, but even that she would now happily approve.

Very quietly, so as not to disturb the giant, Simirra stood up. She used the shadows to make her way toward Martu. He was busy with his ropes and seemed surprised when she squatted down in front of him, as though he had forgotten her. She was pleased afresh and smiled at him again.

He smiled with her. Very practiced at being the master, the expression was not false. "What are you doing, Simirra?" He whispered. "Don't you know who they are?"

She tilted her head at him, rounded her eyes. "Who are they, husband?"

"The spies. Shinar will pay a lot of gold for them!"

She slowly drew out the knife. She touched its sharp edge with the tip of her finger. "Enough to pay for my babe?"

That took the grin off his face. She lifted her brows, watching him with so much pleasure. She felt an energy grip her stomach and had a near to unstoppable desire to laugh. Martu was all the while working his hands behind the tree. She let him, allowing time to pass.

"Who is he?" Martu asked, attempting a second ploy and nodding at Arphaxas.

She turned her head very slowly in the direction of her companion who was gnawing flesh at the fire. "The one who will kill you," she replied coolly, "or perhaps…" she tipped the knife at her own breast, "I will?"

The left side of Martu's mouth turned up. It was almost the look to send her past the edge. But he licked his lips with a dry tongue, making a somewhat pathetic sound.

"And what will he do to you, Simirra?   Look at him; he's an animal."

Which was a humorous remark, coming from Martu.

"More than you think," He hissed, answering himself. His eyes darted at the knife.

She closed her hand around it tight, watched him fight the knots. Then she stood, drawing out the moment but careful not to arouse Arphaxas. She rounded the tree to assess Martu's efforts.

"Not quite," she said with a smile and towering above him. Then she squatted back down some short ways away lest he use his leg against her. "He will make you suffer first," she cooed.

"You were always stupid, Simirra."

"Worry about yourself."

He gave the ropes another tug.

She wanted to say "You do squirm like a maggot." but the fire in her belly burned suddenly so hot and her hatred so stark that her mouth actually contorted. She felt her chin begin to shake even as she heard, coming from Martu's throat, a familiar and disdainful chuckle.

That sound seemed to peel off a very thin skin of self-restraint. It was the last insult she would endure and was at him in a flash. She felt the beautiful give of his soft flesh to the tip of her knife when she was suddenly picked up and flung away.

"Get back, Woman!" Arphaxas demanded.

"He killed my baby!" she shrieked.

Arphaxas towered above her, the raging, reckless woman. But he had heard her. The words digested quickly as he faintly recalled the long ago scent of innocence. He merely glanced at Martu, an ordinary banal man and not worth his trouble. With no more a thought than that, he dispatched his scimitar. It caught Martu at the juncture of collarbone and neck. It lodged itself with a deep sounding thud into the tree, waiting to be retrieved.

"Get up," Arphaxas ordered.

He watched her trying to stop her sobbing. She didn't know yet, that the husband was dead. Arphaxas had an inordinately righteous feeling about it, that he'd all but beheaded a baby killer. And when the woman looked around, she saw him with his head lolling to the side, lying on the blade as if it were a cushion. She scrambled back the distance he had flung her on hands and knees. She took the dead man by his bloody coat and shook him.

"Simirra!" Arphaxas barked. He grabbed her again and jerked her away. He lifted her and held her, feet dangling, directly in front of himself. He found that he had to control his own breathing before he could speak.

"Let it be."

She blinked and looked at him, her face red and pinched. He set her down on her own feet and she balanced herself with a hand on his chest.

"I wanted to watch."

He felt his jaw twitch. He cleared his throat. "Find some more wood," he insisted, "and wash off your hands." Then he went back to the fire and the charred remains of what had been rabbit, or perhaps a pig and fought to quiet his thumping heart.

ISCAH WATCHED IT ALL, ONE GHASTLY ACT AFTER AN-other. But the story was told – a dead babe, a murdered murderer, an efficient assassin and a pitiful grieving mother. She wiggled away from a rock that was turned, its sharp edge out, against her hindquarters. Her shoulders ached too, where her left side was pulled far to the right. The woman, whose name was Simirra, had gone in search of water. A horse whinnied. Water splatted somewhere behind her and Iscah supposed she was washing off blood.

So now it all made sense and with the villains dead, they would be soon untied and she could look after Kittim's poor head. But the man in the dragon's cape was just sitting by the fire. She squirmed again.

"Be still, Iscah," Madai hissed. She shot him a look.

"There's something about him," Madai warned, nodding at Arphaxas.

"The dead man killed her baby," she explained, realizing he hadn't understood their speech. "They'll let us go now."

Madai's face proved that he was as aghast at the revelation as he should have been, and still he shook his head at her like some cantankerous bull. That was when Simirra returned with an armload of sticks. She dropped them by the fire, strangely subdued, vaguely afraid of the man, Arphaxas. Well, she couldn't be blamed for that.

Ignoring Madai's hisses, Iscah turned her attention to Kittim, who was coming round again, praises to God.

She gingerly touched the raised place on his head. "Are you muddled?"

"See what they want," he whispered hoarsely.

"But, are you hurt?"

"Iscah…"

"Alright."

She wiggled back to her spot against a tree and nearer to the woman. "Simirra," she whispered.

But Simirra did not seem to hear and had the appearance of someone that had been too many nights in the wild.

"Simirra," Iscah tried again.

The woman glanced up, looking confused as if Iscah had been only a part of the inanimate forest.

SIMIRRA STARED AT THE GIRL, THINKING HOW ODD WAS the sound of her own name, which cut the quiet and the vast sort of nothingness that had come upon her. The rage in her belly had left her feeling faintly sick, but quite vacant beyond that. Perhaps it would have done her better to have witnessed the moment that Martu lost his head. Perhaps she might be…

"What does he want with us?" the girl was asking. Then she squirmed, trying perhaps to wiggle out of the ropes.

Simirra turned her head slowly toward Arphaxas, being vaguely wary of his hearing. But he seemed busy at the fire eating something the spies had had cooking. It gave her time to decipher the meaning of the girl's words. Simirra shook her head ever so slightly.

"But…"

"Be still," Simirra heard herself whisper.

"I am sorry about your babe," the girl tried again.

The words were quite inadequate, but there was something deep about the tone. Simirra felt it reach through to her wound. And that started it bleeding and raked the glaze off her eyes.

"Will you be quiet!" she snapped. And the girl was, looking startled.

"He will have gold for you," Simirra finished dryly.

The girl's face was such a canvas of emotion. It might have once evoked… pity.

"But why?" she was asking.

Simirra sighed. It felt heavy, coming from deep parts of herself. Her belly felt quite wretched and she had an unexpected longing for her father. He had been a kind man. He would not recognize her now.

She looked at the girl again; confused, frightened and young. Her father would have bent down and smiled and told her about his one God. He would have meant to do her kindly.

"What is your name?" Simirra asked without bending. The girl's face relaxed some. "Iscah," she answered. "Well, Iscah… you are spies."

The girl's mouth dropped open.

But Simirra heard the noise of the red giant. She looked back at him. He was standing, turned in her direction. She knew how his eyes would be glaring slits of green, though the dragon hood hid his face by its shadow. But she was suddenly very tired with every rage poured out like a river – with this new and unwelcome compassion she seemed to have found for the girl. Beyond that, enough days were passed for her breasts to shrivel and milk to dry, enough that her belly hugged her backbone for want of food. So why did he think she would care for the threat in his eyes?

"There is a reward for those two." She muttered. "An edict…"

Arphaxas actually hissed. The outline of his face was just illuminated by the fire and its ferocity was breathtaking. But it was just that look that ignited her. How should he demand her silence? Did he suppose she would cost him the reward? That killing Martu had granted him a… possession?

She was not cold and terrorized as she had been that night of the storm. And… their agreement was satisfied. She was, in fact, entirely free and would never be owned again. As if she had been three women in the course of this one hour, she was revived.

She looked back at the girl on the ground in her muddy, ripped dress with her tangle of hair. "He'll take you to Calneh… for the reward," she finished boldly.

Then she straightened her back and pulled her coat tight around herself.

She walked away from Iscah, away from the fire, feeling Arphaxas all the while glaring at a spot between her shoulders. She found a place on the ground to sleep; perhaps a spot not chosen well but her legs seemed to wobble some. She picked the place free of rocks and lay on her side. She lay facing the tree with its corpse of Martu slumped on the ground. Simirra's cheek lay on the cold, damp forest floor. She was a distance from the dead man, but eye to eye with him, as though they were in a great giant's bed together.

THE NIGHT WAS VERY LONG. MADAI SPENT IT AWAKE, uncomfortable and watching, for the events of the night had been both catastrophic and astonishing. Divine providence – for which he'd been gullible enough to believe – had proved a perfect ground for the ambush. He had been both freed and recaptured by a wild dragon-clad man. Kittim had been bested. There was a dead man; beheaded, tied to a tree, and a crazed woman who threw daggers. Yet each such happening must pale beside the aspect of murdered babies.

"No," came the flat sound of the woman's voice. Madai did not know the two stranger's language, but her refusal was clear enough.

The man in the dragon was insisting and she was angry again.

"Kittim," Madai whispered. The only positive of the night being that his friend was sitting up.

"Madai," he answered.

"What is he saying?"

"He wants her to go to Calneh after the priest."

Which certainly was the last thing Madai would have expected. "What priest? Why?"

"Namim."

His body literally felt the shock of that name. And he might have been in Shinar again for all the remembrance it provoked – all the vile crimes of Nimrod's new religion. He could still taste it at the back of his throat. He shook himself, visibly, and reminded himself that Nimrod was dead and the Shemites were victors… Except that the priests and Semiramis had survived. So, here was the cost of that, Namim, like a vine of poison growing back from a deeply buried root.

"There is set a price for our heads." Kittim finished.

And Madai remembered the assassins sent after Noah. How well the eyes of Shinar followed its enemies!

But he also remembered the daughter of Shem who had whispered him a warning in Nimrod's temple. She had declared that a new corruption would arise from Nimrod's death and that Madai must expose it, carry the truth back to his own shores. Was Namim a part of this new corruption? But of course.

"What new lies have been invented?" he hissed.

"A god is born," Arphaxas interjected. Like an uninvited guest he was suddenly standing above them.

Madai's head shot up. The stranger had been watching them, listening…

understanding! A chill ran through him like an icy river.

"What god?" Kittim asked as if Arphaxas inserted into the discussion was non-eventful.

But Arphaxas turned silent, watching them. Certainly, such a man would enjoy being informed of a secret. "Son of Nimrod," he finally chuckled.

"There is no son of Nimrod," Madai volleyed.

Arphaxas expelled a profanity.

"Tell us," Madai demanded. "I was warned once about a lie."

"Tammuz," Arphaxas replied coolly. He looked directly at Madai. "Son of Shinar's Queen, a-bed with Nimrod's ghost."

"Blasphemy!" Kittim declared.

"So you do speak," Arphaxas replied, turning his head ever so slightly. "Which one are you?"

"I am Kittim."

"Kittim," Arphaxas played with the name on his tongue. "Not that it matters."

Simirra stared with incredulity at the red giant, and from whose control she had silently stolen herself. He spoke the foreign tongue of such nobles as these who had come with laden camels and in finery. Indeed, nobles as she once had been when her father was alive, before the decree, before Martu who was, even now in the cold, gathering flies.

She would never have suspected it. As she was made a new woman, was this Arphaxas a new-born man? His mastery of horses had been a surprise – this brutish dweller in forests – and now, this command of fine speech. And though she could not understand what was said, indeed she must acknowledge that he spoke more to them in one span than he had to her in all the days that she had kept his fire. He had, as well, betrayed an emotion. The realization sparked a sense of betrayal in her, preposterous though it was.

Her hands went to her breast; it was the place her pain had traveled. She watched Arphaxas use foreign words against the one called Madai, like weapons.

He had demanded something of her also. Arphaxas was indeed more complex than a simple savage, and he wanted the priest. He wanted the gold. He wanted her to fetch it. Well, she would not! It would certainly be more difficult than he could know – persuading the priest of a great city, looking as she did and cast off. All of Calneh knew that now.

It was precisely that thought which changed her mind. She was born to a family more worthy than all the shop folk of Calneh. She had been daughter to a great man – condemned and deserted to the likes of Martu! Yes, she would do it. She would take Shinar gold away and give it to a wild man.

She wet her lips and looked at Arphaxas again. He was taking Iscah by the arm and pulling her off the ground.

"Take the girl," he demanded, shoving her forward, "To prove they are captured."

Simirra squared her shoulders. "Even with the girl, it will not be easy. Look at me." She held her arms out, exposing muddy, bloody breeches and matted hair. "I will need clothes."

THE GOWN SHE CHOSE FROM THE CAMEL'S PACK WAS finer perhaps than any she had owned, though she would certainly never tell it. She took the time to wash her hair and comb it through with a fine perfume. She felt the soft folds of silk fall across her skin, running her fingers along the lines of a lily embossed with silken thread the color of a morning sun. The gown itself was blue, such a color as to enhance her skin and highlight the midnight black of her hair.

She came back into the camp fully bedecked. She walked across the dirt as if it were marble, toward Arphaxas, with sufficient grace to enchant a stone.

"I am ready," she announced.

"Good. If you do not come back, I will hunt you down and send you to your husband."

They were the red giant's parting words to her.

CHAPTER 8

SUCH A PLEASANT MORNING AFTER SO PLEASANT A night! Namim was beginning to understand Nimrod's penchant for the flesh of youth. This girl was someone's child, but as Namim had never had a child, at least before Tammuz, he could not comprehend the angst that shone in the mother's eyes when the girl was chosen, which had been an honor after all. She was twelve, if she was a day. Namim would not stoop so low as Nimrod had stooped. Twelve was a woman in Shinar.

He stretched. Now that he had rediscovered the pleasures of womanhood, his horizons had widened by half.

Well! Today was only getting better! It seemed his mission would be soon accomplished and they might all return – tomorrow, perhaps. The spies were caught! He had just been told, and he was already plotting the added benefits they would assure him with the queen.

He called in his little servant. She had been the first to tend him, and the first to give him a warm bed. And when he had tired of her, for their wait had been too long in this provincial nook, she had brought him her cousin.

And this lovely, fresh lass had serviced him through the night. Perhaps he would take them both home.

He hurried through his morning's business, taking time only to encircle his eyes with blackened henna, they being his most winsome feature. The girl brought his clothes and removed his discard.

His morning devotions were also hastily made; it was his son, Tammuz after all, to whom they must all pray now. Surely that bought him an indulgence or two. If all the world should honor Nimrod as spirit father, he knew the truth. He chuckled. Somehow it was amusing.

"My Lord," came a tenuous voice at his outer door. It was the under-priest.

"A moment!" Namim furled his white tunic across his shoulders and opened the door. Greeting him was the shaved, bent head of his assistant and an arrogant, beautiful black-haired woman.

She was wearing clothes of the finest silk, cut and sewn by the finest skill and fitted to her form in the finest way. The gown was brilliant blue, nearly royal – possibly royal – and matching the blue-black sheen of her hair.

That she was in his outer chamber completely escaped him. Conventions seemed to be changing every day.

"My Lord," she breathed, inclining her head but slightly. "I am your servant."

'Indeed,' Namim thought as she was certainly no servant. But her boldness appealed to him. "Surely it cannot be you who has caught my spies," Namim crooned.

Simirra smiled daintily. She dipped her face again, though this time with a handsome flush. "Why no, my Lord. I'm but a Lady." She lifted her face to look into his painted eyes. "I am Simirra, wife of Martu, a great warrior of Calneh. I carry a message."

"My Lady," he said. "Your husband is a fortunate man." He cleared his throat and looked behind her. "So then, where are my spies?"

"A morning's ride, my Lord."

"A morning's ride? Lady! Bring them here!" He snapped, suddenly irritated by the beautiful face. Simirra was blessedly calm. She set her mouth in a way meant to suggest nothing short of seduction.

"Please, my Lord. My master is shy of cities. And he does not wish to be marked as the man carrying the gold – bandits, you know."

"You said your husband was a warrior."

"My husband, yes." She smiled the seductive smile. "I did not say that the man whose message I carry is my husband."

Namim felt himself a-flamed. So bold a woman! He touched her silken sleeve with his finger.

"My Lord!" Simirra tittered. "All in good time." She took a step back. "Your position," she whispered with an excess of concern.

Namim was sweating. He hoped his eyes weren't running. He needed his henna pot.

"I will be just there," he pronounced. He backed into his room, calling to the under-priest as he began to push the door closed. "You will bring the Lady wine," he said.

"And my friend?" Simirra interjected.

Namim looked across her shoulder at the younger woman. He had not noticed her before, waiting beside the outer door. She was nearly again as lovely, and wearing a gown of equal worth. It was getting better all the time.

"This is Lady Iscah," Simirra continued. "She is my proof. She is companion to the man, Kittim and to the man, Madai. It is these two you are seeking, is it not?"

NAMIM'S FINGERS CLOSED AROUND THE DOOR, HOLDING it open at the sound of their names. How it brought him back! Yes. This temptress had means to the most reviled of foes. He took a deep breath and as he did, was instantly inhabited.

"Alert the guards, Sidon," he snapped. "We will travel with this Lady. Now!" His voice rang with an authority that belonged to another.

Simirra turned to Iscah with a flourish. He was hers! No matter what came of the girl's companions. The priest with a penchant for burning babies was in her grasp.

With the evening sun just perched above the trees, there came a sound of hoofs against the forest floor. Madai and Kittim sat, both aching of back and numb of limb. They were still bound fast and in the same position all through the night and the whole of the day. Their captor had frequently visited them to check their knots, though in every other way they seemed forgotten.

Arphaxas straightened his back and lifted his head at the sound of the horses. Madai pulled at the ropes a last time before watching to see who might be coming and how many were guarding the priest.

"Have you prayed?" Kittim asked in a whisper.

"I have," Madai answered simply. If Kittim were right about dark powers set against them, and Kittim was usually right, then being misguided into the ambush could be set aside for the time. He wiggled his toes, coaxing blood back to his feet for they had been dead of feeling for half the night.

"Get up!" he heard their captor demand.

But Madai could not get up. Arphaxas jerked on his arms, lifting him by sheer strength. "You will make me rich today."

He pulled Kittim to his feet as well. Madai lost his legs, went to his knees and was dragged up again. "Stand!" Arphaxas hissed.

Madai wobbled, being shot at by his own blood finding its way back to his toes.

SIMIRRA EMERGED FIRST FROM THE TREES, RIDING HER mare. Then came Iscah. Madai thought first that they had been unsuccessful in bringing Namim until six surly looking soldiers came into view. It seemed they had not appreciated their night's ride. They were not half the soldiers that Nimrod's army had been; little more than men for hire.

Four white-clad servants followed the guards, carrying an unwieldy litter draped at all sides by curtains. It brought Madai back to his days in Shinar with a loathsome distaste. He could all but smell Namim, could see the white faces of little girls taken and drugged and sitting on enormous thrones. He could see Nimrod's face again, taste his food. He could remember the sound of Palapa's voice, pleading, afraid. Lastly, came a youth whose job it likely was to serve the priest. That recalled to him Tazek, an equally pitiful soul. He yanked hard at his ropes.

Kittim looked at him then, as if to quell the storm that was brewing.

The guards seemed to swarm the clearing. Madai had a too close view of their horse's hooves and the men's breastplates jangled when they moved in the saddle. One of the soldiers pushed past Simirra, who had led them in, jostling her horse with his own.

"Remove that body," he snapped at Madai. "The High Priest comes."

Madai only stared at him, thinking what a ridiculous order it was, as he was clearly bound and hobbled.

Arphaxas stepped in front of Madai. He set his feet apart and folded back his cape, revealing a well-used scimitar. "That priest boy can do it," he retorted. "This one is mine till I am paid."

The boy, less than nothing to the guard, was sent about the grizzly task. Madai heard him retching in the trees after he had pulled on the body, leaving a smear of Martu in the leaves.

"Let me see them!"

Madai recognized that voice. The man poked his head out even as the retching started again; appropriate fanfare, in Madai's opinion.

"What is that smell?" Namim covered his nose.

"A dead man," Arphaxas replied.

"Not Madai?" Namim was quick to ask.

"As you see." Arphaxas nodded in Madai's direction even as Namim found him with his eyes.

NAMIM PINCHED HIS NOSE SHUT WITH HIS SQUARE OF silk. The smell of death mingled with the scent of Shinar perfume and came near to gagging him. His eyes watered, but he could see Madai clearly. Bile rose in his throat, which he coughed to force back down. He took a moment, collected himself and came out of the curtain-draped litter.

"Ah, yes. The Japhethite." He said, arranging the folds of his robe.

He crossed the camp slowly, deliberately, as if to assure himself that he commanded the scene with adequate menace.

Madai wondered if he realized that he still bore the print of his pillow on his cheek.

"I see you look well." Namim crooned. He spoke the Japhethite tongue of the region. And though it differed from the Family both in structure and accent, it was decipherable.

He all but collided with Arphaxas as the man stepped purposely into Namim's path. "They are yours," he growled, "when I am paid."

Namim looked up at the man wearing the dragon skin. "I will see who speaks to me," he demanded, finding comfort in the guards that had swarmed them.

But the giant only peered at the priest from the confines of his hood. "It's cold, priest," he replied. A guard stepped closer, making their proximity quite tight indeed.

It was like a meeting of roosters, each baring their spurs.

"Then stoke your fire, atoyak, and step aside; this is the High Priest."

Namim smiled, finding the power of authority quite pleasant. He crossed to the campfire and rubbed his hands above it. They trembled slightly as he was full of the inhabitor. He was always affected in such a way when first entered.

But it brought him such confirmation.

He watched the man in the dragon cape acquiesce. He watched him move Madai and Kittim to the tree that belonged once to the headless corpse, which was amusing. He would have his revenge for Tazek and savor every moment! Were there day enough, he would make for Calneh and sleep in his own bed, two heretics richer.

But it was late and had been such an arduous journey. He could not decide if he wished to share his litter with the servant boy or the raven-haired woman. Perhaps neither, he was suddenly quite weary.

"I shall retire," Namim proclaimed abruptly. He tipped his head toward the giant. "And you shall be paid tomorrow."

MADAI WAS GLAD OF THE SUN'S SETTING. HE CONTIN-ued to fight with the knots, but found it quite useless as Arphaxas had moved them to Martu's tree and retied them with heftier rope. He could feel the sap leaking from the cleft made with Arphaxas's blade. His body was sore, he was starving and there came the man in the dragon cape. Madai was not glad to see him.

Arphaxas knelt beside the tree. He tugged at the bindings and planted his face nose to nose with Madai.

Madai could smell supper on his breath. The dance his belly performed was one part hunger and another good part revulsion.

"One more night," he hissed at Madai.

Madai clamped his teeth together, refusing Arphaxas a reply. Instead, he turned his head, watching Namim close the drapery of the litter. He watched the whole thing sway as the priest arranged himself for sleeping.

He looked at Iscah, glad she had been fed and covered with a blanket. He prayed she would sleep and be forgotten by the band of Shinar's men. And for the second time, cursed himself for bringing her.

ISCAH WATCHED ACROSS THE TOP EDGE OF A SCRATCHY and odorous blanket. Though the ride to Calneh for the priest had been all but silent, she had not found the woman, Simirra, unkind. A piteous tale of a murdered babe would bring any mother to revel at a near be-heading, being that it was the murderer's head. That she kept the company of a dragon-killer, one who tracked men for profit, was something else again.

She watched the man, in height no more than Kittim, and yet there was a thing about him. Perhaps it was the dragon skin. He was checking Kittim's bindings now, yanking with not a mite of mercy. And they had not been fed. Iscah felt for the cold piece of meat hidden in her belt. It was more than half of the meager scrap thrown at her. She knew she had Simirra to thank for even that. It seemed an impossible effort, getting it to Kittim, with the guards and the litter bearers and the dragon-killer, though she would certainly be ready if the opportunity should come.

When Arphaxas got up, she thought perhaps it was her chance – that he would find a place to sleep. Instead he knelt down in front of Simirra. A queasiness crawled into her stomach, watching Simirra respond to the man.

She seemed not afraid, but expectant. He leaned in toward her so close that the hood of his cape hid the woman's face. Then he took her by the arm and lifted her up. She leaned on him like a lover and they, together, strolled into the forest. The estimation Iscah had so newly formed of the widowed, childless woman was instantly diminished. The guards beside the fire were watching too, and finishing a carcass of young swine. They laughed that sort of laugh – the kind that pollutes the atmosphere. Earnestly, she prayed to be ignored. But they seemed absorbed with drinking and a good ways gone at that. There was rustling in the forest after that, or perhaps Iscah imagined it.

Her nose stung, the kind of sting that can warn of tears. She blinked and rubbed her knuckles across her face. She was not for crying tonight! Somehow, a rescue must be performed and she was the only one they weren't paying attention to. She glanced around at the guards, less vigilant now, with Arphaxas and Simirra in the woods. There was snoring coming from the litter, the disgusting priest, who reminded her of those first days at the temple of Gerar. They all carried the same odor. There was a fist size rock lying near, which she pulled in and under her thigh. Then she lay across it and listened, waiting for all the guards to fall asleep.

IT HAD BEEN QUIET FOR A WHILE. THE GUARDS HAD passed a night without sleep as much as she, and she was completely exhausted. If she would dare it, it must be now. She squeezed the rock to reassure herself and pulled her knees up, ready to… do something. Only there was suddenly leaf rustling and feet coming out of the forest and into the camp. She peaked across her shoulder. Arphaxas! She waited for Simirra; but the woman did not reappear. Perhaps he had beaten her…

Iscah eased herself back against the ground. Now she would have to wait for the giant to go to sleep! She searched for a comfortable position and found herself watching the trees for Simirra, though the woman was tarnished now, in her estimation. If not that it was taking Arphaxas a while to settle, she might have made good on her plan. But her eyes were uncontrollably heavy.

A COMMOTION WOKE ISCAH. HAVING BEEN IN THE DEEP-est depths of sleep, she tried to make sense of what seemed to be happening. The dragon man was dancing, his silhouette leaping, spinning in the light of the fire. He was almost graceful, swinging his curved blade back and forth. She heard it swoosh as the guards slowly, one by one simply toppled over without a cry nor any fuss at all. Stunned, she watched firelight reflect in the spreading pools of blood.

It was no dream. She lay very still, that he would not turn on her.

A rustle sounded from Kittim and Madai's direction and she tried to cry out, to warn them, but – as if she were a mute – no sound came. She only had her rock, which she clutched with ferocity.

She heard another scraping. It was from behind and she turned to see the person she had thought to be Arphaxas remove the dragon's cape. It was, in fact, a ruse she had seen before, and instantly she knew it was Simirra in the giant's garb. She knew as surely, that the happening in the woods had been a ruse as well, meant to put off the guards. It had worked very well. But now she was confused; if it was the gold he was after…

She watched Arphaxas wipe his scimitar with painstaking care, as if the sword were what concerned him and all else had been an unremarkable event. He did not bother a second look at the slain men, trusting in his own efficiency. He did not look to Kittim or Madai, nor did he speak to Simirra, who was his partner in the scheme.

Instead and incredibly, he started toward the litter. Despite what was known to her of priests like Namim, she felt culpability in what would happen next. For she had no doubt of it.

A path was lit by the moon as if a night's spotlight were provided and she watched Arphaxas with horrible fascination, going behind the cart and eventually out of sight.

ARPHAXAS PINCHED THE FINE DRAPERY BETWEEN HIS fingers and delicately pulled back the cloth. Then he sat back on his haunches to look at the sleeping priest. The night air was cool. It would wake him soon enough. Arphaxas waited with a sort of calm. A smile creased his face, watching as Namim groggily clutched at his covers. Arphaxas diligently pulled them away. The priest's eyes shot open and he yelped at the sight of the giant man looming above him.

"Sidon!"

"No one to hear you priest," came Arphaxas's voice, as smooth as lamb's milk.

He watched Namim sink back against the bed. "Sidon!" he called again, with a crack in his voice.

Arphaxas cocked his head, listening to the silent night. He turned up the left side of his lips in a sympathetic half-smile as there were no guards arousing, nor litter bearer or underling priest.

"Where are they?" Namim's lips mouthed the question woodenly. Arphaxas shrugged.

"What do you want? Here!" The priest reached for something under his pillow. Arphaxas grabbed his wrist as Namim pulled out a bulging bag of coins.

"The reward," Namim whispered against the fear and the tight circle of fingers around his arm.

Arphaxas scarcely glanced at the bag, savoring instead the way the shadows had found Namim's eyes, giving his shaved head the appearance of a scull – amusingly prophetic. Arphaxas finally released Namim's wrist and took the bag, cupping it in his palm.

"You think it's gold I want, Priest?"

A sort of whimper escaped Namim's lips, sweat born of fear on a cold night beaded above them. "What do you want then?"

"Only this," Arphaxas whispered back, quiet as the grave.

He watched again as expressions passed the priest's face. He watched the man's eyes calculate, dart back to his own and calculate again. He tried to memorize each tic, every sweet fear that entered the priest's brain and passed across his face. It was a glorious moment, long in coming. Slowly he sat back on his heels as Namim seemed to wilt into the litter's purple brocade. The priest's body quaked with cold and terror. Arphaxas leaned forward, almost gently, and pulled the brocade robe up to Namim's chest and then to his chin. He felt the clammy skin of the priest's beardless face with his knuckle.

"Better?" he asked.

"I can give you more than only gold," Namim whimpered. "I am a king-maker."

Arphaxas threw back his head and laughed. It was an ugly laugh, replaced as quickly with a look to vanquish the expectations of even the most valiant.

It was time.

"You make worse than kings," he hissed, pale green eyes resting on Namim like a snake. He slowly stood, stretching his full seven feet above the bed and jostling the litter. He found the hilt of his scimitar and pulled it smoothly, silently from its scabbard. He held it aloft, trailing his eyes across the gleaming blade as affectionate as a caress.

"It will be quick, Priest," he said in a low voice. "You do not possess my soul." He looked back at the man. "You never did."

The head of Semiramis' priest was severed cleanly and quickly, as promised. But not before a look of astonishment passed its eyes, a spark of recognition, an old desire.

MADAI HAD ALSO BEEN WATCHING; AT THE PRIEST'S FIRST startled cry he was fixed on the litter. He heard a nasty laugh and after that only silence. He fought the bindings that affixed him to the tree all the more urgently and could not make sense of what had assuredly happened to Namim. What could their mystery captor want with a Shinar priest and these guards dead? His wrists were torn and every struggle against the ropes was another cut, and got him no better freed.

It seemed but an instant and the stranger re-emerged from behind the litter, sheathing his weapon. Madai's sweat sprung up on him, cold and dreadful in the night air.

"Is he dead?" Madai growled, hearing his own voice sound with more force than their situation deserved. Arphaxas looked up, appearing startled, which gave Madai another shot of confidence.

"I held claim to his life," Madai growled again, suddenly overwhelmed with remembrance of his captivity and all the parts that Namim had played.

And yet Arphaxas turned away as though he had not bothered to hear. His hand rested comfortably on the hilt of his sword like a familiar nook. He did not respond to the challenge in Madai's voice, impotent as it was in the circumstance. He simply reclaimed his dragon cape from the woman, Simirra, and swung it across his shoulders.

He bent then, slowly and with no menace at all, to take up the knife that had once belonged to the dead husband, Martu. He took it by its tip and flexed his wrist, seeming to test the balance of the blade. In almost a dance, he turned, and before Madai could dodge or duck or respond at all, the knife was air-borne, launched with expertise from Arphaxas's fingertips. It impaled the earth just to his left and Madai knew of certainty – and to his wonderment, that his captor's aim had been true.

"My claim was first," Arphaxas spat back.

He bent again, taking up his pack and started for the black horse. The wom-an, Simirra, was instantly on her feet, scrambling behind. She grabbed at his cape.

"You are free, woman," Arphaxas objected, shaking her off. "Your husband is dead."

"And so is the priest," she insisted.

Arphaxas stopped at that. He looked at her. "All who killed your babe," he countered. "You should be glad."

"But I am the one that came for him. It is known. Will you send me to do your work then leave me as bait for the jackals?"

Stunned, Madai watched the drama as if he and Iscah and Kittim had ceased to exist for the giant. "Wait!" he insisted, even as Iscah was beside him, using Martu's knife to saw through his bindings.

"Ssh" she whispered. "Let them go if they will."

"What do you mean, your claim?" Madai all but yelled, standing up. "Who are you?"

But the dragon-man ignored him, again. Madai watched him take up a bridle, pull it round the stallion's head and fasten it behind his ears.

"Who are you?"

"You may travel with us," Kittim suddenly interjected, his voice calling out in the dark.

Arphaxas threw a saddle over the horse's rump, ignoring them all, even the woman, Simirra, who was frantically preparing her own horse. He pulled the cinch tight, let the animal exhale and pulled again.

"You have made an enemy of Shinar," Kittim continued, nodding at the dead guards.

Madai could not see Arphaxas's face in the dark, but he could imagine it as unmoved as stone. "Yes." the man affirmed, swinging up on the horse.

"I see you are not afraid," Kittim continued, "though you should be."

Arphaxas snorted. "Are you afraid then?" he asked over his shoulder.

"We have a protection of which you know nothing," Kittim replied evenly.

And Arphaxas reacted in the expected way; he laughed.

"Who are you?" Madai demanded. He had not meant to let importance leak into his voice and was instantly sorry because he could see a sort of satisfaction settle on the man's frame.

"My name is Arphaxas," came the cool response. He clipped the horse with his heels, his want to be shed of them all quite obvious.

But the camels snorted and kicked at the black stallion. Arphaxas started to rein around them... but stopped. He seemed suddenly intrigued by the camel's lumpy cargo. Madai was across the camp and grabbing for the camel's halter before he knew he had even meant to move.

"What is that?" Arphaxas asked resting his foot on a protruding object.

Madai planted a proprietary hand on the pack just beside the blood-spattered boot. "It is mine," he insisted.

"What is it?" Arphaxas sneered. "A talisman?"

"It's a bone."

"More than a bone, I think."

"It is a proof," Kittim answered and Arphaxas turned in his saddle. "Of what, atoyak?"

"The flood."

He laughed again and Madai felt poked at by it.

"You are still a dreamer, are you?"

Madai heard the question and did not hear the question. He watched Arphaxas looking back at him with a hint of smile. He pulled his hand back, somewhat dazed. "Who are you?" he asked again.

"My name is Arphaxas."

"I have known no Arphaxas."

The night was silent after that. He was vaguely aware of Simirra riding up from behind.

"Let me see you," Madai insisted, feeling a chill borne less by the night than by the suggestion that he was known by this stranger. He could bring to mind no man to fit the figure Arphaxas made on his horse. Perhaps he had ridden with Shem... but he could recall none belonging to the tribe to match him.

"What was your first claim on the priest?" Madai probed. "Did he escape you in battle at Shinar

Arphaxas removed his foot from the stirrup and pushed against Madai's chest. "Get back," he demanded. Madai grabbed for man's boot. "Are you a Shemite?"

Arphaxas pulled his leg away, catching the stallion in the flank. The horse shied sideways and reared back, flailing at the air. Arphaxas clamped his knees against the animal's sides, keeping his seat but dropping the hood of his dragon cape onto his back. The moon caught the red sheen of his hair.

Madai blinked as inconsistent bits of information raced through his mind and out his mouth.

"Tazek?"

CHAPTER 9

*T*HE CAMP WAS SILENT, EVEN THE REBELLIOUS stallion. Madai could see Arphaxas staring between the animal's ears, staring down at him with rage.

"I told you my name," he hissed.

Madai expected him to pull the hood back over his telltale hair, but he did not. He bore the genes of The Family in a hedge of red. But this man was so unlike the one he had met in Nimrod's court. It seemed all together impossible, and yet here he was, Tazek buried beneath the scowl and the muscle. He could easily flip in Madai's vision, back to Arphaxas the dragon-man, and no piteous Tazek, who had been servile and abused, afraid and bitter, the toy of a dissolute priest. How did so seemingly weak a vessel contain latent so ferocious a man? wonder Namim was headless.

"You will call me Arphaxas."

Madai watched the moon cast shadows across the man's face – Tazek, though greatly changed, brother of Palapa, Palapa, who had saved his life.

"I am going home, Arphaxas," Madai said quietly. "To The Family. Will you come?" Then he watched the man who was quite a stranger after all, sit motionless, stiff, like a pillar wrapped with dragon.

"You are repaid, for Palapa's sake." His whisper sounded more like a growl in Madai's ears. "She loved you. But to me, you are atoyak, and she is dead because of you." Arphaxas moved then, leaning forward. "I have a claim upon you as well. So, consider Japhethite – do you really want me at your fire?"

"I do."

A very slow and slight smile played at Arphaxas's mouth. It did not reach his eyes, which were slits of contemplative green.

THERE IS A SORT OF RHYTHM BORN OUT TO A MAN'S DAYS. At even the most calamitous event or exhilaration there follows, with precious little exception, stretches of absolute dullery. Such were the days which followed the extermination of Shinar's soldiers and its priest. An uneasy civility settled upon them, advancing toward the Sea as though such blood-letting were common place, with no dread curiosities remaining of Arphaxas's life and character. They each passed the days guarding their own trepidations in silence.

It was hot; a late autumn's last stamp upon the season. For Simirra, the first thrill at Martu's death had faded in the immediate circumstance of hunger, fatigue and monotony. Vengeance was a fickle lover it seemed. The less travel-worthy blue gown had been exchanged for the old leggings and vest. They were stiff now and smelled. That was a fortnight past, an eternity.

Arphaxas rode ahead of her, a fixture now more than adversary… or protector. She'd watched the black stallion's tail wage a hopeless battle against pernicious insects. Perhaps the insects were why the man was still covered in dragon, which seemed a hot excess on such an afternoon.

She swatted at a spearfly settling boldly on her arm.

That Arphaxas had killed so many had not surprised her. She'd seen him do it in the grove before, taking down those dart-blowers from Calneh as if they were children. But there was such an ease with which he could do such a thing, not unlike Martu. He would be so defined were there not that tone in his voice when he had told her to 'let it be'. She frowned. He was not as he appeared, not the brute and he knew the Japhethite tongue. She did also, but she had an education.

Besides that, there were her own problems. She could not return to Calneh. She was the known messenger sent to retrieve the priest, who was certainly discovered headless by now, and with the gold missing. Arphaxas had it, of course. All her previous circumstances were lost. Calneh was… dead to her.

The baby – she would not think about that.

She jerked her eyes from the mesmerizing quality of the stallion's relent-less tail to the girl riding the bay.

Aten, what an audacity: naming a beast after a god! That Iscah was brave, amusing as well, was also proved along the way when she had been sent after Namim. She might have been a kindred spirit at any other time. But it is hard to be a friend whilst you nurse a thorn.

Pity the girl loved the man, Kittim, as he did not love her back. Not in such a way as she loved him. With such a promise of womanly beauty, despite her unruly crown of hair, there was scarce little to explain it.

A seam in Martu's legging was starting to rub a sore in her thigh. Sweat was making it sting. She must ask Iscah for something fresh tonight, which was but a further proof of such a fall from her former life. She patted Basar as though to remind herself that she was once no beggar. As for Madai and Kittim, she could recognize the trappings of wealth but Shinar did not lack for gold. What then would arouse such a disturbance in the far-off capital as to hunt them? Surely they could not be part of a rebellion of Shemite shepherds! Namim had said so, but she did not believe him.

She was a fortnight with this company now, riding toward the sea. She had seen it only once when she was very young and her father had taken her to the shore. That was very long ago. She remembered the trip now as a winsome tale of someone else's childhood.

The spearfly had come back for more. She let it dine. If she let herself, she could be drowned in melancholy…

As if the girl had heard her musings, Iscah dropped back and came along beside. There was a look of genuine excitement on her face, in exact opposite to her own feelings. Simirra estimated that the sunny smile was, in any case, no insignificant feat.

"We are coming upon a wondrous valley!" Iscah chirped. "I do recognize it."

"O?" It was all Simirra could manage.

Iscah pointed toward an area of rolling hills ahead of them. "Behemoth lives there," she confided. Which sent a chill down Simirra's spine. She pulled sharply on Basar's reins.

Iscah turned in her saddle. "Nothing to fear, Simirra," she said. "Behemoth is an eater of grass." She smiled, brilliant with confidence.

"Who has told you this, Iscah? I have never seen Behemoth, and I have not always lived in a city."

Iscah pointed to her own eyes. "I saw her myself," she proclaimed.

Simirra pursed her lips, fighting with the ache in her shoulders.

Iscah nodded determinedly. "Tis true."

The older woman looked at the hills again. They were no longer green, but golden and with an abundance of seed-topped grass.

"Behemoth was very much larger before the deluge," Iscah continued undeterred, "very much!"

Simirra sighed. "And how would you know that?"

"I've seen its bones," Iscah answered, leaning way over, spanning the distance between Simirra's horse and her own.

"Now I know you're spinning a tale!" The older woman allowed herself a thin laugh, finding that it felt nearly foreign after all that lay behind her.

"No, it's true, Simirra. When we were with Job…"

"Ah! Don't lie, girl!'

Iscah sat squarely back in the saddle. "Why would you say such a thing?"

"You tell me that you know so great a man?"

"Yes."

"It is not seemly to put on airs, Iscah. You may be rich…"

"I am not rich! And I do not…. put on airs."

"Lord Job is an important man, Iscah. So important that news of him is known. Just in spring, it was rumored that he is ruined."

"So he was."

Simirra raised an eyebrow at Iscah.

"Yes," Iscah confirmed stiffly, looking thoroughly insulted. "Though Mighty God is restoring him even now."

"You are telling me that you know a man of such nobility as Job?"

"Believe me or no." Iscah touched Aten with her heel.

"Wait." Simirra stopped her. "You are saying that you know this man?"

"I do know this man. This was his horse. He gave him to me."

Simirra studied Iscah's face. It was just indignant enough to be telling the truth. She sat back and left Basar to direct himself, forgetting behemoth, feeling both slightly ashamed to have offended the young girl and reminded but again of her fallen station in life. That this company knew one so renowned as Job...

"Iscah," she coaxed. "Iscah, I am sorry. It is only that I cannot imagine... though your caravan comes from the east... but I have never met a man who actually knows the Lord Job. Many would wish to. But he is very important. Very important! Why, even my father, who was a great man once, would never have presumed..."

"He would have been welcomed," Iscah declared coolly. "Job is very hospitable. He believes in the One True God, you know. And your father..."

Simirra stiffened. "My father was murdered for your One True God," she snapped.

Iscah heard the words spoken so bitterly and yet with such pain. It instantly banished all her newly born indignation. She could relate to orphans. But she was also curious, despite the improper taste of it. How might knowledge of the One True God survive a pagan city? Though, of course, it had not.

"Yes,' Simirra continued. "A true believer."

"I am sorry," Iscah replied quietly.

"It seems all my family is dead for one god or another."

Iscah's sensitivities were stung at that... If it was a truth, still it sounded a lot like blasphemy. "There is just One God," she said quietly as she could not stop herself.

Simirra looked at her then. "You may find, little Iscah, it is not so simple... I was once as you are."

And despite the dead father and dead babe, Iscah felt her prickles rise again. She had lost a father too, and mother as well... and virtue. She turned away from Simirra to look at the valley that had so short a time ago promised her pleasure. It seemed there was a disturbance between them, she and Simirra, that would not be tamed. It also seemed to have sucked her free of joy.

They settled into silence again after that. The heat of the day had finally reached its peak and was beginning to ebb at last, which was a great relief. But Iscah had an almost urgent need to be somewhere else, anywhere. She clucked at Aten. He responded instantly, trotting away.

He trotted past the camels. Iscah urged him on to the head of their little caravan and to Madai, who could always be counted on for conversation.

"Can we ride all the way to the lake?" Iscah asked him without preamble. She leaned toward him as she had leaned toward Simirra and whispered, "Behemoth."

He looked over at her with a pleasant expression and nodded. "You recognize it too?"

It had been just the change she needed. His response was like the fresh smell of spring air and she smiled back. She pushed her hair behind her ears and nodded at the surrounding hills. "We've come a long way."

"We have."

She felt the muscles of her neck begin to relax. It was pleasant again. She could hear the start of a night's chorus of bullfrogs, the certain sign that marshes lay near. She could hear the sound of soft earth under their horse's hooves. It was a perfect end to a miserable day.

But still, there was the mystery. It had remained unspoken, un-approached and this was, perhaps, an opportune moment to approach it. The day had been long; the journey longer, full of atrocities and untold secrets. Madai and Arphaxas had not, in fact, spoken again of the mysterious Tazek.

"Madai," she whispered. "Tell me about Tazek."

He looked as surprised as a wide-eyed owl. As quickly, his face came cloudy. He was, in that instant, so inaccessible, so reluctant that she was immediately sorry to have asked.

"It's part of Shinar," he muttered.

"Of course," she answered quickly. "But," she could not stop herself, once started, "But who is Tazek? And Arphaxas… so wild."

She could see that he did not intend to answer.

"They are odd partners," she pressed quietly, "he and Simirra, do you not think so?"

"Odd indeed."

"I wonder how they came upon each other…"

"You should ask her, perhaps," he replied quietly.

She scratched her head, needing the diversion and had the stray perception that it needed a good wash. "I have insulted her thoroughly," she mumbled.

His expression changed again, looking like his old self, slightly amused; decidedly relieved. Iscah felt relieved too and somewhat absolved of her crime, both crimes.

A slight breeze picked up. It was quiet again and she was glad of it, for she had insulted Simirra and stumbled upon testy ground with Madai, all due to her curiosities. It was somehow no longer… acceptable to be at odds with Madai. Though what of questions should provoke such a cloudy look she could not understand.

"Will we reach the valley by dark, do you think?" she asked him.

He turned them onto the rising slopes and nodded. "Just through that pass."

Directly ahead was the last color of a sun being eclipsed by the hilltops. The sound of the frogs was louder now and if she imagined enough, she could almost hear the reedy call of a behemoth mother on the wind.

THEY BUILT A FIRE OF GREATER SIZE THAN THE AFTER-noon might have predicted, as the night was cold. Madai watched Iscah start toward the reeds at the edge of the lake and remembered her penchant for frequent bathing, even in a chill. Arphaxas had built a fire of his own that even his woman did not venture to share. Instead, she followed Iscah to the water's edge.

"The women are bathing," he heard himself announce in Arphaxas's direction and felt himself go pepper-fish red at the inane comment.

Arphaxas looked up with the exact expression Madai would have predicted. He glanced at the lake and shrugged.

"I'm glad you are with us," Madai tried again. He also tried to keep his eyes off Arphaxas's fish, though it was difficult. He was exceedingly hungry, but with no expectation of sharing.

Arphaxas took a bite of very hot fish, and retrieved one of its slender bones, pulling it through his lips. "Why is that?"

"I," Madai paused, "I wondered what would happen to you… after Shinar."

"I escaped," Arphaxas replied flatly.

Madai nodded.

Arphaxas tossed a fish head in the fire.

"If not for you, Palapa would be alive," he declared, licking his fingers.

Madai had not expected that so soon. "It was not in my control, Arphaxas," he muttered quickly. "She would have been sent to the temple." Arphaxas looked up. "She would be with me now."

"You know what was done in the temple."

Arphaxas's lips stretched across his face with a surly smile. "Still the high one? You do not know what was already done to her."

Madai stared, seeing a filled out Tazek, very much the remembered boy at this moment. But he had to concede that what Arphaxas had said was indeed true. He could only guess what was done to both of them and that would likely not be grievous enough, for there is a depth to evil that the un-initiated cannot imagine.

"You should know that she died peaceable." he finally revealed.

"How would you know that?"

"There was a true smile on her lips. I saw, I held her."

"She was dead, atoyak."

"You've seen the face of the dead," Madai retorted. "They do not all die peaceable."

Arphaxas waved his hand at the air. He chewed on the edge of his mustache where perhaps there was a lingering taste of fish and Madai watched the man remember his sister. But when Arphaxas looked back, it was with bitterness. "She believed in a one true and good God, you know. Like you. Both fools." He glared a minute, then stood up. "See how she was saved?"

"Do not suppose there is just this life," Madai grabbed Arphaxas's arm as he spoke.

Arphaxas looked down at his hand. "I do not think on such vanities," he hissed. "I leave that to priests."

"I don't believe that, Tazek."

Arphaxas swung back around. His hand shot up to Madai's throat, and clamped around it with blistering ferocity. He pushed his face nose to nose. "I would not presume on old associations, Japhethite. I can snap you like a chicken bone now."

Madai could feel the truth of that. "I do not."

The expression on Arphaxas's face shifted as he chuckled, "Your arrogance is still astonishing," he finally replied watching Madai with cold eyes, and dropped his hand.

Madai took a quick step back. He felt his neck, then found his knife before he spoke again. "Palapa was right."

"You will not speak of her again." Arphaxas growled.

"She was right, Arphaxas. Surely you don't believe in Namim's gods." To which Arphaxas expelled an incoherent snarl.

Madai let his hand slide away from the knife. "I have talked to Noah," he began.

Arphaxas blinked. Madai could see that the man, who seemed another fellow all together than the Tazek he had known, was surprised. Madai watched his eyes flicker with quick deliberation. Then the man chuckled again, but only after his face was betrayed by that look.

"Lies are hatched every day." He finally replied.

"I thought the same," Madai replied quickly, "but I can tell you, Arphaxas, that he was the father of Shem.

All of Shinar knows the Shemites. You know the Shemites."

Madai watched him. But the passions, which had etched his face before, did not reappear. "You invite danger, Japhethite. I am no friend to the Shemites."

"They did not kill Palapa. A man of Shinar did, one who hated me."

Arphaxas closed his eyes. "So you are guilty twice." He turned abruptly to walk away, seeming suddenly tired.

"Wait, Arphaxas," Madai reached for his arm again. "There is a One True God. Palapa is not lost forever."

"Don't speak to me, Japhethite. I do not want to kill you tonight." He walked away from Madai then and out into the dark, away from his fire.

SIMIRRA AND ISCAH HURRIED THROUGH THE REEDS. IT was uncommonly cold and their hair was wet. Iscah laughed, tripping through the mud, determined to put their afternoon's tension aside and glad to provide the woman clean clothes. She noted that Simirra left her dead husband's leggings at the water's edge with designed finality. Iscah watched her knot her hair at the nape of her neck with the grace that The Lady might have used, knitting up her own heart a bit with envy. They continued on then, weaving through the rushes, anxious for the fire and something to eat.

Iscah suddenly stopped, putting her finger on her lips, "Ssh," she whispered. "Listen." Simirra stumbled into her, "What?"

"Something is walking."

"Behemoth?" Iscah heard anxiety in Simirra's voice.

"If it was Behemoth, we would know," Iscah replied. She pulled Simirra down and they looked through the reeds in the direction of the sounds, which were now unmistakable to Simirra as well.

"A man," Simirra whispered.

Iscah exhaled softly. "Of course. Kittim. He leaves the camp every night to pray."

"Come, then," Simirra replied, standing up. "We will not spy."

"No. Certainly not." Iscah stood as well, straightening her clothes.

BUT IT WAS ARPHAXAS, AT THE WATER'S EDGE LOOKING across the lake. He was wearing his dragon cape, with the hood laid flat on his back. He was pondering something. Iscah carried on toward the fire, but Simirra stood watching. The great red giant that had treated her as an animal would... was crying. His matted beard sparkled with tears in the moonlight.

MORNING ANNOUNCED ITSELF BLUSTERY. IT WAS COM-ing quickly autumn, the season of color with a winter at its heels.

Madai knew they must hurry to the sea. But he was sitting on his robe and watching Arphaxas this morning. The man was squatted beside his fire, waiting for a speckled trout to cook. The fish was nearly ready; he could smell it. But Madai was considering a dilemma of greater substance than simple hunger. He was prepared to bring a Banned home with him, one that announced a fondness for killing him.

How would his Patta respond to a Banned? Or Tiras? Or Togarmah? In truth, Madai had once cast his voice against a friend – poor Laeden – a broken wretch laid hold by the Banned and tempted away. Madai knew this one as well, this Arphaxas – knew his story. The salient difference, perhaps, was that the choice had been thrust upon Arphaxas as a child and it had reaped a costly harvest. That Madai became a part in the reaping was also a part of the current dilemma, the guilty part.

Arphaxas was finally pulling the trout off the spit. He looked neither right nor left, but only to the fish. He ate it quickly. It left Madai with the uneasy reminder that within this man dwelt no generous heart.

A tiny hand suddenly clamped on his shoulder.

"Madai!' Iscah's excited voice whispered in his ear, "There."

She leaned over, turning his head with her hands to face him toward the lake. Indeed at its center rose the slender neck of Behemoth, in silhouette against the dawn. It was turned in their direction, as though it remembered them.

"Does she have a calf, Madai? Can you see one?"

"I can't see much, Iscah, move your fingers."

She leaned away, and Madai rose to his knees. "I only see the one," he answered. Iscah clapped her hands together. "I knew she would be here!"

"She would not want to disappoint you."

"O!" Iscah complained, "Don't laugh. I'm just glad she is still here! After we have seen the bones of those drowned others, it is very good that such a wondrous creature is still alive!"

"Saved in a ship," Madai responded, glad to have his worries interrupted.

"Which you and Kittim have seen, and I have not! Shall not, if we must go west!"

He laughed.

Madai's laugh carried across the water to the keen ears of a behemoth mother. She bumped against a calf, which was hidden from view by her very great bulk, pushing it toward the far shore. She moved gracefully, arching her neck to touch the top of her baby's head. Then she snorted across her shoulder at the two who watched from shore. There was a fear of humankind placed in her now, by the Maker, and she was a diligent mother.

Iscah wrapped her arms around Madai's shoulders in her own glee. "Isn't she grand?"

Madai reached up to pat Iscah's hand. It was the only gesture he allowed himself. Her hand was tiny and cool and she soon pulled away to rest both of them on his shoulders. They watched the great beast together, quitting the lake for the reeds.

"So, you were right," a second voice sounded beside Iscah, and Madai turned his head to find Simirra standing there. "I should believe you, I see."

It was, for Madai, an unwelcome interruption, even one so handsome as the Calnehan. She was wearing something of Iscah's and it was a good deal more attractive than the trousers of a man. She had an astounding beauty, really, and tall for a woman. She seemed no rightful companion for Arphaxas at all.

"I am so hungry," Iscah announced. "Where is Kittim? Do you think he is fishing?"

"I'll find him," Madai answered. "And bring you something to eat."

She tightened her hands on his shoulders. "O thank you, Madai! You are always so good!" It was an off-handed remark, sisterly in tone and entirely disappointing.

"So then," Simirra continued. "If it is true of that beast, then I will believe that you do know Job."

"As I said."

"He is a legend."

Iscah turned to her with a friendly look. "Why do you say that, Simirra?"

"Everyone has heard of Job. He is very rich and very wise."

Iscah lifted her brows. "Do you want to hear about him because he is very rich, or because he is very wise?" And she had to allow that Simirra blushed at the question.

"Why… wise, of course."

Iscah sat on Madai's mat. She smoothed the folds of her robe as she had seen Job's Lady do many a time. It was an unconscious gesture and a part of her now. "His wisdom comes from the One True God," Iscah warned, having broached the subject with Simirra a time before.

Simirra did not look to be still in an ill humor, though her voice was chilly when she said, "Men are obsessed with gods."

"Well they should be," Iscah replied easily. "It is God Who has made them. But there is only One. And, He is jealous of His throne."

"A despot?"

Iscah's brows arched again, higher this time. "Is it not a kindness to demand that men follow not after myths?"

"Certainly. But whose myth is true?"

"You sound like Madai!" Iscah exclaimed. Arphaxas looked up from his fire.

"He came looking for truth," Iscah continued. "And … I will add that he found it."

"From Job?"

"Yes… a part from Job, and a part from Noah too."

Simirra laughed, but Iscah did not blame her this time. It had been a surprise to her as well, and were Kittim not a part of the adventure, she might have been more skeptical, indeed. She simply nodded and made room, as the woman sat down beside her.

"I know, Simirra. It sounds impossible. But Madai and Kittim both met him."

"Who are Madai and Kittim to me?" She asked.

"Well, they are a great deal to me!"

Simirra patted Iscah's hand, seeming sorry for the question, which was of small compensation to Iscah – being so often patted like a child. As for the tale of Noah, she was both entirely convinced and equally offended.

"Forgive me." Simirra hastily replied. "Of course they mean a great deal to you. And you believe them.

But," She paused, looking across the lake. "But, Noah would have to be… hundreds of years old!"

"Nine hundred."

"Well."

"Yes, nine hundred. Kept alive by half his life lived on the first earth. Kittim told me."

Simirra's eyes all but screamed her disbelief even as she asked – perhaps to be kind, "The first earth?"

And Iscah told her the tales of a time before the great deluge when the earth was wrapped in mist which fed the grass and the streams and the throats of beasts and men; when beasts ate grass and not each other. She told of long lives, of men who talked with God and walked with Him, of Adam and Eve, of fallen angels and serpents.

Arphaxas heard the conversation as well, with equal parts of scorn and curiosity.

Madai cleaned his arrow, then took up his three silver fish through the gills. He slung his bow across his back when Kittim stopped him with a hand on his shoulder.

"Wait," Kittim said.

"I'm hungry, Kittim."

"It is a good time to talk."

"There's time aplenty for talk."

Kittim bent to pick up his catch. "Perhaps," he answered slowly. "But with enemies at our tail, such times should be… taken."

Madai frowned.

"We each have a mission," Kittim began quickly. "You must carry truth away from this shore..."

"Yes."

"We are nigh to the shore."

"And you, Kittim," Madai frowned uneasily as he asked, "what about your mission?"

"Nearly complete," Kittim answered carefully.

Madai studied him. He seemed no different, but there was a tone in his voice not to like. He had turned to look at the mountains. They separated the sea with its sandy regions from the high deserts of lands just traveled and from the far boundaries of Shinar.

"You will not sail with me," Madai muttered, finally unable to keep himself from asking.

"It will be time to return to my Master."

Madai could only stare at Kittim's back. It was the moment to ask a myriad of questions but it must be that his tongue had gone to stone and all the questions he'd stored up seemed to have flitted away. There was only this coming goodbye that was sitting on his heart, heavy as behemoth herself.

"You are well equipped, my friend," Kittim said quietly, pointed toward the mountains.

"Still," Madai found his voice, "I had hoped…"

When Kittim did not answer, Madai let the breath escape his lungs with a sigh. "You will tell Iscah goodbye?"

And even that question, Kittim did not answer.

CHAPTER 10

*A*CHILD WAS WRAPPED IN PURPLE AND GOLD. HE was watched every moment of every day and night and suckled at a generous breast. Tammuz's nursemaid had a boy-child of her own, who would be at risk if she could not feed them both.

Semiramis held the child, Tammuz, only to croon at him and find herself in his little face. He had the nose of Namim, which was regrettable. But today Semiramis had been told news, and the dimensions of Namim's nose would soon become irrelevant, as people do forget. It seemed his litter had been found. The gold bounty was missing, the guards were dead and so was Namim. It was a terrible affront, as the man had been high priest in the service of his child-god – Tammuz. With the priest gone, that was how it would stand and no one beyond herself to know his parentage. She could even be persuaded to forget.

There only remained the affront. It was against Tammuz, himself, and she could not let it remain un-avenged. She cared little about Madai and Kittim. They were a small part in the plot against Shinar and were returning west. They would disappear from her shores to be remembered by no one. And yet there was a persistent inkling that they should be stopped.

She gave Tammuz back to the nursemaid. "Put him to bed," Semiramis told her.

She watched till the woman was gone, then turned to the courier, who had by now developed a bead of sweat on the end of his nose.

"Rise," she told him.

He set his eyes no higher than her feet.

"Bring me Admah," she demanded, an order he was most happy to obey.

SEMIRAMIS EXAMINED SHINAR'S NEWEST COMMANDER. Admah was not the caliber of Nimrod's old guard, but they were all dead. This man was brought and bought and bent a knee to them who paid him.

"The rebels will be stopped," Semiramis demanded, spoken to the top of an abundant garnishment of hair. That Admah smirked to be in service of so notorious a woman was irrelevant, for he would do her bidding.

He underestimated Semiramis, but that was irrelevant too.

"We will catch them in the great wadi, west of Calneh, my Queen."

"No," she replied simply. "They are far escaped and you are well behind them." She rearranged the robe across a belly that was not quite shrunk from childbirth. "But we know where they are going. They shall pass through Sodom to the Great Sea. That is where you will stop them." She studied the shoulders that supported the head, deliberating as to their width. "They were ashore at the village, Gerar,"

"Yes, my Queen."

"Ready your fastest men," she continued.

"The village, Gerar?" he asked.

Semiramis thought she heard some doubt in his voice. It was a tone she was hearing one too many times since Nimrod's demise. But Admah was a strong man, as she had only just appraised, and attractive in his own way and there were not many of his sort left after the terrible defeat. She had stooped to Namim after all. But she was Queen and could not excuse even the scent of insurrection.

"Gerar." She affirmed tersely. She watched his jaw clench, a sign that there were unrestrained passions in the Commander. "Admah," she continued in a tone less severe and with hopeful seduction, "you may rise."

He obeyed quickly, which pleased her too.

Smiling now, she had a good long look at him: younger than Nimrod, eyes not so intelligent perhaps but a healthy jaw. There was a rawness about him which she found appealing. She would pinch her diet till he returned and find a new hair dresser. What she lacked in youth she could enhance with wealth. But she would not bring him into confidence; to tell him that Madai himself had divulged his point of coming ashore was unnecessary. There was still the allure of supreme power, which she was too shrewd to surrender.

"You will be greatly rewarded, Admah," she crooned the twofold promise. To which he inclined his head. "My reward is your pleasure, my Queen."

ADMAH BACKED AWAY FROM THE DAIS AND ITS MIDDLE-aged monarch. He had not missed the inspection of her eyes. It gave him no small ambition and was not so high a price. She was not so repellent of face and form as gossip rumored. Not so bad at all.

CHAPTER 11

ARPHAXAS KEPT A POSITION BEHIND MADAI AT ALL times. It was somewhat troubling – being always followed by a seeker of revenge. It was a situation Madai learned, with time, to tolerate, and with more time, to ignore. They moved quickly, beyond behemoth's valley and past the cave where they had first shared a burnt yam with Tutan.

THEY DID NOT TAKE THE ROUTE, WHICH WOULD HAVE passed them by the ancient river, Pishon. It spared Iscah mourning their good Eastern friend once again. It did seem another life-time ago that she had traveled this route. So much was seen and known and loved since then. Her dear Kittim. She could watch his straight, square back for miles; the way his dark hair curled, and was growing too long.

That she had not spoken of such things – most assuredly not spoken of them – did very little to dampen her hopes. Her expectations were long ago transformed from devoted servant to well-loved wife. She sighed, feeling the length of the journey already passed. Nothing was spoken, no gesture made to provide the right moment. If only she had spoken garbed in silk and with the scent of lilies in her hair! Now, on this long trail, they all smelled of camel, excepting of course Simirra, who somehow remained a beauty.

And here they had crossed the long distance from Job to the city, Gerar! It was molded after the great cities of the Shinar plain and lay across the sand but a few days ride. The second of her life's calamities had come upon her in that village as second wife to Hamonheb. He had been the vehicle of her rescue, purchased at the temple with its smooth-skinned priest. She might have been more generous of heart toward Hamonheb, but she had been terrified, a child newly stolen.

And so it was a pleasant surprise as Madai turned her more westward. It was only that Kittim would join Arphaxas and Simirra to sell their camels and wares in Gerar that damped her relief. She supposed they did not entirely trust

Arphaxas. But the priest, En-Utu-Aten, was most ill disposed toward Kittim and that she did not forget. She reminded herself that he had been always kept safe. Arphaxas's sword would ride with him. That gave her a greater degree of confidence. She watched them break away eastward without complaint or concern.

It lay with her and Madai to find his boat, which had been left in the reeds beside a muddy canal, some distance away. How well it came back to her, the night she had led them away from Gerar in the dark and past the tar pits! The boat they would surely need to make a sea crossing and reach Madai's kinsmen – where he meant to take the leg bone of behemoth, turned to stone now by waters of the deluge. And he meant to take ark planks with assurances of a One True God. All such things as everyone knew, being but a few generations past the days of Noah himself. Only Madai's clan lived a far distance away. Perhaps they forgot. When she thought of it in such a light, she supposed she must grant Madai a noble cause, one that cost a great deal, fraught with dangers as well. Indeed, had it not been for this purpose, she would still be slave-wife to Hamonheb. That Kittim – being bound by some invisible tie – would follow Madai across the sea, meant that she must as well. And she did not know about the sea as she knew about the plain.

She blinked back a sudden and unexpected emotion. To cross the sea... It would take her that last step away from a well beloved Papa and Mama. A presumption that they were dead these many years by Sabean swords lost its certainty at such an irreversible course.

Iscah patted Aten's neck. She readjusted her seat in the saddle and squinted against the setting sun, which she blamed for the quiet trickle starting at the far corner of her eyes. She swiped at them with the back of her hand. She would set her mind on new adventures and help them find Madai's sea craft. It had been made from the thick hide of a great grey sea cow, oiled and rolled and buried in sand. Its cypress skeleton was left amongst the reeds with only God to guard it, praise His Name.

A BOY SAT ATOP THE WALL OF GERAR. HE WAS OLDER now than when he had first watched the foreign yellow man kill their dragon, but he still kept a watch – from time to time. There were men from Shinar waiting for them too. They came with sacks of gold, always appreciated on the frontier. Gerar was a village hoping to become a city and populated by ambitious men. Its temple, bathhouse and square mimicked the city of Shinar in all but size.

The boy could read the intentions of the men as one reads the weather. And he knew his fellows. Their dragon was dead; their thanks, once brilliant, was burnt out. Time passes and so does gratitude. Besides, Gerar's priest, En-Utu-Aten, was no friend of the strangers. He had been glad to see them gone so long ago, and now happy to help the Shinar captain catch them. In that regard, the priest had spared nothing, denied Commander Admah nothing.

But the boy, Fadil, still retained the quiet quickening in his heart that Kittim had given him when he confided that there was, indeed, a One True God and that he and Madai were only men. They were the men that had killed the fire-breather that once besieged the city, perhaps, but only men just the same. Fadil was no short-lived friend and he did not know men who shunned praise, except for the western strangers.

He was seeing a caravan now, a small one, but with a short string of camels and three horsemen. He raised his hand to shield the glare of the sun from his eyes. They were one too many for what he remembered of Kittim and Madai, and he had only known them to be humble of circumstance and afoot. He was disappointed, but he was also glad. He would warn Kittim; he had decided that already, only the soldiers were well-armed with a vast number, which frightened him and set him to wonder what had so provoked the distant powers of Shinar.

Fadil was just starting for home, having heard his stomach, when he turned back toward the plain. Perhaps the caravan had come upon Kittim and his yellow friend. If so, he might intercept them along the way and preempt a dangerous encounter entirely. So the boy slipped down the eastern side of the wall, dropping like a practiced bird from its perch, to start across the distance.

FADIL WAS EATING A MEAL FLAVORED WITH GOOD COM-pany. How surprised he had been to find that indeed, the caravan brought the man, Kittim, and with so much more than when he had left! Though Madai was not with him, there were the camels, most unexpected wealth and hand-some of horses, a surly Arphaxas, in color not unlike Madai, and a beautiful black haired woman. Sorry for the absence of Madai, who had been the actual one with the spear, he was glad of Kittim, enjoying a full belly and the security of a memory not disappointed.

"There are soldiers in the city," he warned Kittim.

The stranger, Arphaxas as he was told, looked up with surprise, even as Kittim nodded, looking back through his fearless eyes.

"They are from the High Queen herself," Fadil continued. "They have brought gold and they are after you." He wanted to ask whose dragon they had killed now, and thus upset the order of ambitious men, but he was yet in awe of the enigmatic man.

"Semiramis," Arphaxas muttered. He looked up chewing a mouth full of supper.

Fadil blanched, hearing The Light of Heaven's queen spoken of with such flagrant disrespect. Kittim grinned. "She's just a woman, Fadil, nothing to be afraid of."

"She has borne the Seed," Fadil replied in a whisper.

"Not likely," Arphaxas grumbled. The boy looked at Kittim.

"She's an ordinary woman who has born a child in the ordinary way," Kittim assured him.

"But the stars…"

"Let me assure you Fadil, the foretelling will occur just as Mighty God has decreed, imprinted there in the heavens. The Virgin shall indeed bear the seed that shall crush the head of the dragon. But it will be by the will of God alone and in His timing. Nimrod was no god and this Tammuz is not his son."

The boy, Fadil, looked as though he had sneaked a round of bread still warm from the oven; as if his ears, having just heard the words, would convict him of blasphemy. "The Lord Nimrod?"

"No god at all. He was the son of a son of Ham, who was a man – the son of Noah who was still only a man."

The colored sphere of Fadil's eyes ringed with white as he heard the name, Noah, and he lowered his chin to whisper, "The friend of the Huwah?"

"The One True God, my young friend. Yes."

"But the Huwah… killed the world," Fadil's reply was scratchy, barely audible.

Kittim's brown eyes held the boy's for a moment with a stern expression, and yet not unkindly. "Not without warning," he insisted.

Fadil seemed puzzled.

"Near to a hundred years of warning. Men had only to love Him."

Arphaxas shuffled in his seat, finished with his meal and his patience stretching thin. "The boy's brought a warning too…"

Kittim and Fadil both looked at the aggravated man startled by the interruption and his irritated voice. "You did say an entire soldier's unit?" Arphaxas pressed impatiently.

Fadil slowly nodded, his eyes round in perplexity.

THE STRETCHING OF WHALE SKIN FELT FAMILIAR, COMfortable. Madai's hands remembered how to ease it over the cypress bones of his boat. It looked and smelled like a rocky seashore to him. His nose awoke the past, recalling with naked clarity, his lost wife and little son who would likely not remember him. He dropped his chin and wrestled with the mast.

"I hope Kittim and Arphaxas get a good price for the camels," he said, clearing his throat. "We need a new sail, no doubt of that now."

Iscah looked up from her part of the work. She had been forcing old sinew through old holes in old sea cow to fasten it to the rim of the vessel – an unfamiliar occupation for her and hurting her fingertips.

"Will this hold, Madai?" she asked, glancing down the river, thinking of the sea.

Madai looked at her work, then up into her face. He heard the fear in her voice, instantly reoriented to the present and to her. "Boats older than this one have served us very well on the sea," he said with an assurance in his smile.

"Must we really cross it?"

"It is a good land, Iscah." He stretched out his hand toward her, though the expanse of the ship was too wide. She looked at it and reached her hand the rest of the way across. He gripped her fingers. "You will see. There are no cities and no skinning of men or burning of babes. We keep the first ways. And we will bring them the assurance that all the star stories are true."

She nodded slowly. He watched her purse her lips, swallow and nod again. Madai knew she was planting courage inside herself. Then she squeezed his fingers back, held them a moment and withdrew her hand. She put her fingertips in her mouth.

She was silent, looking at him before she said quietly, "They do hurt. You will not tell Kittim?"

"Tell him what?"

"That I was afraid." She looked down quickly and picked up the edge of the hides again.

"There is no shame in it, Iscah," he replied. "Were there no fear, then courage is cheap."

She glanced up, slowly a sparkle growing in her eyes and finding her mouth. "So you say." She laughed. "You do surprise me, Madai."

FADIL, BEING NOW PLUMB OF BELLY AND OF INSPIRA-tion, had set about carrying a tale to the streets of his city, Gerar. It would be soon dispersed throughout that there was a caravan on the plain – indeed there was as it could be seen from the wall. The deception was what he said next, that the caravan had come across strangers, the very Madai and Kittim, who were setting sail from the banks of the Gihon, some many leagues south, at the very moment. They were weighted with Shinar plunder and had bought a greater ship than whale-skin, which was likely crust and rubble in the sand long since. It was a lie conceived by the woman, and brilliant in his estimation.

As it was a likely story, the Gihon being a great transport to the sea and men being what they were where plunder is involved, he was believed.

CHAPTER 12

"**T**HE BOY HAS BEEN GONE A LONG TIME," Arphaxas began.

"The boy is shrewd," Kittim replied, mistaking Arphaxas's concern.

"Shrewd enough to convince them?"

"Would you not plunder a palace and need a bigger ship?" Kittim asked.

Arphaxas face remained carefully indifferent at the suggestion, with just his hand around the hilt of his sword and eyes on the city wall.

"We shall not beat them with that," Kittim observed, nodding his head at the weapon.

Arphaxas arched one red eyebrow. "True enough."

"I will persuade them," Simirra enunciated confidently.

Kittim looked at her, there in Iscah's crimson silk. It fit the Calnehan woman well, though she stood a bit too tall so that her ankles showed a silver beaded chain that fastened to a sandal. She looked every inch the courtesan. With a veil of finely spun silk, so delicate it hid not a trace of her beauty; she could convince a king that she was a queen.

"They're coming!" Arphaxas announced suddenly, jumping up. "Kittim..." he turned with the warning, but Kittim was already starting down the hill and toward the grove. "He'd best hide well," Arphaxas muttered.

"Arphaxas!" Simirra snapped. "Come here... help me with this if you are to be a convincing servant!"

He was sure he heard a heavy dose of retaliation in her voice. There was also an effortless manner, however, as though she were familiar with mistress and slave, which did not sit well. He gave her a look of warning, for her beauty was to him, detestable. He better liked her in leather and mud.

But he straightened his straw colored tunic, being ridiculously outnumbered, to take on a character. Slave was a part he was loath to play, being reminded of past and shameful offenses. To recall such a thing knotted his gut and rubbed a raw place in his soul. It did little to endear Simirra, which was unfair. But Arphaxas carried no scale for weighing fairness. The tunic was ill-fitting and stretched too tight across his back. A careful perusal would prove it not meant for him. He guessed the perusals would likely be spared for Simirra.

He stepped in front of her with his hand wrapped once again around the scimitar, supposing it struck the proper note betwixt mistress, servant and approaching soldiers.

He bowed, well before they reached him. Then he stood straight-backed and poked out his chest.

"Welcome," he grumbled the greeting, alltogether inhospitable.

A square-figured mercenary stepped forward, pleasant as Arphaxas. Indeed, Arphaxas knew a man for hire when he saw one, and could read the soldier's rank in the lines of his ruthless mouth.

"Your name!" Admah demanded, "By command of the Queen."

"Command of the Queen?" Arphaxas retorted. "What sort of mission commands names? Do you know my mistress?"

"Forgive my man, Sir," Simirra purred, coming from behind Arphaxas and into view.

Admah's face, which had showed itself roguish, did not lose the quality but only added one. He moistened his lip as he smiled.

"Lady."

"Lady Simirra," she bowed again. "My man is uncommonly diligent when I am approached."

"You will allow this humble invasion?"

"My camp is yours," she murmured, fanning her arm to the side, "if you are in service to the Great Semiramis. You will take wine with me? And tell me what use I may be to the Queen. Arphaxas!"

Arphaxas started slightly, tried to hide it and released the hold he had of his weapon. He went to the camel for their clay pitcher of wine. It was all that was remotely cool, and he grumbled, begrudging its surrender even for their charade. He brought two goblets to Simirra, letting her offer one to the soldier who had the atoyak appearance of a Dedanite.

Admah took the glass in a gulp and offered it up to Arphaxas for more.

"We are looking for two spies," he finally divulged. "Part of the rebellion."

"I thought that was the Shemites." Simirra replied daintily. "They are beyond Nimrod Dagh, are they not?"

"Spies, Lady, spying out the land, spreading rumor, conscripting followers against Queen Semiramis."

"Very vile indeed," she responded thinly. "What service do you suppose I may be?"

He seemed to study his reflection in the wine for a moment before he leaned suddenly toward her – like a blunt-faced bear – and grabbed her face. "Let me see you!" he demanded.

Arphaxas hadn't the time to unsheathe his weapon before he was grabbed on both sides by two of the Commander's soldiers.

"Sir!" Simirra gasped.

Admah tugged off her veil, ran his two hands up the side of her face and caressed her earlobes. "Bring the brewer," he barked.

A trembling man emerged from the company of men. "Here, Commander."

"Have a look," Admah ordered.

Simirra brought her hand up to hide her face and snapped, with no feigned indignation. "Who are you, Sir?"

"I am the brewer of that town, my Lady, Hamonheb."

"Is she the girl?" Admah demanded, pushing Simirra's hand away and turning her head to expose the earlobe.

HAMONHEB BENT FORWARD. HE KNEW IN THE INSTANT that she was not his second wife for whom he had paid a pittance to the temple priest. There was no disk hole in her ear and she was not a scrawny scrap. Hamonheb shook his head.

"You are sure?"

"Not the girl," he managed to enunciate.

"Well, then." Admah said, releasing her ear. "And the man?" Hamonheb shook his head again. "No."

"Then you are not detained," Admah continued with a smile as Simirra refastened the veil, looking altogether enraged. "I suppose you have met other caravans along the way?"

Simirra stepped back, turned curtly and stalked toward Arphaxas. "You will release my man!" she demanded flatly.

"Let him go," Admah agreed.

"And yes, Commander, we have met other caravans," she snapped, "fortunate enough not to venture so near Gerar as myself. I thought it was a civilized port."

"If I do not have what you call a civilized approach, Lady Simirra, I have achieved resolution. I came to know who you are not in the span of five minutes. What I do not know is who you are."

Simirra adjusted her skirt, though it was impeccable. "I am a lady, Sir, a trades-lady and your better, as proved by your conduct."

Admah laughed. He spread his legs. "Tell me about the other caravans, my Lady."

Simirra adjusted her veil next. She sauntered toward a covey of cushions and picked up an expanse of cloth, which she fastened to a reed frame against the sun. "Ask my man," she insisted, carefully arranging a place to rest.

Admah watched her every move, especially as she reclined. It was bold of her to turn her back, bold of her to recline. Too bold to be much concerned over wanted men or a suspicious court. He touched his tongue to his lower lip, tasting salt and preferring the amber hued skin of this lovely merchant to what Semiramis promised. He would remember Simirra after this job was done.

He looked at Arphaxas. "Well?"

The big man shrugged. "Two fellows, one by name of Madai and his woman. We passed them at the Gihon, buying a boat. They bought wine from my Lady Simirra, and something for the woman."

Admah listened with half an ear. He was struggling to direct his thoughts from Simirra, whose near presence was proving a distraction. It was her disdain that needed taming, a contest beyond the temple whores and he had been long on the plain. He walked stiffly toward Arphaxas.

"I was told Madai had a boat, and came ashore at Gerar," Admah suggested. Arphaxas shrugged.

"Commander," came Simirra's sleepy voice. "My man does not lie. May we rest in this heat and perhaps meet again in the cool of evening?"

Admah kept his gaze fixed on Arphaxas. "So you say they will be still on the Gihon River?"

"I believe they were to take it to the Sea."

"Where are they going?"

"Across the Brine Sea. I do not know what mutiny can be made from there."

"It is my business to know. And when they are found, perhaps your mistress will be rewarded."

"She is rich already."

Admah looked at the animals then, and their packs. It was a paltry horde, given his own expectations, and so he retained only an interest in the woman, already thinking about the cool of the night...

"What you say matches what is passed on the streets," he began with a certain arrogance. "The spies were once admired in Gerar as dragon-killers." He made a display of tapping his fingers against a leather scabbard strapped across his chest before he affirmed dismissively. "It was already known to me that they were seen on the Gihon."

He tipped his head toward Simirra. "I will send you an escort, Lady Simirra. I am well situated in the city and they will provide us a banquet." Glancing at Arphaxas as he turned, he issued a last challenge, "And I will be the lady's protector tonight."

ARPHAXAS WATCHED AS THEY LEFT. THERE WERE A score of them, marching back to the city with their Commander, officious as a banti rooster in the lead.

"You've made trouble for us, Simirra," he growled.

"He believed you, didn't he?"

"Because you offered yourself."

"I did no such thing!"

"You know what you did."

Simirra got up, scattering pillows too elegant for a rustic seaport. She stuffed them back inside their packs. "Then you'd better get it all sold. Madai needs sails and dried fish and oil and... sinew."

"I know what he needs. But we needed more time and that atoyak will be back for you Simirra. Maybe I'll give you to him."

She whirled around at that. "I am not yours to give!" she declared.

"You won't stand up to the likes of him."

"I was married to the likes of him."

"Well, it took the likes of me to kill him."

She lifted her shoulder in a petite shrug.

"Well done!" Came Kittim's voice behind them. "We have an afternoon and Fadil will help you, Arphaxas."

ADMAH CAME FOR SIMIRRA HIMSELF. HE WAITED TILL the sun had set and the sky was washed in a soft glow. It had not been easy to wait, but he wished to revise an uncivilized impression. It was his experience that all such animal inclinations as he harbored would be better served, given a slow start.

It was dusk and there was a fire glowing beyond the dunes, so it took him a time to fully realize that the caravan was gone. He expelled a low growl and kicked at the sand, cursing all such women of high society. When this Madai and Kittim were found, he would come back after her with no restraint of civilization then!

Still rumbling, he looked back at the city... there were still the temple whores.

CHAPTER 13

*M*ADAI RESTED A MOMENT AGAINST THE MAST. IT was coming dusk, but he had finally wrestled the stump of what had once been taller, into place. Seeing it pointing a stubby finger at the sky, recalled to him a difficult voyage where it was only the Arm of God that saved him. The great typhoon had dealt him a blow to the head and a broken mast. Though what was left of the mast had seen him safely ashore. He hoped it should, as well, see him home. He turned to look at Iscah, who had pulled and stretched and sewn till her fingers bled. She was sitting cross-legged in the belly of the craft, hands clasp in her lap and watching for a first star in the darkening sky.

"Patta's Torch" he told her.

"Hmm?"

"The first star, Patta's Torch. It was what Tiras and I called it."

A tiny smile formed her mouth as she leaned forward, propping her elbows on her knees. "Tiras?"

Madai squatted down beside her. "My friend," he answered. "We hunted many a ferocious rabbit when we were lads. And if we did not come home after the first star, then Patta's torch would come looking for us."

She laughed. "So you worried your Mama? You've had good practice, then."

"Practice?"

"At stirring up a worry."

Madai chuckled. "So you say," he answered, enjoying the look of her face till she blushed.

"Well, yes Madai. You are a great vexer."

"I have vexed you, I know," he laughed, remembering squabbles past. "But now, as you see, I have been salvaged."

"And you are vexing again!" she declared, settling against the sides of the boat. She gripped her hands in her lap again and looked back at the stars with a trace of childish drama. "So, tell me about Tiras."

"Tiras is my oldest friend, a stalwart believer."

"A good choice of friend."

"Yes. And my Patta and Mamam, all believers in the One True God."

"So they will be happy to see you returned and… salvaged."

"So they will."

"And you are bringing the Ark planks."

"Yes. And the leg bone of behemoth."

She was quiet. He watched her savor the cool, still air. "Yes," she replied thoughtfully. Then she rearranged her sitting again, seemed a bit pensive, even timid as she turned to him part way, "Madai?"

She took such a small part of his boat – ironic, that.

"What is it, Iscah?"

"I am sorry. I have kept an ill will for you, at times, and…" she turned her face just a bit more in his direction, "tis a worthy thing to come so far… after Mighty God."

He felt a great leap in his heart.

"You were badly used, Iscah," he answered carefully, "I would not wonder that I should have seemed the…villain."

"O no, Madai! Not villain! More a…scoundrel." Then she laughed as true as a child. "Only you must admit, with such a fact so quickly born out as Noah's flood, you did take a good long time coming to it."

"How was it born out quickly?"

"By my poem, of course. You did not forget that, Madai…" She was putting on a vexed face with a near challenge in her eyes.

"Yes, Iscah, I should have come to it sooner," he answered, wanting to keep the peaceable atmosphere. "You were a very young thing then, skin and bones really with great moons for eyes…"

And he had said too much. She looked away again. He waited, hearing the frogs start up and knowing he had crept too close to announcing his heart to her. But after a moment she turned back.

"So, tell me about Tiras." She said. Perhaps she did not like the quiet.

"Tiras is a father now," he answered, "and wed to a good, strong lass. His father is named Togarmah and is more zealous than anyone I know for the One True God, at least before Noah."

She arched a brow. Madai knew she was thinking of someone else then, as she always did.

"Or Kittim and Job," he added. "But then, I was speaking of Togarmah. His wife left with the Banned when Tiras was near a babe."

"Who are the Banned?"

"A group of kinsmen. But the deceit was amongst us, Iscah…carried from the tower, from Nimrod himself as I know now. Corruption doesn't just die."

She nodded in affirmation.

"Some of The Family believed it, the new religion. Or maybe it was just what they wanted to do, with all the dancing and… other things. But The

Elders banned them, sent them back across the sea. Tiras's mother went with them. And other people I knew." Madai was thinking about Ido's brother, Sru, who had broken a mother's heart so long ago.

Watching Iscah's face commiserate with an unknown child of an unknown land welled up inside him. He loved her for it, again. This orphaned girl, so unlike Ido, had honed out a place for herself, silently, before either one of them knew it.

"It was terrible for Tiras… without his mother?" she asked.

Madai nodded. "Togarmah was a severe Patta. I know why now…I did not understand before."

"Yes," she answered.

"It was another reason to go to Shinar, and find the Ark."

"Another reason?"

Madai felt his blood drain away and the soles of his feet begin to pulse. He watched Iscah see his face lose its color and quickly looked past her into the night. Though it never really occurred to him to deny her an answer, there was never the possibility that he would divulge the whole truth. Leaving for the shame of Yamma; he would hide till his last days.

"I lost a wife to pestilence." He said it quickly, sounding flat in his ears.

When he felt her fingers touch his hand, he looked back. Tears were in her eyes, and he supposed it was not spoken so dispassionate as he thought.

"I know, Madai," she breathed.

The comfort in her voice threatened to stir up a forgotten well of tears, which horrified him. Surely all his weeping had been rung out of him in the storm, in the boat, alone on the sea and in a rage. That there was any left to be spilled down his face was proved at this moment… and terrible.

"Dear Madai," she soothed, leaning forward to place her hands gently on either side of his face. "Tis no disgrace. It would be, if you hadn't loved her."

There was such a look in her eyes! It seemed to feed the old grief. So, new love did not dispel old love, or old pain. He felt her finger move to wipe his eye.

"There," she said. "I know why you had to come."

Her callous hands felt soft on his face; her eyes shone with kindly sympathies. He swallowed. "You lost kin," he said quietly, "and never doubted…"

She smiled gently. "But then, I am very smart, and no scoundrel."

"Smart indeed," he managed to reply.

They looked at each other a moment before she pulled back to sit in her old place, just beyond his reach. She nestled into the cypress frame.

"Now then, tell me what we will do in this new land of yours, Madai. Are there fearsome beasts?"

He breathed out deliberately, wishing she hadn't moved so far away. But he answered her question as simply as if she were only Kittim "Not so fearsome as Leviathan," he answered. "There will be a great feast I expect, and dancing. I will kiss my son."

Her mouth popped open in surprise. He could see that she was fighting the most feminine of instincts. He was relieved when she did not ask, for Japhet held a most tender part of himself, and weakness aplenty had been already laid bare.

"Yes… you should kiss your son," she finally answered and said no more on it, but slowly stretched. "Will they return tonight, do you think?"

Madai looked toward the eastern horizon. "It's a far way."

"In the morning then?"

"Yes," he nodded. "If Kittim can sell the camels quickly and buy what we need."

"Now that we are settled upon sailing to your new shores," she announced thoughtfully, "I find that I am anxious to leave."

"You are not afraid of the sea, then?"

Iscah leaned back on her elbows. "Now that we are here, and the boat is still sound, I remember how it was to sail away from Gerar. I felt very safe then. And you did cross the Sea alone. Now there will be Kittim and Arphaxas to help."

"And Mighty God," Madai reminded. "I know now that I did not sail the Sea alone. He saved me through a great storm."

Iscah looked taken aback. "Of course," she answered. "So now you are the teacher."

With just those few words, Madai felt himself raised up in her estimation. It was a brilliant gift on this cool night amongst the chirping frogs.

With the side of his face pressed against the ground and from the far regions of early sleep, Madai felt the beat of horse's hoofs. There wasn't even time to rouse himself properly before he heard, and to his own relief, that it was Kittim and indeed, arrived so much sooner than he had predicted. There was an extreme urgency in his friend's voice, however, yanking Madai's brain up to consciousness.

"Hurry!" was Kittim's first word. He dropped a roll of sail on the ground.

Arphaxas and Simirra were quickly beside him, transferring other bundles of goods from the camels to Madai's boat, which displaced Iscah from where she had been sleeping. Only she was climbing over the edge, perpetually tuned to the sound of Kittim.

"Give me anything you will not need," Kittim continued. He hurriedly tied the old sail to his horse and eyed the leg bone of behemoth.

"I need that!" Madai argued.

"We are followed by a good tracker. He will see the difference in weight."

"Who? What do you mean?"

Arphaxas put a last goat stomach, bulging with tepid water, inside the ship. "You are being hunted, kinsman," he grumbled. "And I am yoked with you again."

"Who?" Madai demanded. "Who are you talking about?" It was a question he needn't really have asked, because Kittim had told him the answer weeks ago. But even a demon needed man arms.

"Soldiers of the Queen and one who will not stop. And he's after her too," Arphaxas snapped, jerking his head at Simirra.

She passed him brusquely, wrestling with a bag of rice and skin of beer. Kittim started for the bone of rock.

"I need it." Madai insisted again.

"Men will believe what they chose. It is not always proofs that convince," Kittim argued. He was still for the first time and intent on Madai as if it were only him.

"But you brought me to Noah."

Kittim put his hand on Madai's shoulder. "You are a seeker, my friend, and hate a lie. Not all men do." He tapped his chest with his fist. "It is the heart."

"I don't understand, how could they not…"

"Do you want off this coast?" Arphaxas cut him off. "Because if you do, you will get that boat in the river."

Which was a suggestion Madai could appreciate. He nodded at Arphaxas. "He's right." Then he loaded the behemoth leg into his ship. "It will convince them," he insisted.

They weighted down the animals as best they could, given what time was allowed. Then they drove them off across the plain, with the hope that Commander Admah was turned south toward the Gihon in chase of a rumor.

SIMIRRA WATCHED THE LAST OF HER OLD LIFE DISAPPEAR as Basar scrambled off behind Martu's stallion and into the night. She felt naked again, even in beautiful borrowed clothes, and in wonder that she was climbing into the bow of a provincial whale-skinned boat, a relative antique. It felt like a cyclone had brought her to it, that and the mysterious Voice, which had surely been some kind of madness. What was she doing, sailing with the gods knew who to the gods knew where? She felt the boat lurch as Iscah and Kittim came over the side.

Madai and Arphaxas were leaning against the nose of the ship. She heard a hissing against sand as they pushed it off the shore and through the reeds. Then they each climbed inside and she thought their weight might surely turn them over.

After that came the actual sailing. At first it was with such leisure that they used long poles to move the craft laden with people and food and behemoth bones. Then Madai hoisted his sail with what was a somewhat adequate display of engineering. A cool breeze found them after that and pulled them down the canal. She found she did not need the ribs of the boat where she had first braced herself, hand gripping the slopping side and foot against what seemed to her its spine. She wrapped herself in a blanket that smelled of horse. She did not mind the smell because it reminded her of her father's stable. And she did not mind the night because the stars were brilliant and the breeze was pleasant. She thought that perhaps it would not be so terrible after all. It was a good way to fall asleep after a crazy ride across the sands of Gerar. It seemed safe, in fact, after their midnight's flight away from a Shinar bounty hunter.

Sometime in the dawn, they were funneled into the sea. It was a salty spray that woke her and all the noise of a determined surf. She quickly found her position of the night before; hand against upper rib, feet against lower.

The ship was rising, cutting through a wave and falling back against the sea. Whatever put men in boats by choice?

But Madai was laughing! There was a different look on his face, like he was remembering another part of himself here. He was being pelted with the same spray that was soaking her to the skin and shouting at Kittim that conditions were excellent. She hugged herself at that, starting to sense an obnoxious rolling in the pit of her stomach.

CHAPTER 14

*M*ADAI COULD JUST SEE THE SHORE. HE HAD taken them northward so as to avoid the traffic of fishermen and soldiers. They sailed till the sea started a sweeping turn to the west, as north as the waters would take him. He catalogued it in his mind that perhaps the Brine Sea was in fact a vast inlet. Its girth was most great, shores not to be seen from its center, but ringed with the ancient East and this great forest of fragrant cedar to the north. The south he had seen pocked with mud cities laying claim to ziggurat. Perhaps the peninsula of the Banned was even attached to this land in some way farther west and he thought for the first time that perhaps when he returned home and in the dark days of winter he might try his wits at map making.

They had put ashore briefly on the cedar coast. Arphaxas complaining about the food and Simirra being sick. But only just long enough to kill the stag that had been more curious than frightened and to find a spring of water bubbling up from ancient depths. He was pleased with their progress thus far, being saved from any such storms as had thrashed him before. With the perpetuity of such graces, he could bring them to his lands – perhaps before Simirra found her sea stomach! With all his companions settled and quiet and just himself as company, he hid from his consciousness the dread remembrance that Kittim meant to leave them. Perhaps he had changed his mind.

It was the end of day and he was sailing them near to the shore, skirting its boundaries for the sake of good fishing and a growing curiosity about the dimensions of this Brine Sea. And he was watching the way the evening's wind blew through Iscah's hair as she slept, when Kittim, who had been quiet of late, came up beside him.

"I would like to talk about the bone," he announced abruptly.

Which was an odd remark, given that it was some time past that Madai had insisted on bringing it.

"Even the ark plank," Kittim continued. "You can show a man the sky and call it blue, but if he wants to believe it green… it will be green."

"That's ridiculous."

Kittim shrugged. "Or behemoth. See his bone? If you believe in Mighty God, the heap of bones turned to stone is an evidence that He sent a deluge to wipe the earth clean. If you believe in Hedros, it is his war club that was lost…"

"And if you believe in no gods at all," Arphaxas interjected, "It is a stone beat at by the wind, which looks to fools like a bone."

"You can see it's a bone!" Madai spat back.

"But we are each looking at the same thing, are we not?" Kittim replied, looking from one to the other.

"Men want to know what is real, Kittim. The ark is real; I have the proof, and so the deluge."

"Men want to believe what suits them."

"Why are you speaking like this? We have done it, Kittim, you and I."

Kittim smiled.

"And why would anyone think this is not a bone, or the sky is green?" Madai finished, cutting a look at Arphaxas.

"I did not say I understood it, my friend. Only that it is as I have said," Kittim answered. Then he looked away and at the coast. "There is a good cove for coming ashore."

"But we have just been ashore," Madai answered, now thoroughly confused. "And this is a good wind, Kittim."

He looked at Arphaxas, who, though he had been an interloper in their conversation, might see the sense in keeping the wind. But Arphaxas merely shrugged and looked at the sand bar Kittim seemed to have seen glistening a little in the fading sun. Kittim had an insistence in his eyes that gave Madai little choice and a somewhat sinking intuition. He steered the boat toward the alcove where the waves lapped quietly at the shore.

After a short time, he felt the sand receive the belly of his ship softly, like a gull settling onto the sea for a rest.

It was then Kittim suddenly and deftly stepped over the side of the craft and into the water, thigh high. "What are you doing, Kittim?" Madai cried in alarm. "Help me come ashore."

"There is a good wind, Madai."

Which was stunning to him. Had his friend gone mad? First the sky is green and then he is getting out of the boat on a wilderness of coast. Madai grabbed Kittim's sleeve, which was dripping salt water. "What are you doing?"

"This is a good coast. I shall return now."

"Where is there to go?" He asked, bewildered. "Help me, we will make camp. I can leave the bone…"

"No, my friend, Madai. Take your bone. It does tell the deluge. Only remember what I have said about the will of men. And sail with this wind," Kittim interrupted. The sinking sun was shining orange, revealing Kittim's placid calm, which Madai had always found enviable, authoritative and somewhat annoying.

"You're leaving us," Madai admitted and with that spoken, he was suddenly and surprisingly angry. "It's a shabby way to do it. With Iscah…"

"She cannot come where I am going."

Madai's fingers clenched around Kittim's arm like a lion's jaw.

He only smiled. "I told you, Madai. My purpose was near to complete."

"You will not see my shores, then?" Madai's anger evaporated as quick as it came, leaving him to feel like a child-beggar. He released Kittim's arm. His fell to his side, ineffectual, as the boat gently rocked. "But Iscah," he whispered. "You know she…"

"I have no need of her," Kittim replied, also a whisper and kindly spoken, those unkind words.

Madai stood wooden. What a thing to say, if it did advance his own expectations! And he was feeling the way the ship was just barely planted against the sand and swaying, feeling the wet on his hand where he had taken hold of Kittim, who was standing, waist deep in a beautiful azure sea. Kittim with his inscrutable eyes looking back at him, the friend with whom so much had been shared, so much seen. And even though what had been always at the back of his mind was happening, it had him paralyzed. Kittim was going back to his Master, as he had said.

Kittim smiled again. "You have still a great mission, Madai. But you are going from these shores and do not need my gift of tongues."

"I have need of your friendship," Madai argued.

"You have friends aplenty," Kittim replied quietly. "And I have a great Master. He has need of me." Kittim backed away from the side of the boat. "I will give you a push."

Madai watched his friend lean against the cypress frame and slide them off the sand.

"Mighty God is with you," Kittim insisted. He smiled again and raised his hand. Then he turned toward the shore.

It happened as quickly and simply as that. Madai watched him silently, every argument frozen on his tongue, the way you try to run in a dream. Then the wind caught the sail and pulled them into the sea, till Kittim seemed to vanish against the coastline.

ISCAH TASTED SALT IN HER MOUTH, OR PERHAPS IT WAS sand. Perhaps it was her bones rising up her throat, as she knew by instinct that of sand they were made. She was crumbling into extinction, to be not seen nor missed, and God loosening His fingers, which once had held the mold of herself together. She could close off the memory of her ears hearing the splash Kittim's feet had made when they plunged into the sea. She had, however, no will great enough to erase his final words: "I have no need of her."

Her hand ached, clutching her bundle. She had grabbed it, ready to launch over the side after him. It held clothes chosen so carefully upon departing Job's house. They were garments picked to serve for a wedding, made of gossamer fineness, as fine as Reenah's and turned to ash by six little words. And yet, the useless bundle seemed the only thing of a real substance to her. The boat was inconsequential, so was the sea, so was the dark depths this thin skin of whale protected against. But there was the wind whistling past her ears, pulling at the sail, chasing them away from the shore.

It was that very wind and what it was doing, that set her instantly into a panic. How wide had grown this expanse from the shore? Suddenly, any last impediment of pride was wholly erased. She felt herself hurling over the side, leaving the bundle in the belly of the boat, an unimportant dream extinguished in a moment.

The water was a salty, icy shock of reality.

She couldn't swim, which hadn't mattered a moment ago.

She gasped, sucking cold, salty water down her throat on reflex. The sea was black, churned up by the wind and the season, stinging her eyes, her nose and throat... She coughed, her lungs a pitiful force against the great Brine Sea and only drowning her faster. She felt herself as falling from a great height through liquid sky when suddenly there was a great wrenching up by the roots of her hair. She was ripped up through the water and back into the air, instantly colder by infinite degrees. Breath tasted of salt as she sputtered and gagged. Her arms flailed at the side of the boat, feet kicking spastically against the waves. There were people yelling and a rough grab under her arms to pull her over the edge again.

"What's wrong with you, Iscah?" she heard a woman's voice almost hysterical.

"Get something around her," she heard a man's voice, it might have been Madai.

"What were you doing?" she heard the woman again.

"Leave her alone," she heard the other man.

"She needs a fire," she heard Madai.

"Yes," she heard herself thinking. "The shore."

"Aren't we near the Banned?" she heard the woman.

She felt the boat slow as Madai dropped the sail. She felt it lurch as he and Arphaxas began to pull at the sea with the oars. She was still coughing, fighting to breathe and trying not to retch.

CHAPTER 15

*T*HERE SAT A MAN, PICKING HIS TEETH. HE SPAT, popped the twig at the fire and studied the horizon. He was sandy from hair to foot, his thick breast shield stained with arm rings of dirt and sweat. He smelled of long days on the back of a horse.

He was savoring the dawn, having been sharply awakened by a great black stallion, impossible to catch but still wearing the imprint of a saddle and streaming the reins of its halter behind it, as defiant as its rider had been. It was a second confirmation. That no one could find the boy had been Admah's first clue. Disappeared with his sister, it was said. No other family, it was said. It was also said that the boy had been enraptured of Madai and Kittim.

Admah had divided his forces at that discovery, one toward the Gihon on chance the boy's story was true. But he had remained northward, where the caravan had gone. He had an inkling that Simirra was a part with the wanted men, so he followed her and the red-haired giant with hopes both for the Queen's promised reward and a salient settling of accounts. He had tracked the sandy prints of camel till he came upon them belligerent and wild with thorns in their blankets. It had not been a complicated ruse that led him away from the Sea, but it had cost him a day. It was confirmation that he had been right about the woman, but wrong about following the trail of beasts away from the coast.

Quick calculations convinced him that retracing steps to Gerar where he could find a sea vessel was too costly by days. He had decided to take the overland route to the Cape of Wilds where he would buy a ship from the originals there. Even savages could appreciate gold.

"No fire this morning," he ordered his six remaining men. "We reach the Cape today."

He ignored their grumbling. If he'd been trained a soldier he would not have allowed it. But he knew they were still afraid of him enough to obey and that was sufficient. He also knew they would not likely reach the jutting peninsula by nightfall, but it would make them push the harder.

CHAPTER 16

*I*SCAH HELD HER KNEES TIGHT TO HER CHEST, WHICH throbbed when she breathed. There was a burn running the length of her throat. They had wrapped her in a blanket. Madai built a fire and was fishing... or something.

Simirra had tried talking at first. Arphaxas was hunting in the forest. She shrunk herself down; perhaps if she was small enough...

"Every moment I stay here he is farther away," she was telling herself. But she had been denounced. That seemed to have made her legs go crippled.

There were words he had spoken, the last she remembered in reference to herself and she had been redefined. But she would not cry, would not utter a sound. Humiliation aplenty occupied the very air she breathed even as the Sea had threatened to drown her.

She sat like that for a long time. It could have been an hour. It could have been all night. But it was long enough to be extremely rump weary, feet and fingers numb as well. She let her legs go and carefully, quietly slid her feet straight out in front of her. If Simirra heard, she didn't look. Perhaps she was asleep. But her stomach was telling her she was hungry and achy and even sleepy and broken hearts do not silence any of that. She let the blanket slip off her shoulders and started to stand. The fire snapped.

"You won't find him," Madai whispered.

The voice, after so long in silence, startled her enough to jump. But there was Madai sitting beside the fire, feeding it a length of pine.

"Before, when he would go out to pray, I would look for him," Madai continued. "I never could find him."

Iscah didn't answer.

"I can look at first light, but there is not much time. Winter. Believe me when I say you will not find him."

She bent down and picked up the blanket, wrapping herself up again.

"I know he did not mean to harm you. Kittim was... inscrutable."

"He did not teach me that word," she muttered, trying not to remember the long days of tending Madai's wound so very long ago, when Kittim had used the time to teach her the western tongue.

"Past understanding," Madai replied. "He was a mystery. I do not think his leaving was... an accounting of your worth to him."

"I have no need of her."

Iscah flinched. Madai must know she had heard, though she would treat it as if it never were spoken, surely he would as well.

"Kittim did not... need us. Not as we need," he explained.

Iscah felt the blood rush into her face and she pressed her lips together, unable, unwilling to inspect how Madai's knowing made her feel.

"Perhaps I shall return to Job," she announced quietly.

Madai didn't answer. He continued to feed the fire. She could hear him at it. At least he had stopped talking. She did not know what to do. But standing there as if she was ready for some sort of decision, made her feel... worse. So she went back to her spot and lay down. The sand had gotten cold and she was shivering, but she would not move again tonight, not even to get close to the fire.

"Was she trying to drown herself?" Iscah heard the brogue of Calnah impose upon her sleep. She was mildly surprised at the morning, though she could not imagine why. People do wake up after calamity.

"Be quiet, Simirra," it was Arphaxas with impatience.

"I know she loved Kittim," Simirra finished, ignoring him.

Iscah found herself waiting for Madai to join the conversation. Maybe he was still asleep. She would certainly not open her eyes to find out – all her own wretchedness laid bare. Slowly, she pulled her knees to her chest. She counted her heartbeats, waiting. A slick tear slid from the outside corner of her eye. Kittim had sounded very cold... passionless. How different from that warmth of arms picking her up from the coast of Gerar to place her carefully in Madai's boat, taking her far away from Hamonheb and his old man groping. Perhaps all that business would always prevail upon Kittim, and she was forever unwantable to such a man. It was what she had always feared for herself. But Kittim, so altogether good... A sob suddenly escaped her throat. She choked down a second, tensed her muscles and held her breath.

She heard a footfall near her face. She heard the soft muffle of leather as someone knelt beside her. When she opened her eyes she was startled to see Arphaxas, his bushy red face staring out from the hood of his dragon cape. He was looking at the hole in her earlobe, where the disk of a slave had been removed to leave a dangling circle of flesh.

"Do not be robbed," he whispered. "They cannot have your soul."

She blinked, wiping her eyeballs of tears. He stood abruptly and walked away. It had been bitterly spoken yet somehow she knew, meant as a kindness. She heard him finding the fire where there would be something to eat. Her stomach suddenly rumbled, surprised again by everyday life.

She had just taken the first bite of some sort of flesh, somewhat dry, when

Madai suddenly burst out from the forest and into camp. It was only then that she realized he had been missing.

"There are men to the south," he cried, taking Iscah by the arm, dislodging the meat from her hand. "Get the fire out, Arphaxas. Simirra, come after these blankets."

It was all a mad dash to Iscah, being actually yanked up from her breakfast. She was oblivious to all the accusatory glances of Simirra who was rolling up robes and sleeping mats as frantic as a mouse ahead of winter. She stood motionless, watching the night's camp disassemble and be dumped into Madai's boat like so much rubble.

"Come on, Iscah!" It was Simirra, spitting out her name as an unpleasant bite.

It was Madai ... again... who, and gently this time, coaxed her down the beach.

"I didn't find him," he whispered into Iscah's ear, lifting her up and over the edge of the whale-skin boat.

"How many men?" Arphaxas asked, pushing the boat off the shore.

"Six," Madai replied. He shoved hard against the ship's frame then hoisted himself inside. "Seven." He grabbed Arphaxas's forearm and pulled him up. "They'll be just behind me."

Arphaxas took an oar as Madai tied the sail. There was pitiful little wind.

Iscah might have been a bird perched on the top of the mast, watching the incoherent scrambling of men from afar, for all that she felt. What did it matter, after all. What even did it mean? And what of Kittim... alone now with men just behind them? Her stomach flipped.

"Kittim!" she exclaimed. "He'll be..."

"Better than we are!" Simirra snapped, "If they catch us."

"Quiet, Simirra," Arphaxas demanded, pulling with the oars. "It'll be your Commander."

Iscah turned her face away. They were only words, ineffectual, unrelatable. But she knew Simirra was right. Kittim would be safe. He always was.

"Did they see you?" Arphaxas asked.

"No."

They were all quiet after that. Iscah watched the wooly red man fight the sea with the oars. She watched Madai give up on the sail and take the second oar. She watched them pull with a great degree of determination. And she watched the shoreline shrink in the distance again.

THEY TRAVELED THE NORTHERN COAST WESTWARD without threat or sight of the Shinar commander and his men. It was inordinately still. Perhaps he had only imagined them.

Instead there was the sight of coasts and cliffs that would have given Madai pleasure to share with Kittim. Here now was only Iscah – and two ill-tempered souls – to see the rocky coastline of new lands, the great tall cedars that swayed and creaked in the wind, the spouting porpoise. But Iscah's eyes had seemed to lose their love of marvelous sights. Her lethargy might have become contagious, if not that this night they skimmed the coast of the Banned. It was three days since Iscah had leapt into the Sea after Kittim and they had traveled a winter's wind as many. Dusk had been chosen to navigate the cape and to guard their passing. Even the moon, a mere sickle of silver, hid behind storm laden clouds of which Madai prayed would hold their snow a time longer. He watched the shore line carefully, dark and somber in the distance, knowing there were rocks and Banned to beat against his boat if he came too near.

The voyage without Kittim was worse than even he had expected; their supply of food and drink came alarmingly insufficient, of which Arphaxas was fast to complain. Simirra watched the coastline, hands knit tightly in her lap, and Iscah seemed able to always turn her face away. That the trees now displayed the irrefutable markings of his western terebinth brought him little pleasure. Even the wind that had blown them so diligently westward began to fail, finally to bring his craft fixed upon the sea, heaving and rocking despite the calm. He was wrapped in the cold wet of a pre-winter's night, limp of sails and spirit.

He could not dispel a sense of disquiet. His skin felt almost raw with it, his belly set just on edge.

"Why are we stopped?" he heard the woman's question, heavily intoned with the accent of Calneh but the first words spoken in a great while.

"The wind's gone," he answered.

"You have a paddle," she insisted. "We will wash to the shore!"

When Madai didn't move, she reached across Iscah's knee to hand it to him. "Are you not afraid of these Banned?" she asked.

Arphaxas took up the second oar roughly. Shadows of evening did little to mask the look he gave her.

They each paddled against the tide, which otherwise threatened to bring them ashore. The sea had become angry of a sudden with great waves reaching eager fingers at the coast. Madai scrambled in his mind to remember where he had come ashore in his eastward journey; perhaps he would need to know if they could not win against the Sea tonight.

"We are coming closer!" Simirra's voice rose with urgency.

"Quiet," Arphaxas grunted, pulling hard with the oar.

"O!"

It was Iscah, the first Madai had heard her speak in a very long time. He glanced at her to see her pointing toward their bow. There was a great tall wave, twice the height of his mast, a dark rise upon the water, rushing at them. They would not prevail against the mounting wave but he pulled with all his strength.

"Hold on!" he yelled even as the boat rose, a helpless flotsam. It lifted up, carried as a flea on a beast. Their ride into the arms of the cape was predetermined now.

SIMIRRA WAS SURPRISED TO BE STILL BREATHING. SHE

pulled the heavy coat of her dead husband tight around her throat.

Even as they had been shoved at the shore by that terrible wave, she had felt the earth also tremble. Madai had managed somehow to point them toward a cove whose rocks had not torn them apart. And now, everyone was silent. Also surprised to be alive, no doubt, and afraid of the Banned as she was – the Banned and the last shivers of a quaking earth. Could the misery of this company and its voyage be exceeded? What trouble in Calneh would compare? Surely her first misstep had been stumbling upon Arphaxas and his wretched camp.

She tasted blood in her mouth. And there was Iscah beside her, wrapped like a corpse with her arms tight around her chest. Somehow this was her fault. If they had not lost time pulling her up from the deep then drying her out, if Madai had not cost them the night searching for Kittim who had abandoned them, then without question the wind would have sailed them past this wretched outcrop days ago, past The Banned. These certain savages with whatever terror they might store were waiting out there in the dark. Why, even the earth had turned against them, quaking and heaving, sucking them at the shore.

She was still shivering even after the earth stopped its rumblings. It was the fear, she knew, and that was a new development. When had that started? Why, once she had dared the very Temple of An with only a knife! Was that just a month's time? No, perhaps more, she had lost count of the days.

"Must we stay here?" she heard the words come choppy past her chattering teeth. The surf crashed against the sides of the ship as if to answer the question.

"We'll have no fire," Madai replied calmly.

As though that would make it better! She watched him crawl out of the boat and tether it to the trunk of a tree, which leaned nearly into the water.

"I will sleep here in the boat tonight," she insisted.

"I as well," it was Iscah's scratchy voice, speaking just a second time in the whole length of the day.

There was something satisfying about the girl's cowardice, as presumable as her own. Simirra didn't move, leaving Iscah but a wedge of space to lie in. Arphaxas noticed, and Simirra wiggled to the side. It was inconceivable that the belligerent giant favored this girl! She felt the boat rock as Arphaxas jumped out. She pulled the robe up to cover her nose, fending off icy air, and licked her cracked lip. It would be a long cold night and she was feeling quite alone. Where once she had pitied Iscah, there was contempt brewing. She, herself had stood tall against Martu whilst Iscah had leapt foolhardy into the waves!

THE SHAKING EARTH SEEMED TO HAVE SHOOK THE CLOUDS apart and the sickle moon exposed to light up a patch of the beach.

It was awash with sharp black pebbles and broken shells.

"The gods are having a laugh."

Madai was surprised to hear him speak. "Don't blaspheme, Arphaxas," he ordered.

The man merely chuckled.

"I do remember this cove," Arphaxas continued. "It was where we first came ashore, I and my good parents... Palapa. This earthquake has seen us brought here again. How do you like that, Madai?"

"I think we will have a cold night," he replied carefully, hearing the old poison on Arphaxas's tongue as bitter as when he had still been Tazek.

"I think I will look for our old camp in the morning."

"Then I will leave you here, Arphaxas. I am going home," Madai replied.

He thought he heard Arphaxas chuckle again. Madai watched the man wrap the dragon cape around himself and settle against a tree. He looked like a piece of the landscape, a rock or a gnarled old root.

"Where did you get that?" Madai suddenly asked.

"What?"

"That dragon skin."

Arphaxas didn't move. His head was tucked like a turtle in its shell.

"Where did you get it?"

"Are you the only dragon-killer here, then?" Arphaxas spat from his dark surround. But Madai heard a shift in his confidence.

"A good piece of work, that skin. Did you do it?" Madai watched as Arphaxas lifted his hand. One long finger slowly slipped inside the hood and peeled it back. It lay on his shoulders as a dragon's wing at rest.

"I stole it, kinsman," Arphaxas replied slowly. "I dragged my shriveled leg up to the great Lord's own bed chamber and took it. How was that for a good joke? Whilst the Shemites brought down that whoremonger, I stole his coat and sneaked off on a crippled leg." Arphaxas made a sound, something between a cough and a cackle.

"Good for you," Madai replied.

"Yes, good for me."

Madai suddenly knew Arphaxas was thinking about Palapa who was likely dying at the very time her brother was sneaking off into the dark, hiding in a stolen cloak.

"Why did you tell me that?" he asked.

"Why not? We have no secrets, do we Madai? We both know the other."

Madai looked at the form of Arphaxas, squatted in shadow with a sparkle of curly red hair where the moon touched it.

"I see you are changed, Arphaxas."

"Yes," he slowly nodded. "I earned the right to wear such a cape. I earned the right..."

Madai waited for him to finish, but Arphaxas pulled the hood back up. Madai was glad it was dark. He was afraid that if he could see Arphaxas in the eyes, it would be Tazek's eyes. And Tazek had been a wreck of a man.

"The Banned are changed also," Madai whispered and waited for Arphaxas again.

"Let me sleep."

"They were being killed by a pestilence when I sailed eastward. I think they are not so strong anymore."

"What are you afraid of then?"

Madai hunched his shoulders against the attack. It was not worth the bother! He heard Arphaxas rearrange his legs. Madai, himself was starting to feel the cold. He tucked his hands under his armpits.

"What scares you, boy?" Arphaxas asked again. It was the self-same question Madai had asked Tazek in Nimrod's palace. It had been asked in much the same spirit, meant to bring a man low.

"Go to sleep, Tazek," he answered shortly.

He hadn't realized the old name was spoken and Arphaxas didn't respond. Madai fought off the cold and managed a few hours' sleep. When he awoke it was still dark and his legs felt as stiff as a poorly tanned hide.

AS IF THE NIGHT'S CONVERSATION WERE BEING RESUMED, Madai heard Arphaxas walking toward him, crunching on broken shells and debris brought ashore in the waves.

"You were right, Kinsman," Arphaxas voice carried on the still morning air. "But I don't think it was a pestilence."

Madai jumped to his feet.

"Where have you been?" he demanded, instantly suspicious.

"The old camp." Arphaxas squatted down. "Don't worry. They're gone, your Banned, and not easily."

Madai noticed only then that Arphaxas was back with an armload of sticks. "I said no fire."

"And you are not my Lord."

Arphaxas began to reach for a flint inside his vest. Madai grabbed his hand. "There's the men from Shinar too," he warned.

"Have faith, Madai." Arphaxas laughed. Then he blew a cloud of frost into the air. "I want a fire."

Madai was enraged! There was a knot in his stomach that seemed to burst. He snatched his bow and jumped up, more to stem the mad rush of energy than to go about a purpose. But he had started something, so he grabbed up his quiver and stomped across the beach toward the forest. He would look for this camp of the Banned, not thinking that perhaps Arphaxas was lying and setting a trap. If he had thought about that, he would not have left Iscah alone and asleep.

THE CAMP WAS NOT HARD TO FIND. HE CAME UPON A clearing no more than a dozen paces or so from the start of the tree line, in evidence that the Banned were not so adept at defensive camp placement. He would have thought it was a first and temporary site, if not that it showed the signs of a lengthy habitation. No wonder they had incubated pestilence!

Their campfires were long dead. Their lodges were made in a similar way as the Families, and yet had not been disassembled for a move. Instead, they were tumbled about, perhaps the quake, but burnt long before that.

What remained were stiff, black and singed hides, exposing in places the odd skeletal remains of lodge poles, and other sorts of skeletons – what was left after the scavengers.

It was stunningly quiet. Madai only stood staring, slowly turning till he had pointed his eyes at the scene in full circle. So small – impotent remained the murderers of Ido, and superbly anticlimactic was this end to the defining occurrence of his old life. He felt his heart bang against his ribs, ready to fight a battle long since passed.

If it had not been so keenly felt, this sudden loss of foe, Madai would have known the event for what it was – a slaughter. Instead, he went to inspect a near heap of bones. They were shoved up under an over-turned kayak as if hiding. There was the skull, wedged between the bones of knees, an arm dislodged from its socket and scattered ribs. After the first – he could only describe it a disappointment – there was very little that he felt. He knew he should be alarmed.

Perhaps the Family had sought out their old kin and defeated them after the devastating pestilence. But they would not have left the camp like this. They would have burned the dead as they had eventually had to burn their own.

He knelt on one knee beside the bones. There was a necklace hanging off the spine, which was intact. At first Madai thought the ornament was made from the teeth of an old bear, but when he leaned forward to touch it, he snatched his hand back as if it were bitten. It was not the worn teeth of an ancient bear; it was the finger bones of a human hand, strung together, hanging as a trophy around this Banned neck. The hairs of Madai's head stood up in place even as he remembered poor Laeden, come starving into camp with stubs for hands. Lost rage welled up and out his mouth. It was as much an animal cry as any beast's. Madai kicked at the skeleton, scattering all that was still attached.

He was shaking. He flung his arms wide, looking for something else to attack. But it was already a ruination. So he kicked the bones again and kicked the earth, stirring up a last spit of ash.

"I thought you would be hunting something for me to cook on my fire, Kinsman."

Madai whirled at the voice. He rushed at Arphaxas, crossing the litter of a community's last remains and grabbed him by the throat. "You call me Kinsman?" Madai squeezed the question through his teeth. "These are your kinsmen!"

Arphaxas smiled. He peeled Madai's fingers loose. "So you do hate me after all."

Madai jerked back, bitten a second time and literally shaking before the great red-haired man. Arphaxas was fleshed out, wrapped in muscle and unruly confidence but Tazek just under the skin. Madai took another step back, keeping the green eyes of Arphaxas fixed with his own.

'I'll not give him what he wants', Madai vowed to himself, sensing the challenge. But he did not trust his voice to answer and he would not roar like an animal. So he stood there, eye to eye.

Eye to eye.

Suddenly, randomly, Madai was struck with an awareness that Arphaxas was indeed tall. Before, in Shinar when he had been only Tazek, he had seemed... short. Perhaps it was the lame leg. Madai glanced down at the man's left leg, now straight and strong.

"How did you fix your leg?" he asked abruptly as if he hadn't had Arphaxas by the throat a moment before.

"Running," Arphaxas answered smiling, asserting his self-control as superior to Madai's, "and jumping and eating a lot." He looked purposefully at Madai's bow as if so much wreckage did not surround them. "I'd hoped you would be hunting."

Like a well-placed arrow, Madai was struck again by the man's indifference, surrounded as they were by bones and the energies of preempted revenge. He willed himself remember it was a mere ploy, a delicate jab which he would not return. Instead, he kicked a broken pot with violence rather too great for the benign object.

At last, when he determined his voice might be trusted, he asked the pertinent question. "Who do you think did this?"

Arphaxas cocked his head. He glanced casually about. "A good question," he replied. "Whoever it was has been gone a long time. They could be anywhere by now..."

"Yes," Madai answered shortly, feeling another jab. Anywhere.

He brushed past Arphaxas and headed toward his boat.

"I am going home," he announced.

Arphaxas smiled again, pulled the hood back over his head against the cold and followed behind.

CHAPTER 17

*T*HERE WAS STILL HALF A BRINE SEA TO CROSS, which was not spent in the hold of a typhoon as Madai's first voyage had been. It took a time long enough even to still the quiet fear that had arisen in him at the camp of The Banned. There was a wide sea betwixt his shores and them that had razed the village.

Madai watched for the sea serpent, which had threatened to swallow him, but it did not reappear. Perhaps it remembered the point of his spear, though that was flung out as easily as a husk of chaff by the creature. Or perhaps it had already had its fill of kipper in the moments they sailed through its range. Whatever the truth of the matter, Madai was glad enough. He needed the quiet. He was coming home. And the nearer he came, the less familiar became his companions, even Iscah who remained withdrawn and silent.

Indeed, all the length of the remaining voyage seemed couched in perfect weather and circumstance till what finally welcomed Madai at the coast of his homeland was a herd of green and bronze porpoise. They came close enough to spray at his boat, cackle a welcome and smile in their own human-like way.

But this was not the arrival he had hoped for. He'd imagined stepping once more onto his rocky coast with the hand of Iscah in his own. He'd imagined showing her the height of the terebinth, the way a glacier is the color of the sky, even a snow bear perhaps. Instead, she might have been a bucket inside the boat for the company she had offered since that last night with Kittim.

Even Arphaxas had reacquired his silence. He may well have been alone. It was in fact, a simple, unspectacular beaching that welcomed Madai home.

The boots, which were first to touch the shore were civilized and were Madai's. When he had left this place, he'd worn rustic shoes of leather sewn by Ido's hand. When he left, it was from a coast in spring. It was near to winter now with frost crunching under his feet.

He filled his lungs with piney air. How he had forgotten that smell, how well remembered now and welcome! It was orienting, as familiar as an eagle on a draft from the soaring heights of a fir. Madai left his companions behind.

He vaulted up the bank, finding new joy by the simple use of his legs on the well-worn path to The Family's campsite. His chest was pounding. He was not remembering another morning on this path, when he had drawn water with Ido and had nearly kissed her. He did not think about that day. Neither did he think about Iscah or Kittim, or disappointment. He was thinking about now. He was thinking about seeing his own Mamam's glad eyes and happy smile. He was thinking about the pride on his Patta's face and the feel of Japhet in his arms again. His heart was pumping hard, beating blood into his legs and purest joy into the every parts of himself.

He rushed into the clearing calling their names. He was answered by the piercing call of a hawk, unsettled by the intrusion. He stopped running, breathing fast. He felt his stomach do a quick flip, scanning the vacant site with disbelief.

"They are not here?" It was Iscah. Odd, hearing her voice.

He turned around slowly. She was a jolting sight, standing that way in his clearing, and so out of place.

She was dressed in linen, though it was stained with sea splash. But it was also a sight to forge his old self to the new and a flash of the Iscah he remembered with sympathy in her voice.

"I thought they might still be," he muttered.

"But you do know where they are?" She asked.

He let the thumping in his chest ease up and breath come slower. "I do," he affirmed.

"Good." She answered. Her voice sounded unpracticed and thin in his mountain air. She seemed inexperienced, child-like as if she had only just woken up. The hawk screeched at them again and flew away. She looked up at it, watching it tilt at the wind. She cocked her head to the right. "I hear your river," she offered quietly. "You once said that it sang to you at night."

Madai swallowed. He felt very cautious, afraid of chasing her back inside herself. And he felt his face going red, fumbling with his memory to find when he had spoken so womanly. He didn't answer, but only stood looking at her – Iscah, lost goat herder's daughter, here on his shore.

He heard her sigh. It sounded sad and he knew that now she was thinking about Kittim and how he was not here. She had always envisioned him in this future, though Madai had not heard her speak his name since that night with her in the Sea. He wished she would. Then he would reason with her, explain that her love for Kittim was not exactly what the love of a woman for a man could be...

Madai forced his eyes away, looking back through the trees and in the direction The Family took through the forest at each year's migration. "I thought we might be here before they left," he repeated, steering past the matter of Kittim.

"Where are they?" It was Simirra.

"Gone into the valley," Arphaxas answered her coming into the clearing, which startled Madai, having forgotten them in the moment. But it reminded him that Arphaxas had also been here before, if only a child.

"We'd better get a fire," Madai suggested, shaken to reality. "And something to eat."

THEY HAD GONE AFTER DEER AND SETTLED FOR SQUIR-rel. Arphaxas spoke longingly about the flesh of mammoth, which needed explaining to both women. Simirra asked with the curiosity he would have expected of Iscah. She would have badgered him for an exacting description. She was subdued instead, and they ate in relative silence after that. Arphaxas answered Simirra's questions with as few words as possible, finishing his squirrel in time to reach for the last one.

In the end, Madai regained a balance in his steady familiar earth, which made him a welcome bed though he could not sleep. The fire snapped, sending a spray of sparks skyward.

"It will be a week, perhaps more," he thought as he lay looking up at the night's stars. The Family's fires had been extinguished at least as long as that. He decided it might be best that way, giving him a stretch of time to reorient. His companions seemed less well known to him here. Perhaps Arphaxas could remember himself a boy once, before the banning. And Iscah...

When he thought about Iscah, he thought about Kittim. No matter the time spent and the lengths traveled, Kittim was still a mystery to him. Madai supposed he would remain so, as the Brine Sea separated them now. All that he knew of his lost friend was that he owed Kittim his life and perhaps even his faith. If not for the chance meeting on that far sandy beach, he might never have come upon Noah, nor Job. Perhaps it was providence... That would speak of a God Who sees... certainly.

And that made Madai feel like a lad again, holding up a silver fox for the Mighty God to appreciate, and laying it with importance on an unstable altar built by little boys. He smiled and let himself entertain the notion. He lay face up, arms under his head inviting the settling weight of his quest, which was of greater consequence than even his own disappointments. In that moment, he believed that the Family would be restored their confidence in the first ways. The stars would shout their prophecy the louder.

There in the cloudless night sky was the star map in all its familiar places to bring his assurance. He thought that perhaps he could feel God. It was a bold thing to think – that such a Maker of heaven and earth would not only see, but would swaddle him the way a mother does a babe. He knew it was fanciful, likely born of fatigue and... coming home. He would certainly not tell Tiras.

But the sense of being watched over – it was a comfort.

CHAPTER 18

*I*T WAS AN UNSEASONABLY CHILLY NIGHT. THE STARS were bright, bright enough to illuminate the hillside, bright enough to make the Shinar Captain's bones go slack for what he was seeing. There stood at the crest of the hill in silhouette, seven spectres. In height they seemed as trees. Though they stood and moved about as men, they wore the heads of beasts with horns and manes. It truly was the outer world that he'd come to, with all its legendary wilds proved true.

Remarkably human voices emanated from beastly throats and carried in the wind to the place Admah had hidden himself. He was glad he had scouted ahead, leaving his men in the valley, for they were only Dedanites and very superstitious. Admah was holding his own terrors in check by only a tenuous cord.

The creatures – part human, part beast – had erected a sort of shrine: massive monoliths of stone, impossible by any sort of natural means. What they chanted at the Dragon, whose constellation stood prominent in the heavens, was indecipherable to Admah's experience of language. But they were human words; he was certain of that.

Perhaps it should have been a comfort, that they were not mute beasts. But it was somehow made more terrible to him by what happened next.

They cut themselves and howled at the moon and flung blood at the stones. There came the gurgling scream of some poor creature – he dare not suppose it human for they dug about it searching for its heart, which they shared. It was dreadful to the Shinar Captain, though he was a veteran in battle and nearly a beast himself.

CHAPTER 19

MADAI PULLED AGAINST THE CORDING. THIS length of braided leather that had fastened a new Gerar sail to his boat's mast, had been stretched in the wind but hardened by a salty sea spray and so the tether was brittle. He was using it now to hold an earth-bound sledge together and it threatened to snap each time the little skiff caught on the rocks. Iscah and Simirra pushed as Madai pulled. The steady uphill climb was made all the harder by a heavy piece of rock in shape of a leg bone. Strapped beside that was a thick plank of pitch-coated gopher wood and sundries brought as gifts with his mother especially in mind. Arphaxas refused to help with the ungainly sledge. He, instead, had fashioned a device of his own that he pulled with very little effort. It contained their other belongings, which was, by his argument, all they should have bothered with.

Madai's ship had been sacrificed, its cypress frame refitted into these two sledges. Taking it apart had been a surprising loss to him, proving yet another glimpse of himself as more sentimental than he would have expected.

Even as Simirra huffed and grumbled with various laments about wild ends of the earth, Iscah voiced not a complaint. She pushed the laden sledge uphill as if it were her lone ambition. It was only when the heavy stone shifted, threatening to pull free and squash the women in a downhill slide, that Madai stopped midway up the mountain.

"It feels like snow," Arphaxas carped. "Leave all that and let's find a shelter before dark."

"I know a cave," Madai panted, feeling slightly guilty, "It isn't far. We've camped there before."

"Why must we bring this again?" Simirra huffed.

Madai secured the behemoth leg bone with an audible snap of cording against rock. He straightened and stretched his back and scanned the hill-side. He didn't answer Arphaxas or Simirra, but wrapped the length of leather around his waist and leaned uphill. Years of traversing this trail had imprinted upon his memory and he knew of certainty that the cave must be near. But it was in a late season's blizzard that The Family had last passed a night in the cave, and the terrain did not look the same. It was only as they cleared a thicket of chokecherries that Madai spotted the landmark – a smooth rock face with a narrow, oblong mouth.

He stopped, glad to have found it before dark. Unhitching himself from the sledge, he pointed and announced, "There it is. Arphaxas, we only need your skiff brought up."

"As I have said," the man replied thinly.

THE STARS HAD ALWAYS LENT HIM CONFIDENCE AND NO more so than tonight. Madai was not aware that he smiled, but he did – sitting at the mouth of the cave and looking into the clear dark sky. He was remembering his Patta on another night when all was made simple by a father's assurance. It might have been only last night that he sat with him here, for the stars and their alignments remained the same. It could be relied upon.

"There He is," Madai offered. And though he spoke in Arphaxas's direction, it was spoken mostly to the night.

Arphaxas grunted.

"The Bowman," he explained quietly as if the cynical man's response had been more apt.

"I know it's the Bowman," Arphaxas replied with an edge in his voice.

It catapulted Madai, most reluctantly, to the present and to this one beside him – not a friend, not expressly a foe. "Yes, of course," Madai answered with an appeasing voice. "But do you also know that The Bowman is the One to come from the Virgin, the Crushing Seed?"

Arphaxas stared at Madai as if he were a two-headed horse. He grunted and looked away, sitting cross-legged, slowly rubbing the edge of his cloak between his fingers. "You never surprise me, Kinsman," he jeered.

"I have gone a great distance to prove it true!" Madai argued.

"There is no lack of fools, I suppose."

"I find it a curious thing, Arphaxas," Madai countered, "that you are here."

"You invited me."

"I believe it was Kittim who invited you."

"You did not object. You were very generous, as I remember."

Madai heard the grating, paradoxical sound of a smile in Arphaxas's voice, an unwelcome change to an atmosphere full of peace but a moment ago.

"Do you believe in nothing?" Madai asked impatiently.

The left side of Arphaxas smile disappeared, leaving his lips in a thin crooked line. "I believe men like their gods."

"And you, what about you?"

Arphaxas huffed, "Well, look at me, Kinsman!" He patted his chest fondly. "What god has done this? I have remade myself!" He leaned forward, putting his face in a close proximity to Madai's. "Men can fight for their gods. I fight for me."

Madai believed it. It even sounded prophetic to his ears and Madai would not forget it. He could see Arphaxas's face clearly, could see the work done on his skin by the sun, could see the thin black vein of grime in the fine lines around his eyes and the flecks of muck buried in his curly red beard. He could see mirthless eyes of green above a half-smile. If he pressed his memory, he could just make out a thin, pale Tazek, even now, under the burnish of weathered skin. But indeed, as he bragged, the once weak was now a powerful man.

Madai looked away, angry that the peaceable mood of the night was disturbed, feeling his heart thumping and thrashing like a wild bird caged up in his chest. Remembering, and reluctantly, what Kittim had warned just before departing.

"Think what you will, "he muttered. "Truth is truth. It does not have to be believed to make it so, and all the star stories are true by the mouth of the great Ancient himself. I have seen the Ark and I have seen Noah."

"And I, the Lord Nimrod with his pack of gods."

"We believe in the One True God here on these shores. " Madai reminded him.

Arphaxas expelled a sharp snort. "And my Patta believed in the gods of the forest and the gods of the tower."

"And was banned for it." That bird had grown fierce in Madai's belly.

Arphaxas laughed outright. "That is how you see it. But they left to find their gods too. No less than you." He laughed again.

"You dare compare me with your Patta?" Madai raged. "I believe you remember what was paid to Shinar's gods! Was it a fair price?"

It was a wicked, fatal jab, recalling a father willing to sell a young boy and his sister for his place in a corrupt kingdom. He watched Arphaxas's expression freeze just before an invisible hood dropped across his eyes. Madai squirmed inside a little at that.

Arphaxas put his elbow on his bent knee and leaned forward. "Let me persuade you, Madai," he whispered, "to tread carefully there."

The big man seemed to uncoil then, springing up to his feet with astonishing agility. He retreated to his mat laid out at the back of the cave and scratched around in his belongings. He left Madai alone in a chilly atmosphere.

Madai could not quite conjure back the pleasures of his old memories after that. It was only after a fair stretch of time that he considered; perhaps his first real attempt at persuasion of all things sacred had been poorly done indeed.

MADAI ROSE EARLY AND REPLENISHED THE FIRE. IT HAD been a cold night. He was standing at the mouth of the cave scanning the full length of the pass... again. He assured himself that he would have altered nothing in all that was said last night, even given the chance, with only one possible omission, though it had been true.

"I hope Arphaxas is looking for something to eat," he heard Simirra from deeper inside the cave, "he did not have to drag that wretched bone and I am hungry!"

"Arphaxas is gone," Madai replied quietly.

"Wherever to?" she asked, incredulous.

He shrugged.

"When did he go, that lazy brute!" Simirra demanded.

"In the night," Madai answered, turning. "I will get something to eat. These are my mountains, have no fear."

"But where has Arphaxas gone?" Iscah asked, sitting up. Madai came for his bow.

"He made a choice."

"What do you mean?"

"Last night. We talked and he made his choice."

"What did you say to him?" Iscah demanded, a rise in her voice.

Madai leveled his eyes at her, hearing that tone again. It brought him back to a time when she had considered him a heretic. It did not sit well with him; it brushed him against the hair.

"This is where I sat with my Patta once, with all my people in this cave." He said slowly and not in answer to the question. He scanned the rocky surface of the cave walls. "We are not so many as I once believed, seeing Shinar. We are few, in fact."

Iscah did not respond, but only fixed her eyes on him.

"We cannot be divided," he finished. "Truth is truth."

She raised her eyebrow, hinting clearly and without her words that he had been no different once.

"Arphaxas. His way would divide us," Madai insisted.

"So, you made him leave."

Madai was not sure if it was the look or the tone that bit him worse. "No," he answered, more defensive than he liked. "He was gone when I woke up."

"He is a brute – deserting us!" Simirra charged again. "If you had seen him, living in a dirty cave like a beast."

Madai turned toward Simirra, having nearly forgotten her. There was an accusing, unappealing aspect about her.

"And yet he saved you?"

She inhaled sharply.

"But he saved us all! What with Martu…" Iscah insisted, glancing at Simirra. "Don't you remember? What did you say to him?"

"We talked about God, Iscah. Arphaxas does not choose Him."

"Of course not," Simirra responded tightly. "You cannot be amazed by that. He is little above an animal."

"I knew Arphaxas before you," Madai suddenly revealed, surprised to find himself at the man's defense. "I knew him in the courts of Shinar where he was no beast."

Both women were stunned by his passion and completely silent.

"He had been sold as a slave," Madai continued, directing his speech at Simirra, "and had the knowing of many tongues, as you, Simirra, and as Kittim. He was sold to buy favor with the King." Madai walked away from them. He walked toward the mouth of the cave again, drumming his fingers against his thigh, at odds with himself. He looked at the clouds. They were a dark grey, promising snow. And he remembered himself but a day past, stepping onto the coast of his homeland with joy in his heart and happy prospects.

"How would it be?" He suddenly wondered, as if he had not been the last night's aggressor, "to be so little valued?"

"Then he has suffered." Iscah whispered.

"As have we all," Simirra chimed.

Madai frowned at her and finished the story quietly. "His parents sold him."

"What did you say?"

"To gain standing with the King of Shinar," Madai turned to look at Simirra. "But that does not alter the course. He made his choice last night."

"How do you know he's left?" Iscah asked. "Perhaps he is only…"

"I know."

"But…. sold by his own Papa," she persisted.

"He will not serve The One True God, Iscah. How can I bring him into The Family? He is a Banned."

Simirra stood as though frozen in place. "You shall desert him too, then?" She spoke, aiming her accusations this time, at Madai.

"He is the one who left, Simirra," Madai responded sharply. "And a minute ago he was a brute."

She bent down then, and pulled up her night's covering to throw across her shoulders. "You have never been betrayed," she muttered, so quiet Madai did not know she had spoken.

"I will not take the corruptions of Shinar into The Family!" He insisted at the air in general and to Iscah in particular.

"Do you forget, Madai? I was also a slave of that place." Iscah said it carefully, stoic and quiet.

It was stunning, like the frigid spray of icy sea. Her eyes were piercing, like some soaring bird of prey knowing things only a bird could know, things denied to men with feet on the ground. No winsome maid, no brilliantly curious and delighted heart shone at him, but a seasoned spirit. He felt his own heart stand still. Indeed, there were greater depths left to be known of her. It made her of a greater substance than even he had imagined and he loved her more at the moment than before. Perceiving the truth of that, he was suddenly terrified.

"That was different," he felt his wooden lips reply. She merely lifted her chin.

"I don't think we can find him," he finished quietly. "And it will be winter."

Her eyes released him. She glanced away toward the valley below and Madai exhaled.

ISCAH STUDIED THE LANDSCAPE BEYOND THE CAVE. IT seemed so very vast, a new world and empty so far as she could tell. It ached of loneliness. She thought it was perhaps in sympathy toward Arphaxas who was, as just revealed, a lonely man. She was not surprised that Madai did not comprehend it.

"Who will pull the skiff?"

Iscah turned at Simirra's voice. The woman was suddenly beside her, pinching a blanket closed at her breast and looking out at the scape beyond their cave.

"Very vast, is it not?" Iscah whispered.

Simirra nodded. "What could be so terrible... to send him away? Who does not ask after the gods?"

"There is but one God, Simirra," Iscah answered softly. She heard Madai moving outside, his feet crunching the gravel. Perhaps he had been down at the sledge securing his ark plank again and contemplating the trouble of the second skiff as well.

"That is what my father believed," Simirra whispered.

The response surprised Iscah and, though Simirra had said it before, she had been showing her least attractive side for some time. Iscah trained her eyes careful away from the woman's face and ventured quietly, "You once said that everyone you loved was dead for the cause of gods."

"It is true."

They looked at each other then, with Simirra seeming suddenly different this morning. Maybe it was this foreign forest and the expanse of a great Brine Sea. But she seemed almost... meek.

"Does your One True God speak?" She was whispering again, and nervous.

Iscah blinked. That really was the question, though she had not expected it to be asked by the very earthy Simirra. She took a step forward, nearer the ledge of the cave to think. There had been a time with Tutan at the head of the Pishon: his assurance that God had traveled along beside him on the way. Had Holy God whispered that in Tutan's ear? Or... how did Job know God would walk with him on the earth again, in flesh? She had believed him, certainly, at the time. But how did he know? She remembered Madai saying God had talked to Noah, telling him somehow that a boy would not die, and most obviously telling him to build a great ark.

She turned slowly, back around to see Simirra with new eyes. And then she considered something that would have been, previous to the question, preposterous. "Has He spoken to you?" she asked.

"I don't know." The woman replied with fear in her eyes. "I heard... something."

"What did He say?"

"It said I should run."

Iscah frowned, feeling surprised and curious, suspicious and slightly jealous. "Surely it was someone having sport with you," Iscah offered.

"I thought it was a real person at first. I looked; the voice, it was so real. But there was no one. Now as I think of it, I do remember that He said my name...

Simirra."

Iscah watched as the moment replayed itself to her. A longing passed Simirra's face.

"No one has said my name like that," she finished softly. "My life is likely saved by that voice."

Iscah hardly dared to breathe. "What do you mean?" She whispered.

"I was going to kill Martu myself. I'd gone to the temple to do it. And then at home, before Martu returned; I was taking too long, It said I should run." Simirra focused her eyes to look at Iscah with a degree of fear. "What do you think it was?"

A long shuddery sigh pulled up through Iscah's throat. And she had an unwelcome, teary sensation. It had somehow become less welcome to share Mighty God since Kittim was gone. It was as if none should have so dear a piece of God as she, and especially not Simirra, whose very air smelled of pagan.

"I do not believe in conjuring," Simirra continued. "Father and Mother's God did not save them… but, perhaps…"

"Perhaps He saved you," Iscah forced herself to confess. "Do you really think so?"

Again the flutter, like generosity set loose in her heart. Iscah took hold of Simirra's arms. "God is very great, Simirra. Who can know what He does. Perhaps… perhaps He wanted you saved."

Tears sprang in the woman's eyes and Iscah knew she was thinking about the dead baby. "He does love me, then…"

Iscah's fingers tightened on Simirra. No, it was much more than the child. She suddenly wrapped her arms around the older woman, unabashed and full of new-found charities.

CHAPTER 20

T HE TRAIL THEY FOLLOWED WAS AN ANCIENT ONE, used by herds before the scattering and by sons of Japheth after. It gave the most efficient route into a valley protected from great gales of snow with sentinels of ragged peaks to the east and west. It allowed as easy a trail as could be found whilst dragging a skiff weighted with treasures of immeasurable worth.

Madai found himself thinking about Arphaxas a lot. He was at odds with himself over the man; knowing it was a thorny business to bring in a Banned, but feeling tied to him none-the-less. He reworked that last conversation over and over in his mind and with differing speeches, looking for other outcomes, though it really didn't help.

"I provoked him," was what it always came to.

The fact that Arphaxas was an enemy now, and at his rear did not improve Madai's pondering. That it was an exposed back, which worried him most, made him less noble perhaps than the original crime. But Madai was, and more than once, sure they were being followed. It wasn't a footfall or snapping brush; it was a sense. It made him haul the sledge a little faster to go a little farther every day before night. He was surprised that Iscah and Simirra did not complain about that. There seemed a sort of truce come between them, a camaraderie that he envied, reminding him of Kittim, whom he greatly missed.

Upon passing a certain and recognizable assembling of granite boulders wedging the river in, Madai came upon the final and eastern slope of their journey. It would be their last hard climb. It brought this business with Iscah to desperate heights, how she had commiserated over Arphaxas and blamed him for the man's leaving. She had looked at him with knowing eyes, eyes that had seen grievous things, but never would tell it all. In that moment she had taken a step away – very much farther than how Kittim stood between them. He could not enter the Family somehow, with such a distance left.

"We will stop here," he announced.

The women stretched their backs, ready enough.

"Help me bring the water, Iscah," Madai said when they had stopped for the night, because he was unfamiliar with awaking love, and it was how he fell to it with Ido. Iscah did look at him oddly, but he supposed that was not a rare occurrence between them. They left Simirra to unpack the blankets and to coax the most out of their night's fire.

The river was at its finest, the boulders enormous and the way somewhat difficult. It had cut a deep gorge, and Madai turned where the downward climb was steepest. Iscah had the goat stomach in one hand and balanced with the other. He reached up to steady her.

With not the least hesitation, she wrapped her fingers around his hand. She did it unabashedly, as if it was nothing, which was so much less than he wished for.

"Does this remind you of the Pishon?" he asked, somewhat blithering but hopeless to think of anything else.

She looked up because she had been watching the ground, careful not to slip. She smiled. It was not a brilliant smile but neither was it empty. Using him as a fulcrum, she climbed to the top of a boulder. From its somewhat hazardous perch, she quietly surveyed the length of the river.

"Yes, I think it does," she answered.

His heart beat too hard when he looked at her, the way her cheeks reddened in a crisp mountain air and how she got a look of shine in her eyes. It was nearly as if she might emerge from the doldrums set upon her by Kittim's swift and unexpected departure.

"It smells good here," she said. "The way it smelled on the Pishon."

Then he saw her face change. "O, Madai! What is that?" she asked, raising her arm with the goat stomach still clutched in her hand.

He looked across his shoulder to see what she was looking at – spears of fireweed, which were just losing their topmost petals. Knowing how she loved a marvelous thing, he should have already told her about the knee-high blooms. They spread across the mountains to turn them scarlet in autumn. But he hadn't thought of it.

"Fireweed," he answered proudly. "Did I not say you would like it here?"

She looked back at him as if he were a child and she the parent. "Very beautiful, Madai." She answered.

Then there came a look on her face to tell him as plain as her mouth could, that it should be seen with Kittim.

"Kittim was bent entirely to his master," he said abruptly, surprising them both. Her face went ashen and she pulled her fingers out of his grip. But she was still standing atop the boulder and had to grab his arm for balance. "I'm sorry, Iscah," he sputtered quickly. "I just… " His voice trailed away.

"Do not be vexed. I am quite well."

He studied her face at that. It was closed, not as it had been last night telling him with fierceness that she had been a slave of Shinar once; daring him imagine what that could do to souls. He could not decide which distance he hated most.

"Will you help me down?" she asked and let him lift her off the rock. It was not at all what he had had in mind.

But he kept hold of her hand, stubbornly, to lead her the last way to the river. It thundered past, just beyond their feet, with a roar.

"It shall be cold," she warned evenly.

"Yes." He agreed, all his expectations turned to naught. "Help me hold the skin open." Which she did obediently, holding one side of the bag open and him the other. Together they held it against the current, filling it almost instantly with such a glacier's melt. They pulled it out together, a heavy plop on the river's edge. Madai tied it closed.

He stood, and with a great courage required, dared to trap her eyes with his own. Then he smiled tightly and rested his hand on her shoulder. "You will try to be happy, Iscah?" he asked.

He could see that there were speeches aplenty in her mouth and behind her eyes but they would surely not be spoken. She slowly turned her face away after a moment to see the flowers again. He would prefer a bout with a dragon to this, surely, as he hadn't a clue what to do next. But a curl had escaped her braid and was lying on his hand. It was a terrible distraction. If he were to fix her to memory, it would be as she looked now, though it was far distant, gazing at his meadow. He lifted his forefinger, just enough to touch the edge of her jaw. She turned at that to give him a rather sad smile.

"Of course I shall be happy. I am well, as I said." Then she paused and looked down. "I should never have thought ill of you, Madai. You are a stalwart friend."

It was somewhat better than the distance, though barely, but he replied with as much optimism as was felt in the last moments, "Then I will tell you now that we are near to the winter's camp sight. We will be there tomorrow."

"O," she pronounced with relief, "I know that shall make you very happy! The end of your great quest."

"Yes."

"You can tell them all about finding Noah and all that he said."

"And you can tell your poem, Iscah. That is a proof too."

She nodded at that.

"And you are a second witness to Job's hill of bones," he continued. "I had not thought of that."

"And Tutan, with his markings."

"Yes," she agreed, "from as far away as his East!"

He watched the merest hint of enthusiasm surface, a tiny seed.

"I would not have thought of that," she said again. "Perhaps I can be a help. Well, that is a mission, is it not? And I was just thinking that..."

"Thinking what?"

She shook her head. "No matter, Madai." She patted the top of his hand, which still rested on her shoulder. "We have a mission."

She was ready to go; he could sense it. But he tightened his fingers a moment. "You don't blame me, Iscah?"

"For what?"

"Arphaxas," he answered, afraid because it probably had been his fault.

She had looked confused when he asked, and now she seemed relieved and a little like the old Iscah, explaining away a latest foolishness.

"I was surprised this morning," she said. "And I was not thinking about your kinsmen, as you were. Arphaxas did make a choice, though he could have used some more teaching," which was the only rebuke he could detect in her speech and it was not so bitter, as he knew it was the truth. "Your mission is very great," she continued. "And perhaps he will come back anyway, in the end."

She let him help her back to camp after that. And they passed a peaceable night with the last of rice and eastern dates and western river fish. Perhaps it was not everything he might have hoped for, but it left him more glad of heart than he might have expected, given all that had occurred. Tomorrow would be their last day's march. Evening would bring him home.

CHAPTER 21

*B*LEACHED WHITE AND ARCHING AT THE ORANGE glow of sunset, there were the trophies of many winters past. A pile of ivory tusks proclaimed him home, even at this distance. It was to him, this ancient structure, as significant a monument as any tower of Shinar. Beside it, opposing black in color, stood The Family's altar, dark lignite stacked in height to a man's chest and meant to offer up in fire, the Provider's Portion. These two constructions were the winter's valley to him enshrined. He watched the camp, smelled his old life, and took a moment to savor it.

The huts did look a trifle more dingy with their shaggy skins. But they were as well, the familiar comfort of home. He looked for the ceremonial lodge, their Place of Gathering, both to orient the camp and find his father's shelter.

"There's something wrong…" he muttered. He pushed through the shrubby, scratchy willow denuded now of its leaves and into the clearing. He stopped there and looked a long time.

"What is it, Madai?" Iscah whispered. "My Patta's lodge is out of its place."

"They all look alike," Simirra scoffed quietly.

That was when he spied a woman. She was dressed as any other woman but had a particular way of moving. She was starting toward the loom positioned at the front of the door and carrying the tamping rod she used to thread the wool. It suddenly was of little matter that his Patta's lodge was at the edge of camp.

As if a long ago birth cord somehow still attached his Mamam to himself, she glanced up to look their way and stopped mid-stride. He watched her free hand rise to her breast even as he started toward the camp, forgetting the sledge, which bumped along behind him rattling all the gifts of silk and raisins, stone bone and ark wood. It pulled him up short, too weighty for a single man to pull. With no little effort, Madai disentangled himself and finished the distance at a lope. He grabbed his mother, whose face was brilliant with surprise and the language of purest joy. He wrapped her up in his arms, tamping rod and all, lifting her off the ground in a great hug and long awaited.

"My son!" She cried, " My son!"

She smelled of stew with cameron root and wet wool and earth and smoke. She was tough and solid to the touch, swaddled in a tunic of fur-lined lynx. "Mamam!" He bent his face into her hair where he was not ashamed to hide his tears.

When he drew back to look at her she was the same, praise to Mighty God, light blue and sparkling eyes in the fair face of his Mamam, the one to love him first.

She was laughing when he put her down and reached up to wipe his cheek. "We must find your Patta!"

"Madai?"

He heard the voice, the ever-steady underpinning and looked up to see his Patta, coming at him in a new bear robe. Ashkinaz lost the coat half way and grabbed them, he and his Mamam, in both his arms.

"O, my son. Praise to the Most High, you are home! You are well?" He pushed away to look at Madai. "By the Arm of Mighty God," Madai answered – the best of answers.

ISCAH FELT HER HEART THUMP HEAVY INTO THE PIT OF her belly, producing a vague queasiness. It was fear as surely as her palms had gone damp. A long day, pushing Madai's skiff had brought her here with an aching back. She should have felt more relief that there, through the brush, lay Madai's village, looking like an ant city, great oval mounds of black and grey. Only it was not relief she felt. There had been no going back from the moment they took sail, and yet – here it was, real. Here it was, an insignificant human habitation, flimsy against elements, mammoth and something called saber cat.

"O!" Simirra gasped beside her. "Is that where we have been going?"

Iscah nodded, almost afraid to look at the woman who had been very long in a city.

Madai's claim that something was wrong had been of little reassurance. That was when a woman had come from one of the hide mounds, which at a closer proximity had the look of some enormous woolly beast, and looked at them. The woman gave out a loud shriek and came running, wielding a long flat stick.

Madai had met her midway between the camp and tree line – after dumping the sledge. He had grabbed the woman who was now crying with her arms wrapped around his neck and waving the stick rather dangerously in the air behind his head.

She was dressed as one would expect, coming from such a hairy house. She had three long thick braids, somewhat faded, but looking once to have been the color of sand. Another came fast behind the woman; he could only be Madai's father. A furry robe was lost on his way toward them, giving him more the appearance of an actual man; very tall, bushy of face and enormously happy.

They stood that way, the three of them in a kind of six- legged dance, weeping, laughing, words muffled and tangled up together. It struck Iscah how used to Madai she had become; he in his civilized appearance, since coming upon Gerar's bathhouse. She remembered how he had looked at first. He had been dressed like his father with a voyage upon the sea to make it worse.

"My son!" the man was saying, and praises to God.

The mother looked up again, and disengaged herself. She seemed to look Iscah directly in the eye, even at this distance. Her expression changed, likely to mirror her own, and then she said something to Madai.

The father looked up to the line of willows and saw them for the first time. The woman lifted a hand, the one with the stick. Iscah watched them all three start their way. She breathed in sharply, realizing only then that she'd been holding her breath.

"Well… we are here now," she heard Simirra mutter.

"Come, come," the mother called even before she'd reached them and stretched out her arms. "Madai, you have brought us new… friends?"

The father was smiling and would have spoken as well, but all the hide houses seemed to have given birth. Before he could speak or Madai could answer, they were joined – surrounded in fact – by a crowd of tall, fair-haired people, all looking quite the same in Iscah's estimation.

"MADAI!" EXCLAIMED A SOMEWHAT OLDER AND SEEM-ingly important man, "you have returned!"

The elder spoke with a short and quick cadence. They were the first words Iscah heard spoken by these western peoples and were what she would have expected their leader to say. It seemed, however, that they were not spoken with quite the pleasure she would have expected. But perhaps it was not their custom to gush.

She turned her head away, feeling oddly disappointed for Madai. She surveyed the other's faces. Indeed, they were light of skin with the same yellow hair as Madai. No… she thought, varying degrees of yellow, some like Arphaxas. But they had the same light eyes. She felt herself blush, remembering how she had thought Madai's eyes so beautiful. His were not so different from all the others…

She turned her attention to their dress, all in one sort of beast or other, which recalled her own home to her, when she had been but a simple goat herder's daughter. Only these furs were heavy, a testimony that this valley would be cold.

"And who have you brought us?" The elder was asking. She felt his gaze on her and heard a dubious note in his voice.

"They are his wives," Madai's father quipped with startling haste.

Iscah had thought she would understand the speech of these people, as Kittim had taught her. She had, after all, spoken Madai's tongue all this long journey and understood Arphaxas as well. But she was certain that Madai's father had said that she and Simirra were his wives.

"His wives?" Simirra whispered at Iscah. The two women looked at each other and then at Madai, both with alarm. "If he doesn't set it right," Simirra declared quietly, "I will!"

"Yes, Toban. Indeed my son has brought two beautiful daughters home to me," the mother instantly proclaimed. She dropped her stick, bustled around the men and took them each by an arm. She stood facing them, back to the crowd with an intense expression. Then she leaned forward and kissed them both on the cheek.

The moment would be strangely fixed in Iscah's mind – at such a declaration and the mother of Madai kissing her, looking very tall. She should be protesting and yet she was struck by the dignity of the woman, fine boned with an almost translucent skin and blue eyes. There was a hint of red in the braids that hung long on a rather flat chest.

"But…" Simirra began.

"My daughters!" the woman quickly reaffirmed.

The Elder nodded at Madai with what appeared a better judgment even as Madai's father took the tether of their skiff up off the ground.

Another man made his way past the Elder with a slight jostle. "Madai is home, Toban, and with all that he has seen and learned," the man said. "But he is surely tired. Will we let him be the son of Ashkinaz tonight? And these new daughters, should they not know their mother?"

"Togarmah," the Elder affirmed in a grunt, nodding his head. "Certainly so." He turned toward the others gathered around them. "And we shall ready a feast!" he declared, "to welcome this son of ours home, our truth finder!"

The chief elder gave Madai's shoulder a resounding slap, reclaiming his authority and setting miles worth of dust into the air. "You've come at an auspicious season, my boy," he declared. "The morning star on a wing!"

Iscah watched what had been a scratchy tension stretch near to snapping between the three older men at the mention of stars on wings, and Madai looked aghast. It was a disconcerting introduction. He had promised her a peaceable coast, a Family where God was God. But it would be so like Madai to have gotten it wrong. Of course, then there was the part about being his wives…

CHAPTER 22

*I*SCAH AND SIMIRRA PUSHED AGAINST THE SKIFF again as Madai pulled it across the camp. Simirra thought some of the men might have helped, and yet she supposed it may be women's work here on this barbarous coast. She was relieved that the village did not smell, though the hide tents might still offer their own offenses. She pushed as hard as she ever had pushed, feeling blue eyes follow them.

Their women wore hides as well as the men. It was making her feel exposed in the thinner stuff of civilization and it was feeling like a very long way to the family's tent. Simirra caught the gaze of a woman especially striking – one with a certain air about her, as though she were important – or thought so at least. Simirra knew in the instant that this one would be no friend, though she was not looking for friends. But she was not looking for enemies either. And this woman with the stormy expression was surely shooting them fire from her eyes.

Perhaps she was a lost lover of Madai's.

When they reached the tent from which the mother of Madai had emerged, Simirra was more than glad. It was a rather large domed construction, more substantial than desert tents and seamed with thick cords of leather. The hides were turned hair side out and had been removed from a creature of enormous size; the mammoth no doubt of which Madai and Arphaxas had spoken with greatest reverence. The rather curious edifice to be seen in the center of the village was constructed of massive tusks and had likely come from the same beast. Simirra considered herself an educated woman, having once seen a creature with such a tusk, with great ears and an undulating appendage on its face, though it was not so large nor so hairy as the once owner of these tusks must have been.

Madai stopped in front of the tent. He was studying it too, as she might – returning to a beloved home.

When he bent to pull aside the flap, which served as its door, she held her breath, dreading the aroma she was sure to meet.

ISCAH PUSHED ALONGSIDE SIMIRRA. IT WAS A SURPRIS-
ing turn to feel camaraderie with the Calnehan woman. That had happened, of
course, in their discussion of God's speaking. It did match her perception of
things, that Mighty God should care when even a pagan has lost a child.
Perhaps it was because Simirra's mother and father had once served Him, and
been cost their lives for it. It was a terrible world, after all, she was coming to
believe.

MADAI HAD TO BEND AND DUCK HIS HEAD TO COME
through the door and into his old life. Forgotten for the moment were such
travesties as omens of wings and morning stars. Instead, smells spanned the
years he had been away. There hung the mammoth skins, stretched on poplar
yearlings to make his father's lodge cozy if somewhat dim. There was the glow
of embers and his mother's crock above the fire filled with stew, smelling of
musky meats and woody herbs. There sat his own little son.

The boy was cross-legged on a hide bed. He was holding a miniature bow.
Madai remembered the bow; it was painted red. Ido had done it.

"Japhet," his mother coaxed. "It is your Patta!"

The boy's eyes came round and his mouth popped open. He jumped up
instantly, nimble as a hare, and scooted up to hug his Grand Mamam's leg. He
peeked around her, clutching the folds of her tunic in a tiny, tight fist.

"Patta?" a little voice squeaked.

Madai's eyes took a moment to adjust in the dim. But he stared at the child,
more nervous than he'd expected to be, and squatted down. He leaned forward
slowly, searching past a forehead of curls for the toddler he remembered. He
reached out carefully to cup the child's face in his hands. "Yes, Japhet." His
voice caught in his throat, "I am home."

Japhet was motionless, but Madai could feel his little heart, beating so hard
as to be felt through his own fingers. He had the fair skin of the girl Madai had
loved very well, with an abundance of dun colored speckles across his nose,
eyes the color of clear morning sky. It was a singular moment, apart from time.
Unexpected tears filled Madai's eyes and he waited before speaking again. He
watched every tick on the child's face to see if his son would wiggle away or
accept him. What the boy did was arch his back to stand straight and take one
step forward. It was a mark of courage, one that Madai knew he had his own
Patta to thank for. He scooped Japhet up in his arms then. He hugged him tight
to his chest, tight enough to smell smoke and a little dirt in the child's yellow
curls, tight enough to bring the boy to squirming. Japhet pried himself away to
look his Patta in the face with a hopeful look of pride.

"Did you sail the Great Sea?" he chirped, enunciating very well for a lad
of five.

IT WAS MORE THAN SIMPLY TOUCHING. IT BRIDGED FIRST
and somewhat unpleasant impressions of a smoky and close interior. There
was also the quite delicious smell of food, reminding Iscah's stomach to make

itself known. Only that would be ignored for the moment, for the child looked so much like his father, with just those rosy cheeks and yellow hair and hopeful eyes. She could feel herself smiling. It was a testament to character, as Iscah knew she should never have so glad a homecoming herself.

Madai had leapt whole-heartedly into a story. It was the quickest way to a little boy's heart; to anyone's heart that loved an adventure. She found herself listening to stories that she'd been a part of herself as if they had been brand new.

"The sea touched the sky in every direction, Japhet," he was saying. "I could not see the land."

"Sea monsters?" the child asked in a squeaky voice.

Madai laughed. He picked the boy up again and hugged him. He looked unlike Iscah had ever seen him look before, and laughed with a great freedom – and pride. It was more than being newly home in high mountain air, which smelled of pine... and food.

"Yes, sea monsters."

"Like the Songs of Ashkinaz?" Japhet asked, tripping lightly across the difficult name. It was not the song of his grandfather, but of his grandfather's grandfather, telling of a perilous journey during the days of the Great Scattering when men had fled their brothers. It had been a confusing time, speaking new tongues, spawning suspicion in a civilization already bloody with conflict.

"Those songs are true, my son, as true as what we know about the stars."

"But tell me about the sea monster."

Madai laughed again. Iscah listened to this new story, glad it had not been told before they set to cross the Great Sea for the reason of a fearsome eely serpent. If it was no embellishment, then the creature had been a size as to take Madai up in one bite. She glanced at Mineo who was listening with horror, hearing for the first time that all her mother's trepidations had been rightly owned.

But the boy was wide-eyed with wonder. So this was his Patta! Mineo moved to her cooking pot.

"Let your Patta eat, Japhet," she said.

She brought them bowls of stew then, and Iscah reached for one gladly. Her stomach rumbled. It was delicious, hot and smelled of onions, sage and meat. It tasted like something her own mother would have cooked if goats grew to the size of ox.

Japhet sat wedged up against Madai, ignoring his bowl with a look to say 'stew is boring'. Iscah scooped up another bite. She suspected Madai had gained an extra appendage for some good time to come.

"What about the dragon?" Japhet interjected between obligatory and miniscule sips of broth. "Well, I did not do that alone," Madai replied, putting his bowl down.

"O?" Mineo asked. "Not alone?"

"No, Mamam," Madai answered. "I was kept all along the way and saved by the Mighty Arm of God Himself, just as you said."

Mineo beamed. She did not need to reply for the look on her face. "And I met a great friend. His name was Kittim."

"Kittim?" his father asked. "A Japhethite?"

"He did not look like us," Madai explained. "But he spoke our tongue and served the One True God."

Madai stopped. The look on his face changed and Iscah wondered if he felt the loss of Kittim as much as she did. She waited. She watched as his face went pale under the sunburn.

"What is it, Madai?" His mother asked.

"Kittim was always a mystery," he muttered. "He said his master had sent him to seek out a man… Do you suppose..?"

He didn't finish the question, but Iscah was suddenly filled with indignation at such a suggestion, even unspoken. Surely Madai did not think Kittim had been sent to seek him out, so great a man as Kittim! Jealousies were piling up inside her at an alarming speed.

"And did he help you?" Mineo was asking.

"More than helped," Madai answered. "He had the knowing of all the tongues of all the peoples we met. And he had the… steadiness to wait me out, to let me find Mighty God again."

The lodge was quiet. A log crumbled in the fire, spitting sparks against the bottom of Mineo's cooking pot. Japhet was fighting hard against eyelids that wanted to close.

"Tell us everything you learned, my son." his mother asked.

"Everything you and Patta always told me," Madai answered with a boyish grin.

Ashkinaz coughed. He could have swallowed wrong, or he could be hiding an unmanly emotion.

"But surely you learned more…"

Madai reached out and touched his mother's arm, unsettling Japhet from his dozing spot.

"Here, boy," Ashkinaz spoke for only the second time and reached for Japhet. "Let your Patta eat and go lay down." Anticipating the child's reluctance to do such a thing at such a time, his Grand Patta took him up and deposited him gently on his mat. Japhet's protest was surreptitiously made, being grown at a time when obedience was a vital part of survival if you are only five in a dangerous world…and already sleepy. Iscah watched his eyes pop open only once, likely to see that his father was really still there.

"I learned more than even you had hoped," Madai answered with a smile. But that was when someone else came into the lodge.

"Tiras!" Madai exclaimed with surprise.

"You don't mind?" the new arrival asked of Mineo.

"You're like Madai's brother," she answered happily.

"Iscah," Madai said to her, "this is my great friend, Tiras. Yes, and like a brother."

She was surprised to be remembered at such a time. Perhaps he was asking that she not begrudge him a friend beside Kittim, and as near as a brother. She smiled at the new-comer, feeling a little shy.

"Madai was just telling us what new things he has learned of God," Mineo began.

Tiras sat cross-legged beside his old friend and took the cup Mineo offered him.

Madai told the story that Noah had told. Iscah did not grow tired of it. She watched their faces show the same disbelief she had felt at first, and watched as they became convinced and then amazed. No cold before the deluge – which was near to outrageous in this land of ice and snow – and no rain, beasts that did not eat each other, stars that sang. But when he told about Eve, the longing she felt for an air that did not smell of death and rot, it was quiet that answered him. A very small thing, Iscah thought. But it is often the small things that prick. They sneak through to the heart while one is guarded against the large.

"Noah knew Adam?" Tiras asked slightly incredulous.

"No. But he knew men who did. And he kept a very important scroll. It is "The Account of Man through Adam, the clay of Elohiym". In it are the names of forebears, names that you carry in that pouch around your neck, Patta."

Ashkinaz fingered the leather bag, which carried a small stone for every forebear. It held Japhet's stone and Madai would wear it one day after Ashkinaz was no more.

"They make marks on leather which speak each word," Madai continued. "They do not need songs but they may read it." He leaned toward then and whispered significantly, "On this scroll are the names of all the forebears of the One Who will be the Crushing Seed."

"They know the Bowman?" Ashkinaz asked, amazed.

"Noah only knows through whom He will come."

"How?" Mineo asked.

"Mighty God tells him," Madai finished cautiously, sounding somewhat uncertain about it himself. "But God has spoken to Noah before," he added hastily, "about the Ark."

"Certainly," Mineo answered.

"He must be very old..." Tiras began.

Madai smiled, hearing the noise of unmistakable doubt.

"It was the first earth," Madai explained. And then he explained that.

MADAI FINISHED BY TELLING ABOUT TUTAN; THAT HE married an unlikely lady who collected birds. He told about Job. He told the story of Nimrod, which perhaps he should have told at first for he was the in-famous tower builder and corrupter. It was he and his city that had so exercised God as to confuse the tongues of humankind, at least Iscah thought so for she held a thoroughly pitiless opinion of the place.

In fact, Madai talked well past the time that Simirra had finally succumbed and Mineo had made her a place to sleep. It was only then that he told about Arphaxas, how he had known him as some other boy in Shinar and how he had come into their camp with Simirra. Iscah was glad Simirra was asleep because Madai told about her dead babe, burned for a terrible god of Baal. He told that Arphaxas had left them at the cave for a disagreement because he had once been a child of the Banned. It troubled her again, wondering if he was safe. Though Arphaxas was dreadfully adept at killing, he had been kind to her in a brusque, reluctant kind of way.

They talked till she thought there could be nothing more to say. That was when Madai finally asked with a certain degree of anxiety in his voice, "What is this of second wives?"

A brilliant shock, like a web of lightning in a summer storm, raced through her stomach and pulled her upright, back from encroaching sleep.

"And why is your shelter set here, so far from the Place of Meeting?"

Mineo gently smiled, not tired at all. "You have been away a long time, my son," she replied.

"Togarmah..." the father suddenly interjected.

"Surely he can wait," the mother argued. She turned to address Iscah. "Will you tell me, Iscah, about the woman with the birds?"

Iscah was hardly recovered and certainly not able to speak before so many strangers. She had not always been so... shy. It seemed in fact, a new development. But she felt terribly insufficient here in this rustic tent.

"There is something in here I think you shall find beautiful," she said instead, digging into a bundle. "There is a bird woven in a silk, which came from the East. Madai got it for me." Iscah felt herself going as red as the garment she was searching for. "We are not his wives, you know."

"Of course you would not both be his wife," Mineo replied sympathetically. "But it is not safe for unmarried women here."

"It's time to go," Ashkinaz interrupted again.

"Perhaps so," Mineo agreed.

"Where are we going?" Madai asked, confused and alarmed.

"Togarmah is waiting with the others for us, in his lodge."

"It is very late," Iscah heard herself say.

Mineo looked at her kindly. "Yes," she answered. "It is better so."

They watched as Madai and his friend, Tiras, and his Patta quietly left. That was when Iscah realized she felt on shaky footing without him on this foreign shore and in this musky abode where it was not safe for unmarried women.

CHAPTER 23

*T*OGARMAH'S LODGE WAS DARK, THE FIRE LOW AND no one speaking when Madai was suddenly jumped from behind. He was too stunned for any kind of defense and it was too instantaneous to feel betrayed. The assailant was draped across Madai's back, arms tight around his chest... and laughing.

"Kessed!"

"You yap rat! We thought the sea dragons had you!" The young man quipped, letting him go. "Quiet, Kessed," Togarmah warned.

Madai's young friend chuckled. He wrapped his arm around Madai's shoulders again, gave him a shake, and ushered him forward, into the circle of men. They were no great number assembled, and mostly old. Madai inventoried the group: Togarmah, Tiras of course, Riphath the bear and his son (he was given such a name for the silver bear he had killed with a flint knife). There was Kessed – and Madai was more than a little surprised to see old Tiptri, not just that he was still alive but that he should share in such a group. Then there was Tiptri's son, Guran, doubly astounding, for these others were the most devoted to the first ways. Tiptri and Guran were father and brother to Yamma. And Yamma had led the way to new devotions. She was, as well, Madai's great shame.

"You must tell us what you found, Madai," Togarmah quietly insisted, with no perfunctory welcome.

"Not before I know what has happened here."

"In good time, my son," Ashkinaz replied, "but these men have been waiting a long time and in no little danger to know what you've discovered."

It was too late for so much mystery. But he knew the tone in his father's voice. It was the same as when he was a boy, the Little Hunter with blunted arrows in his quiver. So he began again to recount his tale as though Tiras and his Patta had not already heard it.

"I found the Ancient," he announced quickly. "The Nua himself, though it is said "Noah" in the East." He must admit that he did not grow weary of seeing their amazed expressions. "Yes," he affirmed. "Still alive. And I went to the top of Ararat, the greatest of peaks to come inside the very ark!"

Togarmah had to quiet the group at that, though they were small in number, for their astonishment.

Madai frowned. "What is this, Patta?" he insisted. "What are you hiding from? Why is your lodge out of its place?"

"There is a new order," Togarmah finally answered the question with the added ingredient of grit in his voice. "We who hold the first ways are... set aside."

"We have only waited for your return, my son," Ashkinaz interjected softly.

"Before we could separate ourselves," Tiras finished. He nodded grimly at his old friend, "We'd best be gone quick, now that you're back."

Madai felt the air snuffed out of Togarmah's already stuffy shelter. And though he had known that there was a thing greatly changed in the village, he could not have suspected the loss of The Council.

Here with such a revelation as he had to tell, it was too ironic. Whatever could have changed this life of theirs that had always remained the same steady rhythm of mammoth in winter and fish in summer? The stars held their alignments; their stories vouch-saved by the greatest of Ancients.

That the stony man, Togarmah, and his own Patta should be set aside was no small rearrangement. That they should speak of separating from the family, willingly flee the safety of numbers was inconceivable.

"What are we running from?" Madai asked.

"They've been waiting for you too," Ashkinaz answered mysteriously.

The assembled men held the same grim expressions as if they were one, at his Patta's statement.

"Who's waiting? The Banned?" They were Madai's old phantoms and all he could think of. "But they are burnt out."

"No, Madai," Tiras replied with an ominous voice, "the Nephilim."

The look on their faces was so tragic as to be nearly comical. Madai would actually have started to laugh if it were only Tiras telling him such a high tale. But there was Togarmah, and he entertained no humor at all.

"Why would you believe such a thing as that?" he had to ask.

"Because it is true, my son."

It was the worst possible answer, as it had been his father's who would not lie. "But..." he sputtered, "Nephilim are from the days of Nua."

"And here again," Togarmah assured him. "But, if you have talked to Nua, then perhaps you know how they can be fought against." ** Gen. 6:4

"Togarmah," Ashkinaz interjected. "It has been decided. We do not fight; we leave. Look at us, we are too few."

"And we are old," Tiptri added, which produced a chuckle from Madai's father even at so grim a matter.

"Wait!" Madai insisted. "Why do you think they are Nephilim?"

"Their shortest is ten feet tall, my son. Their tallest have six fingers on both hands."

"And powers," Tiras added.

"Perhaps that is a trick," Ashkinaz argued.

"Perhaps," Tiras conceded. But Madai could see his old friend did not believe it. "Two lads were hunting," he continued. "Only one returned to tell us…" Tiras stopped mid-sentence, seeming uneasy.

"Tell you what?"

"That they saw one of them," Tiras blurted, "outside the caves. He had the head of a bear!"

At that, Madai did laugh, though it must have been difficult for Tiras to repeat so ridiculous a tale. "You know scared boys can't be believed!"

"Scared boy, Madai. Only one came back."

Madai was quiet, feeling chastised and rightly so, for some mother's son would not come home. It had happened in his own family when his last live brother was killed. "Even still, the boy was scared." He persisted.

Tiras merely nodded, but there was a set to his eyes that told Madai he would not be shaken from the belief that a Nephilim stood some greater height than ten feet, lived in a cave and with the head of a bear. He had never known his friend to be fanciful nor superstitious.

"Where is this cave?"

"They live to the north, in the caverns there. And they are most interested in your quest, Madai," Tiras answered as if their interest in him should be another alarming piece of news. "Where did they come from? When? What do they want?"

"They want to live with us," Guran answered, speaking for the first time and causing Madai to turn. He bore a striking resemblance to Yamma.

"Do you remember, Madai," his father answered, "when I said that unmarried women are not safe here?"

"They were not safe here before the Nephilim!" Togarmah spat.

"Sit down, Madai. We will tell you everything."

Madai obeyed Tiras, finding it ironic indeed that the telling tonight would be to him and not from him. He would listen, but then he would reassure them all, for he had seen Nimrod fall and he had seen the power of God in the home of Noah… power to best Shinar's assassins, to travel the Brine Sea and to fell a dragon.

"The Nephilim were here this spring when we came into the valley from the shore," Tiras began. "Waiting, as if they expected us. They were living in the caves of the Fire Mountain and live there still."

It was a place Madai knew well, long supposed to be the source of the sulfur plains and feeding it a caustic brew. "A dangerous home…" he muttered.

Tiras shrugged. "It is said they ride the back of dragons," he offered as though to explain the daring of such living quarters.

Madai laughed. "Now I know your confidence is robbed by fear," he exclaimed. "No one may ride a dragon!"

"How do you know that?" Guran scoffed with just that trace of jealous pride to remind Madai he was indeed Yamma's brother.

"Dragons live in Shinar," Madai explained, "and they will not be ridden."

"It is no matter, Madai," Tiras continued. "What is known of them is terrible enough to believe what is said of them."

"What is known of them then?"

The men grumbled amongst themselves. "We have only spoken with two," Ashkinaz answered quietly, "and they have heads of men. They come … whenever they like. They bring messages from their leader and we cannot hunt as we did, leaving the women without a guard."

"They say they are interested in the Seed," Tiras continued with that edgy voice and Madai suspected he had been greatly worried over Kiellet, perhaps even little Naru. "They came to know the star stories from the Banned and the exacting site of our shore. They have been welcomed by Toban and the council of elders."

"The new council of elders," Ashkinaz gruffly corrected. "The old ways are no longer followed here."

"And the Nephilim are interested in what you found on your journey. "Tiras repeated.

"What new council?" Madai demanded.

"You do not know, Madai," Togarmah sneered, "But the virgin has been born a son. The Bowman lives among us now."

Old Tiptri was weeping.

"Yamma has born a child, my son. She was no man's wife."

"She was betrothed to Uke!" Madai argued, "And no virtuous maid."

"Uke was driven from among us, as you know, Madai, more than nine months before the child was born."

"You cannot believe she is the virgin of the stars!"

"Of course not, Madai," Tiras interjected. "But many do. We are the remains who stand against her." Madai looked at Guran, and at old Tiptri, unlikely rebels against their own sister and daughter.

"Remember, Madai," Guran offered as if to explain, "we know her."

Again, Madai felt a most inappropriate urge to laugh. It was a stunning audacity to claim herself The Virgin! But Yamma was not for humility. And she was champion of the forest spirits and temptress. Every lad had had his fancies for her, excepting perhaps Tiras.

But in the face of his coming home from such a journey! Yamma would have her own laugh over that.

With the old ways overthrown for the religion of the forest and the fabrication of a virgin birth – it was the same story Nimrod had spun! And, if there were Nephilim in the valley…

He stared aghast at their faces, knowing that he had returned none too soon. He had returned with the truth; a truth to save them. And… he could prove it.

"I will tell what I found on my journey," Madai assured them. "And set this all to right."

"What? That the prophecy of the stars is true?" Togarmah argued. "Yamma and Toban are in agreement.

There is not a man amongst us to claim the child. We know; we have searched out every lodge."

"Then the culprit will not confess," Madai reasoned. Togarmah shrugged. "Of course."

Madai stood up. He paced to the edge of Togarmah's lodge and back. "And the Nephilim?"

"They want what we know, they want what you have learned. They want to live amongst the people that have brought forth the Seed," Guran replied ironically.

"It is my belief, my son, that they are ridding the earth of virgins."

A silence fell upon the room, settling to the ground like winter air. The men's faces were stark, reflecting a fear for their virgin daughters.

"There was a maid," Ashkinaz continued grimly. "We think she was one of the Banned. She came to us from the Fire Mountain – with child. It was too big and she died with it still inside her."

Once again there was silence as if dread of this errant tribe had pursued them too long. "What did she tell you about the Nephilim?" Madai pressed.

"She could not speak," Ashkinaz said quietly, as if he would respect the memory of a mute girl. "There were markings on her body, Madai… past savagery. She had a wild look in her eye all the days she lived among us."

"The Banned are massacred," Madai suddenly told them. "O? We had not heard that."

"The Nephilim," Togarmah muttered.

"Now that you have returned," Tiras insisted, "We must leave this valley. We must leave tomorrow, if the Nephilim wiped out the Banned."

Madai looked at his friend, Tiras, who would brave a saber cat to bring his wife its heart; who hunted mammoth before his day of marking; who had always been the leader between them – the bravest and wisest.

"But I have the proof, Tiras. And the telling of the star stories from Nua himself! I must tell all the brothers. Then we will stand against these Nephilim!"

"Precisely so, Madai!" Togarmah agreed.

"But you have not seen them!" Tiras sounded as adamant as Togarmah.

"And you have seen only two of them. Perhaps they are the biggest two and you do not know their numbers… or their strengths?"

"You forget the new council, my son."

"They can be persuaded."

"Of what, Madai? They believe that Yamma has born the Bowman."

"Then you must tell the truth," Madai was glaring at Guran. "Tell them Yamma's ways. Tell them who is the child's father. She kept your father's lodge."

"We do not know who the father is," Guran growled. "There was Uke…"

"And what was done in the forest," Madai insisted.

Guran shrugged.

"Men will believe what they chose to believe," Ashkinaz reminded his son. "And now Yamma leads beside Toban."

Madai sat down again. He stared at the fire. His head sat heavy between his shoulders. "There is a Truth," he muttered, "and more powerful than these Nephilim."

He felt his father's hand on his shoulder. "You are tired, my son. This was too much to hear in one night. But Tiras is right. It is time to depart our brothers."

"They are brothers no more," Togarmah snorted.

CHAPTER 24

*I*T WAS DAWN. MADAI HAD PASSED AN ADVENTUROUS NIGHT OF dreams and restless sleep and he was being awakened by a racket. Coming out from the tent, he saw that a great amount of packing had been accomplished and he supposed that perhaps it had begun even as he came last night from Togarmah's lodge. It was then he recognized that these few, faithful to the old ways, had indeed been waiting, biding the time for his return before they would leave. There was a plan agreed to and already set to motion. Sledges were being loaded, mammoth hides pulled down and lodge poles tied together. Guran had old Tiptri tucked into his skiff already. It made Madai wonder about Guran's mother, though she had very likely died, having been almost blind and very old. He went back inside to put on his boots.

He was just pulling the cords tight when he heard an unmistakable voice. It sent his stomach plunging to his toes. Quickly he scanned the lodge with trepidation for he was suddenly afraid that Iscah might be witness to the meeting, as it was surely now upon him. But he was alone. He wondered briefly where she was, and Japhet, where his Mamam and Patta were, for his father had also been very late in coming home.

He heard his Mamam's voice then. "Madai is still asleep," she was protesting.

"He shall be glad to see me, good mother. He has sailed the sea, has he not, to find what the stars have to say? And here I am! The Answer, Mother of the gods!"

"There is One God," Madai heard Iscah's voice, very strident, "He Is, and with no beginning!"

So Iscah was just outside, and within earshot! Madai flung aside the skin, which covered his father's door at the very time Yamma came through it. The others tried to follow, but someone stopped them. Such an affront: to be stopped at one's own door! And then the flap dropped back down to close him in alone with her.

"Who is that, Madai?" were the first words from Yamma's mouth. "Another wife?"

He was struck dumb. Yamma was followed behind by Tiglath, the scout Madai had admired so long before.

She did not turn, but kept her eyes steady on Madai's face.

"I am quite safe here," she said. And when Tiglath did not leave, she told him to. Madai took a step back.

Her lips parted in a soft smile, "Another wife?" she asked again.

His mind raced to remember exactly what was said last night. Were unmarried women unsafe for cause of the Nephilim? He could not remember in this exacting moment with Yamma standing there, looking somewhat ordinary, at least beside what harbinger of shame she had become to him. She reached out, laid her palm on his chest and he knew then that she was not ordinary at all.

"You are happy to see me, then," she proclaimed quietly.

She still had a trick of rounding her eyes and looking quite innocent in her deerskins. He felt breathless, his heart beating too hard. It took him a moment to race back over all he had learned last night, not the least being her most spectacular of lies.

"You are no virgin of the stars," he proclaimed, hearing the choked sound of his voice. She laughed. "So you remember." She took a step forward. "I am full of power."

The announcement was so unexpected it took him aback. But here were her softly upturned lips, her blue eyes telling him she was full of power. She was always the most beautiful of maids and for a moment he remembered seeing her in the forest, the second look he had taken because she was so beautiful with painted skin and only eagle feathers for clothes. He could feel it again, here after everything he had learned. He could still feel that power; not just the lust of an adolescent boy, but the power itself... dreadful. He stepped quickly back again, as if he were burned.

"What power?" he demanded.

"Why, I lead beside Toban," she calmly replied as if it were so simple as that. "It is a good arrangement."

"The new religion?" he accused.

She sighed. "I had hoped you were not still the unlearned boy, Madai. You have seen Shinar, have you not?"

"What do you know about Shinar?"

"We are not so provincial as once we were," she crooned. "There are great ones among us now, have you heard?" She waited, then she turned her head slowly, admiring the tidiness of Mineo's lodge. "I know there was a council last night."

"The old council, you mean."

Yamma looked back at him with what he read to be a slight hurt in her eyes. "Surely you do not also resent me. Is that why they are leaving?"

Madai was again unsure. What had befuddled his thinking? Was it best to deny the plan to go, though surely it was plain. What reason should he give? Was it because of the Nephilim or the 'virgin birth'?

"No matter," she continued, sounding recovered. "They are old mouths to feed. I am happy to see Ashkinaz is not so unwise," she looked again at his parent's belongings, yet to be packed. "Or, perhaps that is your doing."

"I hold no sway here," he managed to mutter.

"No? They begrudge me, you know," she continued. "After so long a wait for the Bowman; you would think they would be grateful."

"Your child is no Bowman, Yamma. We both know that."

As if she had waited for the moment, she turned to take a graceful step toward him. Her eyes were no innocent pools of blue now. He watched her take a moment, slowly stroking a long yellow braid that trailed down her breast. "Would you like to see him, Madai?" she finally asked.

"Why should I?"

Yamma put her fingers softly against his chest. "Because he is yours," she replied.

MADAI'S EARS WERE BUZZING; HIS KNEES LOCKED IN PLACE. HE FELT as if he were the weight of a mountain. All the lodge was a blur, all but Yamma. He knew she could see his own face going white. She took a step closer even as he could not move being rooted in place by the wicked mirth of her glittering eyes. And suddenly his Patta's lodge was swarmed by a presence most palpable. It found home in her slight body. He watched as she wrenched slightly to the side and bottomless depths reached her eyes. He stumbled. She smiled.

Netted by such a huntsman, he did not hear the commotion outside. But Iscah rushed into the lodge at that very moment and with the turbulence of a thunderstorm. Madai was stunned, astonished to see her at such a moment, in such an atmosphere. Tiglath and Mineo chased behind her, Mineo shushing and grabbing for her arms; Tiglath trying to stop them both. But Iscah, stirred by a passion, would not be stopped. It allowed Simirra, for all the confusion and of all unlikely souls, to wrestle her way between Yamma and Iscah and whatever confrontation was doubtless upon them.

Madai was all but paralyzed; it had happened so quickly and at last. His Mamam and Iscah had both heard the revealing of his infamy, and they would surely be struck down by Yamma's terrible power. Still he could not move, could scarcely breathe and Yamma knew it. She was looking at him as if they were alone, only their two souls swimming together in an air thick with her dark lord. In her eyes there was a glimpse, an unveiling of under-worldly secrets.

"Madai!" Iscah cried. "What is she doing here? This is your father's tent! Don't you know what she's done?"

Madai's heart was pounding as he made a choking sound, more a gasp.

"Hush, Iscah," Simirra demanded sounding uncommonly concerned as if she too knew what powers were at play.

"Guran has told us everything!" Iscah declared fiercely.

Yamma peeled her eyes from Madai's face. It was as though a thorn were removed. "What do you mean?" She asked Iscah with an icy voice.

Even still, with her gaze turned aside, Madai's head was a-buzz as with a thousand angry bees. Could they not feel her? And yet Iscah stood against her, un-assailed.

"Your mother!" Iscah accused. "What you did to your poor blind mother!"

Yamma turned ever slowly back at Madai. "They are unruly, your wives," she hissed. "You may be released of them… if you like."

"We are obedient and strong!" Madai heard Simirra protest.

It was an announcement that seemed to amuse Yamma. She wet her lip, not unlike a serpent.

That was when a scene came before Madai's eyes. It filled the lodge with a keener substance than flesh and bone and he was immediately set free of Yamma's hold. He was not disoriented, but simply removed, as though this lodge were made less real by the vision. He might have been there again, standing witness to the death of Shinar assassins who were, all five of them, frozen in the forest by an early blizzard. They had come with their spells and arrows and malice to stop the voice of Noah. Unseasonable snows had stopped them – as loud as any proclamation. It had been the witness of God's Strong Arm.

As quick as it came, the image was gone and he was in his father's lodge again, seeing Yamma instantly diminished. Simirra brushed past her then and actually put her hand on Madai's arm. She patted her own belly with a kind of satisfaction.

"And we are loved," she insisted, intimating a lie of her own. Passions ticked across Yamma's face.

"No," Madai replied evenly, "I will not be released of them. I will keep them."

There was a visible contorting in Yamma, uncontrolled fury making ruin of a once lovely face. "But, will they keep you?" she threatened. She whirled around, facing Iscah and Mineo. He watched her bite back the truth of her own child, because, as he suddenly realized, she could not confess it and remain the virgin mother.

He should have been glad.

He watched Yamma fling aside the hide door with a flourish. He did not see her actually leave, as there was Iscah's face now, commanding all his attention. She looked so willful, so triumphant and righteous, having exposed some dreadful deed of Yamma's. There was a brief moment when he felt ablaze with pride for her. However short-lived, it was intense and made the facts of the matter all the more terrible.

Yamma was no virgin ruler, hers no star child. It was the truth to set all the Family back to the One True God. It would save their numbers, numbers enough to stand against the Nephilim. But if Yamma had given him the weapon of truth to unseat herself, she had, as certainly, wielded the deathblow to all his hopes of Iscah. And what, O what could he ever tell Japhet?

CHAPTER 25

O N THE QUICK HEELS OF SUCH REVELATION, THERE
came across the camp outside, a hush. Madai was suddenly
aware that all the bustle which produced the noise of busyness,
had gone silent. He heard the crying out of an old man, all that broke the sudden and unnatural quiet. He rushed outside.

He passed Yamma as though she were no consequence at all, but was stopped by such a sight! There stood a creature of enormous height and odor. It stood in shadow with its great bulk blocking the sun. It stepped sideways and into Madai's path. It was a man – of sorts. He bettered ten feet and was most woolly. His parts were all that were covered, and them by a hide of bear. The creature's own head had such an appearance as the bearskin, with hair somewhat rusty in color. Planted upon that was a second head – the most enormous rack and skull of a great red stag. The antlers of the stag tilted slightly forward, filed to sharp points, when the creature lowered his face to inspect Madai. His hand, indeed appendaged with six fingers, had tumbled over a sledge. Old Tiptri, still strapped inside, was pinned, cheek against the rocks.

"You are Madai?" the creature actually roared.

Behind him was another like him; taller, in fact, and wearing the head of a bison. The horns of this shaggy ox arced very wide, like a tree's great branches. The fact that they were not some sort of beast-man did nothing to comfort Madai at the first shock of his seeing them. They towered above the Family by quite more than a head and filled the air with a stench.

"We have been waiting for you," the second Nephilim bellowed.

Ashkinaz emerged from the crowd. He came to the sledge; directly in front of the man wearing the red stag.

"He is old," Ashkinaz protested, turning his face upward so to see the creature in the eye. "Let him up."

Madai stepped forward to add another against the giant, for his Patta had never looked so small, nor so righteous.

The Nephilim sneered. He removed his six-fingered hand. "That is your weakness, Ashkinaz."

The very name of his father sounded grotesque to Madai, being uttered by such a mouth. And it was too terrible that they should be so familiar as to know his Patta's name.

"And yours, Malak, that you have no pity," Ashkinaz retorted.

The giant, Malak, slowly pulled back on the sledge. Madai heard its leather bindings creak as it was set upright by only the hand of this Nephilim. Tiptri fumbled with what was lashing him to the sledge and attempted to pull himself out. Madai took him under the arms and the old man was freed. There was quite a look on Tiptri's face. Madai would have expected terror, but the sinewy little man stood as straight as his bent shoulders would permit.

That Tiptri stood to defy the giant was an act of courage, which provoked a kind of guttural response from Malak, perhaps a terrible laugh. For Madai, it was confirmation that all the truth was owed to such men of The Family who could find courage, even old Tiptri, to stand against these creatures. Madai knew that he had hardly a choice but to claim Yamma's child.

"Lord Malak."

It was Yamma. Madai heard her approach from behind. She pushed around him and came to stand directly in front of the giant.

The Nephilim ran his eyes across her.

"You will come to our feast in three days' time?" She asked in a pretty voice. "We shall receive our brother, Madai, home with a grand style." She seemed quite confident before the man, Malak, standing near him yet far below his chin. "You and your tribe are very welcome. We shall learn together what was discovered in Shinar."

There came the same rumble from Malak's mouth and Madai was certain now that it was a beastly laughter, for there could be no more ludicrous display than Yamma's tidy invitation. Malak shook his head, the way the stag does to display its spread of antlers; not a refusal, but a marking of territory.

"You will not leave, Ashkinaz, not before Naphal sees this pup of yours." Malak barked, tipping his head at Madai, "And he is tired of this waiting. Tonight – have the feast tonight and with plenty enough to eat." he demanded of Yamma.

A slight frown arched above her eyes. "Of course," she replied calmly. "I would not have you hungry. But for that we need three days. And," she added, "It will take that long for the beer. The nights are colder."

Malak grunted. His eyes flitted across Togarmah's sledges, upright and set to be burdened down with sundries. Madai watched him calculating, weighing perhaps the luxury of good beer. "Arba will stay," he announced abruptly. "No one of you will try to leave."

If Yamma found it an unsavory demand, it did not show. Instead, she smiled at the bison-crowned Nephilim with just enough deference to produce in Malak another of his rumblings. Arba actually licked his lips.

"Three days," Malak grumbled. He surveyed the tops of their heads. He seemed to inventory their lodges, their campfires, their children hugging tight to mother's legs.

Madai watched him slowly turn away then with a confidence that more than equaled his size. His back was broad as a five stone spear and had the look of a boar, down to the ridge of hair that ran down his spine. The length of his stride was very great and made the speed of his departure quite amazing, though at a walk. Men of the Family that Madai knew very well to be brave, stood deadly still.

Yamma expelled a long breath. "Tiglath," she said stiffly. "The Lord Arba shall keep in your lodge whilst he is among us. Lord Arba," she nodded at the giant.

He rubbed himself with the sort of dedication as a bear with fleas. Then he shoved past Tiglath in the direction of Yamma's lodge like a proprietary buck. Madai watched her blanch white. It was the first time he had ever seen such a thing in her as this cold, authentic fear.

"Get the child!" she hissed at Tiglath.

Arba passed a stew pot along the way to Yamma's shelter. He bent over it and sniffed. Then he took it off the coals with one large hand. The woman whose ill fortune it had been to cook, shrank away. He considered her a moment, but seemed to find the food more appealing. He squatted right down in front of the fire, fishing out hunks of meat with his fingers.

Mineo shuttled Iscah and Simirra into their lodge even as the Family's females all seemed to do the same – all but Yamma. Tiglath snatched past Arba with an astonishing obedience and returned with a squirming bundle. The giant hardly noticed, occupied with his tasty pot of stew.

MADAI WATCHED THE NEPHILIM, MALAK, DISAPPEAR

into the trees. There was heavy silence to fill the space he had left behind. Madai put his hand on Tiptri's sledge, disguising even from himself that it was to steady the thrashing in his chest.

"How many are they?" he whispered only when the stench of Nephilim started to fade.

"We have seen just those two," Ashkinaz replied, "and others on the mountain. But we do not know their exact number."

"Perhaps they are not so many, then."

"They were using the Banned to breed," Togarmah interjected somewhat heartlessly, reminding Madai of the mute woman.

"And still you know their names?" Madai hissed.

Togarmah's jaw clenched at the charge.

"Who is Naphal?" Madai pressed, leaning in.

Ashkinaz shook his head. "He is their chief elder. They speak of him as a god but we have never seen him."

As if on cue, the Family's chief elder, Toban, stepped forward, a blanched face among many. He emerged from the little group that had stood at a distance from Tiptri's sledge. Madai turned his disgust at him. "Why have you let them stay?"

"What could we do?" Toban complained. "You see them…"

"But if you knew what they were…"

"They are Nephilim, my son," his Patta interjected. "And we shall leave them this valley."

Toban looked surprised. "Leave us, Ashkinaz? But you will diminish our own numbers!" Toban's voice was steadily rising. "I would not think that of you."

"You do not keep the first ways, my old friend," Ashkinaz replied sadly.

"I've been watching for the Seed, as have you, Ashkinaz. How can you say we do not keep the first ways?"

Yamma actually put herself between the two elders. "Your squabbles will wait," she demanded. "We have just three days to ready a feast."

"You should not have involved Malak!" Ashkinaz charged.

"You know he has been waiting for Madai." Toban countered. "He would be here, invited or not. And you will not leave us."

"You're both afraid!" Yamma scoffed. "Malak and Naphal are also seeking the Promised Seed as well as we. And…that one is born among us!"

HEARING HER AND SEEING HER, MADAI WAS ASTONISHED that she had ever held him in such a grip only in this last hour. Perhaps he would let Yamma rule her pack of believers and simply carry on with his Patta's plan to leave. But even as he thought it, he knew that like a man fighting the currents of a spring flood, he must lay bare the lie. And they must defeat the Nephilim. If the Nephilim waited for the Promised Seed it was not for good, of that he was certain.

He stared at Yamma's lodge, where Arba with his bison skull had disappeared. This homecoming, so long awaited, was too terrible and changed from what he had hoped. Stiffly he forced his body to pivot away and looked at the far hills. In that direction lay the path to the sea, the meadow where he had passed a pleasant time with Iscah. A sudden and unmanly urge to weep came upon him. Surely, there had been too much revealed.

He needed a place to ponder; he needed the time to ponder; he needed Kittim. "There are boar feeding at the Knuckle," Tiglath was saying.

Yamma scarcely acknowledged the scout "Get them then," she ordered.

CHAPTER 26

*I*SCAH WAITED FOR HER EYES TO ADJUST TO THE DIM interior of the lodge. She was still shaken by the sight of the two Nephilim. They were creatures only spoken of in whispers; dark sons of spectres, all such tales as she did not truly believe; but she was shaking anyway.

"They are only men," she told herself, hardly more terrible than the Anak who had killed and sacked Tutan's caravan though these giants did wear antlers and she could not miss the six fingers.

She sat heavily on a bench beside the fire. She knew it should be no surprise that there lived evil men here as well as Shinar, but she had hoped Madai's telling of his shores had been more… accurate.

Because there was also what she had learned about Yamma. It was a villainous deed to cast out a blind, aged mother. The woman had died in one night in the cold whilst husband and son had been on a hunt. It was surely as terrible as great giants wearing horns. She rested her chin in her hands and closed her eyes, suddenly very lonely for her own lost mother.

She heard Mineo rustling about and looked up. How did she fair, having watched her son and husband stand against the giant? Madai's mother was first poking at the fire, then retrieving earthen cups from a corner as if it was any morning. But when she reached the cup toward Iscah, her hand had a bit of tremble.

"I still have water for tea," she said quietly. "I do have honey as well. It's in that pot." Iscah went to get it, a willing partner in Mineo's quiet charade.

"It is fortunate I was not packed up," Mineo continued. "I was letting Madai sleep."

Iscah could not help but see the mother blush. "He is my last son," Mineo explained. "He was with Togarmah and the council very late…"

Iscah extended her cup and watched Mineo fill it with steaming water, as artful as Job's Lady. She watched the rustic woman take up dried herbs from another jar and drop them in her cup of hot water. There was an ant swimming with the tealeaves. Iscah picked it out. It may not once have bothered, sharing tea with an ant, but she would not risk drinking it. She watched Mineo fill Simirra's cup, touching the hot brew to her own lips. It was good, tasting of rosehips.

"Do you like it?" Mineo asked. "It is bloom of fireweed."

"Thank you, Mineo," Simirra offered. "It is as good as any tea I have tasted."

"Yes," Iscah affirmed. It was all she could manage and was grateful that Simirra knew how to act when surrounded by all things terrible. But they drank in silence after that.

She wondered where Madai's little boy had gotten. He was scooted through the door at the very moment by a hand, most likely Madai's, and with a good deal of protest.

"Japhet," Mineo crooned. "Come be with us and obey your Patta."

He flashed a look at his Grand Mamam that reminded Iscah of Madai being stubborn. "Go get your bow then," she conceded, "and play on your mat."

They watched him put one stiff step in front of the other and sit cross-leg on his mat. He had a stormy look on his face and gripped his little fingers as if to say he would only play if he wanted to. Iscah hid her smile with another sip of tea, thinking how simple was the world to a child. When he sneaked his hand across the fox fur mat to find his bow she nearly choked.

"Come, let me show you something," Mineo said, carefully ignoring the child.

She unfolded a small woolen blanket then. It was mostly grey, but with a pattern across it in dots of white.

Simirra put her cup down and ran her hands over them.

"This is the last weaving Ido finished," Mineo said in a hushed voice. "She was Madai's wife. She was a good wife."

Iscah looked at the blanket. It was perfectly square. It was the first organic remnant of Madai's wife, save his little boy, of course.

"We are neither one his wife," Simirra blurted.

Mineo nodded with a slight smile. "I thought as much," she said, studying them both. "When my son marries again, it will be for love." She touched the nubby blanket affectionately. "Not all men do, you know. Some marry for sons, some for the nights. But Madai will marry for love." She pressed her eyes into each of their faces with importance.

"It is the constellation of The Virgin," she finally continued. "Ido wove it while waiting to marry him. She was young and…nervous. But she loved him very much in the end."

Iscah watched Mineo's eyes water, in wonder that she could be thinking about such things when there were Nephilim about. But she reached out to cover Mineo's hand with her own. It was her own offering, having admired Simirra's manners a moment before.

"It is a well woven blanket," she affirmed.

Mineo folded it again. "Ido died before she could finish another."

Simirra looked at the door. "What will we do about them?" she asked uneasily, and mindful of the boy playing in the shadows.

The tone and the question seemed enough to bring Mineo back to the moment. "The Nephilim?" she asked. "Well, we will leave. It's been decided. Though I do not think it will be so easy. I think Togarmah is right. I think it will take a fight." This last she whispered.

"Surely you cannot win against them," Simirra whispered back. "They are quite terrible – sons of the gods."

"They are ordinary men, child," Mineo answered kindly. "Just very evil and … big."

Simirra opened her mouth to argue but seemed to think better of it. Iscah knew the stories too, that Nephilim before the days of the deluge were sons of the dark ones come upon the earth. But she was already decided on that. No, she had seen plenty of human kind quite capable of things most terrible.

"They can be beaten," she insisted. "I saw Madai and Kittim beat a company of bandits, the Anak, every bit as big as Nephilim."

"Patta can do it," Japhet suddenly chirped, looking up at the women.

SIMIRRA LOOKED AT THE BOY, WISHING SHE COULD TRUST so well; even as the two women, both innocent in the ways of the world. She took another drink of her tea, which had gone cold and knew she could not argue with the child in the tent. Besides, Mineo was a kind woman and Iscah little more than a child, herself. Perhaps if Arphaxas had not deserted them they might have a chance. He could wield a scimitar like a devil. It would take a devil, after all, to beat one.

CHAPTER 27

*I*SCAH FOUND MADAI SITTING IN A FIELD OF FIRE-
weed. As she had seen him watch the waves of the sea, he was watching crimson blooms sway in the wind. She had left Simirra with Mineo,
both coaxing Japhet to wait inside for his father's return. Simirra seemed to
have an affection for the boy, which Iscah could well understand.

She stood quietly behind him, pondering. She remembered the way he
looked just this morning, in his mother's lodge with that Yamma woman. Iscah
had seen him being owl-eyed and then... shorn up somehow. Like a willow
staked to the ground in a windstorm, he had withstood her. It was with an
authority Iscah had not seen before in him.

He had stood against Malak also, with his father, to defend an exceedingly
bony old man. Why then, was he so troubled? What had driven him to this
meadow? She had never known him to be a coward, so it was not fear.

"I thought you might be going so far as the sea," she said gently. Madai
turned with surprise. "Iscah?"

"We are almost back to the cave," she said. She came up beside him and
carefully sat down, sharing the rock he was sitting on. "It is easier done without your behemoth stone."

She would have expected him to smile at that, but he looked away instead.
"Your little boy is very beautiful,' she tried.

"He looks like his Mamam."

His answer was quiet. Never had he seemed so distant. Perhaps the smells
of home had put flesh to Ido's bones again and broke his heart afresh. She
looked down at the flowers and pulled at a thick stem. Its petals tumbled off,
leaving behind just the tiny scarlet framework they had been attached to.

"It's autumn," he said, looking down at the blooms piled up at the base of
the stalk. "When all the petals fall, it will snow."

"Well, they are wondrous now."

He nodded and looked away again.

"You are glooming," Iscah said softly.

"I would like it if Kittim were here."

They were words to steal her breath away, but there did not follow that unwieldy inclination to tears, which was a relief and yet a surprise. She did not like the wrinkles that crossed Madai's forehead like furrows in one of Job's fields.

"What troubles you so, Madai?" she asked.

He was staring at the shed pile of crimson. "We've come so far," he muttered. "I tell you, Iscah, I cannot see it happen."

"What do you mean?"

"What was said by Job. That Holy God would come upon this earth to walk with us, as He walked with Adam...Noah's first earth, it sounded very... wondrous."

She would have smiled at his use of her oft-used word, but for the angst she could see on his face. "O," she replied. She found herself staring at the denuded fireweed herself. "Make us holy," she mused. "What you asked Kittim."

"Yes," he looked up. His eyes had a searching, troubled look about them. "And what was said by Enoch, that 'the Lord comes with multitudes of His holy ones'.* *Jude vs. 14 It would be a great triumph, but I can hardly believe it." He looked at his hands. "We were proud to be called The Family... coming from the scattering with our songs, our knowledge of Mighty God, His Bowman." Madai stopped. He looked across the meadow again. "We are no better holy than Nimrod and his court."

"Men will always be men," she affirmed quietly. "How are you surprised?"

"But I am! Who does not want to know the truth?"

She patted his hand kindly. "Madai, you must remember what Kittim said. Men will eat and sleep and worship gods. He will serve the god that serves him best."

"So men do not love truth?"

"Only the best of men do." she answered.

He was quiet a moment before he muttered, "Job said that there were none innocent."

She squeezed her fingers around his hand. "I did not say 'innocent'."

He did not reply to that, but his face turned a ruddier shade.

She could not know the matter of Yamma and her son. She could see Madai's face grow red, but could not know it was for his shame, and fear that her mercies would not survive his confessions. She also did not feel what he felt at that moment – the gap between a standard set and a standard lived out.

"Why did I travel so far then?"

"O Madai!" she quipped abruptly. "Will there always be a 'why' when the answer is so simple? You went to find truth for yourself. You went to discover Tutan and take him to Job where he would marry Reenah and be happy. You went to meet Kittim and to rescue me." She smiled. "You went for that wretched bone!"

She watched the thick vein in his neck pulsing, slowing and finally disappearing. He breathed out slowly and turned around to look at her. There was yet a worry on his face, but the furrows above his brows gradually smoothed, replaced by a crinkle starting at each his eyes.

"That is an important bone," he replied.

"So it is," she agreed. She shifted her seating and folded her hands on her knees. "Now what will you do about the Nephilim?"

Which appeared to startle him and produced the modicum of a smile. He scratched his beard. "I don't know," he replied. "I don't know what they want."

"Well, it is not to learn the truth!"

"No."

"Trickery," she continued. "Kittim would say so too. Let us think. What do you know about them?"

"Only fearsome stories, Iscah."

"Well, there was also such a giant in Shinar," she said, matter-of-factly. "I saw him once, the very night the Sabeans… took me. The Sabeans, who were great fierce men themselves, gave him bags of gold to pass his territory, which was full of date palms and I was very hungry. He had a harem of women and I was actually glad it was the Sabeans that got me. I would say he was bigger than that one in your camp, but I was scared and… little."

"Why didn't you tell me that before?"

"You think you know so much about me, Madai, you and Kittim! Well, you would be surprised!"

Madai laughed. It was a welcome response.

"So, if they do not want the truth," he asked, "what do they want?"

He watched a flicker pass across her face. "It seems rather clear to me," she answered, "if unmarried women are not safe."

It shocked him that she could say it so easy, knowing what was done her. He felt his stomach clench up, and hoped it did not show on his face.

"But why should they care if the women are married or not?"

"Virgins," she answered, sounding experienced. "They always want virgins."

It was blunt, too blunt to stop his face going red again. It was not for the obvious, as Madai did not see an innocent in himself. It was for her, and that she was blameless. She did not even seem to resent his bringing it up. He stared at her a moment longer, long enough for the wind to undo him with the way it blew one curl across her eyes.

He looked away.

"Why did they always want virgins?" he wondered angrily.

He was first angry for Iscah, then for the slave girls on the temple steps of En-Utu-Aten. He was angry for the little maids that Nimrod had deflowered, a monster always wanting younger flesh. He had reasoned first that it was for the malady which whores carried with them. But that was a cold reasoning, one that forgot the maidens. He shook his head to clear it, to ponder the question with calculation.

There was also Nimrod's ruse…

His eyes came wide. "They all want to father the Promised One!" He cried.

"Not quite, Madai," she corrected evenly, calmly as if she had known it all along. "They want to prevent the Promised One."

And, like a bolt from a stormy sky, it was suddenly clear.

They looked at each other, neither speaking, each knowing she had spoken the truth.

CHAPTER 28

*I*SCAH NODDED ONCE. WITH A REASONED LOOK, SHE proclaimed. "You will just have to kill them."

The words seemed to bounce off her lips and across the meadow fluttering with fireweed. How simple she made it sound.

"We could use Kittim," Madai muttered.

"You have Togarmah."

It was the way she said it, as though he could set the world a-right. "Iscah," he began…at which she leapt up.

"Let's go to the Fire Mountain!" she cried. "They won't expect it. We will see how many there are and…"

"No! I would never take you there."

"But, we are so near it and you are very good at sneaking about."

"I could never endanger you."

"Do you think I am safe in that skin tent of yours?" she demanded. "I can be the rear guard."

"I brought no weapon."

"Well, that was foolish! What about your saber cat? Did you think about that?"

And things were again as they always had been between them. But she made him want to laugh, even now, pondering a risky, ridiculous scheme.

"I'll take Tiras," he argued. "Later."

"He has his child, and his wife, Madai. What do we have?"

"Japhet," Madai argued.

"Well, you will not have him long if the Nephilim burn you out as they did the Banned. And he will not have you. No, there is no better way. I will not simply wait to be stolen again and I have no one to…"

"Do not say you have no one, Iscah," he warned.

"We can wait till dark then," she persisted, ignoring him. "We will see what we can…"

He shook his head. "No. I will not risk you."

He stood up, tromping on a near spike of blooms. "You are…" If he allowed himself, it could spill out just as the petals had tumbled off their stalk. But he held his tongue and looked down at her. She still had that gritty look in her eyes: tenacity, blind optimism.

"You were so little in that cloak," he mused abruptly, "all eyes and riotous hair. But you always kept up, and talked a lot. Then you cured me when the Anak cut me with that poisoned blade, and found something wondrous all along the way. I'm sorry we didn't let you explore the crystal cave… but we did watch the rainbows in the waterfall at the Pishon… we saw them, you and I, before anyone else. And," he forced himself to keep his eyes on hers, "and then you grew up."

She was turning white.

"I don't want to scare you," he added hastily, leaning down to touch her arm lightly. "I only want…" He let his fingers gently close. "I only want to…" he paused. He took tender hold of her other arm, "Iscah," he began again, holding her at arm's length and square in front of himself, "I loved a girl once. I loved her very well and when she died, it was like I was on… trying to stand in the sea when the tide pulls the sand from under your feet. Not a thing I knew as true… was.

"But I have my footing back," he whispered. "And you helped… Even now." He could no longer read her eyes, but he had come too far.

"I wish you would let me love you," he finished quietly, feeling the words roll off his lips like water in a spring's rushing stream.

She was looking grave. Then she reached up to pat his hand. "Madai," her voice sounded scratchy. "It has been too much, with the Nephilim… you are…"

"I loved you when we were still with Job," he interrupted. He thought he saw her flinch at that.

HE WAS LOOKING AT HER WITH SO MUCH SHOWING IN his eyes. It was a preposterous cruelty. Where there was this wealth of pining after Kittim, there had been no time for, nor the slightest contemplating of Madai. But she could not say, in honesty, that his speech had not pleased her in some part.

He had talked about their journey… and happenings that kept a singular place in her memory as well. She remembered waiting those many long months for them to return, when Kittim and Madai had left her behind to seek the Ark. It was Madai who had come to find her when they returned, and to him that she had yelped with glad surprise. He was the one that came into the Anak camp, and carried her flung across his shoulder to safety. He had persuaded Kittim to bring her when Kittim would have left her a last time with Job. She was aghast, a prickle running down her arms. Was it always Madai; never Kittim?

She tried to envision it. But Kittim was so imponderable and Madai so… ordinary. It was a glimpse of herself to be ashamed of, if she looked too close.

"Say something," he whispered.

His fingers had tightened on her arms. He seemed quite stoic now, somewhat tragic and noble. How full he was of paradox: one moment bewildered, the next defiant and then casting open all his improbable... love. How could it be?

"But," she whispered, scarcely audible, "A father would not take me for even... twenty goats."

Madai laughed outright and she could see him greatly relieved. Well, she was not relieved and how could he be laughing? Then she felt herself lifted up off the rock, pulled into his chest where her nose buried in the end of his beard. He was kissing the top of her head and she did not know how it had happened.

"You are worth all the goats of Job!" he exclaimed.

She wondered, at hearing that, if Tutan had not said something of more charm to Reenah when he had declared his love. But that was a ridiculous thing to think about, as it was she who had brought up the goats. And why should it matter anyway? She had been misunderstood.

"Put me down, Madai," she insisted, both against his chin hairs and arms too tight around her.

"I only meant..." and now she had gone too far to stop. But he put her down and was wearing a beautiful smile. "I am... "she blinked back the tears that had not as yet surfaced, even at the name of 'Kittim'. "I have been... ransacked," she forced herself to finish. But she would not force herself to look at him while she said it, and had turned completely away. "So, you see... the twenty goats."

She felt his hands on her arms again. "I would take it all away, if I could," he said. "But – and I say this on oath, Iscah – you are the more beautiful for it."

She could not have heard properly. But then, Madai had always been the last to understand a simple fact.

She felt herself slowly turned around. He did not look confused. He looked, in fact, ardent. "Beautiful," he repeated.

"Madai!" she sputtered, literally shaking herself free of his hands. "You always do surprise me!"

He kissed her, wrapped her in his arms again and kissed her! His whiskers scratched. And then he let her go.

"Will you be set apart for me?" he asked.

"What?"

"Wed me, Iscah."

"But, I do not love you."

"You do," he assured her – again that beautiful smile. "You do."

"But, there are Nephilim..."

It was the last thing she said before Madai was grabbed from behind and made utterly defenseless.

CHAPTER 29

*T*HEY WERE IN A TANGLE. MADAI FELT HIMSELF toppled sideways, Iscah still in his arms. Together, they were shoved behind a boulder and into thorny brambles by someone very large. Iscah was stuffed up under him – everything dark now, their assailant blocking out the light with his body. But Madai could see, from the corner of his eye, the scuffed scales of a dragon cape.

"Be quiet!"

"Arphaxas?"

"Be quiet! They're just behind me!"

Madai was finding it difficult to be quiet. He could only breathe in short gasps and didn't know how Iscah could breathe at all. But, now that he was listening he could hear cracking branches in the forest – not stealthy hunting – and a feral squeal of swine. It was alarming how insensible he had been, preoccupied and reckless.

Arphaxas held them against the brambles a good while after the noise of giants chasing prey had passed.

Iscah came up gasping and pure white.

"Arphaxas! Where did you come from?" she cried, and "God be praised, how close they were! What would they have done?"

But Arphaxas's eyes were set on Madai. "Iscah should not be out here!" he scolded in a rough, hushed voice.

"What are you doing here?" Madai charged with a similar tone.

"Roaming."

They glared at each other though Madai was first to yield. "Where have you been?"

Arphaxas scratched his head and looked at the forest where the Nephilim had been after the boar.

He was standing spread legged and listening as if he were not gone these many days, looking fit and fed. Madai was not surprised.

"Iscah is not safe when they are near," was all Arphaxas answered. "Let's get out of this clearing."

ONCE IN THE COVER OF FOREST, ARPHAXAS EXPLAINED simply, "They plan to wipe you out."

"As they did the camp of the Banned," Madai agreed. "I can only praise Mighty God that they have waited this long."

"They have been waiting for you, kinsman. The Banned knew your quest from one of your own; Uke he was called. The Nephilim learned that you had sailed to Shinar from them and... "

Madai frowned, suddenly suspicious. "How do you know all this?"

Arphaxas laughed. "So, now you think I am a spy! No, kinsman, even I would not ally with them." His expression quickly changed. "The Nephilim are not... ordinary men. No. But after I left you, I stumbled across an old... friend."

Madai went suddenly cold, launched after by an unreasonable fear. Had Arphaxas somehow talked to Yamma? Did he know about the babe and did she know things about the Nephilim? But Arphaxas did not seem, at the moment, vengeful; instead, he was somewhat reluctant, glancing cautiously at Iscah.

"I am quite prepared to hear the worst, Arphaxas," Iscah proclaimed. "Madai and I were just discussing how best to kill the Nephilim ourselves."

A sardonic smile parted Arphaxas's lips and Iscah blushed. "And what sort of 'not ordinary' are they?" she finished, squaring her shoulders against the impact of a red face.

"It is said that Nephilim are sons of spectres," he replied, looking at Madai, "and should be kept apart from maids of men."

"Where did you hear such ridiculous tales, Arphaxas?" Madai quipped.

"Do not mock what you do not know."

"Shinar?" Madai pressed. "Did you hear it in Shinar? You know how superstitious they are!"

"Nephilim have a great power."

"They are ten feet tall! Of course they're strong!"

"I did not say only strong."

"Don't talk madness, Arphaxas. It is facts I need to know – what they're after."

"Beyond burning camps?"

"Spectres will not be flesh," Iscah suddenly asserted, and Arphaxas stopped. He looked from Madai to Iscah, waited a moment and shrugged.

"It was Admah," he said abruptly, "the captain of Semiramis's army. Remember him?"

"Of course. He is the old friend?"

Arphaxas nodded. "Well, they'd taken his eyes."

Madai heard Iscah gasp. "They killed him?" she whispered.

Arphaxas looked at her again with the same censored expression. "I found him stumbling about. And," he continued, "I took care of him. He talked before..."

"He died?" she asked.

Arphaxas looked suddenly uneasy. He actually shuffled his feet in the leaves and shrugged.

Watching the little drama between them, Madai was amazed. He would never have suspected Arphaxas capable of... delicacy, but he had shown it in speaking to Iscah and Madai felt a sudden and ridiculous rush of jealousy.

"What did Admah say?" Madai asked abruptly.

It took Arphaxas a moment to turn and with no remains of kindness showing. "That they will kill all The Family," he replied evenly, "except the strongest maids. They will leave behind no virgins. You should take her away from here, Madai."

Silence followed that announcement.

"Why were they waiting for Madai?" Iscah asked.

Arphaxas turned his head slowly, waiting a moment before he answered. "They hate the Promised Seed," he replied simply.

"But what..."

"They will stop Him being born."

"But they cannot know..."

Arphaxas held up his hand to stop her question. He pulled the hood of his dragon cape over his hair, which was being blown by a growing wind. "It will be dark," he said. "If you will not bring Iscah away and come with me, you should go back now."

"O! But you will come with us!" Iscah argued. "Simirra will be glad you are safe. She was sorely vexed for you, Arphaxas, when you left."

He croaked out a bitter laugh. "You are the innocent, Iscah!"

"She will come with me," Madai proclaimed. "And there is one of them in camp," he continued, speaking of Malak's guard. "I'd like to hear what you know now. Here."

"He will come with us, Madai." Iscah insisted. "And tell everyone."

THE WIND HAD WHIPPED UP QUITE STRONG AND DARK had fallen quickly as Arphaxas had warned, which was in itself an added irritation. Madai would not have brought him here at all had Iscah not refused to budge without him. That Togarmah was now glaring suspiciously both validated Madai's position and satisfied his ego. And though his father's lodge was one of the largest, it had become quite close with the old council assembled inside.

Arphaxas had been a surprise to them. Indeed, too many strangers at a time starved of trust. Ashkinaz and Togarmah both remembered him as a red haired boy, he and a sister. They remembered his Patta and Mamam those years ago, run off with the Banned. And that was not a helpful recommendation.

"I knew him in Shinar," Madai explained. "He was a captive."

"And one of the Banned."

"As a child and not his own doing," Incredibly, Madai heard the defense come from his very mouth. "He helped me escape the Queen of Shinar," Madai continued, "but that can be told later. Arphaxas knows about the Nephilim."

"And how does he know them?" Togarmah asked suspiciously. "Why was he not with you when you arrived?"

Madai could well understand Togarmah, who was watching him askance – Arphaxas – standing a little apart and in the dragon skin with a shock of wild red hair. He did not have the size nor the fingers of Nephilim, but the aspect of untamed ferocity was certainly there. It was enough in itself to warrant mistrust and Madai could have let it go at that, which would have assuaged that niggling bite of jealousy just awakening. But then, there were weightier matters at hand.

"I'll go," Arphaxas growled, starting for the door. Madai moved to stop him, but it was Ashkinaz that took him by the arm.

"Wait." He said. "You are welcome."

"Yes Arphaxas, sit you down," Mineo encouraged. "You are Madai's friend. We would not have you in the cold night."

"We can be none too cautious," Togarmah grumbled. "No more meant than that."

"Of course, Togarmah," Mineo continued, kindly. "Will we have warmed ale while Arphaxas tells us about Nephilim?"

Togarmah looked round the circle of faces, avoiding the women as they had never before been admitted at council, and grunted.

Madai could only admit that Arphaxas received the steamy cup from his Mamam's hands graciously, though perhaps it was more to do with his mother than the man, himself. Madai watched him drain the cup and accept a second, ale glistening in his beard like copper. Arphaxas merely held the third cup, as if to drink warmth into chilly hands.

"It is the singular purpose of the Nephilim," Arphaxas finally announced, "to stop the coming of the Promised One."

"Yes, we have worked that out," Togarmah grumbled, having stretched his patience to the last. "They will use up the virgins before…"

"That and worse," Arphaxas insisted. "They will pull down every strategy of the Huwah even to blotting out the promise – rob its memory from all the earth. That is their… obsession. End not just the promise, but the knowledge of the promise. All that still sing the star stories, they will destroy."

"They cannot take the stars from the sky!" Iscah blurted.

Arphaxas looked at her and just opened his mouth to answer when Madai stopped him with another question, "But they killed the Banned… why kill them? They did not follow the old ways."

A murmur passed amongst the council, hearing for the second time that their lost kinsmen were no more; awaking even sympathies for a once-enemy, one that did not seem quite so grievous beside the terrible giants.

"They remembered," Arphaxas coldly replied.

"But they were banned for heresy!" Madai insisted.

Arphaxas gave Madai a glare before he answered stiffly, "They told the same story. You do forget that. But the Nephilim believe, of themselves, that they are the rightful gods of the earth… stars of heaven so to speak. They will not bear the strategies of Huwah."

"You will not profane His Name in this place," Ashkinaz warned.

"But," Iscah interceded, "they cannot think they will overcome Mighty God? If the Seed will be born, it will be born."

Arphaxas was running his hand across the hilt of his scimitar, an irritated twitch. "Ambition breeds its own madness," he answered cryptically.

"We are to believe you know all of this how?" Togarmah interjected, casting Iscah a silencing glance.

"Yes, Arphaxas. How do you know this?"

He shrugged. "I was… nearly captured."

"And you escaped. You'd have us believe that?"

"With the help of a friend."

"What friend had you amongst The Nephilim?"

Even his own Mamam did not try to stem Togarmah's rising suspicion at the suggestion of friendship among the dreadful hoard. But Arphaxas was not inclined to much patience.

"You are wasting time," he complained.

Togarmah put the point of his spear under Arphaxas's chin. And though he stood half a head below in height, he did not appear the lesser. "Yes you are," Togarmah snarled. "You will tell us how you've come to know the Nephilim or I will find the back of your skull with the pointy part of my spear."

Madai saw Arphaxas's hand close on his scimitar. "Wait!" He shouted. "Arphaxas, tell them."

The wind howled. A piece of hide covering the outermost of the lodge was loose and snapped against the side. The fire popped. Togarmah slowly removed his weapon but kept it pointed at Arphaxas's throat.

"Tell it now," he demanded.

Arphaxas stepped back and sat down, as they both had risen, facing off like competing stags. "There was a war in Shinar," he said dryly, "The sons of Shem defeated Nimrod and all his armies."

"Shem?" Togarmah scoffed.

"Armies lost, priests escaped with Nimrod's Queen," Arphaxas persisted, "and his gold. Gold buys new armies. She's had a son too, Queen Semiramis, born her by Nimrod's ghost."

"What about the Nephilim?" Togarmah demanded.

"The army's commander was a Dedanite, Commander Admah. He was a stupid man but the Queen sent him to find your kinsman here, and bring him back to Shinar."

"What could she want with Madai?" Ashkinaz asked doubtfully.

"She rather liked Madai," Arphaxas replied with a thin smile, "but I believe Admah claimed that he was a spy sent by Shem to unseat her new little king. That is how we first met Admah, in Gerar."

"Gerar?"

Ashkinaz glanced at Simirra with a suggestive smirk.

"Gerar is a city on the coast," Madai quickly explained. "The first city I came upon and where I left my ship. I separated from Arphaxas at Gerar, to ready it for sailing. And it is at Gerar that Arphaxas did me a service, sending Admah off course, in the wrong direction."

"Yes, well he was not entirely stupid," Arphaxas admitted. "He followed us here with half his men. The Nephilim found them, killed them all but Admah," he paused but a second, "I suppose it was a point of pride. Admah did not divulge Semiramis, nor his purpose here till they put his eyes out. It would have next been his tongue, but he needed that to speak. They left him on the far side of the mountain for the saber cats, only I found him first."

"This commander, this captive told you all about the Nephilim's plans?" Ashkinaz asked doubtfully.

Arphaxas shrugged. "He was with them some time before they turned him out. It was one eye at a time, as he told it."

"Where is he now?" Iscah asked nervously.

Arphaxas stood and stretched. He had an almost casual appearance, standing there with the light of the fire reflected in the scales of his dragon's cape, but Madai could see tension in his face.

"Nephilim," he replied tersely. "Out hunting. They found us. I escaped. He couldn't."

"Then they know you know," she whispered.

"How many are they?" Togarmah barked.

Arphaxas turned his head slowly toward the older man. At that moment, he did indeed look one with the beast whose skin he wore.

"Admah knew of seven," he answered. "I'd been watching from above their cave for a time before I came upon him and I did not see more, though there were women, one or two."

Madai heard Iscah gasp. "Then you heard the captain being…"

"Only seven? Why, we are eight here!" Togarmah exclaimed.

"Surely there are others who will fight with us," Madai asked quickly.

"The trouble, my son, is that we do not know who to trust," Ashkinaz replied.

"We trust no one who is not here tonight," Togarmah spat. "The divide amongst us is most severe."

"We are eight, then."

"You will not win a fight," Arphaxas insisted. "Do not forget, they overcame a soldier's regiment from Shinar itself."

"We hunt mammoths!" Togarmah proclaimed proudly.

The men of an age to fight looked from one to the other: Guran to Arphaxas, Madai to Togarmah, Ashkinaz to Riphath and Tiras. Riphath's son was the eighth among them and was but thirteen.

"Perhaps we can leave in the night," Old Tiptri suggested.

Ashkinaz rested his hand on the man's shoulder. "I wish it were possible," was all he replied.

"The Nephilim sleep in a cave," Arphaxas continued, "now that it's cold. There is but one way in; I have investigated it."

"So, that will be our point of attack," Madai confirmed. "Agreed," Togarmah snapped.

But Arphaxas held up a hand. "They will not be bested with spears and arrows. They are cunning, more mighty than ordinary men."

Togarmah grunted. "We are mammoth hunters!" he declared again. "These Nephilim are…"

Madai watched Arphaxas uneasily for there was a thing on his mind that he was not saying. "Charge against them if you like," Arphaxas revealed. "I will not."

An increasing grumble rose up among the men, especially Guran who, having joined the old council against Yamma – his very sister – considered himself owed a voice and at a greater risk.

Arphaxas put his empty cup on the ground. He moved toward the door at all the commotion and pulled the hood of his cape back over his head.

"Wait!" It was Ashkinaz, preventing his leaving again. "Tell us your plan, Arphaxas."

"This is not my fight."

"But it is!" Iscah chirped. "You have come to warn us!"

Madai was struck again at the way Iscah had of stopping him. The large man had turned to look at her, green eyes glittering from under the dark of the hood.

"And I have warned you," he said quietly.

"If we do not kill them, then they will kill us," Madai interjected. "They will take her. You've said as much."

He watched Arphaxas go still as one of Nimrod's stone statues.

"I would see them drunk with beer and then attack," he said at last.

"You will help us then?" It was Simirra's voice, full and demanding, and surprising Madai, for there was unexpected admiration in her voice. But then he supposed she knew, and far better than any, that Arphaxas possessed remarkable skills, he and his scimitar.

"Attack them when they are drunk," Guran grumbled. "Not an original plan."

"And smoke them like bees," Arphaxas added.

"Very simple," Togarmah declared. "Too simple, I think."

"Not if you use Stupor root," Mineo interjected mildly.

CHAPTER 30

*A*BLIND WRETCH SAT AMONG THE SHARDS OF A BRO-
ken pot. He was in the cave again; he could smell it and feel the
ache of cold. His fingers were burned where he had grabbed at
scraps of food tossed too near the fire. But he was working a shard of clay, one
of the sharpest, despite the pain. He had forgotten himself, for he was no one.
He was only a belly needing to eat, a few bones needing to be warm, flesh being poked at.

Now he was a hand with a piece of sharpened clay. He would have wanted
two 'blades', one for the giants that took his eyes and one for the dragon-man
who had not killed him outright. When the Nephilim were upon them, he had
begged to die for he could not escape.

An insect was buzzing about his face. He would not flick it away for fear
of finding his empty sockets.

That was something to send him over the edge and he must be sane enough
to take one of them to the under-world with him.

CHAPTER 31

*I*SCAH LISTENED TO THE WIFE OF TIRAS. SHE WAS talking about her little girl, Naru, named for Ido's mother. Naru was six and headstrong. Perhaps she was like her Grand Mamam, Kiellet was saying. She could not say it to Tiras, for his mother had been a part of the Banned. But she supposed he was thinking it. Should she consider it with him? Would that be better than having it niggle at him?

Iscah thought it was something better left to another time, for there were Nephilim. But they were waiting the three days Yamma had insisted upon. It did seem interminate.

Why was she anxious to have the fight upon them, if there would be a fight? Perhaps it was made the worse by waiting – this tension. Better that than what Madai had proposed amongst the fireweed.

She was back at that, which she found quite annoying when there was such trouble ahead.

"Ido was quite young and fancied herself in love with Tiras."

What?

Iscah shot her a look. Then she looked at Simirra and felt her own face going red. But it was dark in here, darker than Mineo's tent and perhaps they couldn't tell.

"Young love is the cruelest," Simirra was saying, which also strayed profoundly from the last that Iscah had heard.

Kiellet smiled. "Yes. Though I never loved a boy but Tiras, from my earliest. He was set apart for me, and I for him."

"A good system," Simirra replied.

"Not marry for love?" Iscah asked.

"There is love and there is love," Simirra remarked coldly.

"Mamam." It was Naru. "I want to play."

"Your Patta says 'no'," answered her Mamam with a firm and yet smiling voice. "We want you close – for when we leave."

The little girl pursed her mouth. There was an argument in her eyes that could be seen even in the dim but she went back to her pile of sticks.

"What is she playing at?" Iscah asked, better than glad to be done with love talk.

"She is shaping arrows," her Mamam replied.

"O! You are a brave girl."

Naru beamed at Iscah when she said that.

"Will you show me?"

The little girl moved aside and Iscah sat with her on the ground. The sticks were quite straight and sharp, hardly a child's toy, which reminded her afresh that this was indeed, a land of wilds.

"I kept my Papa's goats," Iscah said, reminded of a far ago time in her own life.

"What is papa's goats?"

"Well," Iscah stuttered. "They are animals which we keep for their milk and hair and meat. My Papa is like your Patta."

"O." The girl studied the point of one of her sticks. "Papa... Patta." She said with the cadence of a song.

Then she looked up. "How do you keep animals?"

"They are tame."

"Tame?"

"Not afraid. I led them to the springs and to new pastures when the grass they were eating was eaten up."

Naru nodded. "O."

"And I had a dog."

Naru cocked her head.

"You're funny," she said.

Iscah laughed. "A dog is like a wolf, but tame. He was my friend."

"I would like a wolf," Naru chirped. "How do you get one?"

"Perhaps we will ask your Patta and Madai when..."

"When we leave!" Naru finished. "Mamam, Patta will get me a wolf!"

Kiellet came to kneel beside her child. "Do you have a new friend, my little Naru?"

Naru nodded happily and took hold of Iscah's hand. She would not be distracted for long from her own wolf, but it was working for the moment.

"And now we will go to our Cousin Mineo's lodge. There we shall prepare the last of her seed grass with the last of our mammoth and talk more with our new friends."

Iscah's ears perked at the mention of mammoth. It was a meat for which she had been both dreading and curious.

"We will make rice with raisins," Simirra suggested. "It will be like a celebration." Iscah looked at the Calnehan woman. How peculiar, to talk about celebrations.

MAMMOTH WAS NOT SO BAD. PERHAPS IT WOULD BE BETTER if it were left to stew. Iscah was thinking how they had not brought all the spices from Tutan's caravan. That may have helped as well. But she was certain she would not be soon hungry.

The rice was sweetened with honey, interspersed with raisin and the best part of the meal. It was all that made the night any sort of a celebration, with the exception of Kiellet who had an inordinately cheerful spirit. Tiras was worried, Ashkinaz stoic, Mineo busy. Madai ate with the relish of a boy being granted his favorite meal, and Arphaxas – who should be glad to be amongst them again – was sullen. But then, he did always seem sullen.

It was Simirra who was not herself. She was intermittently angry and sociable. She was coy at times, offering Madai another piece of meat, and distant. Iscah would never understand the woman. She was a pagan, but then, so had Reenah been…

"TELL ME ABOUT THE ROOT OF STUPOR," ARPHAXAS asked as the night wore on.

Mineo put down her ladle. "I have some here," she said reaching for a small bundle of twisting roots tied to a rafter. "They should be kept apart," she continued, "but I'm careful."

"We use them if there's a saber in a cave or a bear," Ashkinaz finished. "Burning Stupor will make a bear stagger. But bears are big. It will kill a man."

"So we smoke them to death," Arphaxas muttered. "Brilliant if it works."

Mineo offered him another bowl of rice. Iscah thought she actually saw him smile. Perhaps he wished his own mother had been like Madai's. Perhaps that was what lay between them. 'No,' she decided. Their hostility had been from the start.

"You were a friend of Madai's in Shinar?" Mineo asked.

Iscah saw the look that passed between the two. But Arphaxas merely filled his mouth and nodded. Madai gave his mother a guarded look.

"Madai said you saved him from the Queen?" Mineo asked.

Arphaxas glanced at Madai. "It was my pleasure," he replied cynically, a tone which Mineo ignored. It was the moment Iscah came to admire her most.

"You shall always have my deepest thanks, Arphaxas. You have helped bring us back our son."

Iscah caught the red climbing up Arphaxas's cheeks. It matched his hair and somehow wore off an edge around his eyes.

CHAPTER 32

*I*T WAS THE NIGHT OF THE FEAST. THE LAST THAT Madai had spoken with the Old Council was the noon meal. They had parted a bit uneasy, final strategies agreed to, apprehensions left unvoiced. But the three days Yamma had insisted upon were passed.

An aroma was filling the camp, of roasting and brewing, a merry atmosphere. There was a good deal of pleasure taking, as in the aftermath of a successful mammoth hunt. But this was not a successful mammoth hunt. It was a coming together of The Family and Nephilim, near to blasphemy. Madai would like to have thought that this festivity was in anticipation of the telling of his quest, but he had his suspicions it was for the party alone, perhaps to appease a foe. And it made him melancholy. It did not seem that he had been gone so very long as to change this camp so very much.

He looked at the ground. There lay a great bone-shaped stone, larger than the equivalent foreleg of mammoth. Madai bent and traced it with his finger. A victim of the great flood lay before him, disentangled from those many others that had been caught in the death struggle of the first earth. It was forbidding; a thought to send a man to his knees.

Beside it lay a singular length of gopher wood; a piece of the ship to which the second earth owed its rebirth.

They seemed at the moment, paltry proofs. But there were the writings of the Maio, which he had learned from Tutan. There was Job, there was Noah himself. That was when Madai thought about the scroll again. On it were recorded the names of forebears who would bring to the earth the Crushing Seed. Tiptri's name was not on it; another proof that Yamma did not bear the Promise. He started to sweat, hoping that perhaps he did not have to reveal himself. He would use the shameful truth only as a last device.

That realization bolstered his thinking for the moment. Sitting here, at the entry to the Place of Gathering, he was alone. There was laughing, there was preliminary eating and drinking. In fact, the mood of the camp reminded him of a similar feast held before – and in his honor. It had been in the city Gerar, where he and Kittim had countered against the fire-breather. It had been Kittim with the foreknowledge, somehow, to lead the beast to tar pits where it sank to its own death, whilst chasing them for theirs. And the city was mad for them, hailing them hero-gods; in the end, forgetting them in their own revelry. So it felt tonight.

He was alone. The old council hadn't arrived; perhaps they were formulating their last tactics. The final disagreement amongst the men had been one of timing but Togarmah was convinced in the end to wait for the feast… how else to cripple the Nephilim with ale?

Where were his Mamam and Patta? He was so deep in the doldrums, he was wishing for Kittim, his stalwart friend. And where was Iscah?

He searched the crowd for Arphaxas. When there was eating, he could always be counted on. But even he, and no great friend, was not to be seen. Madai scanned the village once again. There were familiar faces, and yet unfamiliar for they reminded him of drunken banquets held on pagan shores.

He looked down again at the ark plank, desperate to suck out of it, some breath of inspiration.

"One does not reach Elohiym by possessing old timber."

The words caught him unsuspecting, as though spoken afresh and from Shem's mouth and just beside him.

The warning to set no great store in relics hit the pit of his stomach like a sour piece of meat. "Surely I have not made it a god," he whispered, suddenly terrified.

He snatched a look at the merrymakers as if they might have seen a budding idolatry. They ate and drank on. Only what was just laid bare to him was worse, a stinging humiliation – that even he might make a god of life-less things… this piece of ark. Perhaps it was the more profane – for he had seen Noah's face shining in the Presence of the One True God.

"No, my son."

His very hair prickled.

"You've not made these things your god. You are weary and sorely vexed and are laid after by the evil one."

He turned his head, ever carefully, to see his Mamam. She had emerged from the shadows at an opportune moment – as mothers are apt to do. She reached up and ran her fingers through his hair as if he were a child.

"You did not expect to bring us such good news unopposed?"

"Yes… no. But The Family…"

She simply smiled; that mother's smile. "Come sit with me," she urged, and pulled him toward a fat log that was waiting its turn for the fire. She laid her hand on his chest tenderly.

"In here," she whispered. "Is where you know Mighty God – and where the enemy takes its aim, that old snake."

He was breathing shallow now, shaking his head. "But I have seen things," he argued. "I am bringing Truth."

"And so the opposition."

"You sound like Kittim," he almost chuckled.

"Hmm?"

"My most mysterious friend…who helped me. He knew the strange tongues of all the peoples we came upon…a great help, a great friend, and yet I knew him very little."

Mineo's fingers had found his hand, and closed round it tightly. "Where is he then? You've brought us Iscah and Simirra and that poor Arphaxas. Where is this friend?"

Madai smiled faintly. "I wish I knew; returned to his master and with a paltry goodbye. He took Iscah's heart with him, I am afraid."

"Nonsense," Mineo replied tapping his hand. "She shall be a good wife to you."

It was a stunning remark.

"You needn't answer, my son. I have seen it. And you need have no guilt for Ido's sake. She would be glad. Iscah is a lovely child." She was smiling with the shine of tears in her eyes. She patted her fingers on his. "But we were speaking of more weighty troubles. The Mighty God – speak what you have seen and know… He will help you. He will be with you."

"You have always said that, Mamam." Madai exhaled. "I thought… when I proved the truth, it would be the answer to finish every trouble."

"O, this world has troubles, my son. But you will be upheld, for Mighty God has promised it! You know, in here," she tapped his chest again, "that it is true. The snake does not win. Listen to the sound of God and recognize the snake when it hisses."

"So," he breathed, "I am not failed."

She laughed softly. "You have always chased God, Madai. He shall not let you fail." He kissed the top of her head.

"You will be safe," he insisted, wrapping his arm around her. "When we are after the Nephilim tonight, you will take Iscah and Simirra to hide in the grove and you will be safe."

"Of course, my son. Togarmah and your Patta are working it all out. Why, look! They are coming now."

THE BLIND WRETCH SHRANK AGAINST THE WALL. THE cave was all sharp edges, left as it had cooled, molten rock aiming a course down to the valley, a web of empty veins. It was no warmer than any other cave in the region, despite what was at the heart of its mountain. The Nephilim had been making ready for hours. There would be a slaughtering tonight, which was making them forget about him for the moment. Odd he could still be made glad by anything. The wretch could see only by his ears and they had told him that someone new was here. This one had come of his own will, which was amazingly suicidal. And when the man spoke, the wretch gripped his sharpened shard till his fingers bled because he recognized the voice.

The smoke made Arphaxas's eyes water. It made it hard to make out faces and lent the cave's occupants an ominous appearance.

"I know you have plans for tonight," he charged, "You will burn the camp."

"Who are you to come here?" One of them growled back. It was Malak, his face painted blue with berry mud.

"Your very good friend." Arphaxas replied pointedly. He stood with his side to the fire, in such a way that his dragon's cape shone in its light. It had been oiled with bear fat, rekindling an old splendor.

Malak started to laugh. It was no ordinary laugh, coming from no ordinary throat. "You're no friend to us."

Arphaxas shrugged. "Perhaps you ought to hear me before you decide that."

A new voice emanated from the shadows. If Malak could growl, this one could bellow. "How do you know our plans?" It insisted.

Arphaxas watched a great hulk rise to stand above its company by a head. He wore a wild ox upon coarse red hair and the canines of three sabers around his neck. The ink of a squid was scraped in a permanent pattern from collarbone to chin and across his shoulders. He wore a thick ring of gold on his sixth finger.

"Because it is what I would do," Arphaxas answered.

The Nephilim reached him in one step. There was a shrewd intelligence staring at Arphaxas through eyes the color of night. The huge man bared his teeth with a calculating look, perhaps his version of a smile.

"It's what you would do?" he mocked. "Who are you? Are you not one of them?"

"I am for me," Arphaxas replied evenly.

The Nephilim grunted. He possessed no weakness as far as Arphaxas could see, no involuntary twitch, no stray expression or eye darting. He merely stood there, studying. He studied Arphaxas's height, his scimitar, his dragon-cape, even his hair.

"Where did you get that?" he asked, poking at the cape.

"Nimrod of Shinar."

"Who? That old pretender?"

"So he was," Arphaxas agreed. "He is dead now. So you see, I am your ally." A rumbling rose around the fire.

Naphal bent to put his face in Arphaxas's face. "You are no god killer," he growled.

"And Nimrod was no god."

The Nephilim truly smiled at that, and stood up straight. "What do you want, son of the earth?"

"To set my lot with yours."

"Of course you do."

Nephilim do not chuckle, and yet their rumbling changed in tone to approximate it. Even with such an urge to step back, Arphaxas held himself in place. He did not underestimate Naphal's barbary, standing where he was…

having come upon Admah. But Arphaxas had planned this out patiently.

"Why squander them?" He asked, expertly infusing his voice with reason. "Don't lay them waste tonight. Breed the maids. Use the men to build your cities. What is a god if there are none to worship him?"

Arphaxas watched Naphal's eyes contemplate. "Are you offering yourself?" he sneered.

He let his mouth form a stiff, ironic smile. "I have their trust." Arphaxas pressed. "I understand their ways. I know how to give them just enough... because a willing slave is the best kind, you see.

"As for religion," he shrugged, "They are already part way there. Bring in Yamma, bring them all."

A heavy crease formed above Naphal's brows. "I take what I want."

Arphaxas nodded. "Indeed," he agreed. "But, even the Huwah granted a man his will."

He all but held his breath at that and felt for his scimitar even as he watched the first appearance of rage in the Nephilim's face.

"What do I care about that?" Naphal spit.

"I hate the Huwah," Arphaxas insisted quickly. "And I am of The Family. I shall be your mouth to them and ferret out the rebels. I will deliver you Madai, and his father and that fool Togarmah. You will never control them."

"You think we need them delivered?"

Arphaxas didn't answer and gripped the hilt of his sword.

But Naphal was looking curious. He pushed his face all the closer to Arphaxas. "Why would you betray the seed hunter?"

"Madai? I am owed a debt by him," Arphaxas sounded bitter. "For killing someone... I loved."

Naphal laughed. "You sons of Noah are all the same." He put his finger on one of the scales of Arphaxas's dragon cape. "I can snap you before that flimsy blade leaves its scabbard."

Arphaxas heard the gravel shift as Naphal repositioned himself. "Who bred Yamma?" he asked abruptly.

Naphal showed a first sign of surprise. His eyes darted at Malak.

"She has a son." Arphaxas declared. "He has six fingers."

YAMMA RAN HER EYES ACROSS MADAI. HE WAS VERY beautiful... always had been. He spoke with such an easy authority, standing there beside his ridiculous proofs.

"What is sung of sea serpents is true," he was saying, describing such a great long creature with spiny teeth and the strength to take up a boat with its jaws.

Yamma had had no womanly feelings since birthing the babe, but Madai's recounting of his fight against the sea serpent was arousing her. And when he began about Nimrod, she was near to beside herself. That was when Malak stepped out of the forest. A new Nephilim was with him; it must be the famous Naphal.

This new giant was of a greater height even than Malak. They had their faces painted blue. They wore their talismans, Malak with his red stag and Naphal his ox. She had never seen a Nephilim without his head ornament, not even that once when her son was bred. She felt torn between a desire to contemplate Madai and this new giant.

"Job also told the story of the flood," Madai continued, "both in words and with paintings, which were upon his walls. He is greatly blessed of Mighty God, with flocks of sheep the size of caribou herds. They ride the back of beasts there, called horse and camel also, most efficient."

"You must make a song about Job." Came a voice from the crowd. Yamma knew that voice – Tiras – who was the son of the sanctimonious Togarmah. Yamma decided at that moment to remove him from Madai for she could not win against the sway of their friendship.

Madai laughed. "I leave that to you."

"Tell us what you've brought," Ashkinaz called.

And here was another impediment… though it was a proposition a trifle too thorny, removing an elder of his renown. She would ponder it later, an accident perhaps.

Madai lifted one end of the first relic. It looked exactly like a huge bone.

"This was one of many," he began. "It is the leg bone of a giant creature, behemoth, turned to stone and buried with a great herd of many other kinds of beasts…all the lost remains of the first earth. I would bring you Nua himself, for he does live. But he is very old. You must believe me for this is proof, and because you know me. I would not lie. I am the son of Ashkinaz. I have seen all that I say, and much more."

"You say Nua is alive? You have seen him?"

"He lives at the Mount of Ararat, in a house of stone. It is roofed with ark wood. This ark I have also seen – of more enormous a size as any boat we have ever sailed."

"You're a mythmaker!" Tiglath shouted.

His companions laughed.

It rubbed against the hair – hearing them laugh – because Tiglath was a mole beside Madai. Yamma glared, identifying the culprits, though they were all a part way drunk.

"Men lived long years on the first earth," Madai explained. "It was the air, heavy, filled with dew. It kept no cold or even rain and protected them. Their first years in such a place preserve them still perhaps. We also have such songs, do we not, telling of men who lived many hundreds of years? They are proof that these first songs are true."

He laid the bone down and moved closer to the fire. He seemed invigorated by his own words and Yamma felt herself waiting for him, against her own will, to speak again.

"What about the star stories?" Ashkinaz prompted him.

Madai looked up into the crowd for his father. The fire reflected onto

Madai's face, shooting Yamma with old desire. That was when Malak came up behind her. She had lost track of the Nephilim in her swooning. But he wrapped a proprietary arm around her waist and lifted her off the ground.

Yamma thrashed. She tried to wrench around to claw him in the eyes, but his arms were like a terebinth. He was breathing heavy against her ears, beastly sounds. When he put his other hand on her mouth, she froze, afraid to be snapped by accident, for he did not want her dead – he only wanted her.

This was a coup. She should have known.

CHAPTER 33

*I*SCAH SAT WITH SIMIRRA. THEY SAT BESIDE A PIT OF coals from which a young boar had been removed. The air was full of such an aroma! Their beer however, carried the unpleasant suggestion of something dead.

"I have never seen Madai like this," Simirra whispered. "He's more excited about that bone than he would be a woman!"

"Don't be common, Simirra."

"Why? It isn't common to tell the truth."

"He is speaking about things sacred."

"You're being very vengeful."

Iscah shot Simirra a look. "I only think you should be more… respectful."

"Perhaps," Simirra acknowledged.

"Well, I should think you would be. You have been spoken to."

"Perhaps."

Iscah exhaled in a somewhat dramatic fashion, putting her elbows on her knees, leaning her chin into her hands and excluding Simirra from her vision. She fixed her attention on Madai's story, waiting for all the parts that shot her through with shivers.

"And this is the leg bone of a creature that walked the first earth," he was saying. "A behemoth, as called by Job, a very beast that may have lived in Eden when Mighty God walked there. We have seen a living behemoth with our own eyes, in a valley of the East, a more fearsome beast also, Leviathan…"

A pair of legs stepped into the path between her line of sight and where Madai was standing. He did not wear the buckskin trousers of The Family, but a length of leather like a kilt, leaving just the abundance of hair on his legs to keep him warm. She followed his body upward, more than a little stunned to be staring into the back of a Nephilim. She heard Simirra gasp.

They'd slipped into the camp with a quiet unexpected of such creatures. Their hair was near the color of Arphaxas's, darker perhaps but nigh to red. They wore their horns, of course, but Iscah was prepared for that. She was not prepared for the way their legs flexed, showing bulky muscles or the way their necks met their shoulders… as any ordinary men.

When her hands started to throb, she forced her fists to open. Her heart was pounding and sweat was running down her back. She hugged her belly, suddenly queasy with the smell of roasting boar. Terrible hate engulfed her then, and recollections of past despoilings. Those perpetrators had been so like these.

"Iscah!" Simirra whispered, pulling on her wrist. "Sit down." And Iscah sat back down, not knowing she had stood.

"You look… ghastly, like you think you can fight them yourself."

Iscah was shaking. She could not trust herself to answer. But she would fight them herself, and certainly lose. She shook her head and looked at the ground where her feet were shod in shoes that were quickly falling apart, bits of the last of The Lady's kindness to her. Lost daughter's shoes; a chilly thing to think about now.

"Come away," Simirra whispered.

"I want to hear," Iscah whispered back.

"You've heard it all. You've even lived a part of it."

Her heart was slowing down. She tucked her feet up under the leather dress she was wearing. "I'd like to hear it again."

"Do not forget, Madai wants us in the grove before… you know."

Iscah nodded. And when she looked back, one of the Nephilim was gone. The other hadn't moved. He had the manner of a tree, planted in a spot. But the one in the way was the one that had left, and she could see Madai again.

He was about to laugh, telling about the Hemp Bridge and how it swayed. He mentioned Leviathan again, leaving out Lemmeri, the kitchen maid, though that was a good story.

She thought he should have told the bridge part first, before telling about the bone as it was only natural to tell the start before the finish. But perhaps he was too excited about the bone. And then he jumped in his telling to the Ark plank, holding it high so even the children could see it. He was talking about the Ark, a sore point with her, being left behind as she was. Iscah sighed, she would likely never see it now…

"The ship was made of three levels," he was saying. "Many seekers have come, as we came. It was as big as Winds Cliff and black; made of trees," he spread his arms out "of a greater girth than any I've ever seen. You would not believe it."

The giant moved, stepping once again into her line of vision. The sight of him did not well up her hatred as he had done at first, for she had been surprised by him then. Instead, his standing there incited an instant alarm. He was clenching and unclenching his fists, acting like the wild ox he was wearing and ready to charge. When Madai told them about Noah's 'Book of Adam' and the forebears of The Crushing Seed, she thought she would have to stand up and shout, 'Stop, Madai, he's going to kill you right now!'

But Madai shifted his telling again, back to Noah himself, the very old man who was fond of beasts. She darted her attention back to the Nephilim, who seemed to have calmed himself. They were no small menace, these pagan giants. The attack would have to happen tonight and she was afraid for Madai again.

"The first earth must surely have been a wonder, a paradise." He was saying. "Nua spoke of it with...a great longing. And Eden, before the serpent; such a grievous loss, he said, for it was recounted to him by them that knew Adam... more a loss than we can know, to lose the Presence of God."

Madai stopped. He was letting them ponder that. Iscah forced her thinking from the Nephilim, to ponder that herself.

"There was no rain," he continued. "But only a mist to water the plants, which all the creatures ate. They did not eat each other... and the stars declared the glory of God... they sang."

Iscah felt chills down her arms.

"What I remember, like I am hearing him now, is when Nua asked the simplest of questions: 'What of absolute love is so terrible?' He asked me that the first night and I could find no logical thing to say."

She thought he looked undone, staring across the crowd.

"What is so terrible about such a love, about such an earth, about such a God? It is not that there are storms to freeze us and quakes that crush us or bears to eat us...because there was none of that on the first earth. Still it was not enough for men. Surely, He gave us all good things."

Madai blinked. Iscah heard a catch in his voice. She saw him nigh to overcome with passion. He just stood there after that, looking into faces and the one-time boisterous Family was silent, looking back. Perhaps he would persuade them after all.

CHAPTER 34

SIMIRRA WATCHED IT HAPPEN. WHAT A PITY Arphaxas wasn't here to see Madai's story make its impact. He had always scoffed. Simirra thought he was jealous, for he certainly was not simply ignorant. She could feel Iscah beside her, calm again and near to enthralled. There was a certain longing in Simirra as well, having had a brush with the divine, or so it was possible. Iscah believed it. Perhaps Simirra would believe it too, though she hadn't felt nor heard a thing to match it since.

But tonight, Simirra knew she must keep her wits about her. These Nephilim were no beings to be lightly taken. Be they born of devils or merely devils of men, there was a chance they were invincible. She had heard the tales.

If Arphaxas were here, she would convince him to steal away before the fight, and bring Madai and Iscah.

Madai would not be agreeable, she was quite sure, and would require a heavy hand. But Arphaxas was gone. Perhaps he had already stolen away. It was likely.

Then the first plan must be carried on. She frowned.

The Nephilim were not drinking. It was only men of The Family, returning time and again for the brew. A disagreeable grumble rose up her throat; they did not deserve saving! Still, there was Ashkinaz and Mineo, most kind of souls.

"I will return," she whispered to Iscah. The girl turned with an absolute shine in her eyes and nodded. "Do you have cups?" she asked of Mineo.

TOGARMAH HAD HIS EYES ON THE ONE CALLED NAPHAL, known of though never seen before tonight. He was their leader; there was no doubt of it. If Togarmah was not a poet, he was a warrior and a pragmatist. The signs were clear: this Nephilim was bent on their destruction. He could see it in the way Naphal was standing, tight as a saber ready to spring. Togarmah hoped they had not waited too long.

But he comforted himself, knowing the Nephilim had been waiting too and for the same man. What they needed of Madai's discoveries, he could not be sure. He was equally unsure of Arphaxas, whose face he did not find amongst the crowd. That they'd delayed their attack till tonight, and at Arphaxas's urging, made him profoundly uneasy.

He was made the more so by a scuffle which caught his eye. It was not that he would have Yamma rescued, for she had danced with fire. It was what it meant, because Malak had returned to find Tiglath's lodge and emerge with Yamma's babe. Why would he do that? You did not need a babe to take a woman… unless the babe was important.

He quickly counted the giant hostiles amongst them. There were six – Malak having disappeared – and they were not drinking – a vital part of the plan. Their faces were painted blue. They were watching Madai as though he were the mouse and they, pit vipers.

Suddenly he knew. It would be tonight. As it was the plan to attack the Nephilim after the feast, so the signs were clear that the Nephilim had a like plan against The Family. Togarmah was certain and to his credit, grieved to have been right all along. Where was Arphaxas? Why did the giants not drink? Why did Malak come back for Yamma's child?

What fools they had been, listening to Arphaxas! What a fool he had been, letting them persuade him. Instead of the Nephilim besotted, it was The Family, drinking their new ale like yearlings at a mother's breast.

He had no sooner thought it than he saw Madai's Mamam and one of the pagan women receive a skin of beer from old Tiptri. They snaked through the crowd toward the Nephilim. Mineo carried the beer and the pagan carried the cups. She pressed one into giant paws and turned her face up at each Nephilim with the sort of persuasion that only a woman can wield. Only Naphal refused her.

In the end, there were five Nephilim guzzling old Tiptri's newly brewed beer. His beer had always been the tastiest and the most potent. Perhaps Guran had brought him a handful of tick berries, not enough to make it bitter but just enough to double the ale's effects. Togarmah counted the times Mineo refilled the cups as the night turned chilly. He watched the chin of a first Nephilim drop to his chest. That Guran was a clever fellow.

MADAI STOPPED SHORT OF EXPOSING YAMMA'S DECEPtion. There came quite an irrepressible joy upon him when he began to speak, and when he felt no longer compelled by it, he stopped talking. It seemed the thing to do.

He hadn't noticed when a majority of the youth consumed a quantity of Tiptri's brew. He hadn't seen it when Naphal slapped clay cups out of his fellow's fists and tried to make them stand. Nor had he watched the five stagger off, or seen the look Naphal shot across the camp at him before he followed his band of drugged Nephilim. What he did see was the way some brothers did listen and were glad by what he told them.

CHAPTER 35

NAPHAL ROARED INTO THE CAVE. WITH HIS MEN drunk, he'd have to wait for the village to sleep before he took them. He kicked Arba in the gut. He clubbed another across the back and stepped a heavy foot on the chest of a third.

"Where are you, Son of Noah?" He bellowed. "I'll have your head for supper."

Somewhere in Naphal's reckoning he had always known Arphaxas was false but he was swayed by the prospect of worshippers. He blew frost in the air from his nostrils, more than aware that Ashkinaz's pup had spun his story with palpable effect.

"Bring me that god-killer," he demanded, shoving one of the giants.

The Nephilim slapped back, too drunk to appreciate who'd given the order.

Only the slaughter to come stayed Naphal from removing his head. Instead, he smashed the offender in the back with his boot, sending him to the ground. He glared into the shadows for Arphaxas. Naphal's eyes could see in the dark nearly as well as the light, and there was no one there. There was no sound of defiance, which would surely have come from Arphaxas's arrogance, and no whimper from the eye-less Shinar captain.

"Where are they?" he bellowed, frost billowing like smoke from his mouth. He kicked one of his men in the face.

"The big one was gone when I got here," Malak's very sober voice came from behind.

Naphal spun around. Malak was adjusting the skins, which covered his loins and the yellow-haired witch was behind him. She was squatting on the ground with a bundle of furs beside her. Naphal narrowed his eyes at his second in command. He spit on the ground.

"You weren't drinking then," he rumbled. He wiped his mouth. "Bring me the woman."

Malak bristled. "She's mine."

Naphal reached his underling in one step. "I want her now."

"She's mine."

"Arba," Naphal cocked his head at the only Nephilim not yet snoring. "Get her for me."

His third in command shook his head to clear it, so vigorously that he lost his headdress. Malak glared. With Naphal looming above, it was only his height that separated their two faces. And it was only a lack of foresight that stayed Malak's hand at first, for in the heat to get at Yamma, he had leaned his spear too far away. It was sheer arrogance and an expectation of things to come that stayed Naphal's hand.

Arba eyed them both, somewhat beer-fuzzy before passing behind Malak to scoop Yamma up as easy as if she were a pebble. She grabbed for the bundle of furs just in time to hug it against her chest. Arba brought her round Malak to set her back down, wobbly beside Naphal.

Naphal spread his lips across his face in a Nephilim grin. It gave him satisfaction to see Malak's acquiescence and raw pleasure to watch the fear in Yamma's eyes, to see her heart beating wild in the veins of her neck. He was curious about the skins she held so ferociously. His single hand circled round her waist.

"Where's the soldier," he demanded of Arba.

"He's dead," Malak replied defiantly.

"Did you kill him?" Naphal accused.

Malak shook his head slowly.

"Must have been the god-killer then," Naphal sneered. "You should have checked the ropes yourself."

He crossed over drunken Nephilim, making his way to the back of the cave, dragging Yamma and her bundle behind. He found the terebinth trunk they'd dragged up the mountain to fasten Arphaxas to. And he found the wretch, blood congealed in a pool beside it. There was a single clay shard beside him and a flake of obsidian, sharp as any blade.

"Took him all night," Arba muttered, having followed his leader.

Naphal could smell the blood. He could also smell the Shinar captain's rotted eyes. But he could not smell fear from either man. The wretch had wanted to die, no doubt, and The Family's envoy had granted the request in payment for having his ropes sawed with a bit of sharpened rock. Naphal shrugged. Arphaxas would die in an hour or two, however long it took to sleep off the beer. Malak's witch would amuse him for that long at least.

"Keep a watch of Malak," he ordered.

Arba grunted, disappointed of sleep but loyal as a dog.

Yamma had stopped struggling, for which he was somewhat deflated. When the bundle of furs started to wail, he was surprised. When he saw the child, he grunted, remembering Arphaxas's claim. He pulled at the boys little hands and counted his fingers. Then he made her lay it on the rocks before he jerked away what was left of her dress.

Chapter 36

WHEN ARPHAXAS CAME UPON THE FAMILY, THEY were all but asleep. Just the heartiest few were finishing the last of the beer. It disgusted him. He could see the lodge of Ashkinaz on the far side, incandescent with the glow of their fire.

"Madai!" were his first words, as he bent to enter the low doorway.

"Where've you been?" Togarmah hissed.

Arphaxas ignored him. "They'll not be coming tonight," he declared, "but they'll be coming."

"They drank a lot of beer."

"Spiked with tick berry," Guran added.

"It will work, Arphaxas," Simirra insisted, sounding unreasonably and unusually optimistic. "I brought the big one ten cups myself."

Arphaxas turned to look at her a moment, surprised at her tone. "I've seen you with your sword," she added.

He was quiet a moment before he explained, "I gained us the night, but not much more. Whatever we do, it'd best be now."

"What do you mean?" Togarmah asked suspiciously.

"I went to them," he replied calmly, "offered them an enticement."

"They might have killed you, Arphaxas!" Iscah cried.

"And left us a man down." It was Togarmah. "What enticement?"

Arphaxas smiled his crafty smile. "You, Kinsman."

Madai raised his brows slightly. "You're sure you gained us tonight?" asked pointedly.

"They'll be done in," Guran insisted. "It's seen to."

"Can we not just get away?" It was Tiptri again, comparing the strength of their fighters against the giants.

Patta," Guran argued, "They will come after us."

"They will come after us," Arphaxas agreed. "We know the Promise."

"Where is the Stupor?" Madai suddenly asked.

"Stashed near their cave," replied Arphaxas.

"Good. Iscah, Simirra, warn the others. You know who, then hide in the woods where I showed you."

"What others?" Arphaxas asked, disturbed.

"Some were persuaded."

Arphaxas shook his head, frowning. "Do what you will then, but don't get me killed."

ARPHAXAS LED THE WAY. HE WAS ARMED WITH ONLY HIS scimitar. There was just the original eight of them: Arphaxas, Togarmah, Tiras, Guran, and Kessed, Riphath the Bear, who left his son to guard the women, Madai and Ashkinaz. Madai could not fault Riphath leaving the boy, for he would not reach the giant's waist.

It was a distance to the Fire Mountain, which they covered at a trot. But they crept up the side of the mountain, guarding their noise, cautious for a watchman. They came upon no one, which encouraged Madai's expectations to find them asleep.

It was dark. Stars were hiding their lights with winter clouds to help these sons of Noah, at least Madai thought so. But it was bitter cold. Even that would benefit because there would be fires, and with a Stupor root or two... He put on his mitts, fingers nearly numb and knowing he needed to feel if he also needed his longbow. It was bumping against the back of his neck with assurance. He hoped Iscah and his Mamam were already in their hiding place... just in case.

Arphaxas dropped to one knee. It was the signal that they had come upon the cave. Black as the night was, Madai was glad Arphaxas knew the precise location, had already been inside – if it was to use him as bait. When Arphaxas turned his way, the clouds drifted just enough to catch a moon's gleam across his face. Madai's breath caught in his throat, as the dragon-clad man gave him a sly expression. Madai shuddered, remembering the bitter Tazek he had once known. He went suddenly cold, and not with the weather.

What if they were being lured even now? What if the Nephilim were waiting for the only men of The Family who would resist? He was completely covered in a film of cold sweat the instant he thought of it.

"Patta," he turned to whisper the warning. But it was too late, Arphaxas had sneaked to the mouth of the cave. When he actually went inside, Madai knew they were betrayed.

With one smooth and practiced movement, Madai reached for an arrow. He notched it against the string of his longbow. He pulled it back, feeling his winter's mitt just kiss the side of his face as the string came taut. He held it, elbow high and motionless, waiting for the first silhouette to emerge.

"They're gone!"

The cry of surprise startled them all, ringing shrill in the cold, thin air. It was Arphaxas. He emerged from the mouth of the cave making a great racket coming across the rocks. Madai's fingers had waited for the moment and released the arrow. It struck Arphaxas's dragon-cape as it flapped like the wings of a predatory bird behind him.

"Atoyak the gods!" Arphaxas swore. He lunged, grabbing Madai's bow to twist it away. "Couldn't wait?"

"I... "

"They're gone," he spat, repeating the alarming discovery. Arphaxas turned away then to look pointedly at Togarmah. "They'll be at the village," he proclaimed.

Iscah had watched them leave. They'd seemed capable inside Mineo's lodge, big men, men who hunted mammoth.

And they were confident. But outside, with the rest of the village asleep and the cold and a wind that was whining she thought they'd seemed quite insignificant. She watched till Ashkinaz, who was at the rear, disappeared through the trees. Mineo had watched beside her.

"Arm of God," Mineo had whispered.

Iscah had quietly taken the woman's hand. They'd watched the woods together till Simirra reminded with a practical voice, "We have to get the others, Iscah."

Though Simirra warned against it, Iscah had a torch and was at the last elder's door. He was a friend of Tiptri and one of the select few convinced by Madai's tales. The rest had been silently roused and were waiting in a grove of red cherry with Mineo. It was a cold night. They would need to hurry because they were mostly women and children and old men. She was happy there were more that believed Madai for it did make him glad. She had just started to call when a rustle, somewhat distant in the brush, caught his name in her throat. Something was thrashing through the forest toward the village. She froze, hand gripping the torch like a weapon. She strained her ears to identify it, hoping for the sounds of a bear or something equally unlikely to wish for. It was panting – the human sort.

She suddenly remembered her last impression of Madai, looking eager for the job of giant killing.

She dove behind a cache of wood stacked outside the elder's door. She fought to control her breathing, which was making a great commotion there in her hiding place. Still there was the torch and she scolded herself for not obeying Simirra. Perhaps she could use it into the eyes of the first Nephilim when he finally appeared.

Branches cracked.

A human form suddenly stumbled into the clearing. It's clothes hanging in tatters, all but naked. "O!" Iscah gasped and stood,

The woman's skin was also in tatters, as if the tip of a very sharp knife had been used on it. Rivulets of dry blood gave the appearance of a dark braided river and there was a pack clutched in her arms, a feral expression in her eyes.

"Yamma?"

The woman hugged the bundle up under her chin, gripped it tight.

"Yamma, what's happened to you?"

She was shaking, jaw clenched, lips purple. Iscah pulled off her coat, her own hands shaking with left over fear, and reached to put it around the woman's shoulders. Yamma jumped away with the alacrity of a scared rabbit.

"Yamma," Iscah repeated in a soothing voice. She held her coat out at arm's length. "Here. It's cold."

Yamma cocked her head, a strand of yellow hair, also bloody, fell across her face. She studied the coat as though it were something foreign. Then she studied Iscah.

"You're Madai's woman," she managed to hiss through chattering lips.

"N...no," Iscah stammered, taken aback. "Have it, Yamma." She gave the coat a shake and the freezing woman reached for it.

With the coat in one hand, Yamma suddenly seemed uncertain, cradling the bundle in her left arm. She crooned at it, then smiled, baring her teeth at Iscah.

"Want to hold him?" she asked.

Iscah was afraid to come close enough for that. Yamma looked entirely mad and yet it was a child there in her arms. And it did seem a reasonable thing to offer as she would need both her arms to put on a coat. Iscah reached out quite cautiously and Yamma tucked the package gently into her arms.

"He's Madai's," she announced happily, pulling the coat on, hiding her tatters of cloth and skin.

"You must come with me," Iscah prompted gently.

"What?" Yamma replied, peeking up at the girl. "Don't believe me? It's true." She took the edge of the dirty blanket in her fingers and gently folded it away from his face. "Want to look? He is beautiful like his Patta."

Iscah looked down at the bundle in her arms. It was extraordinarily still.

"Yes, beautiful," she agreed. "Now come with me. We'll get you both inside."

Yamma sniffed. She smiled. Then both women froze, as the forest seemed to erupt around them.

NAPHAL WENT STRAIGHT FOR THE BONE. IT SUITED HIS sense of irony. While Madai had levered the socket end against the ground to lift it, Naphal wielded it like a club. It took the tempering admonition of Arba to stop his frenzy. "Remember the women," he said.

Naphal dropped the bone just as the lodge pole he'd attacked gave way. It must have fallen directly in the fire because dried skins caught flame like a torch. It was caved in at the door and Naphal heard a woman's desperate scream, terrified about being roasted alive.

The Nephilim shrugged. "Call the others out," he ordered. That was hardly necessary.

Naphal watched the sons of the earth, jolted from sleep and confused, stumble out of their hovels. He would never understand men's partiality for dank, dead houses. Give him a breathing mountain.

As if in validation of such a preference, the fire fully engulfed that first unlucky dwelling. Them that didn't awake at the first scream could hardly ignore what agony followed second. She had good lungs. It was a shame.

But he grinned with approval anyway. There was probably more she flesh here than they could feed. Just feeding their seven could prove a challenge – especially in winter. Perhaps some of the bucks could be used as hunters. The old, they'd club and also the whelps.

"Two each," Malak was shouting as his comrades went about the terrified Family, dragging women away from their homes.

"Save some bucks," Naphal ordered impulsively as Malak chopped at a protesting father.

It went quickly. Unsuspecting, just waking and partially drunk, the village was effectively without defense.

NAPHAL WAS USING THE BONE AGAIN. HE WAS CAVING IN lodges, creating such an inferno that they were sweating from the heat. Selections had been made fairly easily and now with all the killing done, there was an eerie absence of human outcry. The women huddled in a tight knot, too stunned to utter a sound; not even to weep. The seven Nephilim had been no raucous mob, but methodical reapers. They seemed revived, having eaten of The Family's meat and rested from The Family's ale. Only the flames roared, dancing across ghostly faces with an orange glow.

Naphal inhaled deeply, having always loved the smell of a campfire. He perused the women – possibly too many saved. He had also explicitly demanded the seed hunter be alive, and also their spy but they were not amongst the bucks.

"Where is that pup of Ashkinaz?" he shouted above the firestorm. "Malak?" But the underling only shook his head.

Naphal tossed the behemoth bone into the nearest blaze. He rolled over a few corpses, searching their faces and decided, in the end, to investigate later. For now, he was tired. It had been a long day.

THE VALLEY WAS STUNNED. EVEN ITS NIGHT CREATURES, rodents and owls and such, hid away. Nothing decried the slaughter but the crackling fire. Every night noise was gone mute; mourning, as it had done since Eden, the curse on the earth.

CHAPTER 37

*A*LL BUT RUNNING ALONG A DARK ROCKY TRAIL, they could see the orange glow in the night sky. And then from a ridge, in the shadow of that glow, they watched a line of captives shuffle behind three hairy giants. Four brought up the rear. The moon had come out to watch, perhaps to light the way. The number of captives was far fewer than half The Family. It was not the best of odds. Tiras knelt motionless beside Madai. Ashkinaz was white of face and Riphath the Bear searched the line for sight of his only son. Guran recognized Yamma's gait even now. His heart was bitter, astounded that she should still haunt the earth with his Mamam dead and likely his Patta too.

"We're too late."

"Are the rest dead, do you think?" No one answered.

Madai turned suddenly at Arphaxas. "So, you gained us the night? Or did you tempt us away?" He hissed.

Ashkinaz put a hand on his son's shoulder. Tears streamed on the old hunter's face, watching the passing of the Family.

"Will we fight ourselves?" he asked softly.

They were quiet after that – smelling fire, pondering fates.

When the last of the captives disappeared below them, Tiras slowly exhaled. "What is the plan?" he asked.

"Kill that one," Togarmah demanded instantly, pointing at Arphaxas.

Arphaxas re-sheathed his scimitar. "Don't be a fool," he muttered.

"You're their spy." Togarmah took a step toward him, brandishing his mammoth spear.

"There is no time for this," Tiras insisted.

"I'll not have him at my back."

"I'll have him at mine. If Kiellet and Naru are taken..."

"I told Mineo and Iscah to hide our women and children," Ashkinaz quietly reminded them.

"I think I saw Iscah."

They all looked at Madai when he said that. It was as if the air was snuffed out entirely.

"Now, before they reach the cave," Tiras suggested.

"The first necks to break will be the women," Arphaxas warned.

Madai looked at Arphaxas, a shadow in his dragon cape. Arphaxas was glaring back, accusing.

"You should have left when I told you to," he hissed, too quiet for anyone else to hear.

So Arphaxas had seen her too. Madai looked away. There was something else, more terrible even than that Arphaxas was right. It was that Japhet and his Mamam were probably dead.

YAMMA SEEMED RESIGNED, ALMOST PEACEFUL TRUDG-ing through the night with the other captives. Iscah guessed it was because of the madness.

"I've just come from there," she had cackled, carelessly. "First Malak, then Naphal. Malak. Naphal. I am Queen of the Nephilim. Malak. Naphal." She turned her head enough to look across her shoulder at Iscah. "But I know the way out," and then she went quiet.

That last had been a whisper, but Iscah had scooped it up like a treasure. And she believed it; however else had Yamma escaped? The babe was stiff. It had been dead a good while. But Iscah did not betray it and she did not ask for her coat back, though she was exceedingly cold. She did not pity what was likely done to kill the babe nor to strip Yamma of her deerskins for the sound of killing and burning were fresh in her ears. Indeed, the ale had not done its magic, for the Nephilim had recovered all too well. She was only glad Madai had left the camp, and only a scarce time before the slaughter, for he would likely be dead except for that. She did not see Simirra, nor Madai's mother, nor Kiellet. That was a thing to be glad for… if they were safe in the grove. She stumbled. She was suddenly very tired and thought raggedly that it must be past the crest of the night and near to early morning.

There was an exhaustion in her greater than she had ever felt before. It wore at the sharp edge of memory – of the carnage that lay behind. Even the whispered scrap of information that Yamma knew how to escape the Nephilim faded by her very fatigue. She wondered vaguely if it were possible to sleep as she walked and what would the Nephilim do to her then? She felt her lips begin to move, whispering a prayer.

"Let him save us," she muttered. "Let Madai save us, let him save us." Her lips opened and closed around the words. It kept her awake.

She trudged on that way for an indiscernible length of time. She was a body with legs that somehow kept her upright and moved in cadence to her prayer. And so she did not recognize it at first when they reached their destination. She could not see the Fire Mountain though it rose directly ahead. All around was dark, both of trees and shadows.

But rocks began to jump in front of her feet, which made her stumble. And she started to feel the blood that trailed warm from some undiscovered wound. She was shaking uncontrollably and remembered that Yamma had her coat.

Vaguely, she thought about that last old believer she had failed to warn. What had come of him? He was a friend of Tiptri. A pine slapped her in the face, sharp with needles.

She also tried to remember the way to that meadow of fireweed where she had found Madai. It seemed a world ago. It was near the Fire Mountain. The way had not been so difficult then. Her foot caught the heel of the woman in front and they both stumbled. Anonymous arms helped them up.

"Not far now," she heard Yamma whisper, owner of the arms.

"How would you know?" the other woman whined.

"Been there," Yamma crooned. She tucked the edges of the blanket around the stiff form of her child.

They reached the incline. What was difficult before was torturous now. Iscah stumbled again. She was on her knees, grabbing at brush and rocks, pulling herself up a rocky trail and profoundly grateful that it had not as yet begun to snow. Madai said not till the fireweed lost all its petals. But the wind was howling now, glancing off the mountain like a rock-slide. It was bitter cold – and so dark. She could be so easily lost…

Iscah snatched a quick look behind, finding that she was now at the tail of their procession. She stole a glance forward to see Yamma's head bent above her baby. Perhaps it was too dark a night to matter. Then she sidled to the right, scarcely planning it and into a thicket of what proved to be spike berries, named for the thorns, which ran the length of their stems.

A sort of growl sounded to her left and a very large hand grabbed her ankle even as she crawled face first into thorns. He yanked her away, across gravelly earth. Her skirt bunched up, exposing her skin to rock's sharp edges from breast to foot. He grabbed her arm and jerked her up. He put his hand at the base of her neck and shoved. She fought very hard not to pitch forward and not to cry out. It was all tried and failed so fast as to almost never have happened, except for the way her skin burned from the dragging.

"Get in there!" He barked. She could still feel his finger marks on her throat.

Wherever "in there" was, she could not tell, but it was surely their camp for she could smell it now.

Iscah's head pounded as she lifted her eyes. Was it possible that this dark could produce some place darker still? For there it lay, deep in the shadow of a bonfire which burned in front of the black gaping mouth of a cave. She very nearly laughed. To have waited till now for her grand escape – ludicrous indeed.

She felt herself picked up. The Nephilim dragged her in the crook of his arm the last of the distance. He dumped her with the rest of the captives who had huddled around the fire. They were a woeful lot, seeking a sort of primal consolation beside the flames. She closed her eyes.

"What have you done, witch? The whelp's dead!"

Iscah flinched. Was she asleep? She peeled her eyes open, scratchy lids. She heard quite hysterical laughter in reply.

Yamma. She closed her eyes again. It didn't matter now, the woman was mad and the baby had been dead all night.

Slap.

Scream.

Iscah's eyes popped open again.

It looked like Yamma was dancing by the light of Nephilim fire. But it was one of the giants trying to get at the baby. Yamma was dancing away from him. It suddenly seemed too terrible to sleep through.

"You killed him!" The Nephilim roared. He was the one called Malak.

Iscah was awake now.

Yamma seemed as mad as she ever had seemed. She did not answer, but to snarl this time and clutch her lifeless child and bare her teeth at the raging giant. He snatched at the babe.

"Leave it," another creature demanded. He was a Nephilim of greater stature and malice than even Malak. He wore his kingship in his voice. He did not need a crown, but wore a skull and horns of the wild ox, none-the-less.

"She shed your knots!" Naphal accused.

Malak glared back with a look to hint at some larger story. "My son's dead!" He countered.

Naphal shrugged. He shoved Malak aside and took Yamma by the wrist. She shrunk at his touch, all the courage of her madness fled away. He looked down at the baby then back at Yamma.

"We'll have to get another by her," he remarked darkly.

"Kill her," Malak demanded.

"No," Naphal barked, asserting authority. "We'll see what's in her belly first."

There was nothing left to horrify. Iscah was only cold. She watched as Naphal gave Yamma's belly a rather sensual caress and let her keep the corpse.

ISCAH LET HERSELF BE HERDED WITH THE REST, GLAD for the anonymity and the warmth. They were being pushed to the back of the cave where there was a second fire. It was gigantic and Iscah went to her knees beside it. The flames licked at the frosty air, but also made the farthest corners the blackest. Strangely, it made it less dreadful to Iscah, for when she was warm she determined to hide in its cleft. Her fellow captives were little more than dark and shapeless forms.

They lay down all around her, too exhausted even to whimper. She wrapped her arms around herself and felt her eyelids close. There is a tired great enough even as to dim the most terrible of happenings. She was just sinking into that place when the giants came busy again. Did they never sleep?

They were grabbing and pushing, sorting out two men that they had kept alive. She hoped it wasn't for gouging out eyes as she seemed to remember

Arphaxas talking about that. She shuddered and lay very still, trying not to make noise when she breathed. After a time she felt the subtle drift of sleep again, along with the sinking observation that Madai had returned to a family going extinct. No, perhaps not, for his friends had gone on the raid. Where were they now? She tried to imagine being rescued but it was an exercise too strenuous to carry on.

And then the giants started snatching women. She balled herself up against the rock, feeling every sharp edge of its volcanic walls, unashamedly thankful that she was not among the chosen. She closed her eyes again and covered her ears.

SHE MUST HAVE SLEPT. IT WAS STILL DARK. THE CAVE was silent though a bit less chilled, when she was jolted awake by a hand on her mouth. Her head spun with the notion that it was Madai performing some miraculous rescue. It was Yamma.

The woman shushed her, wagging her head at the entrance and the two Nephilim standing guard at the mouth of the cave. They were silhouetted against the light of their fire. The second fire, which had kept her from freezing through the night danced its waning light across Yamma's grinning face and the stiff bundle she still clutched at her breast. All the feeling that woke in Iscah was a dread to be so near the Nephilim's mad woman and dead child.

Where had her pity gone?

It was only after the first flush of waking to such a dire and unchanged circumstance, that she began to hear the quiet breathing of the disoriented and undone – a faint whimper, a soft moan, an occasional snore and she remembered the women chosen in the night. And she was relieved, glad really, to feel the angst that welled up inside herself.

"I know the way out," Yamma hissed.

"Hmm?"

"I did it before."

"You were here?"

"I told you. Keep your wits if you want to get out of here." She sounded quite sane. "It was him that brought me here, while Madai was talking."

Iscah looked where she had pointed, but she needn't have for Malak's claim on the child had burned itself into Iscah's brain. She might have believed the child was made with protest, but somehow she could not. There was a darkness to the woman that went even beyond killing aged mothers. Iscah could hear Yamma's breath very close and her skin prickled. She would rather have had the madness than the evil.

"Over there," Yamma whispered. "And be silent. We must get past them," she pointed at two women asleep on the ground.

"You don't mean to leave them?"

Yamma came so close to her ear that Iscah could feel the woman's nose. "Don't be a fool. I'll not risk waking him."

She had meant Naphal of course, whose wild-ox skull cast a rather large shadow against the walls of the cave. His breath came with the rhythmic regularity of deep sleep. His night's activities had gone long after the rest had given it up. Iscah thought she could see someone still beneath him, used up and crumpled like a down pillow spills its feathers. No indeed, Naphal must not be awakened.

Even still, it was too terrible to desert the rest.

"We cannot leave them behind," Iscah argued again.

"Stay then."

Yamma pulled away. Like a sprite, she seemed to disappear into the shadows and Iscah reached out to find her again.

"Wait."

Yamma put her fingers on Iscah's mouth, playfully this time. "I want you to live," she sang quietly. Then she took Iscah's hand and led her as if they were children in a game, creeping past the sleepers – inordinately quiet – like a spectre that could see in the dark. She laid Iscah's one hand against the cave wall and pulled her by the other. Iscah felt every sharp edge and contour till they came to an oblong opening little bigger round than her own head. Yamma's breath was in her ear again.

"In there," she warbled quietly, "fire mountain's door. I've been here before, with my little Madai." And then she dropped Iscah's hand.

The light of the fire undulated against the cave walls and ceiling, occasionally enough to cast a shadow, enough for Iscah to watch Yamma just pushing her baby into the shaft as far as her arm would reach and then to wiggle in herself.

Iscah found herself standing there alone with Yamma disappeared into the side of the rocky wall. She might have thought she dreamt it, if not for the sound of grunting and kicking – and it growing ever fainter. A woman moaned...

Only Malak was awake, he and a second guard, but they were far at the entrance.

MADAI THOUGHT HE COULD FEEL SNOW IN THE AIR. HE pulled his bear robe closed and watched the cave. There was Arphaxas beside him, still in dragon skin. His Patta was on his other side.

He felt an unreasonable joy that Iscah was captive and would not venture past that good news to consider other fates, not even Japhet's. What his Patta thought, or Tiras, Madai could not work out. They neither one spoke again on the matter, but wore a hunter's stoic face.

"Where's the Stupor?" Guran whispered. "We can take the two at the front from here."

"They've got captives," Togarmah hissed.

Guran looked thoughtful but a moment. "They're better dead than... taken."

"Had you not better ask them that?" Ashkinaz countered. "Yamma could be down there."

"Better she be dead."

196

"If you will have revenge, boy, it will wait till this is over." It was Togarmah who spoke, more perceptive than Madai would have thought.

"Then what will we do, Patta?" Tiras asked. "If Kiellet…"

He hardly moved in answer, but to turn his head and put the Nephilim in his sights. "There are seven. When we kill those two, there'll be five."

It was happening too fast for Madai; they'd only just taken position above the cave. Their first plan had certainly not worked and he was afraid that Nephilim might kill prisoners when attacked. But to wait would only bring the morning and what would they do then?

"We will beg the help of God," Ashkinaz interrupted the silence. "And after that we'll kill those two."

Madai was watching for his Patta's face to glow with ethereal light as Noah's had glowed. It would have made him feel better. But the prayer was short.

Togarmah and Tiras both stood up, entirely satisfied.

"We go for the one on the left," Togarmah declared. "Ashkinaz and Madai, the right one. Guran, Kessed and Riphath, watch for what comes out."

Arphaxas also stood. He drew his scimitar, which might have been humorous given the distance, if it was not that Madai scarcely trusted him.

"Wait!" Arphaxas hissed. He pointed with the sword.

A shadow was visible rising from the earth above the cave. It was made visible, a brief moment only, by a slight break in the clouds. They watched, dumbstruck as a second emerged. It was possible that they were two of the women; they were certainly not the Nephilim. Another appeared, and then more – one at a time.

"Where are they coming from?" Guran muttered.

"I thought there was only one way out." Madai glared at Arphaxas who merely shrugged.

They waited after the last figure appeared what seemed an interminable length of time. They tried to count, but could not agree on the number. The shadows had appeared and seemed to vanish in the briefest instant.

"They'll be going for the village."

"It's burned."

"Where else would they go?"

"They'll be lost in the dark."

"These mountains belong to us." It was Togarmah, being dogmatic. "They will not be lost." He skillfully aimed his arrow. "Ready? Now!"

MALAK AND ARBA WERE HIT SIMULTANEOUSLY. A PEN-chant for covering just their loins left only muscle to stop the obsidian arrows. Malak was struck twice in the heart; Arba once in the heart and in the soft of his throat. Mammoth hunters do practice a good aim.

Kessed and Guran watched for the others. Riphath watched for his son. It was, however, two impeccable kills, and hardly a sound escaped the giants as they died.

Arphaxas sheathed his sword. "I'll get the Stupor."

"Let's kill them like men," Togarmah retorted.

"Wait," Ashkinaz put down his bow. "If only one of us is lost, it is one that will not bear another son.

Nephilim are giants. The Stupor is… prudent."

Madai wished his father did not always seem to agree with Arphaxas. He hadn't seen Iscah escape, but then they'd been only shadows. He would not torture himself.

"Use it now or not at all," Arphaxas warned. "It will be light."

Togarmah eased his grip on the longbow and glared at them.

"One will be lost regardless," he complained.

"Why do you say that, old friend?" Ashkinaz asked.

"The one who takes the root."

"It doesn't happen that fast."

"Do you think we will simply sneak in and not awake them? It is nigh to dawn."

Ashkinaz lifted his head eastward. "Not yet," he muttered.

Arphaxas simply started down the mountain. The rest hurried after him and the way was rocky making a difficult job to do it quietly.

Arphaxas found the Stupor where he had hidden it. He gathered it up and started his way down again.

"I'll take it," Togarmah said, stopping him.

"You don't trust me."

"You are young. You can still father sons." The two men glared a moment.

"There's good sense in that," Madai interjected quietly.

"If they are awakened, it will not work anyway," Arphaxas argued. "And I am better with this." He nodded at the scimitar.

He removed his dragon skin at that and laid it with a degree of sentiment on the rocks. Then he crouched forward and started the last distance toward the cave. It was not a conscious thought, but sat at the back of Madai's mind, that Arphaxas may be providing them a sacrificial act.

WHEN ARPHAXAS HAD GONE, THEY POSITIONED THEM-selves as if by instinct. With the cover of a rockslide, Madai waited directly opposite the opening; Ashkinaz to his right and Togarmah his left. Tiras and Riphath disappeared into the dark. Tiras had always liked a perch just above an entrance. Guran and Kessed fanned to the far left and right.

Then they waited.

Madai watched, waiting from above for Arphaxas to appear in the clearing below. It seemed to take forever. But a shadow emerged after a time and crept toward the bonfire. It bent and examined the two dead Nephilim who had used the fire to keep warm through a cold night's watch. The fire seemed to shine a singular light on Arphaxas, rising to creep past the bodies. Still, there were no sounds of awaking from the cave. Arphaxas deposited half his load in the outer fire and quietly stole inside with the rest.

They waited again.

Surely Mighty God was with them, because Arphaxas emerged a moment later, less his cache of roots. Then he disappeared quickly, back into the dark. Madai listened for him, coming round the rocks and through the brush, but Arphaxas was a practiced stalker and reappeared silent as a phantom.

"There's more in there than just Nephilim," he hissed. "Who? Who's in there?"

"I couldn't tell, but…"

Madai jumped up. "It'll kill her," he cried and dashed for the cave.

He found the first giant sprawled across a woman's body. Her head was twisted and she seemed to be broken. In the instant that it took Madai to determine it was not Iscah the Nephilim was awake. It was Naphal. He rose up like a great bear and wrapped Madai round with powerful huge arms. Arphaxas's scimitar caught him in the side and he loosened his grip just enough that Madai broke away. The Nephilim king bellowed and grabbed for Madai again even as the cave erupted with angry roars from other waking giants.

Naphal's horned skull was dislodged from his head as he swung an arm back to knock Arphaxas away. He spread his great arms wide and whirled around as Ashkinaz joined the fight in his son's defense. The three of them were sent sprawling, the wound from Arphaxas's scimitar but a nip.

Madai heard Togarmah's voice and suddenly everyone was in the cave, sharp blades were everywhere at once. He rolled, just avoiding Naphal's foot to his skull. He hit the back legs of one of the just awakened Nephilim and the giant stumbled, knocking Naphal against the cave wall.

Madai fumbled quickly for his spear. He was after Naphal, but caught the second giant instead. Madai drove his spear precisely through the creature's back all the way to his sternum.

A man shouted, "Back here!"

A woman screamed.

A shadowy mass roared and climbed across the screaming girl, straight for Kessed. Madai aimed for the giant's side and had time to deliver a second arrow before being crashed to the ground under a great weight. His assailant did not need a weapon but grabbed Madai by the hair and banged his head against the ground.

His brain must have been scrambled as all the mayhem went silent and everything black. When his vision cleared, it could have been but mere seconds for there was Ashkinaz towering above with a huge rock in his hands. The father bashed the giant's head, and followed him to the ground, bashing him again. Madai wondered, slightly addled, how many bashes it would take.

There was yelling from the back. Arphaxas leaped to cut free two men that had been taken along with the women. They came together at the Nephilim with bare hands, Arphaxas with his scimitar. Madai jumped up.

The slightest of dizziness, he grabbed for his longbow again. There was bedlam, a woman shrieking past him, arms grabbing, giants cursing and roaring. The Nephilim raged, great in strength but the target of arrows mighty enough to bring down a mammoth.

In the end, having been roused from a heavy sleep after a long night of butchery had proved a weapon against them, though only two of the Nephilim were slain and none of The Family. Naphal and his last two men, one with Madai's arrows wagging in his side, had their backs together, facing out in three directions. They were each holding a thick square of leather, like the head of a giant drum. It was held in front of the body with an ingenuity that was impressive, a kind of portable defense. Madai found himself trying to analyze the leather; what sort of beast had grown it and he was dizzy again. He blinked to readjust his eyes. He sucked in smoky air.

Stupor root.

Madai refocused. He assessed himself in a panic: still functioning properly, but there was a sort of wobbliness in his head. The arm, which held the bowstring taut and the heel of the arrow in his fingers, felt heavy.

He blinked to clear his eyes, surprised that the Nephilim seemed quite steady and on their feet despite the smoke. Walled in by their shields of hide, they seemed to be merely waiting.

"How shall you die?" Madai shouted at them. It was to stave off the root's affect and distract before it became too obvious. Perhaps Stupor did not affect Nephilim. He glanced at the others. Guran gave his head a shake.

And Naphal smiled.

"I smell Dragon's Tail." He sniffed, pulling the smoke into his lungs. "It delivers us to the stars." He inhaled again, directing a sneer at Madai. "We visit our god there. Perhaps our god is stronger than yours."

Ashkinaz took a step backward. Tiras also. "Come away, Madai." His father urged.

It was possibly the only choice. Still, they held the three Nephilim in check by seven mammoth arrows trained in their direction. Madai tried to think. How long could they keep the aim true? How long till he lost his strength?

"Madai…"

"Don't be a fool," Arphaxas growled and moved backward.

So, together they backed away. The smoke was doing something to Madai's legs, so much that he had to think very deliberately about how to move them. Indeed, he felt the fool. Their advantage of numbers would soon be no advantage at all. He heard one of the giants laugh. They appeared to know it too

Madai coughed, his eyes streamed but the morning air was starting to clear his head. The others did not seem so affected as he had been. Perhaps he had entered the cave with passions too high and fears for Iscah too strong. The Nephilim had not followed. Malak, the first to die, had proved the effectiveness of their arrows. His body at the entrance to the cave bore them witness of that.

They reclaimed their first positions in the rocks successfully. Morning's light was upon them and they had but to wait. When the wait came long, Madai remembered that there seemed another way out for they had watched a certain number of human forms seem to appear out of the earth in the night. It was his hope that Iscah was one of them.

"Arphaxas," he began.

That was when Naphal began to shout. His curses were unspeakable, vile, and he described atrocities yet to be performed. Madai wasted an arrow, striking the earth at the mouth of the cave.

"Still out there, Whelp?" Naphal laughed. He called out to his god and offered him Madai's first son. But all that emerged from Fire Mountain was the dark smoke of Stupor Root.

The more they howled, the more Arphaxas paced. It was a waste of energy and a distraction, until Madai remembered the be-heading of the Shinar priest. That had been an exercise of passion, a long awaited revenge.

And Madai considered that the gods of these Nephilim were not unlike the gods of Shinar. Arphaxas muttered indecipherably.

A cold blast of wind came suddenly. It nearly pealed Madai's coat off. They had no fire and a frigid north blast came roaring off the mountain, funneled into the gully and at the mouth of the cavern. Arphaxas turned to face it, then abruptly started pulling up brush. It was autumn dry and studded with thorns. He raced down the hillside hugging the brush against his body, and hurled it into the Nephilim's outer fire. Ashkinaz and Togarmah yanked brush. Tiras launched a substantial fallen branch. In a short time, it was no campfire but a pyre. The smoke billowed thick and white, carried by winter's arms deep inside the mountain. And even Nephilim must breathe air.

THE ONE WITH MADAI'S ARROWS IN HIS SIDE CAME OUT first. He came with a roar and his leather shield and brandishing a sword as wide as his arm. He was quietly run through with the arrows of six men. Naphal appeared next. His sword was at the throat of his last cohort, a shield made of living skin. Both men were coughing, their lungs filled with the smoke of Arphaxas's brush and their dragon's tail.

Togarmah simply used his spear to impale the first Nephilim, exposing the second.

Naphal towered above the fallen giant. He pealed the spear up through the dead man's chest and brandished it, dripping blood, in the air above him. Perhaps the hunters were being cruel, but Naphal was struck with no less than seven projectiles, none of which were immediately fatal.

Madai and Arphaxas reached him first. He was on his knees, using the spear as a prop and perforated with arrows like a porcupine's quills. He glared fiercely at Madai.

They ringed him. They studied him in proper fascination.

"You think you've won, son of Ashkinaz?" Naphal's voice was remarkably strong. "You will not. Perhaps I will return."

"You have a mortal wound."

Naphal's lips twisted into a half smile, exposing bloody teeth. "But we will always hunt the Seed."

It was more than a boast. It had the sound of a curse or an ages old conflict.

"So you do believe there is a Crushing Seed," Madai challenged.

The giant seemed insensible to his wounds. He actually smiled. "Of course."

"He is coming, then."

Naphal's nostrils flared. Spittle formed at the corners of his mouth. "Of course not!" he howled.

Arphaxas stepped back. He raised his scimitar. Naphal followed the movement with his eyes.

"Watch that one, Whelp," he warned just before the scimitar sang.

CHAPTER 38

*I*T WAS VERY DARK HERE, WITHOUT A FIRE. THERE were unknowns about her, all save Mineo and the old man, Tiptri. The night was also cold. Winter was coming and Simirra did not know this new land, did not know how terrible or long the winter might really be. She was shivering, cringing in a hidden grove of trees rooted in these lonesome wilds. Even the red-haired Arphaxas in his dragon's cape was probably dead by now. She was indeed alone, like a stable horse amongst asses.

The instant she thought it, she felt a mortifying rebuke. It was an undoing moment, to look behind the veil at one's own self. She was glad it was dark.

But there had been other senses at work. She had heard the slaughter of a people, smelled the razing of their homes. She had done what was asked of her, helping Mineo to bring these who believed what her own parents had believed – here to this grove. It was rather ironic, she thought, and slightly comforting. She studied them. She recognized the old man. He had been strapped in his sledge and tossed about like a piece of worthless chaff by the Nephilim, Malak. Still he had risen to defy the giant, as an ant against an anteater. It was senseless, and yet somewhat to be admired. These few, though hiding out quite like moles, had needed reminding that there was nothing but living they could do now for The Family. They were The Family. Again the old man had risen, standing straight as he could to reason that it was their duty to carry on the star stories for children yet to come.

And Mineo, was she not quite a lovely woman despite her circumstance? If she wore a beast's dead skin, it was soft and warm. If she wore plaits like a horse's tail, her hair was abundant, needing three braids. If she cooked musky meat above an open fire pit, she offered it to strangers with a liberal heart

It suddenly seemed to Simirra that perhaps a duty rested to her as well. Mineo was likely alone now, without husband or son. There was only Madai's little child who was of more trouble than help. The thought stung like a slap. Why, she would have fought all Hades for her own lost babe!

"Praises to God Tiras is gone," Kiellet whispered beside her, hugging her child close.

"And pray they be made safe," Mineo concluded quietly, which was what the old man began to do. They were mostly old folk and children and women, those that kept the old ways, as Madai described it.

Now he was probably dead, he and those too few others who'd gone to kill giants. She supposed it was them that were killed instead, even Arphaxas with his shiny scimitar, who had not run away after all. She did not know what had become of the girl, Iscah, who was as near to friend as she had.

"You mustn't gloom, Simirra."

Mineo's soft words came unexpectedly.

"They are in the Hand of Mighty God. He will preserve them."

That it might be true was Simirra's greatest doubt. Surprising her, she realized it was also her profoundest desire.

STILL THE NIGHT WORE ON. IT WAS ALL SILENCE NOW. Even the stench of singed mammoth hide proved it could be endured. All night's little sounds; hunting owls and harping insects, were mute. One might hear the last of summer cherries wither in the cold for all the quiet.

"What's that coming?" Someone suddenly hissed.

The sharp snap of brush in the dark was a mighty noise to Simirra's ears. She jerked her head toward the sound, caught unaware by fright.

Mineo stood up. Simirra grabbed at her, ready to pull her back down.

"Simirra?" Came a cautious voice calling from the dark.

Mineo started forward when Simirra stopped her again. "Wait."

"But it's…"

"Better to be sure."

"Iscah?" Mineo answered anyway.

"Are you all there?" Iscah's voice was coming near.

"This way," Mineo called back.

They were exposed now… Simirra shrugged. If it were Nephilim sending Iscah to flush them out, then she would face it with these few who must be her people now. The rustling through the forest came closer. It sounded a goodly number. They were doomed.

"O, my child!" Mineo gasped as a knot of shivering women came into the grove.

There were six of them, standing in a huddle, clinging to each other, perhaps too stunned to talk. "Praises to God!" Mineo exclaimed. "But… you are bleeding…"

"They took us to the caves," Iscah panted. "But Yamma knew the way out – a shaft. It was very tight with sharp edges."

"Yamma?"

"Where is she?" someone grumbled.

Simirra frowned. She felt very like that voice had sounded. Of all The Family, it was Yamma she would least wish to be saved. She watched closely as a shadow-form emerged from behind Iscah and wearing the girl's very coat.

She was carrying a package of old skins. Someone else grumbled that it would be Yamma with so many others lost.

"The Nephilim took you?" A nervous young voice asked. "To the Fire Mountain?"

"Did they…"

"We left seven others behind," Iscah sadly confessed. "Why? Were they…"

"We would awaken the Nephilim… if we had tried…"

Simirra heard the guilty sound of Iscah's voice and knew her well enough to imagine she would suffer with it for some time when she should be glad to be alive at all.

"The Nephilim are beasts," Simirra interjected. "Be thankful you're alive. If they'd wakened there'd be none of you here." It was reasonable.

"Yes, you're right," Iscah agreed far too quietly. "Then they were…"

"Here, Iscah, you're freezing. Someone find her a coat," Mineo insisted. "They're all freezing."

"They took us straight from our beds," one of the girls chattered.

"Yamma," Simirra demanded, "give them one of those skins." The woman hugged her bundle tight.

"It's her babe," Iscah whispered.

One of the older women came close. "The babe? Let's see him," she demanded. "No one's seen him yet."

Yamma pulled away.

"Yes," another began, "if he is The Bowman, we want a look."

Iscah stepped between them. "Simirra," she said, her voice suddenly commanding "Find Yamma a place to lay down."

The other woman huffed. "She's no virgin mother. It's only Toban that believed it."

"There were many more that believed it," Mineo corrected. She patted the woman's arm. "We'll not do this now, Eedaal. We that keep the first ways have survived. It's enough. And these maids are tired and cold. We must find them something warm."

"We can't have a fire!" A quavery voice insisted.

A shuffling began as someone at the back came toward the newcomers. "I want the father's name." It was Old Tiptri. He bumped past Eedaal. "Who is the father, Yamma?"

"Keep him away," Yamma whimpered.

The sound of her voice surprised Simirra because there was no contempt in it or strength of any kind. But it was Tiptri that Simirra had a sympathy for. She put her arm around him as if to hold him up.

"Perhaps she will tell us all later."

"She's been the shame of her Mamam and me, brought us very low," he argued.

Eedaal, seeming somewhat ashamed herself, took Tiptri's arm. "Come away, old friend," she urged. "Mineo is right; there'll be time for this later. We none blame you nor her Mamam. 'Twas likely Tiglath that put her with child, I'd say. We'll find out tomorrow."

Old Tiptri strained against both women a moment, as though he would get at his daughter. But he stopped, seeming to change his mind.

"We'll see when Guran gets back," he declared and hobbled away.

Mineo and Eedaal, who was really no unkind soul, set about finding something warm for the six to wear.

"Are you alright, Iscah?" Simirra asked. "You are freezing. Why is she wearing your coat?"

But Iscah ignored her. "Will you rest?" She asked of Yamma. Simirra could hear a careful note in Iscah's voice, which was an instant cue that there was something amiss with this pagan. "I shall watch over your boy."

"Madai's boy!"

Yamma actually hissed, and seemed to energize at that declaration. She looked away from Iscah and squarely at Simirra, all her wooden posture exchanged for a triumphant look.

"I had him first," she sang.

That was when Simirra remembered the impulsive proclamation she had made with her own hand on her own belly. Though it should matter very little, she found it quite unsavory to affix Madai with this creature. Simirra clenched her mouth shut but could not stifle her eyes.

"Won't you let Simirra see him?" Iscah asked with an unsuitably sunny voice.

But it made Yamma smile and Simirra realized then that she was quite mad. She seemed to retract her claws just enough to pull the blanket back.

Simirra's breath caught at the sight.

Yamma looked dotingly at her child, as any mother would do. With the dark and all the shadows, it was hard to see the expression change in her eyes, but Yamma sat very still. And she looked at it a very long time before she finally extended her arms toward Simirra.

"You may take it," she declared rather flatly, "I must sleep."

Simirra recoiled, but only slightly before she reached out. She took the child. It weighed so little in her arms. A swell rose up, like something forever present but persistently ignored. It was a most inopportune surprise for her. She closed her eyes, blocking out the sight of the red haired infant.

"Give him to me," she heard Iscah whisper and opened her eyes.

She let the girl remove the little body from her arms. She must gain a hold or she would actually unravel, now when she had just determined to be of good use.

"We should do something with him," Iscah whispered. Simirra nodded, watching Yamma carefully.

"I'll get Mineo. She will know what to do."

It was all the jolt Simirra needed to bring back her senses – and was a terrible suggestion. With this new slander… it was quite more than Mineo should bear.

"Let's have a better look at him," Simirra suggested pointedly.

Yamma sighed. She readjusted her body, asleep instantly as though she were the innocent.

"What?"

"Mineo mustn't be told what Yamma is claiming."

Iscah frowned. "They know this is not the Promised One."

Simirra shook her head again. "No, that he is Madai's son. She cannot be told that."

"But that is ridiculous. Who would believe such a thing?" Iscah stopped. She paused a moment. "Besides, this babe was very young."

"That is it precisely, Iscah," Simirra pressed, "it gives a question, even you."

"But… no. She is…"

"A temptress and a pagan." Simirra gave Iscah a look. "And Madai is only a man."

ISCAH WAS VERY COLD. HER ENTIRE BODY STUNG. IT WAS covered in a web of sharp little cuts. She shivered and glanced at the sleeping Yamma, a woman who had probably saved her only for a moment's improbable gratitude, hugging a coat tight and cozy. She was not aware of the moment that she had left off seeing her as loathsome, but only a poor mad soul hugging a dead child. Somewhere in the dark, stumbling back she supposed. Iscah laid the baby down – feeling suddenly disheartened. But of course she would be disheartened. She was tired. Only she did not like the sound of Simirra telling her that Yamma had been a temptress and Madai just a man.

"I shall see then," Simirra insisted.

"What?"

"There is something about that boy…"

Iscah shook her head dogmatically, but Simirra pulled back the blanket anyway.

"Where do you think they are?" Iscah asked, ignoring the thing that Simirra was doing.

She did not see the woman's expression when she looked up. "Who?" Simirra asked, "Arphaxas and Madai?"

Iscah nodded.

"Perhaps they are waiting in ambush," Simirra suggested half-heartedly. And Iscah knew she did not really believe it.

CHAPTER 39

TIRAS OUTRAN MADAI. MADAI OUTRAN ASHKINAZ and Riphath but they all reached the ruin of their camp, smoldering now, just waiting for a wind to start a flame again. And three ghosts of women were there, those who'd been so lucky as to be saved by the Nephilim, but unlucky enough to be used that first night. Madai had the vaguest sense that they'd escaped during the fight, all but the poor broken women he'd first come upon and them that were crushed in the melee.

They seemed dazed, sifting through the ash and were wearing only what they'd been taken in. A young girl glanced up as Madai reached the village. She ran at him with black, ash-covered hands.

"They're all dead!" she cried. Ashkinaz gave her his coat.

"Have you been to Cherry Thicket?" he asked.

Her face seemed confused, grubby with soot and tears. She wore the expression of a stunned animal in the immediate first seconds of a mortal wound. Her face slowly registered the possibility.

"I hadn't thought of that…"

And together they all ran toward the grove.

AN AUTUMN'S LEAF, WHICH HAD CLUNG SO STUBBORNLY to its cherry branch, finally gave itself up to the wind. It sailed past Madai with a flourish. It was a stunning yellow-red, insignificance to him. He and the others had stopped at the edge of the grove, both afraid and desperate to know.

"Mineo!" his father called anxiously.

Madai could not bring himself to cry out names. But a face suddenly appeared, full of joy. She came racing toward them.

"Kiellet!" Tiras cried. He grabbed her up fiercely. "Naru?" Kiellet was sobbing. She was laughing.

"You are alive!" she cried.

Riphath's son also appeared, jumping at his father like a child though he was thirteen. "They're all safe, Patta," he announced proudly.

"Good boy."

All safe? Madai recognized the words even as more of The Family appeared. He counted faces, all the one's they'd sent his Mamam and Iscah to warn, all but...

"She is with that woman," Simirra whispered, taking his arm, pulling him into the cherry grove.

It was all he heard... the essence of Simirra's remark. He had the sense of his father beside him, hardly breathing... afraid as he was afraid. In an instant they were running again, ducking branches when he heard a sort of gurgle in his father's throat. And then his Mamam was there, looking joyous, coming through the brush.

"Praises to God!" she and Ashkinaz each cried.

"Iscah?" The question escaped his lips of its own volition.

His Patta grabbed his Mamam. Mineo managed to circle Madai's neck with her right arm as she was lifted up. "She's well. Madai..."

But Madai was already into the bushes.

IT WAS NOT UNTIL HE CAME UPON HER THAT HE FELT THE fear turn to relief. And she was looking up, looking straight into his eyes as though she had sensed his coming. She had an expression on her face to make his heart race.

"Iscah?"

She stood up and that was when he noticed someone else. The woman had wakened when Iscah stood. She smiled at him.

The pounding of Madai's heart turned sick in his stomach. His mouth went dry.

"She saved us all," were Iscah's first words to him.

He was struck with a wild panic. "Here Iscah! Come away from her!"

Yamma smiled again. She stood as well, and took a step toward him.

"They took him, Madai," she said. "And gave me that." Yamma pointed at the small bundle on the ground.

He could hardly breathe. "Come away, Iscah."

But it was Yamma that came, and Iscah was looking at him strangely.

"It's a Nephilim baby!" Simirra spat, having followed behind.

"What?"

Yamma spun at her. "Quiet!" she hissed.

"What did you say?"

It was Guran. He was with Old Tiptri. Arphaxas was with them and Togarmah and all the rest. They were all there as if sprung straight out of the trees. Guran jumped at his sister with a crazy, jolting step then abruptly stopped – as if he came upon some invisible obstacle. It was, in fact, the wrappings of the child. It lay, a little noticed bundle, as though discarded at the base of a cherry tree. He stared at it, and slowly dropped to his knees. He pulled back cautiously on the swaddling cloths.

"Well?" Togarmah inquired tensely.

Guran looked up. "Six fingers," He affirmed.

Old Tiptri was shaking but today he did not weep for shame.

Guran let the cloth drop back across the still little face and stood up. "Get away from her!" he ordered Iscah.

Madai was suddenly lifting Iscah up by the arms, not sure how he'd gotten there or whom he was saving her from. She felt stiff and unyielding.

"No!" she cried.

And he was equally unsure whether the response was for Guran or himself.

"Is that why you killed our Mamam?" Guran was shrieking. "Is that why you'd have no other midwife? Did you kill her because she saw that... thing?"

Yamma turned to him for the first time. She seemed vague at first, till she contorted her face into an actual snarl and growled at him.

"Guran!" Ashkinaz grabbed the brother's arm to stop him.

No one expected it of Old Tiptri. He was at Yamma's jugular with the sharp edge of a well-worn hunting knife and the speed few would expect of an old man.

Madai watched it all happen, holding Iscah with too tight a grip as his fates changed by the instant – a dead babe, and not his own.

'Let it happen.' That old voice in his head prodded. But Tiptri's hand was shaking and Madai let Iscah go. He sprang at him, grabbed his wrist and pulled him away.

"No, Old Father," he heard himself say. "You will be undone."

It was so silent after he spoke that he could almost hear the leaves rustle as they settled to the ground. Only the wind whined. He held the old man and looked in his eyes, which were startled at first, then confused and finally... relieved. The ancient father, being of two minds, slowly exhaled.

Yamma chuckled. There was a wild look in her eyes, standing defiant with all the remains of the Family around her.

"What'll we do with her then?" Guran muttered, looking slightly aghast at his father.

"Help your Patta, boy." Ashkinaz led Tiptri to his son.

Madai put a steadying arm around Iscah. Tiras held both his daughter and his wife. Riphath was stoic beside his boy as Guran slowly moved his father away. It was then Arphaxas found Yamma.

It was also the moment of concession for Togarmah, when he received Arphaxas as one of them. It was a long deserved and efficient execution. Yamma was round-eyed, powerless. She looked enormously surprised.

"Arphaxas!" It was Mineo speaking for them all.

She dropped to her knees beside Yamma, quick enough to hear a last expulsion of air between her teeth.

Mineo pushed her hand right into the wound, feeling for the rhythmic pulse of Yamma's heart. "Arphaxas?" she asked this time, turning to look him in the eyes.

He wiped his blade.

Guran was stunned, not disapproving precisely, perhaps just preempted. "Come away, Patta," he urged. The old man had sagged somewhat. Guran had him under the arms. Tiptri was staring at the three of them,

Arphaxas, Mineo and a body of Yamma. It was all red down the front and he seemed slightly bewildered, conflicted by an act that he had only the moment before designed for himself. Then he blinked, stood a little straighter and looked up at his son.

"Where will we go?" he asked quite sensibly. "Everything's burnt."

"We'll go back to the caves along the river," Ashkinaz answered him. "Where we waited for the ice to melt."

It was a reasoned exchange, necessary and pragmatic even with a corpse at their feet. "Yes," Togarmah agreed. "When Toban brought us away too early with his Divining."

"Where is Toban?" Mineo asked in an uneasy voice.

"In the ashes, I expect."

ASHKINAZ AND TOGARMAH WERE AT ODDS. THEY WERE so few and apportioned unequally, women to men. In the end, it was decided to seek out their brothers to the north, where they had moved to live in houses of stone. It was a solution preferable to multiple wives, as Mighty God had only made a single Eve. A resolute dogmatism seemed the better course after so much lost.

A second dawn was upon them since the defeat of the Nephilim, since Yamma, and Madai watched as The Family collected their few belongings. Even so, it was a better stash than he might dare to hope. He was watching his Mamam as she tied up a pack. She splinted it with a plank of wood... the Ark plank! How very like her, to rescue a son's treasure at such a time.

Madai pushed his forefinger against the tip of the arrowhead. It was not his best effort, but they were in a hurry. They would indeed spend the winter in the cave, and then venture North. He hoped there would be obsidian there.

He spied Arphaxas having the last bite of a young range hog. He supposed it was fitting, as he'd been the one to kill it last night. He'd also killed something else, for which Madai was grateful, inelegantly so.

"We are going back to the cave, Arphaxas," he said, approaching the man. "It's big enough. We may even make it before the snows."

Arphaxas sucked on the last bone.

"I think not, Kinsman," he said rising.

Madai closed his fist tightly around the arrowhead. He frowned, feeling both too indebted and too culpable for a full-blown argument. He carefully avoided the tidy mound of dirt, all that remained of Yamma, his last impediment.

"Why will you not?" he asked.

"It has seemed my lot to... spare you."

"Winter is nigh." Madai argued, playing at ignorance.

"Too close quarters."

"Do you forget the cold, Arphaxas?"

Madai said it just as a frosty draft blew back the hood of the dragon cape. Arphaxas turned to face the wind. "I do like it fresh."

"Come with us."

Arphaxas turned slowly to face Madai with a vague expression. Then he chuckled. "You are benevolent, Kinsman," he replied ironically.

Which poked at Madai's conscience, a little like a lad being caught in a crime.

"And I grow weary of... peoples." Arphaxas muttered.

"What are you talking about?"

"I find that I do not mind killing." Arphaxas replied cryptically staring off into the trees. "Perhaps I should. With people comes killing; Nephilim, a baby killer for Simirra and Nephilim whores. Why, do you think?"

"Why what?"

"Why do I like it?"

"Because they were evil."

Arphaxas smiled coldly. "Precisely whose evil are we talking about?"

"Evil is evil. You know the first ways, Arphaxas."

"You mean The Huwah?"

"You know I mean The One True God." Arphaxas shrugged.

"The Huwah, then."

"How can you use that name?"

He shrugged again.

Madai pulled his coat tighter. He was feeling the wind and hearing the voice of his Mamam looking for him.

"Go to her, Kinsman."

But Madai could not leave Arphaxas somehow. "You must come too."

Arphaxas stared a time before he answered with a degree of sincerity, "I fair better alone."

"We aren't meant to be alone."

Which brought a wicked chuckle up through Arphaxas's gullet.

"So you say, Kinsman. There was that," he nodded at Yamma's grave, "and a wife – before my sister." He glared at Madai. "And who will you have now? Simirra? Iscah? Both?"

It was a step too far. Madai made an aggressive move forward when he saw Arphaxas's eyes glint. He stopped himself.

"We are none innocent," Madai replied stiffly, an unplanned admission.

But Arphaxas had revealed something of himself as well, though he did not respond.. "I did Palapa no harm," Madai insisted.

Arphaxas was stone still and silent.

"She was killed by an enemy of mine, that is true." Madai continued. "I would have stopped it, if I could."

Arphaxas turned away at that. "You've always thought well of yourself, Kinsman."

Madai put his hand cautiously on Arphaxas's back. "Not so. I am a low man."

The dragon man continued to face away. He let the wind blow against him.

"But I did no dishonor to your sister," Madai finished.

He felt Arphaxas grow stiff at his touch, then exhale.

"Did you once tell me that she died well?" he finally whispered.

Madai was taken aback by the plea in his question. "She did."

Then the big man turned around. He stared into Madai's eyes. They were in quite a close proximity and Madai took a step back.

"This second earth of yours," Arphaxas whispered, "is no mercy. Your Huwah – if He spared the Nua – He spared us for this piece of hell." Then Arphaxas appeared to feel the cold for the first time and pulled the cape close.

Madai looked uneasily at Yamma's grave, hers and the Nephilim baby. They had not buried them together, unwilling to lay the guilty with the innocent, even one as had six fingers. He smelled the burnt village in the air. He remembered Ido with the plague. And then he remembered a winter, only the winter last, that he had passed with Noah himself.

"But..." he blinked back unexpected emotion, looking at Arphaxas. " Mighty God meant us for Eden."

The wind whined back at him. He thought for a moment that Arphaxas would simply turn and walk away.

"Which is why I serve no God," he said instead.

The words shocked Madai.

"Your All Mighty God is not so mighty after all. And," Arphaxas continued after a pause, "it seems neither was the god of the great Nimrod. So… who rules the world but men?"

"The Promised One will." Madai's answer surprised even himself. But it was a realization as clear as a summer's sky. Perhaps that Promised One would also make men holy… even himself.

"High tales," Arphaxas scoffed. "What good God makes such a race of beasts, eh Madai?"

"It takes a great strength to leave a son to his own passions, his own will. Would it not be easier to hobble him to a stake and save his mistakes?" Madai pressed.

"Ah… the fruit of that tree."

Madai succumbed to anger at last. He just opened his mouth when…

"Madai once stood where you are standing."

Both men started at the sound of Iscah's voice.

"Your Mamam sent me after you, Madai," she continued. "And here I find you in a disagreement with Arphaxas. You two must mend this grievance."

"Arphaxas will not come with us," Madai explained, a little like a boy caught in mischief.

"And he said very much more," she replied.

Madai felt himself go red.

"About such unknowables as you used to ask."

"Do not be troubled, Iscah," Arphaxas interjected. "I prefer the wilds."

"Ridiculous man," she countered. "Do you think it's only the likes of you with questions? Does one ponder? One asks."

She sat on a stump beside the smallest grave. There was something in the way she did that that reminded Madai of a stubborn little girl.

"There is God and there are…spectres," she continued. "Madai was there and saw it when Noah talked to The God, so He is quite real." She laid her hands together on her lap. "And there is that snake from Eden, of which you know very well for you mentioned The Tree so do not play at ignorance. But that one – the dragon – is quite real as well. He spits fire as dragons do and slithers about if he needs to hide. I do believe he hid inside poor Yamma." She paused. She seemed very certain. "And so we choose. We must, for they each vie for us. They are outside this world of ours… making havoc or making peace."

"And which makes which?" Arphaxas asked in a voice meant to be stronger than it was.

"Arphaxas!" she chided, "That is an indulgent remark."

"It is a valid question."

"If you cannot work that out yourself, then you are less clever than… a wild ass."

Arphaxas laughed. But he knelt down in front of her and looked in her eyes. "It's all so simple to you."

"Not at all," she retorted. "We do all have our… troubles."

His laugh turned to a rather tender smile.

"So, are you staying?" Madai quickly intervened.

"Of course he is," Iscah answered, holding Arphaxas's gaze. "What questions we have can be pondered later… in our cave. You remember, Arphaxas; we've been there before. And besides, Simirra is asking for you. She does complain that you shirk the work that is the dullest."

He looked at her a moment longer. The wind had blown his hood again and whipped his hair about. "Very well," he replied quietly. "We will ponder it later."

He stood up. He brushed past Madai. "Do her no harm, Kinsman," he muttered as he passed.

MADAI WAS LEFT ALONE WITH ISCAH SITTING ON THE stump. It was an unlikely occasion but the winter was near and so would be Arphaxas in that cave. Madai had seen his manner when he talked to her. "We are few now," he began carefully.

She looked at him with a smile. "I think he will be persuaded," she replied.

Madai nodded, made quite uneasy by the remark . "Arphaxas is clever," he replied vaguely.

"He has been irreplaceable since..," she stopped before she finished in a subdued voice, "since Kittim."

"Yes…"

"It is well and proper that you should teach him, Madai, because you were once as he is. He has saved us by the Hand of a God he does not trust, and you shall save him."

"Will believing save any of us, Iscah?"

"Are you being ridiculous now? What about walking the earth with Him, as Adam in Eden. I know you thought so a moment ago." *Job 19:25

Madai chuckled. Perhaps it was nerves. Perhaps it was relief, but he dared to sit beside her on the stump. "They will be waiting for us," she said abruptly, fidgeting beside him.

He took her hand. "Iscah."

"Yes?"

"I asked you once… if you would wed me." He felt her go tense beside him.

"Madai…" she whispered, sounding uneasy, glancing at the graves.

He closed his eyes and turned his face to the sky. How elusive she could be, and how inept, himself.

He swallowed.

"I have loved you since… it was in Job's great room, after Kittim and I returned and you were so grown and… beautiful. I asked if you knew what could make men holy. I do still ponder that… And just now, when you scolded Arphaxas, I remember the way you always tried to make me…"

"Be reasonable," she finished.

He smiled, always caught unexpectedly by her wit.

"But you loved Kittim," he continued, holding her hand a little tighter. "Only I don't think it was love, Iscah, not as a woman can have for a man. I believe it was… admiration."

"There was much to be admired."

"There was. I miss him too. But he has left us, Iscah. He has gone to his master to do… whatever he does. And now, there is just you and me."

Her head was hanging, examining their two hands as if they were the height of astonishing. Madai had the daring to take her chin in his other hand and turn her to face him.

"I will be very tender toward you. Surely you love me a little." He watched in horror as tears sprang to her eyes.

"I hadn't thought about that," she said softly, "till lately, with you in the meadow and the fireweed." He thought the sound of his heart should drown out her quiet voice.

"And the thing about the goats. You see," she blinked but, with a great effort, held her eyes on his. "I am afraid."

That was a grave admission. Even Madai, terrified as he was, could recognize its enormity. He carefully put his arm around her shoulders.

"I will be brave for you," he said.

"Do not play with words. You cannot be brave for another." She complained. "You have not been ransacked. You have not been... bedded by... men you cannot remember." Her chin quivered a bit before she clenched her teeth and swallowed. But she lifted it to look him square in the face. "I would like to be consecrated," she said firmly.

And though she pulled as if to dislodge his arm, he held her with an insistent, slightly indelicate embrace. "I will not ransack you, Iscah. I will not even bed you, if you don't want."

"Then why wed?"

He squirmed a bit because it was a good question. And his own blood was pounding in his ears with a familiar urgency.

"I just love you," he managed to say.

She blinked and swallowed again. "As Tutan loves Reenah?" she asked.

"At least as much."

She stared a moment then did an astonishing thing. She slowly leaned her head into his chest.

ISCAH FELT THE THUDDING OF MADAI'S HEART AND SHE felt her own flitting about inside herself – a little like a confused bird caught indoors. But his nearness was not entirely unwelcome.

She thought again about their journey together. How it was Madai to catch Sabta when he would steal her, and Madai to carry her through the Anak camp, and Madai to argue with Kittim to bring her. It was Madai at the waterfall when they stood in its icy spray with a rainbow and Madai who would have her without the twenty goats.

She looked up, trying to see if she loved him. There was a look of fear in his very blue and beautiful eyes, with flecks of green that shone when the sun hit his face. His beard was quite filthy, but his skin was fine and wanted touching. He had an eyebrow that raised more on the right than the left. She watched the lump in his throat slide up and down as he swallowed.

She decided that she had no knowledge of husbands, not really, for Hamonheb had been merely the one to remove the slave disk from her ear, and bed her when he was drunk.

She thought about the rest of the days of her life. It may be lonely to be consecrated. Tutan had decided so.

And she had tasted alone before...

She remembered them first coming upon Madai's coast, how he had been so anxious and leapt up the rocks looking for his family. She had been anxious for him, which seemed unimportant till now. But she had spied some very interesting crannies at the shore, which were not explored. She would like to. She would like to see them with Madai in spring. He was good company on an adventure.

And she was not fond of cowardice, as it served no one well. She pondered the possibility, tentative at first, that if she did not love him now, she could probably love him later.

Perhaps he read that in her eyes, because he carefully touched his mouth to hers.

And in all her past experience, for she regarded it as vast, Iscah – who was a lover of marvelous things – had never experienced a touch so surprisingly marvelous as his.

CHAPTER 40

CYNWRIG SHIFTED STIFFLY ON THE PLANK BENCH. He was not a man for elaborate talking, but he had talked well into the night. He looked into the faces of the two healers, recognizing that he had been many years and a Great Brine Sea away.

"So," he finished, somewhat embarrassed by the length of his tale, "the story of Madai."

"O, I am very glad he won his love at last." Corinne whispered. She blushed, looking suddenly self-conscience. "And I have heard the legend of the Jews also," she blurted, and blushed redder still, glancing at Paul. "I mean…"

He smiled across the table at her.

"I mean…Noah…" she sputtered.

Tirones made a scraping sound with his boot against the ship's plank floor. Cynwrig turned, having all but forgotten the Romans guarding his door. He looked little more than a boy with baby white hair peeking out from his leather head gear. Perhaps it was the hour of the night, but Cynwrig was disposed to think better of him than he had at the start. He would like to ask what was causing the lad's amusement as it was clearly painted across his face. But for the Centurion with him, Cynwrig would have ventured it and inquired from what part of the world he had come with such hair.

"You smile, Tirones," Paul remarked kindly, asking what Cynwrig had not dared. "Did you enjoy this brother's story?"

The rather new recruit glanced at his superior cautiously. The Centurion gave a slight nod, though the young soldier actually appeared little reassured.

He cleared his throat. "Sir," he began, then seemed unsure as though it was no proper address for a prisoner of Rome, even so famous a one as Paul. "We tell of a flood, the giant, Ymir kilt by Odin. It's his blood to drown the world."

Corinne covered a chortle with her hand.

It was mere confirmation to Cynwrig that superstition ran the ranks of the Roman legions.

"So, now you know the real story," Paul confirmed.

The boy turned red as Cynwrig's hair.

"And what flood tales have you, Centurion?" Paul continued, looking at the older man.

To Cynwrig's amazement, the Roman replied like a human. "Many a tale, Citizen, from many a port."

When Paul leaned forward as if he would wait for the soldier to recount one, the Centurion merely returned his gaze. Though perhaps it was the hour spent retelling the tradition of his people, Cynwrig thought there rested between the two something peaceable.

"I have heard this story of the Jews as well," the Roman eventually replied.

Paul nodded with a knowing look as if they shared an improbable secret. It was, by any measure, a step too far for Cynwrig. The Roman may respect the healer, but not the other way round.

"I have preached through the night before," Paul suddenly announced, a random remark and catching Cynwrig by surprise.

Luke chuckled. "What my brother means," he began, "is to say that we are ready to answer you your questions, be it late or early."

Cynwrig could not stop himself glancing at the Centurion, a disagreeable admission of the soldier's authority. "The Crushing Seed…" Arthfael proffered. "Is it your Christ?"

"The Christ has already crushed the head of the serpent." Paul replied simply.

"What? But how?" Arthfael glanced at the Centurion too, suddenly wary.

"At His resurrection," Paul clarified. "Jesus The Christ has led captives in His train." **Eph. 4:8

"What?"

"He's bought us, my friend, by his dying and saved us by His rising."

Cynwrig and Arthfael looked at each other. They glanced at the Roman again.

"Who killed him?" Cynwrig asked in a hushed tone, cutting his eyes at the Centurion.

"It was pre-planned, my friend, before the creation of the world."

Cynwrig frowned. It was late; he had a Roman on his boat and a quantity of untaxed cargo in his hold.

There were mysteries coming from this healer's mouth. He'd already counted two in just the last minute

"God knew it when He put the stars in the sky, Cynwrig," Paul continued, "or do you doubt your own stories?"

He hadn't thought of that, but then he had just heard that the Crushing Seed, the One so long awaited, was dead.

"So where is He?" Cynwrig asked. "Show me the tomb."

"But I told you that He has arisen."

A wry smile bent up the corners of Cynwrig's mouth. "In the ether-world," he suggested.

"In His flesh," Paul argued. "Remember, brother, Jesus was seen eating; He could be touched. He walked this earth again."

"Though I am as rot, I shall walk with Him in my flesh," Arthfael whispered the words of Job at his brother.

They looked at one another in silence after that. "It's late," Cynwrig finally announced.

"But you do not believe?" came the timorous voice of Corinne once again. "You have seen the father of my master healed, and my own mother."

"Is it too hard for your Creator God?" Luke asked, sounding reasonable.

Cynwrig was fighting with himself, being predisposed to believe a fanciful tale. That penchant of his did not beat back the waves of a very real and often angry sea. It did not buy a ship so fine as The Madai and save him being cheated.

"I have preached through the night before," Paul repeated kindly. "Your star stories are born out. I will show you how, and you may go back to your own shores to teach your own people. I will not go there."

He looked at the Centurion again. Cynwrig knew by the look, which passed between them that Paul would be delivered to Rome by this Roman, perhaps for the last time. It was a revelation of sorts that simply came to him and made this chance meeting with this mysterious man perhaps not chance at all.

"It is a worthy purpose, brother," Paul said as if to confirm what Cynwrig had only just been thinking.

"A purpose like Madai's," Arthfael muttered, having always been the romantic.

"Yes," Luke affirmed, "Like this worthy forebear of yours."

"O, but we are not come of Madai," Arthfael replied. "We are from Arphaxas's seed, he and Simirra." Corrine looked up, suddenly interested in an unexpected romance.

"But that is another story," Cynwrig interjected quickly.

"And there is much to teach you, brother," Paul agreed. "If the good Centurion will allow."

The Roman rocked back on his stool and nodded.

"Cynwrig?"

With a gesture to mirror the Centurion's, Cynwrig settled in his seat and leaned forward, more anxious than he would ever own to be persuaded.

"Will you pray, Brother Luke?" Paul asked.

The hairs of Cynwrig's neck stood up. He did not close his eyes or look away, but watched as Luke lifted his hands to the rough-hewn ceiling of his boat.

"My Lord," Luke began and Cynwrig was glad he was seated for the force of those two words in his tiny captain's quarters. "Empower your servant, Paul." Cynwrig started to tremble. "Breath on us. Open these ears, these hearts of your children."

Was the tide rocking their boat? Cynwrig tried to remember the time.

"Carry them through the days of their lives…"

What? What had he missed?

"So the nations might believe. Might You shine Your Face upon them with the tender mercies of Your love and to You, the only wise God, be glory forever through Jesus The Christ, the Crushing Seed…"

About the Author

Kathy Frias lives in east Texas with her husband, Robert. Kathy is a graduate of Harding Christian College in Searcy, Arkansas. When asked, Kathy says her greatest achievement is the good character of her three sons, and that was accomplished only by the Hand of God and the help of her excellent husband.

The Seed Hunters is her second published book.